D0433578

This item is to be returned on or before the last date stamped below.

LK

F

Practising Wearing Purple

PRACTISING WEARING PURPLE

Margaret Graham

HUTCHINSON
LONDON

First published in the United Kingdom in 1999 by Hutchinson

Random House (UK) Limited
20 Vauxhall Bridge Road, London SW1V 2SA

Random House Australia (Pty) Limited
20 Alfred Street, Milsons Point, Sydney,
New South Wales 2061, Australia

Random House New Zealand Limited
18 Poland Road, Glenfield, Auckland 10, New Zealand

Random House South Africa (Pty) Limited
Endulini, 5A Jubilee Road, Parktown 2193, South Africa

A CiP catalogue record for this book is available from the British Library

Papers used by Random House UK Limited are natural,
recyclable products made from wood grown in sustainable forests.
The manufacturing processes conform to the environmental
regulations of the country of origin.

ISBN 0 09 180043 9

Typeset in Plantin Light by SX Composing DTP, Rayleigh, Essex
Printed and bound in Great Britain
by Creative Print and Design (Wales)

For Chris Hancock and Sherie Williams Ellen
who, like me, are practising wearing purple.
Next on our agenda is a 350-kilometre cycle ride
across Israel for charity.
Well, why not?

Acknowledgements

With thanks to my daughter Kate who skydived in New Zealand and saved me from having to experience it first-hand, and to Chris Hancock and Sylvia Fortnum who helped so much, and of course my thanks to wonderful Fowey – but forgive the liberties I've taken. There is no Journey's End, nor, as far as I know, is there such a pub run by Joe.

CHAPTER ONE

Kate Maxwell had tried protesting carefully, pointing out that the stopping distance between two moving cars was two seconds. She had also tried ignoring it, concentrating grimly on the scenery instead. Today she almost screamed, 'Why don't you just get into the poor woman's boot and be done with it?'

She didn't, of course, but relied instead on the advice given in a book she'd bought on improving communication between husband and wife. Reveal your feelings, it had suggested. 'It frightens me when you drive so close to the car in front,' she said.

'Don't be so bloody silly.' Peter accelerated even closer.

Back to the scenery. She vaguely recognised the streams of shops, houses, and the parked cars that squeezed two lanes of traffic into one. Pillock. Pillock. Who was the pillock? The author, or her?

Her, obviously, from the pressure of Judy's fingers which were digging into her shoulder saying shut up, Mum. Just shut up. Though what she actually said was, 'Not far now, Dad. We've loads of time.'

'What's that supposed to mean?' Peter pushed the car in front even harder.

'Nothing, Dad.' Judy's voice was eager. 'It's just really great that you could bring me, it took ages when Mum drove me up for the interview. We're in really good time.'

Kate continued to look out of the window but sensed the glance Peter gave her. 'Yes,' she agreed, 'I'm glad you're here.' She turned to the front, looking no further than the BMW's dashboard, her foot pressed into the floor. 'Really glad.'

Jude's fingers eased and she read aloud from the map that the university had sent. 'Next left, then right, then we're there.'

'Well done, Jude.' Peter jerked to a stop at the lights. There was the sound of the indicator, and the radio you could only half hear because he didn't like loud noise in the car. If the kids had wanted to listen to something he would turn it up, but switch off the two front speakers. Kate shouldn't let it annoy her, she really shouldn't. After all, he spent so much time in his car, one way and another, and had learned what made that part of a stressful job tolerable.

She reached across and touched his arm. 'Sorry, I'm a bit jaded.'

As the lights turned from amber to green he accelerated round the corner, mumbling, 'Been a difficult time. Tough on Judy, too. Not the ideal start to uni.'

'Next right, Dad. Just here.' Peter took a gap in the oncoming traffic that Kate would not have risked. He ignored the horns and powered towards the Edwards Hall sign which was only a hundred yards on the left. Judy's fingers were pressing into her shoulder again, but there was no need. In the driveway cars were bumper to bumper, struggling to park. On the radio someone was muttering faintly.

The hall of residence was concrete, probably built in the seventies; the windows could do with a lick of paint. Kate tried not to notice Peter tapping the steering wheel. She really had to sort herself out, learn to deal with stress. She breathed deeply, another trick she'd read about in a book. It failed. She brushed her hand through her deep brown hair, which she'd had cut short in an effort at sophistication a few months ago.

'Over there, Dad.' Judy pointed out a car that was leaving.

He swung the car round, beating an Escort to the spot. It hopefully did not contain a potential friend for Judy. As he prepared to back in, Kate ventured, 'Perhaps frontways. We've all her stuff to unload.'

Lips compressed, he realigned, parked, switched off, checking his watch. 'Chop, chop, I've a plane to catch. Need to leave for the airport within the hour.'

It was the houseplants, which Kate had wedged in a huge cardboard box in the left-hand side of the boot, that held them up. It was too weak and collapsed, so she and Judy had to ferry them up in dribs and drabs. Each time the hall monitor who stood in the entrance smiled. It became embarrassing. There were only so many things you could say. 'My daughter's doing biology.' 'Gosh, don't get cold, that wind is keen.' Finally there was only the rubber plant, the fig, and the spider plant which showered babies. 'Last ones,' Kate said to the hall monitor, who nodded. Judy strode ahead, irritated.

Her room was on the third floor. There were no lifts, but all the better for the thighs, Kate told herself with each step. Reaching Floor Three, she and Judy pressed through the growing ranks of students and parents, and headed for Room Seven. Outside Room Five a girl grinned at Judy, pointing to the plants. 'I guess you're Biology. So am I.'

'Great,' Judy said.

Kate and the girl's parents smiled at one another. The father wiped his brow and grimaced. 'Bad as moving house. Put my foot down about the number of plants though.' Kate nodded. The world was full of smarty-pants.

Judy called over her shoulder to the girl: 'Are you going to the freshers coffee thing? Great, we'll be there in a minute.'

As they entered her room Peter turned from setting up the word processor. 'If you'd put them in several smaller boxes in the first place you could have brought them up half a dozen at a time.'

Judy dumped the fig, and the mother and babies on the desk, before taking the rubber plant from Kate, saying quickly, 'We should be heading for the refectory or Dad'll miss his flight.'

Kate touched the shiny leaves, concentrating on them. 'Your grandmother used milk to buff these up.'

Judy stood next to her, quite quiet for a moment, and when she spoke her voice was unsteady. 'I'm really going to miss her. I'm so glad she didn't die while I was turtle tagging in Greece. It's as though she waited for me to come home, scheduling it to fit with my university start. Death to order.' She had to stop for a moment. 'I hate to think she won't be swanning around this Christmas in a crazy purple dress. Dear old Barbs.'

Kate squeezed her hand hard. So hard.

Peter said as he sat at the desk booting up the computer, 'That's one facet of my mother I won't miss. I mean, it's as though she flipped when Dad died. Bloody purple, bloody abseiling.'

For a moment there was only the sound of the computer whirring and humming, then Judy broke free of Kate's grasp

3

and went to her father. 'Poor Dad. Yes, you're right, it was weird but perhaps it was the illness. I wonder if it started long before we realised.' She touched his shoulder, leaning against him. He came out of Word 6, shut down and sighed, then stood slowly and put his arm around her. Judy said, her voice muffled, 'But she was always so brave.'

They were both so alike. Tall, dark and striking. Kate longed to be held, too, needed to be held. Peter patted his daughter. 'She's OK now, Jude, that's the thing to remember. And she didn't suffer, she just slipped away – all quite natural. And she'd had a good life.'

Still Kate watched him. Natural? *Natural?* The word, when repeated, lost all sense. Slipped away? Her arms felt heavy with the weight of Barbs, her thoughts were fragmenting as they had done since the day, ten days ago, when she had 'slipped away'. And now her chest was hurting. It was normal she told her patients at the surgery. It's what happened when a heart was bruised, or even breaking. 'It might be normal, nurse,' one old man had said. 'But it bloody hurts.' He was right.

Pete double-parked just a few yards from the entrance to the airport and hurriedly grabbed the map. 'I'll talk you through the route back to the motorway again.'

Kate glanced over her shoulder at the Volvo they'd boxed in. 'It's all right, I've written it down.' She waved the slip of paper at him.

He continued to describe the route nonetheless, tracing it with his finger before reaching over to the back seat for his grip and briefcase. He leaped from the car, hurrying around the front whilst she slid across into the driving seat, her eyes on the mirror. The driver of the Volvo was flashing his headlights.

She started the car, indicating, about to pull away, but there was a knock on the passenger window. It was Peter, signalling for her to lower the window. As she did so, the Volvo flashed again. Her stomach knotted. Peter leaned in, taking his time. 'Good luck with work tomorrow.'

Instantly Kate forgot about the Volvo, forgot everything but the thought of the Medical Centre. In the awful darkness which seemed to have fallen she whispered, 'I can't face it.' This time the Volvo hooted. She jerked back to the present and automatically turned the key, but the engine was already running. There was a grinding sound.

Peter snapped, 'For Christ's sake!'

She broke out into a sweat. 'Sorry.' She depressed the accelerator just as a hotel courtesy minibus swung in front of them. She stamped on the brake. Now she really couldn't move; surely the Volvo driver could see that?

Lots of Japanese hurried out, clustering at the rear door as bags were distributed. Taxis were sweeping past, stopping, depositing passengers who scurried for trolleys. Peter was sighing. The Volvo was hooting. She wanted to scream.

Peter said, 'Of course you can face it. Work'll get you back into a routine, do you good.'

The Japanese had found trolleys and were threading their way to the entrance but the minibus was still blocking her. Do her good? How could he think that? She blurted out, 'I'm tired after it all, upset. I can't bear to think . . .'

He cut her off. 'Of course you're tired, but you're not the only one, for heaven's sake, and being back at the surgery will take your mind off it. Besides, we need the money. God knows our outgoings are enough already without this latest round of university.' He was checking his watch. Any minute now he would bring in Simon. 'I mean, Simon's PhD set us back enough, and you've had all those weeks off while Mother was . . .'

She turned on him as he shook down his sparkling white cuff, and heard herself shouting, heard a terrible rawness. 'What about you? She was your mother after all – don't you care, don't you miss her, or feel guilty? How can you just ignore what happened? And what about me? I need . . .'

The Volvo hooted. She stopped, appalled at herself. Peter pushed himself back from the window. 'Good God, Kate, get a grip. She was my mother, of course I care, but she'd expect me to work. She'd know it was best. Guilt doesn't come into it. Now, come on, buck up. Life's got to go on.'

She felt sick, felt herself breaking out into a sweat again. Life's got to go on? But it was less than a fortnight ago. It was all less than two awful weeks ago. The Japanese were inside the building now and the minibus was pulling away into the traffic. She didn't care; she had to try again or she might come to believe she was imagining things, just as she had before. Irritated, wary, he was beginning to move away, but not to the trolleys. Oh no, he travelled light, to avoid the carousel – he made them all travel light. It was always just one weekend bag. But now she needed him to stay, anyone to stay for just a moment. She called, 'I'll pick you up from Bristol.'

At this he spun round and hurried back, leaning into the car, but not in support. Now it was her turn to pull away. His dark eyes became darker still as they narrowed, and his lips were so thin they almost disappeared. 'Oh, so that's what this is really all about, is it – that hysterical bloody nonsense again, and at a time like this! For God's sake, for the last bloody time there's no other woman, but if you go on you'll drive me to it. Good God, wasn't it enough that Mother was ill without you phoning the hotel, checking up on me, causing a bloody big . . .'

He was too close, his breath smelt of peppermint. She gripped the steering wheel. 'No, that's not what I meant. It never crossed my mind.' Kate could hear her voice breaking. 'I'm sorry, I was only trying to help . . .'

It was his turn to interrupt, his hand up as though stopping traffic. 'Fine, Kate, fine. That's helping, isn't it? I mean, it's not as though I've got nothing better to think about than your damned suspicions. Thank you. So kind.'

Her voice was barely more than a whisper. 'I just thought you might be tired. I just thought it might be nice to have someone waiting to bring you home, that's all.' She was almost in tears. But she mustn't. She must push them back. She must shut up. The Volvo hooted. Cars were steaming past. A huge coach drew alongside, its engine humming.

Peter was talking, but she couldn't hear. His hand was out to her. The coach moved. '. . . you're tired, you've bags under your eyes. Get home and have an early night, and forget about all of this. The lift's a kind thought, and I'm sorry to shout, but don't bother, really. The plane could be delayed, anything.' He was straightening, checking his watch. 'Got to go.' He was off.

The Volvo hooted yet again, drawing up to her bumper, flashing. She wanted to run after Peter, turn him around, make him talk, not about other women but about his mother, for God's sake, the mother he had refused to kill.

The Volvo driver leaned on his horn. In the mirror she saw

6

he was her age, fat, with stubble which could not be called designer. His lips were moving. He was waving her away, opening his hands as though to heaven, and suddenly it was as though a dam burst inside her. She leaned out of the window, shouting, 'Don't you know it's an offence to sound the horn of a stationary vehicle, you sad, raving pillock!'

She swung out into the traffic, narrowly avoiding a taxi. Her fingers were shaking, her throat felt swollen. Pillock. Pillock. She turned the radio up, then louder still. All the way back to their Somerset village her heart was beating too fast. She had to get a grip. Had to. Had to.

CHAPTER TWO

Kate was awake long before the alarm was due to leap into life and she lay motionless, watching night turn into a heart-breakingly beautiful October day. Next door, Bertie the West Highland terrier was barking, preparatory to pooing under the hideous *leylandii* hedge Peter had planted three years ago. Barbs had suspected that Kate's neighbour Penny had trained Bertie to do it in protest, and endorsed her good taste.

The shower was good and hot. Her uniform crisp and clean. She didn't check her image in the mirror. In the kitchen she made the tea too strong, toasting bread, sitting at the pine table that annoyed Peter because it didn't match the white kitchen but they'd run out of money. Kate had meant to keep her eye open for a white second-hand one, or paint this, but somehow time had passed.

On her way to the car she looked through the gap in the *leylandii* to Penny and Tom's 'Kosher' vicarage, as Barbs had christened it. There was no sign of life, so Bertie would be in the kitchen being fed Ryvita corners by Penny.

She checked her watch. No, there wasn't time to visit. She ignored Peter's BMW and backed her own clapped-out E reg. Metro out of the drive of the Old Vicarage. The Medical Centre was in the next village, best approached by the A303 if you were in a hurry, and suddenly she was, because the church clock was chiming a quarter to nine.

Ten minutes later Kate parked next to the senior practice nurse's Astra. As always Jan Seymour was in early, a plus point that was surely designed to be noticed by the patients who arrived any time after eight thirty for the nine o'clock open surgery. It was like the starting block of the London Marathon. In their place she'd have left it until nearer ten thirty when the surgery was emptying.

She closed the air vents of the Metro, tidied the glove

pocket, checked through the tapes, anything to put off the moment when she climbed out of the car to meet her colleagues; the people who had helped care for Barbs, who had sent flowers, who had grouped together at the funeral, who'd munched through the sausage rolls. Except for Jan, of course. She was vegetarian and on that occasion a disappointed one. Kate shook her head. She'd done a poor job foodwise, just hadn't got into gear. She still wasn't engaged.

Dr Stuart Duncan pulled up beside her. It was he who had initiated the reserved parking places, he who had announced at a Medical Centre Fund-raising Evening that any patient ignoring said name plaques would be inviting an investigative procedure that necessitated the bent position and stout latex gloves. It had set the slightly strained tone of the evening, and Jan was not amused, though Kate had been.

Stuart had been a prop forward at university, which he'd left horribly recently, and called a spade something worse, but was the best doctor ever. Barbs had adored him, and had spent many a happy moment wondering what his nose must originally have looked like. Kate felt herself relaxing as he came to her car door. 'That's better.' He was opening it. 'A smile. I've missed it over the last couple of months. Now come into the lion's den. You could have had more time off, you know, the stand-in was willing.'

Kate held her smile, letting him close the door for her, but locking it herself though her hands were trembling. 'It's better to get back into a routine. I'm all at sea, somehow.'

'Of course you are, you silly old tart, you're only human.' They were walking towards the posh new surgery. Stuart nodded to an elderly patient who was racing them to the door, shaking off her headscarf as she did so, but they had too good an advantage. Stuart evened the honours by ushering Mrs Murphy – arthritic knee, prone to leg ulcers, Kate mentally annotated – through first. Mrs Murphy's tweed coat held the scent of bonfires and sagged at the hem as always. Heavy gardening not beneficial to either condition, Kate had written up last time, neither is poverty. Jan had insisted she delete the latter. She couldn't remember if she'd obeyed.

Mrs Murphy took only two steps into the waiting room, then stopped, panting slightly, her hand tapping Kate's arm. 'So sorry for your trouble, dear. It doesn't matter that it was in the fullness of time. It still leaves you lonely.'

Again she kept her smile. 'You're very kind.' Mrs Murphy coughed, and joined the queue for the reception desk.

'See you at coffee,' Stuart murmured to Kate. 'Take it easy, there's a good girl.'

Kate waved to those already seated. In the corner the Wendy house was awash with children who looked completely well, so perhaps it was the mothers who needed care. Would the toys that were strewn all over the floor be cleared away as the notice requested? Probably not.

It seemed strange here, the noises unfamiliar when once it had seemed a haven. Penny had said that was a strange term to use, but Penny psychoanalysed everything; it came with the territory, Kate supposed. She passed through to the nurses' room.

The morning was busy, patients were kind, Jan was brisk. As she had feared, Kate was irritated by the minor wounds, anguished by anything really serious, unable to concentrate as she should, exhausted by it all.

At coffee break she couldn't eat the cake bought by birthday boy Dr Miles Edwards. She couldn't stop yawning, couldn't stop swallowing, couldn't sit still, couldn't listen to the inane chatter, but had to pretend she could. At last the break was over, at last they started on the well woman clinic – the blood pressure, the urine samples, the weighing, the HRT or pill advice, the lump and bump worries, and all the time Jan hovered, her eyes double-checking, not bothering to pretend she wasn't.

Then they were on the last lap and the final patient, a very young Miss Henderson, whose leg needed to be dressed, and whose endless account of her boyfriend's redundancy had to be listened to until eventually she was all talked out and limping carefully to the door. 'You've forgotten to write her up,' Jan's voice was as sharp as the pencil she was pointing to the girl's notes.

Miss Henderson hesitated on her way out of the examination room but Kate insisted, 'No, Jan, I was just about to.'

But she wasn't. She was somewhere else, locked into Barbs's

last breath, and it was the third time Jan had pounced, and as she wrote Kate wanted to scream at herself, at Jan and her gimlet eyes, her meticulously made up youthful face. Because she wasn't coping, her mind was too full, and as she wrote she cursed the whole damn medical profession, who been able to do nothing to help Barbs, who had done nothing to stop what had finally happened.

She bent her head to her task, taking too long, but long enough to take herself in hand. She swallowed. Better now. Good girl. Jan was busy at her desk, a phone was ringing in reception, or was it the Practice Manager's office? All quite normal. All as it had been for the last four years, and she really couldn't bear to be here for another minute, wearing this uniform, caring for patients whose smiles would have faded, who would have appealed to Jan, to Stuart, to anyone to dismiss her if they knew what she had done.

Now it was Kate's turn to hover over Jan. She said, looking out across the almost empty car park, 'I'm sorry I wasn't on the ball this morning. My mother-in-law, you know.'

Jan continued to write for a moment, then laid down her pen. She pointed to the cupboard, not even looking at Kate. 'Just check that we've sufficient syringes for this afternoon, will you?'

Kate did so. There were. 'Plenty,' Kate murmured, reaching for her coat, shrugging into it, only noticing now that the younger woman looked very tired and drawn in spite of her make-up. Concerned, she paused. Jan had moved about nine months ago to a new flat which was halfway between here and Bristol, which meant quite a drive, though none of her colleagues had actually experienced this for themselves because there had been no house-warming beano. Was there man trouble, or maybe it was money? Somehow Kate had forgotten that other people's problems existed.

Jan was rubbing her forehead as though clearing a headache and instinctively Kate moved towards her. 'I'm sorry I've dropped you in it over the last few months, Jan, but I just had to take time off to look after Barbs. I do hope you understand, and I'll get back into the swing of it, promise. And sorry, too, that you've had to put up with an agency nurse.' Jan was rolling her neck. Kate touched the younger woman's shoulder. 'Look,

Jan, is everything all right with you? Can I help at all?'

Jan picked up the list she had been checking. 'Oh, don't worry about the agency nurse, she was refreshingly excellent, actually.' Now she was examining her pen as though it was something she had never seen before. 'You know, Kate, if you aren't ready you don't have to return yet. In fact, I'm sure we could fill the position if you felt you wanted to give it a miss altogether.'

Kate stared at her. The pen was catching the light. On and on she watched Jan turn it with those neat, endlessly creamed hands and began to shake, and it was a mixture of everything churning away in her, for surely she was a good nurse. In spite of Barbs she was a good nurse.

The door flew open. 'Still here?' Stuart bellowed at Kate. Jan winced.

'Just on my way,' Kate's voice sounded leaden. He held the door for her. 'You seem to spend your life on door duty,' she managed to murmur as she passed him. 'Bye, Jan. See you tomorrow, Stuart.'

But he was following her down the corridor. This time she held the door for him, but he grabbed it, sweeping a bow as she stepped outside. It had turned into a damp day. She pulled her collar up. A taxi drew into the car park, and she recognised old Mr Barrat struggling out. A special appointment? She hoped it was nothing serious.

Stuart walked her to her car, his voice quieter than seemed possible given the bulk of him. 'I'm going to teach my grandmother to suck eggs and remind you that it's all quite natural, you know, the yawning, the swallowing, the restlessness, the tears that come out of nowhere.'

She stared at the handkerchief he passed her, and only then did she know that she was crying. Savagely she scrubbed at her face, willing herself to stop, feeling a fool, feeling . . . She didn't know what she felt. She didn't know how she should feel, there was just this sense of imploding, of everything spiralling. Stuart had his arm round her and it was what she'd needed all week. It's what Peter hadn't been able to give her, but some men seemed to have their own way of dealing with emotion.

'It's grief,' Stuart said. 'If you'll forgive me for stating the obvious, and because of your involvement you'll feel it even more.' She weighed the words, as part of her seemed to be doing all the time when people spoke to her. Involvement? She turned it round and round, until it was in danger of banging into the sides of her skull. He said, 'As I say, you don't have to come back yet.'

'Peter thinks . . .' She couldn't go on. Stuart waited. She began again, 'Best to get into a routine. Or do *you* think I should leave too?'

Stuart frowned, digging his hands into his corduroys. 'Whatever do you mean? We don't *want* you to leave, we just wonder if it's too soon, Ms Florence Nightingale. Good God, exhaustion comes into the equation somewhere, or it should. Peter should remember that he is not the one who had to do it.'

It? Kate nodded, unable to speak. She fumbled for her key, opened the door and got in without looking at him. It?

At two o'clock that afternoon, Penny led the way out of the New Vicarage to her Morris Minor Traveller, brandishing gin and a large bottle of diet tonic. 'It has to be done, darling. We shall sit in Barbs's living room and toast her before we begin. I shall only have a very small one, as I'm driving, but you will have a plonker.'

Kate laughed, clutching a small cardboard box crammed with black bin bags and cleaning materials. It was a box which would have gladdened Peter's heart had she had it at the university, she had muttered to Penny half an hour ago. 'Little things . . .' Penny had intoned, slapping down the bacon and egg sarnies she had cooked. Kate had always envied Penny's exuberance, and was grateful for it, because when they were together it seemed to infect her as well.

As they reached the car Kate said, 'Give the bottles to me, you crazy woman, before your parishioners see you and think their souls are in the hands of an old soak. It wouldn't be so bad if you weren't in uniform.'

Penny lodged the bottles in the box, then patted her dog collar. She was still proud of it and so she should be, Kate thought. She'd worked hard enough to get it and insisted it was the height of her ambition. 'No bishopric for me. Black is so much more slimming, though Barbs, of course, would have gone right to the top, just for the colour.' Kate believed her, about the bishopric anyway. Penny loved people, she was good with them, a brilliant vicar.

Inside the vicarage Bertie, the Westie, was barking his loneliness. Penny slid into the car, reaching over and opening the passenger door for Kate, who asked as she settled herself, 'Come on, did you really train Bertie to use the *leylandii*?'

'A woman of the cloth cannot tell a lie, so I shall abstain. Mind your own business and clunk click.' The rattle of cans from the back drowned out whatever else she was saying as she drove out of the drive.

Kate craned round, shouting. 'What on earth's in the back this time?'

Penny grimaced. 'Cans of coffee, donated for the tombola. Probably undrinkable, but how can I say no? Sometimes I think the Christmas Fayre is just a repository for things past their sell-by date.'

'It certainly is if you look at the stall-holders.' Kate grinned.

Penny changed gear. 'I shall tell them all you said that, angel face.'

It took only five minutes to reach Barbs's little fifties bungalow, called Lamorna. Barbs had never warmed to the place, which was indistinguishable from all the others in Acacia Avenue. Peter, however, had deemed it more sensible to sell the house she had lived in with his father, Keith, and buy something smaller, thereby bumping up her pension with the interest from the difference. It wasn't the principle that Barbs objected to, it was the 'sensible' bungalow. 'I still have the use of my legs,' she'd protested. 'And my mind. I can still make decisions for myself.' That was two years ago, just after Keith had died.

Peter, though, had a habit of pushing things through, almost without anyone realising, but perhaps it was inevitable, given the nature of his job, Kate had said, anxious to calm Barbs. Besides, Barbs had pretty soon left her mutterings behind and gone forward.

'Hardly sensible, Mother,' Peter had said when he'd first become aware of the list of things that Barbs had decided to do. The first was abseiling.

'Bugger sensible,' she'd said, offending him deeply and astonishing them all. She'd been such a little mouse up until the moment Keith had died. So grey and distant, with seemingly unassailable domestic standards which had led to a sense of permanent inadequacy in Kate.

'I blame you, of course,' she laughed as Penny prepared to back into Lamorna's drive.

'Moi? For what?' Penny was easing up to the garage. 'Hang on, tell me in a minute, let's get as close as possible.'

But now, as Kate twisted to look at Lamorna, the laughter died. In fact, she couldn't think where it had come from, couldn't understand what she had been thinking of. They were coming to Barbs's house to clear it. They were coming to somewhere that had been full of life, and laughter in the face of death.

It was Peter who had gathered up the valuables, what few there were. It was Peter who must have closed Barbs's curtains, but his mother hated darkness. Why did he do that? Why, for heaven's sake?

Penny was out of the car and practically running to open her door. Why? Does she think I won't be able to go in? Kate stared ahead, trying to control the seesaw of emotion, trying to damp it all down, but a sudden anger was forcing its way out.

The hinges protested as Penny opened the car door, and held out her hand to Kate. 'Come on, lazybones, give me the cleaning stuff, you can be seen carrying the booze.'

The anger fled in the face of Penny's smile, and now there was only fluttering. Her patients had so often asked the question: 'When will this grief fade?' In time, had been her answer. But what sort of answer was that?

Once inside the sitting room they drew back the curtains. Kate looked around the colour-splashed room. It was just the same, just as crazy, just as wonderful. The bright red sofa was strewn with vivid cushions, the cane chair too. On the sponged walls were bright Australian watercolours. Were the colours really so vivid over there? Barbs had asked the artist. 'Go and see for yourself,' he'd replied. Barbs had put it on her list, after Yellowstone Park.

In the dining area Penny was pouring gin into Barbs's crystal tumblers. Kate's was strong, far too strong, thank heavens. She leaned against the dusty mahogany table.

15

Penny held up her glass, standing by the window that looked out on the paved terraced garden. 'To Barbs, bless her appalling striped socks, her out of order comments, her utter bad taste, her wonderful brave heart, her . . . Well, to Barbs.' They drank. The gin hit the spot. Penny came across and poured her another. 'I don't think I will ever forget the coffin lining as long as I live.'

Kate smiled slightly. 'The only surprise was that she didn't have the whole casket spray-painted purple.'

Penny laughed loud and long. 'Glory be, yes, it would have been so glorious.'

Kate was running her finger round the rim of her glass. 'She felt compromise was the better part of valour. She didn't want Peter having apoplexy and two Maxwells storming the Pearly Gates at once. Just imagine the two of them sharing paradise. We'd be having endless thunderstorms down here.'

They were laughing, but all the time Kate knew that soon they would have to begin. Sure enough, before Kate could lift her glass to her lips, Penny was bustling out into the corridor. 'Come on, bedroom first, let's do the clothes.' Kate didn't move. Penny called, 'Bring the bottle, you could need it. This is the worst part.'

No, there was something far, far worse.

Penny called, 'Come on, Kate, don't put it off, darling.' At last Kate moved, carrying her gin and the cleaning box, walking steadily down the corridor still hung with Simon and Jude's playgroup paintings and school photographs. Why was she surprised that they were still there? Did she think the fairies had come in and packed everything up? She stopped and leaned against the wall, nudging a picture.

'Kate.'

Penny's voice was loud enough to draw her on towards the bedroom where Barbs had died. She stopped again, just outside the open door. The bed was stripped. Yes, she had done that when Barbs had been taken away. The curtains were closed. She had not done that. 'Draw the curtains wide, Pen.'

'OK.'

She watched as Penny took them to their furthest point. Still standing at the doorway she could see the end fence which would be covered in honeysuckle in the summer. 'Glorious, it's

16

like stepping into a high-class brothel,' Barbs had said as she led Kate out into the sun that first summer, 'all scent, loungers and anticipation.'

The anticipation had centred on the maps that were strewn by a lounger. Barbs was planning her travelling schedule for the next five years: Paris that year, Yellowstone Park the next, Australia the next. The last two were not yet picked out. 'I've decided to do Paris first, to break Peter into the idea slowly,' she'd confided. It hadn't. Then, after the diagnosis, Yellowstone Park had been relegated to the 'things to experience while I still can' list. But she couldn't.

Kate still stood in the doorway. 'Will the bag lady please enter,' Penny called.

Finally she did, stiffly dumping the box on to the bed, taking another sip of the gin, taking the bin bag that Penny offered, watching as Penny checked through the wardrobe. 'What do you think? Are all these to go to the hospice shop?' Penny asked.

'Not the purple.'

Penny nodded, taking a hanger out, disentangling a purple skirt from a black pleated one. Kate looked away. She could remember when Barbs last wore it. It had been at Branscombe Beach, when finally they knew how long she had to live.

'Why not do the shoes?' Penny's voice was gentle.

Automatically Kate knelt, reaching into the bottom of the wardrobe as Penny fussed above her. She found a red pair, and Barbs was there, in the shape of them. She stared up at Penny and whispered, 'I can't do this.'

Penny dropped down beside her, her arm strong around her. 'You did it for your father-in-law, and your own parents. Of course you can do it, this is no different.'

The red leather of the shoe felt warm in her hands, the heel was worn on one side. She wanted to lean into Penny, but she might tell her too much.

Instead she said quietly, 'I cried this morning. Jan said I would not be missed if I chose to resign because the agency nurse was excellent.'

It was dark here, facing the wardrobe, and there was a heavy stale perfume smell on Barbs's clothes. She would have hated that. Penny's arm tightened. 'Bollocks, she's a cow. But you

17

didn't want to go on working there anyway, did you?'

'But that's for me to say, not her.' She sounded childish. She *was* childish.

Penny smiled. 'I know exactly what you mean. It casts aspersions, doesn't it? Unfounded ones, you daft old thing. As I said, she's a cow. Take no notice.'

Kate felt desperately tired now. 'She wasn't always. When she came she was rather nice. People change. Look at Barbs, once so quiet and proper. So mouselike. So . . .' Penny was silent and Kate knew that she was waiting for more, but she was too tired to talk, far too tired.

She dropped the shoe. *Damn it, damn you, Barbs.* The anger was back. It hurt her stomach.

Penny's arm tightened around her. 'I'm here, talk to me about her. Just let it out.'

Kate swallowed, wanting to. Would it hurt? Would it really hurt? Pulling away from Penny she got to her feet. 'Let's do it another day.'

Penny smiled gently. 'Anything you say, boss.' Kate turned away from the concern on her face, because she didn't deserve it.

The black bin bags rustled as Penny stuffed them into the cardboard box. 'Anyway, what did you mean you blamed me? You know, as we backed into Barbs's drive.'

Kate took the box from her, quite calm again. Totally calm, her brain clicking back just a few minutes, because that's all it was, just a few minutes since they were in the car, with the world going on around them. 'Ah yes, I blamed you, because you read her the poem, "Warning". You gave it to her after Keith's death. It changed her life, in fact she said it *gave* her life.'

Penny led the way down the corridor, her laugh soft. 'Her life was ready to be changed, the poem just pointed the way, so I'm not guilty, m'lud.'

Kate stared at her back, the words going on and on. Not guilty. And she ached with envy.

18

CHAPTER THREE

Peter Maxwell sat on the edge of the bed in his hotel room staring out at the lights of Edinburgh. You could almost see the cold seeping into the granite buildings and the frost encrusting the looming castle, though in here the heating was set too high. Hospitals and hotels, they were all the bloody same. He rubbed his forehead and reached for the minutes of the meeting which had gone on far too long.

He leafed through, scanning rapidly. Yes, that just about caught the gist – mainly that the cock-up continued and if that shower of so-called sub-contractors wanted a future they'd have to do some smart footwork. He tossed the papers back into his briefcase which lay open on the bed beside him. He caught sight of himself in the mirror. Well, anyone would look like that after a day like his, a week like his, a bloody month like his.

He was yawning as he entered the shower, and the low pressure did nothing to boost him. Damn it to hell. He dried himself in the bedroom, away from the steam, pulling in his stomach as he caught sight of himself in the mirror. Not bad for fifty. He grinned and tied the belt of the courtesy towelling robe loosely. The hotel room could have been any hotel room anywhere, but he liked that. Functional, impersonal, nothing to have to adapt to, nothing to have to notice, no twee furniture to trip over in the dark on the way to the lav, no nice comments to summon up for an anxious owner over the wheaties in the morning.

Taking a couple of miniatures from the bar he gathered up a glass, heaped the pillows up on the bed and set back before reaching for the phone and dialling an outside line. It only had to ring twice before she answered. He smiled. He knew she'd be sitting beside it, waiting. She'd have been waiting since she got in at 6.30.

'Hello.' Her voice was eager.

19

'It's me.' He held the phone between his shoulder and chin as he unscrewed the tops and poured the gin. No tonic. He needed something stronger to try and wipe out this bloody funny stomach, which felt as though there were a herd of butterflies playing silly buggers.

'Darling, how are you? How did it go today?' He smiled at the concern in her voice, and at the relief. Sometimes he deliberately rang late because it kept her on her toes, kept her here – he looked at the palm of his hand, imagining her lips, her breasts.

'Peter, are you there?'

'I'm here, Jan, but more importantly, I *will* be with you on Thursday. I'm leaving for Paris in the morning, but I can make it back by Thursday. Pick me up from the airport, there's a good girl, at about eighteen thirty hours. I can stay with you all Friday, so you'll organise time off from the Medical Centre? It should be easy now Kate's back.'

'Of course, a whole day. How wonderful.' There was a pause. 'I've missed you so much. It's been too long.'

'I know, I know.' He sipped his gin. The trouble with room bars was that there was no lemon or ice. 'You'll run me back to the airport Friday evening? I've a hire car booked from there.'

'Of course. But darling, you sound tired?'

'Oh, it's only the usual hassle. I've been trying to get it into the sub-contractors' thick skulls that if they don't keep to schedule and deliver on time we're not the only ones facing penalty payments, and more than that, they'll never work for us again.'

'Why are they so behind?'

'Disorganised management and a sloppy attitude on our part.'

'But only until you took over the contract, of course.'

He laughed. 'Well, you could say that.'

'Can't you take the job off them, give it to someone else?'

'Oh, bloody marvellous, and lose more time?' His voice was sharp.

She hesitated. When she spoke again it was tentatively. 'Of course, that was stupid of me, sorry. You've been through such a lot. I just wish I could have been there, to help. Losing a mother is terrible . . .'

He grimaced at his reflection. No need to speak to the girl like that. 'I'm OK. These things happen, life goes on – and on Thursday we'll be able to catch up.'

'I can't wait,' she said softly. 'I wanted to hold you at the funeral, just to hold you. But Peter, I could be at your side giving you the support you really need all the time. I mean, the funeral was pretty ropey, and as for all those weeks of nursing . . . I'd have been able to handle Barbara without neglecting you. It simply wasn't good enough. Kate should have made more use of the Macmillan nurses, and the community ones too. Darling, it just wasn't fair on you for her to move in with Barbs. She really doesn't deserve you.'

He smiled, sipping his gin, imagining Jan caressing his body, and his hand trembled with desire. Jan hesitated a moment and her voice was very soft when she said, 'Peter, let's pay Kate off. Surely we can now that there's your mother's bungalow? We could sell it, sell this flat and leave Kate the Old Vicarage, and have a fresh start somewhere else, just the two of us.'

There was no smile now as Peter rubbed his forehead, not seeing his image in the mirror as he focused only on her voice, a voice that right now was driving him bloody mad with its whingeing. 'Darling, we've talked about this. It's just not the right time. There's Jude to get through university, and my work. I just can't cope with anything more at the moment, I thought you understood all this.'

'Sorry, sorry, I know, I'm stupid. I just sometimes . . . Look, why don't you let me pay a proper rent for this place? All we need to do is put it into joint names.'

'It all gets too complicated.'

'Why?'

'It's easier to have it in just my name.'

'But I don't understand why. I'd never leave you, we'd never have to split it.'

Peter was sitting on the edge of the bed, not listening any more because these bloody women were never satisfied. All he was after was a bit of light relief, for Christ's sake, just another arm to his life, to help him handle work, stress and family, and now she was starting to add to it all, and he didn't need it.

The carpet was red, swirling red, and it felt like the inside of his head. He took a deep breath. 'Look, honey pie, I don't want you to be putting out any more money. I hate having to take even the rent I do. Can't you see that I want to look after you as much as I can to show how much I care? We just have to be patient, that's all, just for a while longer, and then you'll be Mrs Maxwell, and you can travel with me, live the life of Riley. Or do you want out, is that what you're trying to tell me?'

He knew it wasn't, but there was no way he was going to turn this game, and her transitory part in it, into another partnership and it was one way of getting her to shut the fuck up. Besides, she had a cheap roof over her head in a flat he had bought, so why should she complain?

'I love you,' she said, her voice hollow and distressed. 'I wasn't trying to make life difficult for you, just easier. I love you.'

He eased back on the pillows. 'I love you, too. We'll be having the furniture from the bungalow, remember that. There are some nice pieces, things I grew up with, so you'll be living amongst my past, whilst being a part of my present, a crucial part.' He paused, pleased with that line. He must remember to use it again sometime. 'And what's more, I've a present for you too.'

He and his father had bought the Capo di Monte figurine for his mother's birthday a year or so before Keith died. They were sick of the Dresden she'd taken a shine to and thought it might improve her taste. It hadn't. He stared at the glass in his hand. The gin was finished, his bloody gin was finished, and there was this ache in his chest, this thickening in his throat, this tightening of his fingers round the receiver, until they hurt.

Her voice was soft. 'Oh Peter.'

Quite suddenly he wanted that softness. Quite suddenly he wanted to bury his face in her breasts, to feel her arms round him, rocking, soothing, making the swirl go away, making this bloody stupid unnecessary business go away. 'Got to go,' he managed. 'Someone at the door. See you Thursday.'

He slammed the phone down, bending over, rubbing his chest, his face. Oh God. He let his hands hang down and the glass dropped to the carpet; gin, a tiny splash, stained it a deeper red. Good God almighty, what a bloody performance. He reached down, rubbing at the gin until you would not have known it had been there, wishing all the time that it was all this garbage in his head that was being rubbed away. Furious at his mother. Bloody, bloody furious, and wanting his father, because he hadn't asked the impossible of him, but had just died properly. If he was here now they could share a drink, talk about his mother, talk about Peter remortgaging the Old Vicarage to buy the flat with cash. The old man had done it himself without Barbs ever knowing, so Peter could too.

He walked to the window, wishing it opened, wishing he could take a good deep breath because that would clear his head, that would settle everything back down. Far below he could see the traffic, headlights probing the dark, people on their way home. Their lives were so simple, so terribly simple, and he should be one of them, driving to some pleasant house . . .

The musical tone of his mobile registered. He straightened, shaking his head to clear it, trying to remember where he had left his phone, tracing the sound to the closet. He knew it would be Kate. He told her to always phone that number because he liked to be accessible to her at any time, and she'd swallowed it. He never gave her the hotel number now, not after the time he'd checked out to spend the night with Jan and she'd phoned, and what a bloody fuss when he'd arrived home.

He opened the closet and found the phone in his jacket pocket.

He hadn't even realised she'd become suspicious. In fact he still suspected it was his mother who had encouraged her, because the two women had become far too close once Barbs became really laid up. It hadn't mattered, because the hotel manager had played ball and written and apologised for his receptionist's error. It was a tip his father had given him years ago. Same hotel as often as possible, and build up a relation-ship with the staff.

Kate had not only been convinced but it had made her feel bad, and she couldn't do enough; when she had chosen to spare time from the sickroom, of course.

'Hi,' Kate's voice was clear and calm. 'Just thought I'd see how you were.'

'Tired, just about to get to bed.'

'Busy day? There are no big sticks you can use at this stage, are there? But you'll pull it off, you always do.'

The ache in his chest was easing. 'Look, those Swedes *are* coming over, can we do dinner for them? I thought I'd get the boss to join us. It'll be eight, Wednesday next. The full works. Can you manage that?'

It wasn't a question. If nothing else, Kate was a coper, and the foreign customers seemed to like being entertained at home rather than in yet another restaurant.

'Fine,' she said. 'But how are you really? Peter, we must talk . . .'

'Look, got to go, Kate, someone at the door.'

'At this hour?'

'They didn't leave me any towels, hotels are getting sloppy. Sleep well. Jude OK?'

'Yes.'

'See you Friday.'

At eleven thirty Peter was still wide awake. Rolling over he dialled Jan's number. 'Sweetheart,' he said when she picked up the phone, 'I'm sorry I was short. You really will like the furniture, I promise, and the present.'

'I know I will.'

He'd known she wouldn't be asleep; she never was if they'd had words. 'In bed, but not asleep, eh?'

'That's right.'

She laughed gently and he could detect the relief. He ran his hand from his stomach to his thighs, feeling himself tighten. 'Wearing?' he asked.

'Nothing.'

Excitement snatched at him. 'Then do what I tell you.'

CHAPTER FOUR

THE PREVIOUS APRIL

Sitting outside the shoreside café, Barbs lifted her face to the sun. She adored Branscombe Beach and had thought that one day, when her post-Keith hello-life list was complete, she would move to Branscombe village set back in the valley, and walk to the beach every day. In season, when the café was open, she would guzzle flapjacks at eleven, and have two cups of coffee. Perhaps she would even stride here in the afternoon as well, for tea.

But she wouldn't charge up the coast to Beer; it was too serious a hill. Instead she'd take the slightly more reasonable path which wound up past the hotel, and up into the woods and eventually reached Sidmouth. If it was April, as it was now, there would be violets and primroses, and later there would be wild garlic and the hum of heat-sodden insects. Whenever she went, however, she would always divert to the cliff edge and be renewed by the sight of the sea, by the clean air, by the gulls flying free. Stupid old fart.

Kate was shifting slightly. She sat opposite, her back to the sea. Why? They normally sat side by side at the wooden tables, shading their eyes, not needing to talk any more. Their post-Keith friend-ship finally too deep for that.

Perhaps she had guessed?

Barbs stirred her coffee, not wanting it but drinking anyway. As she swallowed though, it tangled with the panic and the terror, and she pressed a hand to her mouth, insisting, forcing, until it was down.

People were crunching over the pebbled beach fifty yards in front of them. Some stoics were sitting on fold-up chairs on the grass that lay between the beach and the café reading newspapers which the wind was doing its best to snatch. Hikers laboured towards Beer, backs bent. They'd still be doing that next year. The violets would return, the garlic too. She was the only one who wouldn't. She stirred her coffee again and again. It was too cold for bubbles to collect at the vortex.

'OK, Barbs, what did the hospital say, and why didn't you let me know it was today? I wanted to come with you. We've been through it together so far.' Kate's voice was strained beneath the calm.

Barbs continued to stir, watching, watching the bubbles. Darling, beloved, gentle, repressed Kate who'd been with her every inch of the way over the last six months, even to the extent of fishing out a selection of perfectly ghastly wigs. Not needed, thank God, and for that she should be grateful. Strong hair, at least she had strong hair. Suddenly she laughed, lifting her head, shoving her flapjack across to Kate. 'Finish that for me.'

'It's not even started.' Kate objected, her eyes never leaving Barbs's. Kate too had lost weight over the last few months, her cheekbones were too sharp, and the grey at her temples was new; she cared too much.

Moved, Barbs looked down. A dog was sniffing around the table, its lead spinning out of the plastic handle clutched by a woman sitting near the shop. 'Give it to the bloody dog, then.' Barbs heard her own savagery, and saw that it had triggered understanding in Kate, but no, Barbs didn't want that yet. She grabbed the Denners carrier bag on the seat beside her. 'See what I bought.' She drew out a pink and purple striped T-shirt, looking at it. Only at it.

'Great,' Kate said. 'So you went to the hospital, had your consult, went shopping without waiting for the sales. When have you ever not waited for the sales? Then you rang me, picked me up, drove me here, not saying a word.'

I might not have time to wait for the sales, Barbs wanted to say. That's what she had scripted, as she had walked from the hospital to the car park. She had known before Mr Zaire had told her, but she hadn't believed. She still didn't, in a way. In another she did, and it was then that the terror choked her. She rolled the words around in her mind again – I might not have the time to wait for the sales. They seemed too dramatic now. She said nothing. Anyway, until the verdict was spoken it wasn't cast in stone.

She watched the gulls above them, the sparrows hopping from table to table. Behind Kate the sea gleamed. She sighed and smiled slightly, lowering the T-shirt. What nonsense. A fact was a fact, stupid woman.

26

'When I became . . .' Barbs hesitated as Kate pushed the flapjack back into the middle of the table. '. . . unwell six months ago, I looked at everything with new eyes. Fifty per cent chance of death made everything fifty per cent more vivid. Today it's so glaring I can hardly see, so I'm going to walk into those woods, into the shade, while you eat that damn flapjack and put on some of the weight you've lost.'

She pushed herself up from the seat, past the couple whose dog was now over the other side of the eating area looking as though it was about to do something unforgivable. Barbs yelled at them, 'It isn't enough to hang on to the end of a piece of elastic. You're still the ones responsible for his arse.' She didn't wait for their reaction, just strode on, trying to beat down the rage because they had next year, and so did their bloody dog, and she had much more to do with her life than they had. For God's sake, since when did life hinge on a poop scoop?

She tore through the gate, into the field, but already the hill was slowing her, already her chest was failing her, already every step was jarring. She felt a hand under her elbow. 'All you need is a broomstick, you old witch.' It was Kate. Always it was Kate, darling Kate with her eyes which lit up the world around her, or at least her mother-in-law's world, though that pillock of a son seemed his usual impervious self. But she didn't want to think of that right now. Instead she would keep to the broomstick.

'Well, at least it would get me to the top with no hassle,' Barbs gasped.

'Calm down and take smaller steps.'

'Have they wound that bloody dog in?'

'Would they dare do anything else? You might return.'

They walked on slowly, reaching the next gate, passing through it into the woods, and she told Kate that nothing had worked, and that she had three months to live, though perhaps it would be a little longer.

They stopped near the violets, and now, under the trees, there was nothing glaring or vivid, it was just dark and flat. They stood arm in arm and nothing was said. It wasn't necessary. Together they watched midges, and the tentative new growth all around. Together they listened to the wind amongst last year's dry beech leaves, and then they walked through the woods to the cliff top, and the full force of the spring sun warmed them as a fishing boat made

27

its way towards Beer, leaving behind a frothy wake.

Barbs said, 'I haven't even half finished my list. Life's a bitch.'

'There's still time.'

Barbs squeezed her arm. 'I'm heartbroken, angry and bloody terrified, and I can't quite believe it. I should though, for God's sake, it was always on the cards.'

Kate's voice was steady. 'How can you believe it when all your, our, reactions are geared to continuation, to the forming and carrying out of plans?'

Barbs laughed a little. 'My word, but what intelligent words you use.'

'Straight out of a book, Grandma.' The steadiness was weakening.

The fishing boat was taking a slow wide arc. Perhaps it wasn't going back just yet. Perhaps it had seen another shoal, or maybe just felt like playing hookey. Barbs watched the boat, hardly daring to breathe. Was it having another chance at a catch? Was it breaking out of a set plan and extending its day, having another bite at the cherry, a romp? But no, it picked up speed again and was soon lost to sight around the headland, and as it went, it took something of hers. Hope, perhaps, that the unexpected could happen.

She stared until the wake began to dissipate, then looked at Kate. 'Is this a punishment for upsetting Peter, for slighting the life I had with his father? Because that's how he sees it, and he's right. But there has to be a time, surely, when you can stop having to fit in with another's perceptions?' She was tapping Kate's arm fiercely. 'But because of the list, have I made it worse for you? Have I made him more difficult, especially by eating into the savings? He wanted me to exist on the interest. There won't be much to leave now, besides the bungalow.'

Kate's arm was round her now, her voice adamant, her hair lifting in the breeze. 'Stop it. You made a decision.' She laughed, 'And a bloody long list which didn't hurt anyone, or not until you sent postcards which made us all feel extraordinarily boring. And no, you haven't made Peter more difficult. It's all quite normal – it's job stress, middle age, just life really.'

Life, eh. Lucky Peter to be troubled by life. Death was a bit more of a problem. Barbs watched an early butterfly chase shadows amongst the gorse. Simon, Kate and Peter's elder child, had phoned from America last night. Darling Simon, so like Kate, or perhaps like Kate would have been if she hadn't married Peter. Wasn't it said that sometimes those separated by a generation could talk more easily? It was certainly true of her and Simon. Though no, that intimated that he couldn't talk to his mother, and that was wrong, they were close, very close, but some things were outside their remit; Peter, for instance.

Last night she and her grandson had talked of him, as they did increasingly. Of his domineering control which was steadily reducing Kate's position in the partnership to zero, of her acceptance of this status quo. As always Barbs had drawn parallels with her own life, pointing out the insidious chipping away at self-esteem which went unnoticed by the recipient, the repression of emotion, until something happened to reveal the toxic situation in all its glory; like Keith's death, and the presentation of a poem.

But last night Simon had gone too far. He had dared to criticise his mother to Barbs, and it was then that she explained the circumstances of his birth.

Hikers clumped along the path, but the butterfly ignored them. Beside Barbs Kate was lifting her face to the sun. It was a beautiful fine-boned face, but often a closed face. It was as Barbs had been with Keith, though worse, for while Keith had just been a bully, Peter had always felt a justifiable bully, one trapped into marriage by Kate's pregnancy. Good grief, though, it wasn't as if he hadn't been an equal partner in Simon's procreation. No matter, it had set the tone – with Kate endlessly scrabbling to appease. Though of course, along with being a bully Peter had been handsome, charming, sexy, just like his father.

And what had Barbs done, to support Kate? Nothing, she told Simon, because she had been too neutered until after Keith's death. It was then that she'd tried speaking to Peter, but how do you make him listen? Simon knew just what she meant. And Kate . . . Well, Kate just said that Peter was under pressure, that he had had to adapt his plans to cope with a family, that he had always done his best for them, that . . . Poor, darling Kate, so many reasons, so little confidence, so conditioned.

Simon had said, 'You must tell her it wasn't her fault.'

Barbs had replied, 'I have, but like me, her life needs a catalyst, and it is her *life, my darling boy.'*

'Are you all right?' Kate's voice startled Barbs.

'Bloody marvellous,' Barbs snapped. 'Why should I be anything else?'

'Where did we put that broomstick?' Kate murmured, squeezing her arm.

Barbs leaned into Kate, loving her too much to speak for a moment, unable to cope with the thought of the life her daughter-in-law led, or the lack of life, grateful for the deep pain which caught at her and preoccupied her as the breeze stiffened, and more hikers passed behind them.

At last it was gone, and Barbs stood straight, searching for the butterfly, but it too was gone. 'You know, Kate, when I drove here I was thinking that I wished there would be a war, that I wished lots of us would die, so that I wouldn't be alone. I am quite astonishingly foul.'

'Don't flatter yourself, you old bat. You're astonishingly normal.' Kate was hugging her gently, taking her hand. Kate's were so strong and capable, whilst Barbs's were so pale, blue-veined, bony. 'Anyway, you won't be alone. I'll be with you night and day, but before that, there's your list. What's left on it?' Kate failed to keep her voice even.

Barbs automatically listed: skydiving, horse riding, Yellowstone Park, Australia, white water rafting, black water rafting.

'Is that all?' Kate asked. 'My word, it'll be a doddle.' She was under control again.

'Come with me to Yellowstone, Kate. We can do some white water rafting.'

Kate smiled. 'We'll see, but first let's book the riding – but not a snorting stallion I'll have you know – and then the skydiving if someone will guarantee a soft landing. But we won't necessarily tell Peter about that one.'

They let the breeze snatch at their clothes until they spotted the couple with the dog walking at the water's edge, way below. 'Shall I call down?' Barbs asked.

'Certainly not. Any tranquillity the sea has induced would be cast aside.' They laughed softly together. Kate said, 'When I'm old and grey I'm going to live with a view of the sea or the river. Now, that would be heaven.'

Barbs nodded slowly, suddenly thoughtful. For another long moment they watched the couple and their dog, and then Barbs said, 'I want you to scatter me here, Kate, but steer clear of couples

30

with dogs. *You must do it, Kate darling, and bring Penny. But if Peter joins you, do make sure of the wind direction. I simply could not bear to end up on his nasal hair.'*

Kate roared with laughter. 'I doubt he'd be too thrilled about that either.'

Slowly they walked away from the cliff edge and took the steps which had been cut into the slope, one by one, but the pain of the jarring took Barbs's breath, and she stopped, white and frightened. Kate came to her, her hand outstretched. 'Hey, Nigel Mansell, take your time.'

Barbs stared at the hand, and then reluctantly she took it, allowing her daughter-in-law to take her weight. Slowly, horribly slowly, they descended the steps until the slope was more gentle. Immediately Barbs shook free of Kate, who turned, walking ahead, waiting for her by the gate, her face carefully noncommittal. The hinges squealed as they passed through into the field which skirted the hotel.

Barbs waited for a moment, looking back at the top of the cliff. So, this was what it all meant, this stupid bloody illness. Two years of independence down the bloody swanny. Well, not if she had anything to do with it. 'Do you hear,' she shouted at Kate. 'I'm not going to be bloody dependent on anything, or anyone again. I won't put up with it. I won't sacrifice myself to this thing. I will be in control, right until the end. I'll decide what's to become of me. Do you hear?'

Kate was shaking her head, half smiling, her arms crossed. 'Do I hear? Along with the rest of the world. But then you always could be counted on as a stand-in foghorn.'

Barbs laughed. 'Oh, my darling, beloved girl.' Suddenly it all seemed better and together they returned to the café.

Yes, perhaps just one more cup of coffee.

CHAPTER FIVE

Kate oiled the baking tray for the salmon *en croûte* she had bought at the supermarket during her lunch hour. Peter had phoned from the airport just as she walked through the door at six thirty to say he was about to pick up the hire car. She checked the oven – it was almost up to heat. Good enough, anyway, and twenty minutes' cooking would bring the time to eight. Just about right. Keeping her eyes on *Coronation Street*, she slid in the salmon, then tipped the mangetout and baby corn into a pan.

She sat on the kitchen chair watching Deirdre following along behind her glasses, and reached for a banana, suddenly hungry, but then it had been a long day. Jan had called in sick and Kate had had to work until six. She peeled the banana. Jan's migraines were becoming more frequent, so perhaps surgery really did need another full-timer. She didn't like the thought of the hours, not now, though a few months ago she'd have been relieved, because it would have helped their finances, which had become more and more fraught.

It would help if Peter's rise had come through, but all the employees were being asked to do more for less. It was outrageous. Her hunger disappeared. Whilst Deirdre and Ken grizzled over their drinks in the Rovers she tossed the banana in the bin, then boiled the kettle ready for the mangetout.

It was as Gail and Sally put their heads together in the café that she heard Peter's car in the drive, and saw the headlights as they caught the *leylandii*. She managed to change channels before his key turned in the lock and was back at the oven as he walked into the kitchen.

'Tired?' she asked, though he looked well, all sort of scrubbed and shiny. She preferred his hair this length, just touching the collar of his blue shirt. It was these coloured shirts that had fuelled her suspicions, but of course, people had a right to develop their tastes, Peter had been quite correct.

Peter rubbed his forehead and kissed the air above her head, looking at the news on Channel Four, answering her question with another. 'Anything world shattering happened?'

'Not a lot,' she called to his retreating back while he groaned and propped his briefcase at the foot of the stairs as usual.

'God, it's been a long week. I'll change and be down in five.'

She was already nodding, knowing the script, but this time she called after him as he climbed the stairs. 'It's a scratch supper tonight, is that OK? I've been working all day.' She waited nervously.

He stopped and peered down. 'How scratch?'

She explained.

He shrugged. 'I was looking forward to soup. It's a muggy night out there and I've been haring around like a blue-arsed fly, and I'm ravenous. Surely there's a tin of something you can rustle up? Better make it snappy, though. John's coming at nine. He's dotting the i's and crossing the t's of Mother's will for us. Be down in a minute.' He was taking his tie off as he went on up.

Kate stared after him. The will? There were all these wheels in motion when Barbs was still everywhere around them, between them, irrevocably between them, but still un-acknowledged, still not discussed.

Even yesterday afternoon when she'd stood with Penny on the cliff overlooking the sea at Branscombe and let the ashes fly on the wind, *it* had all still been there.

'She so loved it when she skydived,' she'd said to Penny; anything to stop the images crowding her mind. They'd stood silent, the empty casket at their feet. Hikers still walked as they had done last April, and there was a fishing boat on the water, the hill to Beer was as steep, the beach as wonderful. Behind them the trees of the wood were impossibly vivid and amazing in this most stunning of autumns.

Any minute, though, their leaves would begin to fall, and in the relentless pattern of the seasons spring would come, and there would be violets again, and primroses. As usual. Just the same. But Kate knew that nothing in her own life would ever be the same again.

Into the wind she had shouted, 'She was seventy and

experiencing so many things, but she was a selfish old bag, and she asked too much of people.' She'd stopped to draw breath, to yank the hair back from her face, unable to go on because of a terrible rage crowding her. But then she'd shouted again and it was almost a scream, 'For God's sake . . .'

She'd stopped just in time. Closing her eyes she waited, then at the touch of Penny's hand she'd looked out to sea, surprised that the sun still shone, the boat was still chugging. 'Sorry, Pen, I bad-mouthed your boss. By the way, how is the Big Guy this fine day?'

Penny had hugged her tightly. 'As well as can be expected given his hours.' Penny had been wearing Paco Rabane's Calandre, her special occasion perfume, and she had left her uniform in the wardrobe, preferring jeans, a duffel coat and a purple scarf for her farewell to Barbs. Kate's scarf was purple too.

Kate leaned into the hug, desperate for the comfort. 'He'll be busier than ever right now, because she'll be nagging him to blow up enough isobars to whoosh her to the Aegean. She loved Greece, it's where she learned to windsurf just before she fell ill.'

Penny had held her tighter, and Kate knew that this was what Penny had been waiting for, and to make her friend feel better she talked and talked about loss, and memories, and laughter, but nothing else.

Kate found lobster bisque in the cupboard and while that was simmering she laid cutlery for the extra course in the dining room, wishing not for the first time that Peter thought food tasted just as good on laps in front of the television. The meal was rushed, and though the sweetcorn would have been better tossed in butter as Peter suggested, it was passable, and the red wine was fruity, just as he liked. He was visibly relaxing and so she could too.

She asked how many Swedes were coming next week. He checked his watch and said, preoccupied, 'I'll find out, but chop, chop, John'll be here any minute.' He nodded to the old oak bureau which doubled as a drinks cupboard.

Kate said, 'We're almost out of gin, did you bring any duty-free? I rather hoped . . .' She let it peter away as she collected the dessert plates, angry with herself. She should have bought some at lunchtime for goodness' sake.

He threw down his napkin. 'You know I like to sleep when I'm flying and I've enough to carry without endless carrier bags.' It would be only one, actually, she thought. 'Anyway, you can get it almost as cheaply at the supermarket. Surely we're not really out?' He was pushing back his chair, irritation in every movement, stepping round her as she picked up a spoon she'd dropped. The doorbell rang. 'God almighty, he's early.'

'Only five minutes.' Even as she spoke she knew she should have said nothing. She usually wouldn't, but things were constantly pushing past her mind, and out. She hurried out with the plates.

Peter followed her closely, muttering in her ear, 'I suppose there's no tonic in the fridge either?'

'If you'd let me know John was coming . . .' Kate stopped by the kitchen table, took a breath. 'Yes,' she said softly, as he turned and headed for the front door. 'Yes, the tonic's always in the fridge, and there's enough gin for a couple of drinks. I'll get more tomorrow.' But he wasn't listening and she knew she was wittering.

She didn't load the dishes, just dumped them by the sink then doubled back towards the dining room, waving to John as Peter took his coat. 'All right?' she called, smiling, not waiting for his reply. She snatched up the gin, grabbed three crystal glasses and waited in the doorway as the men made for the sitting room, calling, 'Your poison's gin, isn't it, John?'

John Livingstone smiled. 'Certainly is, well remembered, Kate. How are you?' He was a small, neat man, married to a small, neat woman called Henrietta. Simon always said that they'd look good perched on a mantelpiece, alongside their small, neat children. Simon and Jude had been at the local independent day school with the Livingstone children and had liked them. Had a solicitor been able to afford the fees rather more easily than a project manager? Obviously, since Henrietta didn't work. Kate held the bottle against her, hiding the gin line, wishing he'd move along. 'I'm fine. Be with you in a moment.'

Peter hustled John into the sitting room and she could hear him putting more logs on the wood burner, but they'd roast.

35

Or was she the only one getting hot these days? Was it that time of life? Difficult to tell in that department, since she'd had a hysterectomy ten years ago.

She rummaged in the dresser for the silver tray, giving it a quick rub with her sleeve. Solicitors breathed the same rarified air as business colleagues and accountants. She squeezed two gins out of the bottle, adding tonic, lemon and ice, trusting John to have more sense than to drink more than one if he was driving.

Peter stood by the marble fireplace and looked hard at her as she entered. She nodded, tapping the glass that held no gin. He relaxed, taking the other two, handing one to John. 'Sorry, old man, not a lot of chance to say "when" tonight. She's obviously had too many years' of cutting up kids' food.' Both men laughed. Kate dug for a smile and found one, but for heaven's sake . . .

John was lifting his glass to them both. 'I'd like to say cheers, but instead I must offer my condolences on your sad loss.'

Peter sat down opposite John, who had claimed the settee for himself. His briefcase lay open beside him, full of neatly stacked papers. He took several, and leafed through them. Kate walked to the patio windows, looking out into the garden as the security light came on. Which neighbourhood cat had broken the beam? Or was it a fox, maybe a badger? According to Peter, security lighting meant a substantial discount on the insurance, so she supposed it made sense. But it was like living in Colditz. Barbs had said that Peter only wanted the neighbours to think he had Old Masters on every wall. Then he had insisted on having them installed at Lamorna, Barbs's bungalow, too. She pressed the cold glass to her cheek.

'Kate!' Peter's voice was sharp. She could tell from his face that he'd been trying to get her attention for some while. 'If you're quite ready, John hasn't all night.'

She sat down in the chair opposite the fire. John was shifting uncomfortably. She apologised. 'I'm sorry, I'm just a little tired. We're both tired, it's been difficult.'

John smiled sympathetically. 'It's a stressful time. I remember when my own mother died I felt as though I was on a seesaw; fine one minute, all over the place the next. And then all these frightful legal bits to deal with too.' He put down his drink and straightened the papers on his lap. 'Now, to business. I'm not sure, Peter, if your mother made you privy to the dispensation of her will. In fact, I'm not sure if you were aware that she made a new will immediately before her death?'

He was looking at them both but it was Peter who sat forward, rolling his glass between his hands, more alert than he'd been all evening. 'A new will? Whatever for, for God's sake? She didn't go barking and leave it all to some damned adventure school or something?' He was laughing, but Kate could see the frown and hear the wariness in his voice. He stared at her, his voice accusing, 'Did you know of this?'

Kate shook her head. She knew nothing of either the first, or the new will. It had never occurred to her to think about it. God, it *was* hot in here. She eased out of the waistcoat Penny had given her for Christmas last year. It was multicoloured. 'So it will tone with whatever shade of purple Barbs is wearing,' the card had said. She smoothed her cream cotton blouse.

John had his hand up. 'If I may . . .' He had their attention again. 'It is quite straightforward. All monies and investments at the time of her death to you, Peter, though we know that they're almost depleted – she got a bit of a spurt on in the final months, and who can blame her. Kate has one purple dress, of her choosing. The rest to be delivered to a charity shop "in the hope that more old trouts will learn there's a world out there". Her words, not mine.' John smiled slightly, tapping the document.

Kate said, 'We've made a sort of start on the clothes.' Peter hushed her with a wave of his hand.

John smiled at her and continued, 'Now, the proceeds of the sale of the bungalow and its contents to Kate, in recognition of all that she did for her during her illness. She has enclosed a letter to me, wherein she has expressed her unofficial requirements, which are that you use the proceeds of the sale to buy a flat or house with a view, by water. She wishes you to let this property, Kate, to enable you to have the time and income to give up your job, and find rest and recuperation. She has also left a letter for you.' He waved it at Kate.

For a moment Kate didn't understand, and then she did, and the breath just went from her body. Disappeared. Then she gasped it back, but it didn't fill her lungs and she was drowning, and all she could see was the gold of John's cufflinks as he passed the will across to Peter. The cufflinks were gold like wheat, like the sun. She made herself take another breath, and another. She saw Peter take the will, and read it and the letter. She heard John say, 'You shouldn't find your executor's duties too onerous, Peter. As you heard, it's all perfectly straightforward.'

As John sat back his sleeve rode down over his cufflinks. Peter, though, did not sit back. He was wearing no jacket, just a light wool sweater, in a fawn which almost matched her trousers. His fingers were pressing so hard they were white at the tips, as hard as her own fingers were pressing the glass she held.

She was still trying to recreate John's words but they were flying around too fast, though she'd heard, yes she'd heard them, but they were insane. She watched as Peter looked at her, his face red with rage. 'This is ridiculous. We need the money from the house to help pay off the mortgage.'

Kate's brain clicked at the sound of his voice. Words sorted themselves and fell into slots either side of the breaths she was taking. Peter repeated himself slowly, as though she was an idiot. 'We need that money for the mortgage, do you hear? I was banking on it.'

The words sank deeper into the slots. They clinked and clanked, and her own thoughts clarified and sharpened as his dark eyes bored into her. When his father had died their accountant had told them not to pay off their mortgage with money Barbs offered them. It was Peter who was the stupid one now. For once it wasn't her. Her voice seemed loud. 'No we don't, you said that we'd lose the tax relief if we did that. You said that we needed to keep it up to £30,000. You said it was best that Barbs put the money into investments to pay her expenses. You said . . .'

'For God's sake, you're not a bloody parrot, are you?' His top lip had thinned, which meant he was going to shout.

Her stomach knotted but John was leaning forward, staring at Peter. 'Just a minute.'

Kate had never heard John speak so firmly, never heard a man cut across her husband, never heard someone defend her other than Barbs and Simon. She watched as Peter turned to him, becoming conscious of where he was, but none of that

38

mattered because she hadn't dreamed that Barbs would do this.

'No,' John was saying, waving away the copy of the will Peter was returning to him. She watched, as though from a distance. John gathered up his bits and pieces. 'No,' he repeated, 'that's your copy, Peter, but from what you've just said we obviously need to talk through a few things. My office, Monday. I insist.'

He was clicking his briefcase shut. Once, twice. Kate watched carefully. John rose. She couldn't move. All she could do was watch as Peter followed him into the hall, then listen to their muffled voices. John's was suddenly sharp. The front door opened, closed. She hadn't dreamed that this was what Barbs would do. Oh dear God. She had her hand to her mouth, pressing hard.

Peter was in the room, standing over her, a buff envelope in his hand. 'A letter from the grave for you. John forgot to give it to you.'

She reached out. He held on to it. For a moment they stayed like that, both tugging at it. She stared up into his rage. It was almost palpable, but then the envelope was in her grasp and he was shouting at her. 'So, this is how you get paid off, is it? What did you do, whinge to her about how hard it is at the surgery? God, you must have been praying I couldn't do what she asked because you knew it would give you a bloody handle, didn't you? Well, it isn't yours, and it wasn't hers to give. It was Father's, he grafted for it, and then it should have been mine, because I sorted out her affairs so that she had something to bloody well leave.'

She could feel his spittle, smell the gin on his breath. But how could he have spare breath to shower over her when she was struggling, in and out, in and out?

He was striding to the door, yelling, 'I'm going out.'

The words were clinking through the slots again. 'You've been drinking, you shouldn't drive.'

'For God's sake, shut the fuck up.' The sitting room door slammed, then the front door. If she turned she'd see the headlights on the *leylandii*, but she didn't. The envelope was still in her hand. It almost matched her trousers.

My dearest Kate

39

By now the shrieking and screaming will either have just started, or perhaps it has finished. He always could do a good tantrum. I'm having to write this while dear old John Livingstone is sitting at the bedside looking uncomfortable. Men do hate illness, but then I'm not its biggest fan. I'm trying to find words, but the drip, the pills . . . I keep coming and going, my dear. You must *accept my house, because it is mine. You'll have all the guff about it being Keith's. In one sense yes, but in another no. I had some money from my parents' estate and it went into buying our first house. Therefore I feel able to divide things as I have.*

I must just rest.

Here, back again. I insist that you honour my bequest. I insist that you do not allow Peter's 'common sense' to prevail. I insist that you take this gift which will bring you time and space to recover. You will not forget but you will come to terms with the fact that you did for me what my son would not, however hard I begged him, and that in order to help me you put aside your own ethics and principles.

Forgive me, I'm tired, muddled. Let me rest.

I can't write much more, dearest Kate, because I want this to be in my own hand. I want this to be me talking to you. I had not intended that anyone should help me, but my timing was bad, I grew too weak or my arthritis too strong. Stupid bottles. Only children can take off these child-proof tops. You were everything to me, dearest Kate. You nursed me as no one else could, you cheered me on, as only you can. One last thing? Well, when did I ever leave it at one thing, when a dozen would do? You must promise me that you will *buy your holiday let, that you will* not *enter that surgery for six months so that you are not constantly reminded, and that should the occasion arise, you will always deny that you helped me die. Make these promises for the sake of your children, and for the sake of my memory. I love you, Kate. I have left you a frock of your choosing. You will know when you are ready to wear it. Perhaps it will be when you go to Yellowstone. I didn't get to cross it off, did I? Perhaps you will do it for me?*

Barbs.

Peter thrashed through the outskirts of the town. It had rained

40

earlier and the spray from the van he had just overtaken had made a bloody awful mess of the windscreen. He pumped the washers, peering through the smears until his vision was clear. He drove for half an hour, then pulled into a lay-by, dragging out his mobile almost before the car had stopped. He was sweating, but it was a damp cold sweat. He stabbed out the number of his accountant.

'Yes?' Alan's voice sounded metallic.

'It's Peter.'

'Pete, for God's sake, you still at your desk?'

'No, I'm bloody not, I'm in a lay-by shitting bricks.' Cars were flashing past. Where were they all going? Probably somewhere nice, damn them. He told Alan the contents of the will.

Alan chuckled, 'She was a card, your mother was.'

'She was a senile old fool, and she had no right.'

Alan sobered. 'Actually she had every right.'

'Fine, well, if that's all the help you can be . . .' A lorry pulled in behind him, and lights went on in the cab.

Alan was saying, 'Calm down. You're obviously worried about the remortgage. Can you get Jan to pay towards it?'

Impatiently Peter shook his head. 'I don't want her paying more than she is and then having a claim on it. She won't last, any more than any of the others, and I want to have . . .'

'Somewhere to take the next one? Why don't you just book into an hotel like you used to?'

'Look, I didn't phone to have you agony aunting me, and anyway, what the hell is wrong with enjoying an investment?'

'You're a bastard, you know.' Alan's voice was mild. The insult meant nothing, they'd known one another too long.

The lorry driver had his television on now – what was it, *Film on 4*? Peter shook his head; the line was breaking up. He shouted, 'Look, Alan, you and I both know I'm up to my eyes in debt. Come on, come up with something. It was your idea to buy the flat with cash by remortgaging the Old Vicarage. Then there's Jude's university, and making good Simon's long haul, and what about my own spending money?'

Alan's voice was soothing. 'Calm down, rationalise, turn things around. There's Barbs's insurance.'

'That'll only just about cover the funeral costs.'

'OK, but remember that when the income from the letting property starts it will help, and anyway, it would be bad business to settle the mortgage now. I've already reminded you of the redemption fee you'd have to pay, so look on it as a blessing in disguise and go ahead and fulfil Barbara's requirements. You should manage to tick over, but you'll have to cut down on your outgoings. They've gone up a lot recently. You're not back to gambling, are you?' His voice was suddenly anxious.

Peter sighed. 'For Pete's sake, I've got enough balls in the air without that.' Anyway, any day now he'd have a win, and then was the time to stop.

Alan said, 'Best to get a property that needs a bit doing to it, cheaper that way, obviously. Better still, get one that's been repossessed. You could be in by the end of November and have four months before Easter to get it ready. Or rather Kate would. She did up your mausoleum, didn't she? It'll keep her busy, keep her mind off you and any hotel rooms you happen to have checked out of.'

He chuckled. Peter did not. Alan continued: 'Then at the end of the season you'll not only have had the income but can sell it as a going concern for considerably more than you paid, and it will be the right time to pay off the mortgage. Easy-peasy.'

Peter felt his muscles relaxing and as he saw the lorry driver moving in his cab he found himself wondering what these guys did when they needed a comfort break. Was there a portaloo in the cab? Alan was saying, 'You just need to convince Kate, appeal to her common sense. But then you seem able to swing most things, so all in all you'll come out smelling of roses as usual, old lad.'

Peter grimaced. 'Almost didn't. I was so bloody mad I had a go at her, and John cottoned on to the fact that she thought we just had the original mortgage.'

There was a silence. 'I hope you're not about to tell me you forged her signature. Who the hell witnessed it? No, on second thoughts, don't tell me. I don't want to know anything about any of it, but have you sorted John?'

Peter was nodding. Outside the rain had begun again and the car was steaming up. 'Yes. At first he wanted a meeting, but I persuaded him that Kate was confused because of shock.'

'He probably pretended to believe you. He won't want to know either. Just tell me it wasn't Jan who witnessed it – she could have you over a barrel if she chose. No, again on second thoughts, I really, *really* don't want to know. Now, if you don't mind I have a bed to go to, and from the sounds of it, you have a situation to recover. Go and be nice to your wife – she's a good sort.'

'For good sort, read a boring menopausal neurotic, or she is at the moment. What a bloody epitaph.'

'Hey, enough of that. It's no good bumping her off – you can't gain from a crime, or not for six years at least, just remember that.'

They were laughing as Alan broke the connection.

Kate had just finished her port. Bugger Horlicks. She washed the wine glass – well, she'd needed more than a drop. She looked up. Peter's car was coming up the drive. The *leylandii* were getting more than their fair share of the spotlight tonight. Bertie would have to gather himself together for a finale grand enough to bring them back down to earth tomorrow.

Her head was spinning slightly, her stomach was turning over, and it turned even faster at the sound of his key. She braced herself, keeping her eyes on the rain beating against the window. She heard him walk into the kitchen, heard him come up to her. For God's sake, relax. He wasn't going to hit her, he never did that. It was just that he got tense, made her nervous, made her overreact, say something stupid.

He was right behind her and she knew she should face him, but then she felt his arms sliding round her waist and surprise stopped her breathing. 'I'm sorry,' he said against her hair. 'I'm so sorry for everything.' He backed away, slumping down at the table, his head in his hands. She turned, and her breath was coming quick and shallow now, and so was his, his shoulders shaking. 'I'm just so sorry. It's all been so much, and I feel so bad about letting you help Mother die, when it should have been me. I don't know what I'd do without you, Kate. You know how I let things get to me, the responsibility, the pressure . . .'

She was at his side now, stroking his hair. It was so long

since he had wanted her to touch him, so long since he had apologised, and needed her. So very long. 'Ssh, it'll be all right, everything will be all right. Ssh.'

His arms came round her then. 'I'm sorry, Kate. You're so patient, always so good, but I just couldn't. I just thought I'd get it wrong, not give her enough, make it worse. You're the one who knows about that sort of thing. You understand, don't you?'

Kate was nodding, and in a way she did, but it wasn't that hard to help someone swallow a bottle of capsules and hold them as they died. The hard bit was to live with it for the rest of your life.

Peter said, 'I failed, but you didn't. I'll always be grateful. I love you, you know, and this has made me realise just how much. I know I don't show it, but I'm so tired, so busy, and there was Mother's finances to manage on top of it all, and the fact that she was dying. It was so sad. She drove me mad but it was so sad, and you were so good.'

He laid his head against her, and his arms were holding her tightly. Well, what did it matter who had done it, Kate thought. They were sharing it now, acknowledging and admitting it, and now she was talking and it was as though a dam was bursting inside her. His arms were tightening and she in her turn held him closer. 'We have no one else we can talk to. We need one another,' she said, and at his nod she felt the awful anger beginning to die, and the anguish abating, and as she discovered the familiar shape of him it was relief that consumed her.

Peter found that his dry eyes were filling, his stomach was fluttering and when he said, 'Oh God, it was all so awful,' he found he meant it and he allowed himself to miss his mother, and cry for her, because she had once been nice, and the last two years were not typical, and could be forgotten.

Kate held him tighter still and it was as though he was a child and his mother was rocking him again, and for the first time he realised how tired he was, how much everything took out of him. She let him weep freely, then helped him to bed.

CHAPTER SIX

Peter was at Alan's house by nine thirty the next day. April, Alan's wife, let him in, and he kissed her on the cheek, asking after the children, one of whom was at GCSE stage, the other dreading his A-level mocks in January. Beyond her the study door opened and Alan beckoned.

'Come on in, but I should charge you double rate for a Saturday. I've only got half an hour; April has a sofa she wants to drag me off to see at Denners.'

He grinned at his wife, who lifted an eyebrow and said, 'A bit more than just see, my lad. I want your chequebook brought into the equation. How's poor Kate? She's had a tough time.'

April was a faded blonde, with the sort of skin that aged quickly, and together with Alan's red hair and skin the kids didn't stand a chance. Peter made appropriate noises before making his way into Alan's study. April called, 'Coffee?'

Both men refused. Alan waved him to the chair on the other side of his desk. 'So, you've made progress with Kate from the sounds of your call and got the promise of a bit of capital when the selling and buying goes through. How much?'

'I told her that £20,000 was the absolute minimum I needed to get things straight, spun a bit of a story about pension arrears.'

'Quite true, because you're sailing close to the wind in that area too.'

Peter didn't want Alan pontificating. 'So, what about. . .'

'The estate agent, and a repossession list?' Alan was steepling his fingers as he did when he was in professional mode. 'The first I've fixed up. Ben Aspers will do the biz at a one per cent rate, after a bit of arm twisting. You're expected at Barbara's bungalow at ten thirty this morning; he'll measure up and get it on the books pronto.' He tossed a business card across to Peter. 'But the repossession list will take until Wednesday. There's this guy I know who faxes or e-mails out a list weekly. I've told him a West Country holiday home with a view of water. These properties don't come up too often on the list, which is non-specific anyway. It'll be up to you, or Kate I suppose, to weed them out. Put yourself on a few agents' mailing lists too.'

Peter nodded and put the card in his wallet. 'I rang around first thing.'

Alan sat back and whistled through his teeth. Peter looked at him. Alan's voice was curious when he spoke again. 'So, go on, tell me how the hell you've got Kate to play ball? Bloody hell, I can almost see your tail wagging from here.'

Peter didn't like Alan's study. It owed too much to April, what with the shag-pile carpet, the files hidden behind a mahogany veneer, the flowery wallpaper, and the Victorian relatives peering out of mock mahogany frames, but then Alan always said that if you seemed to be giving in on some things you could get away with God knows what. He said, 'I've settled her down so much that not only will she release me the £20,000 from the balance between the bungalow and the letting property, but I'm damn sure she'll sell up in October without a whimper. Why wouldn't she?'

'But how did you get her to agree to a repossessed property? I seem to remember that I touched a raw nerve at the Christmas party last year by telling her about a client who made a killing that way. She came back with something about "gaining through the misfortune of others being another nail in the coffin of society".' Alan shook his hand as though it was burning, and his laugh was rueful.

'Well, she hasn't actually agreed to repossession, but she always goes along with everything.' Peter crossed his legs, examining his nails. Well, almost, but she wouldn't be budged on Barbs's wishes, that was the bugger. Just wouldn't budge, so here he was, going through these bloody hoops.

'Peter,' Alan said. Peter looked up. Alan was leaning forward. 'Not always – she hasn't given up the will, has she? You need that balance. OK, a small conventionally bought house would give it to you, but then you won't get so much letting income.'

Peter stretched his arms out, then sat back, refusing to be panicked. 'She'll agree. She's come this far, hasn't she?'

Alan relaxed. 'How *did* you manage it?'

'Give in on something – isn't that what you always say? And she's been on about needing to talk; God, they'd analyse Armageddon given half the chance. So I talked, played on her sympathy, threw in a bit of emotional trauma. You know, the sort of thing you do when you're young and wet behind the ears. It's what Father always did with Mother and it hooks them in, just like he said.'

Alan was shaking his head. 'A shit descended from a shit.'

He was laughing, but Peter felt a rush of anger. 'Hang on, that's a bit rich. Remember Kate got herself up the duff and I've more than done the right thing by them all. Worked my bloody butt off, haven't I, and so what I do with the rest of my life is my business, as long as I don't thrust it in their faces.'

'Your father's maxim, if I remember rightly.' Alan's voice was dry. 'You're like two peas in a pod.'

Peter said sharply. 'Why are you looking so damned sour? You're no saint, after all.'

Alan shrugged, his pale face flushing. 'Hey, no need to take that tone. I didn't mean anything by it.' He swung round to face his monitor which had pride of place at the L-shaped desk. The screen was a mass of falling stars. He fiddled with the mouse and clicked into today's mortgage rates.

Peter's head ached. He'd been up early talking, drinking tea, smiling when he wanted to throw the damn cup through the window, and he didn't need Alan throwing in his twopenny-worth. He checked his watch. 'I'll be needing two per cent estate agent fees to go on Kate's paperwork. Can you fix it with . . .' He reached into his pocket again.

'Ben Aspers.' Alan's voice was cool and he didn't turn round. 'Yes, I daresay he'll do that for you. I gather you'll pocket the balance, not Kate.' He adjusted the monitor, which he'd put on an eye-level stand since Peter had last been here. God, what a big girl's blouse Alan could be, sitting there huffing away. Why shouldn't he have it, as Kate was having the flat with a view, and the break from work? God, what he wouldn't give for that. These bloody women, somehow they . . .

Alan had stopped fiddling and was looking at him, without expression. 'If there's nothing else?'

Peter stood up, shaking his head. 'I'm grateful, Alan. Sorry I got a bit short. It's all been pretty . . .' he searched for a word, '. . . difficult. Mother dying, it's all a bit hard, you know. Shakes you.'

Alan was leading him to the door, mollified, jolly again, saying, 'Keep in touch. I'll investigate ways we can lighten the load, but the balance between the two properties is essential. You're sure she *will* cough up?'

Ben Aspers was a young man with a big moustache. It didn't make him look any older but obviously no one had broken that to him. He and his clipboard went round the bungalow like a dose of salts, but Peter was quite satisfied, because the guy obviously knew his stuff, and the value he put on it was on a par with the bungalow that had been sold on the same road within the month. What's more he had a couple of clients in mind – one of whom was that gift from God, a cash buyer.

Aspers particularly liked the security lights, and said that old fogies were into safety. Peter nodded, of course they were, or should be, and he wished his mother could have heard the estate agent. What a ridiculous fuss she had made about them.

By eleven Aspers was on his way, but not before suggesting that Barbs's personal possessions should be cleared ASAP, as he was fairly sure his clients would want to look at it this week, and perhaps the cushions . . .? He had left the image of the cushions hanging in the air. Again Peter wished Barbs could hear.

'Fine,' Peter said as he walked him to his car. 'My wife can do that on Monday afternoon.' They shook hands. Peter could see the neighbour to the left peering through her nets. He ignored her, checking his watch as Aspers de-armed his BMW. Over the beep Peter said, 'So, if these people you're showing round are already on your list you won't need to advertise, therefore I don't expect to find that on your bill.' It wasn't a question.

Ben Aspers half smiled, but it didn't reach his eyes. He opened his car door. 'That, as well as a creatively structured invoice, Mr Maxwell?'

Peter shrugged. 'We're all in the business of making money. You're getting a good whack for doing very little, and I'll make sure your firm gets some more business.'

Ben Aspers eased himself into the driver's seat. 'I think we'll have a sale set in motion very soon.'

The drive to Jan's was longer than he had expected, but he'd not done it on a Saturday before. He was feeling good now the way ahead was clear again. He couldn't stand chaos, he liked to know where he was going. Organisation was the key to everything, or so his father had taught, and he was right. Peter drew up to a halt before a roadworks traffic light. The JCB drowned out the slight noise from the radio. Cars were feeding through from the other direction.

He tapped his steering wheel. What the hell would his father have thought of Barbara doing this to him?

The lights had changed to green. The JCB was holding them up. He hooted. The driver flicked a V, before jerking out of the way. He roared past, dodging back to his side of the road at the end of the roadworks, and powering on, eager to be there now. After all, he'd needed support too, and no one had given that much thought, except Jan. He took out his mobile phone and called her to say he'd be twenty minutes. 'Just time to find that new negligee, the one you wore on Thursday.'

When he arrived he let himself into the brand-new flat, which still smelt of plaster. He strode through the carpeted but unfurnished living room. Unfurnished but for the Capo di Monte figure he'd brought Jan from his mother's home. On into the kitchen with its bleached units and quarry-tiled floor. It was a room Jan had worked hard on and it showed. The toaster and the kettle were an olive green which exactly matched the kitchen table. He'd have to make her an offer for those when the time came.

She was flicking down the venetian blinds, her blonde hair falling down her back as he liked, the black negligee nicely see-through. He came up behind her, running his hands down her warm body. She shivered and half turned, her face eager, her deep red lipstick thick. His watch caught on the negligee. He kissed her neck. God, a childless body was so different, so taut, so good.

She was putting her arms round his neck, kissing him. He tasted her lipstick and as always it aroused him further. She ran her tongue over his lips, then plunged it deep into his mouth. He dragged her to the kitchen table, shoving aside one of the green chairs, pulling her to him, burying his head in her breasts. Again she shivered, murmuring, 'You're so cold.'

Her eyes were closed, her lipstick smeared; half of it would be on him. He kissed her again. 'Warm me,' he instructed.

She leaned back. 'I love you, I'm so glad to see you.'

He kissed away her words. 'Warm me,' he repeated.

She eased his jacket off as he inched her straps from her shoulders, kissing her breasts again and again. She was looking far removed from the crisp, neat, efficient practice nurse. Maybe one day he'd get her to wear her uniform just as Kate had done for him, in the early days, when she still had a body that made it exciting.

She was stripping him of his shirt, button by button. First one sleeve, then the other. He couldn't breathe. She knelt to do the same with his trousers, staying there, pressing herself against him, using her mouth on him. He stroked her hair, and his breath came quicker and quicker, and it was now that he told her what he had done for her.

She leaned back, her eyes taking a moment to focus, his words registering, and then her joy was evident. 'You really mean it? You've got her to leave? Oh darling, you're so good to me. It's been such a strain working with her, such a relief when your mother was ill.' She stopped. 'Oh, I didn't mean it like that, I just meant that . . .'

Outside a car alarm was shrieking, a child cried – none of them his, and he felt heady with the relief of his world here. He pulled her to her feet. Her negligee fell to the tiles. He pressed himself to her, working his body against her, as she covered his face with kisses, stifling his words, then leaning back, letting him say, 'Well, I knew it was a problem working with Kate, so when I was helping Mother to set up the will it seemed the best way of doing things. I want to make things easy for you, good for you.'

Her arms were around his neck again, her mouth found the part of his throat which seemed to have a direct link to his balls. 'You are so wonderful,' she murmured. 'And I love the

50

ornament. When your mother's house is sold and we've got the furniture we'll choose where it should go together. I love you.'

'How much?' He could hardly speak. She began to show him, and he couldn't wait any longer, but took her on the kitchen floor.

On Monday Kate and Penny each drove a car to Barbs's bungalow after Kate had finished work, and this time it was Kate who led the way, throwing open the curtains which Peter had obviously redrawn after showing Ben Aspers round. But it was Penny who put on the kettle, rooting in the pantry for the instant coffee whilst Kate stood at the sink. Outside the sodden leaves had collected in the corners of the small garden.

While the kettle was boiling they tossed for the job of clearing up the terraced patio. Kate lost, and pocketed the pound coin. 'Later,' she muttered.

'I've heard that before.' Penny was standing beside her. 'All talk and no deliver.' Kate nudged her, then made the coffee, telling Penny all that had happened. 'He talked?' Penny said, amazed and relieved.

Kate smiled. 'Yes. Barbs was right, he did feel rejected by her metamorphosis when Keith died, taking it as a dismissal of not just Keith, but him. He's never said it before, and I just wish he could have talked to her about it. It would have been good for them both.'

Penny was stirring her coffee, trying unsuccessfully to dissipate the blobs of dried milk. She sucked the spoon. 'Well, it was a justifiable rejection, of Keith at least. He was a tyrant, and tyrants should be bearded.'

Kate pulled a face. 'Well, whatever. But she always loved Peter, and went out of her way to remind him. He couldn't see that.' She sipped her coffee. 'It would have been better black.'

Penny grimaced. 'Forget the coffee, go on.'

'So when John read the will he saw it as a confirmation of all that and everything just caught up with him, made him want to talk. It's sort of cleared his head.'

Penny drank her coffee, blobs and all, then said, 'How strange.' It was as though she wanted to say more, but Kate was glad that she didn't. She could never discuss her marriage. It seemed disloyal, and besides, marriages had their ups and downs; it was called life.

Penny lined up the cardboard boxes on the kitchen table and began to empty the cupboards into them while Kate swilled their mugs under the tap. For the first time for months Peter had made love to her last night, and then held her as she drifted into sleep. But it was a sleep that hadn't lasted.

'What he said made me feel guilty,' she said to Penny softly, as she came to help, wrapping up Barbs's favourite teapot. 'I really should have seen how it was affecting him.'

Penny brushed back her hair. 'Will you stop beating yourself up, you did all you could to involve him. He just didn't . . .' Penny was bottom up in the cupboard now, scrabbling for the cheese grater. She emerged. 'He just didn't want it.'

'He said he did. He said he had to resort to showing it in other ways, in putting up the security light, in doing what he could administratively, and every time I see it from that point of view it makes sense.'

'She didn't want a security light.' Penny dropped the cheese grater in the bag. 'This lot for Oxfam?'

Kate wrote *Oxfam* on a label, stuck it on the bin bag and hauled it out to the Morris Minor, waving to Mrs Jenkins who was busying herself at the window of her house to the left. Ben Aspers's For Sale sign looked gleaming new.

The kitchen took a couple of hours, and after a pot of Earl Grey, which they took black, and a shared flapjack, they tackled the sitting room. Kate couldn't bear to send the richly coloured cushions to the charity shop, and shoved them into a bin bag to take home with her, finding room for them on the passenger seat and fitting the seat belt round for good measure. She told Penny as they packed the small ornaments that Peter had suggested the cushions be removed as 'fogies' were the first clients who would be shown round. 'He's after the right ambience,' she said and smiled tiredly.

As Penny bubble-wrapped the Dresden ballet dancers that had been Barbs's prized possessions they ran through all the firms they could think of that would transport the furniture to the local auction house at a reasonable fee once the house was sold. The last one they mentioned struck a chord with Penny. '*I think* they're good. I seem to remember the son of one of my flock used them.'

Kate was sitting on the floor beside the huge cardboard egg box the supermarket had found for them. Three small glass animals lay on tissue paper on her lap. 'I'll give them a ring later but I expect I'll be able to use most of it in the flat.' She stopped, conscious of a thrill. The flat. My flat, one with a view. But then she picked up the giraffe. Barbs, oh Barbs. She wrapped it carefully with hands that for the next few months at least wouldn't have to pump up blood pressure machines, dress wounds, or be reminded of . . .

Avoiding Penny's gaze she placed the giraffe with the Dresden in the box, then wrapped the other two and laid them alongside, as carefully as she had placed Barbs' hands one on the other before the heat had left them.

The anger was stirring again.

But it shouldn't.

He had explained.

Kate smoothed the tissue paper, again and again.

And Penny was right, Barbs hadn't wanted security lights but he never listened. Never ever, to either of them. She must stop this. Stop it. Stop it. Because he listened had last night.

Penny said, 'Packing's like this, Kate. Everything's fine for a while, and then realisation strikes.' She leaned forward and took Kate's hands. 'Hey, I'm here, let it go.'

Kate's voice was reasonable, detached. 'It's tainted money. I can't gain from Barbs in this way.'

Penny was on her knees beside her, another ballet dancer tucked away on top of the glass menagerie. 'Don't be absurd. The will was a validation of Barbs's priorities and her regard for your life, and you. You must honour her wishes. She's bought you space, it's what she wanted.'

Kate wasn't reasonable any longer, she was shouting. 'But you don't understand!'

'I do. I understand you, and I understand her. This bequest stopped her from feeling a burden. You can't spoil that for her.'

'She was a burden, is a burden.' Kate's voice was a mere whisper.

Penny said, 'Of course she was, anyone would think the same, but she was a blessed burden.' Her hands were gripping Kate's tightly. 'I'm glad you've admitted it. Carers so often refuse to allow themselves to think such a thing.'

Kate was shaking her head, her eyes searching the room trying to find a way of escape. She pulled her hands free of Penny. 'Why didn't I notice that she was ill sooner, done something sooner? None of this should have happened, it just shouldn't have happened.'

Penny's voice was gentle. 'There's no quota to be filled. Illness happens, we can't do deals to undo it. We can't rewrite the script.'

Kate was looking at the mantelpiece, hearing Penny's words, but they weren't touching what was inside her head, nothing was touching it. 'I thought that if we talked it would all just go. That if he shared it, told me why . . .' She stopped.

'Why what?'

Kate tried to recover that word. 'Why it had to happen,' she said at last.

Penny's voice was firm. 'I've told you, these things just happen, and now, believe it not, you are starting to heal, and Barbs wants to help with that. Allow her, and allow yourself to accept and enjoy. Enjoyment is permissible, you know. Grief is permissible. Flagellation, sackcloth and ashes went out with the ark, if a silly parson person can slip into the Old Testament for a moment. Come on.' Penny was passing Kate the clock and candlesticks off the mantelpiece. 'Wrap these while we chat.'

Kate took them. They needed a polish. She wrapped them and the action was normal, and slowly she calmed and listened to Penny who was talking about nothing. But as she placed the candlesticks in the box she had the sense that something was wrong. She looked at the mantelpiece, then around the room, getting to her feet; her legs were stiff. She stretched first one, then the other, searching all the time. 'Where's the Capo di Monte?'

It was nowhere. When they moved to Barbs's bedroom they checked again. There were only Barbs's shoes and in their shape was the image of her walk, the way she sat, the way she tapped her foot while she talked. There were her clothes which charted their relationship; the hat she had worn at Simon's graduation, the corsage she had pressed after their wedding. There was a book at the back of the wardrobe, water swollen.

Kate remembered how she had left it on the patio overnight before Barbs became ill, and how Barbs had said – no matter. It obviously had mattered because here it was, kept all this time. But never a reproach.

You were never a burden, she said silently. Even now you aren't a burden. It's me. I can't sort it out, that's all, and I'm driving everyone mad while I thrash about and behave as neurotically as always.

They packed her clothes, all except for the tracksuit Barbs wore for skydiving, and the dress she had worn to Blackpool when Penny and Kate had to be her proxies on the Big Max. Barbs was diagnosed by then, and the chemotherapy seemed to have worked, though she still felt sick. Together Kate and Penny laughed at the memory of the G force, of their white knuckles on the bar, at their screams, at the exhilarating terror which had made them finally understand Barbs's lust to complete her list. It was all so different; so alive, so on the edge.

They laughed, too, when Kate described the look on Jan's face at the distribution of the Kiss me Quick hats.

'She found them deeply offensive, but the receptionists and the doctors wore them all through surgery. Simon wore his for one whole day in the States. Jude too. You know, Penny, I made Jan's day, or even her year, when I handed my notice in this morning.' Kate was folding the dress neatly. 'Stuart was sorry, though. He doesn't want me to leave, and fully expects me back after my "sabbatical" as he calls it.'

'When will you make your grand exit?' Penny was emptying Barbs's drawers and outside the light was failing fast.

'Not as soon as I'd like, because the agency girl who filled in before isn't available until late November, and though the agent had said there was a cash buyer for this place it seems there are problems.'

Penny was opening the top drawer of the bedside cabinet.

The morphine capsules had been in there, in their child-proof bottle. They had been prescribed for Keith, but he was stoic and preferred brandy in vast quantities for as long as he could cope with it. No one had thought to dispose of them. Kate folded the tracksuit, taking great care.

At last they were finished. At last the final boxes and bags were in the cars. At last the door was shut, but Kate could still

55

feel the bottle in her hands, and the capsules she had shaken out, the water she had held to Barbs's lips, the weight of Barbs's body as she swallowed them one by one. 'Don't leave, dearest Kate,' she had whispered. Kate hadn't.

They had sat like that for as long as it took, and it was of Blackpool, and Paris, and windsurfing, and the feel of the wind as Barbs had floated above the earth in tandem with her skydiving instructor that Kate talked. It was of Simon; his students, and Mel, his girlfriend. It was of Jude who was due home from Greece the next day. It was of Peter, and of so many things, and even while she held her, Kate couldn't believe that she had done this thing, and she couldn't believe that Peter had said, 'I won't do it, it's outrageous to expect it. It's not my responsibility, it's yours; it's a medical procedure, isn't it, and you're a nurse.' And Barbs had said, 'I know how much you love me, I know how strong you really are, and therefore *you'll* find the courage to do this for me.'

She had.

CHAPTER SEVEN

THE PREVIOUS MAY

It was a changeable Saturday morning, and the thought of what was to come had made the night seem more comfortable. Moving to the kitchen table Barbs cut her breakfast toast into soldiers, then offered them to Peter and Kate who were sitting, still in their jackets. Kate smiled and took one, but Peter refused, altogether more violently than the occasion demanded, Barbs thought. She glanced at her daughter-in-law who was shaking her head, pleading silently for Barbs to be tactful. Of course she was, anything for the sake of peace, but the poor kid was the one who had to live with sober boots, so who could blame her? For a heady moment Barbs relished her own single state and forbore to comment, barely listening as Peter prattled on.

'Are you listening to me, Mother?' he said at last. 'The lad is here to fix the security lighting today, so how can you go off like this? I put it on your calendar as an aide-mémoire.*'*

Barbs sat down, managing to eat half a soldier, and that was to ease the anxiety in Kate's eyes. The palliative care she was receiving, in the way of capsules full of what looked like hundreds and thousands, took her appetite – or was it the illness that did that? Who cared? All she knew was that she was a weight she would have died for years ago. She laughed silently; she'd share her witty little gem with Kate, later.

'Mother, I'm trying to have a conversation with you.'

'Peter,' Kate demurred, but Barbs put up her hand, his curtness providing grounds for a grand gesture. Flamboyantly she stalked to the swing bin, tipped in the toast, and slammed the plate down on the draining board.

'I heard and I didn't want the light in the first place. Good heavens, what is the point?'

Peter was staring at the crumbs which clung to the swing bin lid.

'Mother, the point is your safety. Anything could happen to you if someone broke in.'

Barbs stared at him. 'I assume you are joking. Do you mean he could murder me in my bed?'

She had Peter's attention now, and Kate's, but then she always had Kate's. Everyone had Kate's. When did she ever give herself the same? Barbs felt her irritation become anger, and didn't want it. Not today. Today she had taken fewer capsules because she wanted to experience it all.

As she checked her pink and purple tracksuit in the window reflection she saw Peter throw up his hands. 'I give up, but he'll have to go ahead with it. I'm committed.'

Barbs said wryly as she picked up her coat from the back of her chair, 'Yes, when he rang yesterday he said the special price was dependent on doing both houses.'

Peter was getting to his feet. 'Well, if it's going to cause all this bloody upheaval I'll pay for both. And by the way, you've just dug yourself into a hole. If he rang you knew he was coming.'

Good God, it was like talking to his father all over again. Just a smack of infirmity and one's child became the adult who knew better, the adult who had to score points. Barbs felt the heat of her anger colour her face. But Kate was between them, helping her to find the armholes, settling the coat gently on to her shoulders, nudging her towards the door, deflecting, placating. For God's sake, girl, confront the bugger.

Kate said gently, 'Come on, we'll be late. Peter, if it bothers you that much perhaps you could stay and keep an eye on the lad?'

Barbs felt a half smile form. Good one, Kate. Sometimes I forget that you do bite back, but so gently I'm not sure he even realises.

Peter was on his feet now, chivvying them out of the front door. She hadn't realised that the wind was so keen, or the sky so blue. 'Can't, I'm playing golf at eleven. Where are you going anyway?'

Kate began to say, 'Just for a bit . . .'

Barbs cut across impatiently, '. . . of a skydive.'

Kate winced. Peter had been in the process of shutting the front door and now he twisted round. 'I beg your pardon?'

The forget-me-nots were out in the bed edging the path, and the lungwort. Against the house the crab apple was going great guns. Barbs marched past them to Kate's car which was parked in the road. 'Tandem skydiving,' she called back. 'So put that in your pipe and smoke it.' Kate was right behind her, raising her eyebrows. Well, OK, they hadn't been going to say anything. And OK, she had been absurdly childish, but it had wiped that superior look off his face, hadn't it?

Barbs watched as her son scuttled towards them, stepping on the forget-me-nots, for heaven's sake. She was pleased to see there was mud on his shoes as he reached them, his face irate, his voice low but fierce. 'Are you insane? Have you no common sense? No thought for anyone else? Anything could happen; good God, you're seventy.' He turned on Kate. 'And you were going along with this, not saying anything. Who exactly is her next of kin; or don't you think I have at least a right to be informed?'

Barbs gestured Kate aside, going up close, very close to her son. 'This is precisely why I didn't tell you, because you'd be carrying on and spoiling everything, and don't you dare turn on Kate. I forbade her to tell you. Peter, I'm not a child. I'm old, and I'm dying and I want to do this, and a dear sweet Dive Master, who is in command of all the facts, has agreed to wrap his legs around me and dive in tandem. It's my last chance for such a physical thrill.'

There was a satisfying silence. Barbs hoped she had said it loud enough for the neighbours to hear.

Peter stepped back, his outraged dignity riding high. 'There really is no talking to you these days.' He made for his car, his keys jangling, calling over his shoulder plaintively, 'It's just that if I had known in advance I could have cancelled my golf and come with you to make sure everything went all right.'

Barbs sighed, taking a few steps towards him. Again so like his father. If bludgeoning didn't do it, try emotional blackmail. 'Like all the other times we've asked you? Peter darling, we would have loved you to come to Paris, but no, you travel there all the time; so it would be just like work. Then there was Blackpool, lunch at the Ritz, the Hampton Court Flower Show . . .'

Peter waved acknowledgement to the security light lad who was calling from the side of the house. 'Be with you in a minute.'

He said to Barbs and Kate, 'I'm a businessman, I can't just drop everything to gallivant off at the drop of a hat. I do what I can in my own way, like ensuring you have the means to do all those things, like keeping you safe.'

Barbs watched him making for the side of the house, the familiar 'Keith' frustration snatching at her, undermining her confidence,

59

taking away her conviction that she was right. Damn, damn. For a moment, she hesitated then called, 'You can install it, but don't programme it. If I want it on, I'll flick the switch.' She whirled round, grabbing Kate's arm. 'Come along.' Her voice was firmer than she felt.

Kate was looking past her to Peter, the same uncertainty in her eyes. Was her stomach knotting too? Oh God, this girl mustn't have a lifetime of it, too, she really mustn't. She tugged at Kate's arm. 'Come along, I can't wait to be clutched close by a young man again.'

Kate grinned as she held open the passenger door. 'What do you mean, again? Or has a toy boy been and gone?' The grin hadn't reached her eyes.

Barbs settled herself in the car. 'Let's not get completely carried away, dear girl. A little common sense, please.'

She could tell that Kate felt uncomfortable when they laughed.

The tandem skydiving firm doubled as a flying school, and over to the left, in front of the ancient oaks just beyond the boundary, was a runway with a fluttering windsock and some decrepit Nissen huts. Barbs wondered if it had once been a wartime air station.

Jimbo, the Dive Master who greeted them after they had parked the car alongside a wooden hut, gave them a potted history as he walked them towards an ancient corrugated iron hangar, and Barbs congratulated herself, picturing the young pilots he talked of lounging about, waiting to scramble. Then she slowed, ashamed of the panic that still returned again and again, ashamed of the anger, and the sense of grievance, ashamed of the fear of death, of pain, because at least she had had a life.

Jimbo pointed to the windsock. 'A perfect day for it,' he assured them, stopping at the entrance to the hangar, waiting for a moment to watch one of their small planes take off. In spite of what Barbs had told Peter, she hadn't shared her condition with the Dive Master. She had merely said that this experience had long been an ambition. She'd explained to Kate that she couldn't do with the strain of a conversation that stuttered and started, faltering at every reference to the future, and at everyday references to health.

Another plane approached for landing and put down, bouncing once, twice. Jimbo tutted. 'We won't do that to you, Mrs Maxwell.'

'Barbs, please.' Barbs smiled at the boy, for that was what he was really. Only thirty or thereabouts, and blond. Quite handsome, or did all men look good in those sort of jump suits? Uniforms were strange, they could make someone into something they weren't.

Jimbo said smiling up at the sky, 'It's even a bit cloudy. Now, diving through cloud . . .' He left it at that.

Barbs scanned the sky. There was cloud and blue sky in equal measure. 'We're still going?' Her anxiety showed.

Jimbo laid a hand on her arm. 'We'll go, and it will be superb. We've only one other jumper, Ben's already taken him through the procedure, so perhaps we should get on.' He checked his watch, smiling at Kate as well as Barbs. 'Thirty minutes to takeoff. Lots of time to change your mind.'

Barbs said firmly, 'Lead on. Kate, come with us.'

Jimbo led the way into the hangar, and across to where another young man in a jump suit was chatting to a middle-aged man. 'What is this,' Barbs whispered to Jimbo, 'the mid-life crisis and geriatric day?'

He laughed aloud. 'No, the mid-life crisis and life's just beginning day.'

It was Barbs's turn to laugh, and while she strode on Jimbo asked Kate quietly, 'Is she feeling all right? Thank you for getting the doc's note of permission.'

Kate said, 'She's fine, and I'm grateful to you. I wasn't sure whether I should phone and put you in the picture, but it seemed rather unreasonable not to. However, she would have eaten me alive if you'd then refused.'

Jimbo was watching Barbs as she shook hands with the other two men. 'Cannibalism has its place.'

Kate laughed.

He continued, 'Everyone has a right to a list. Just hope mine's as interesting. We'll be fine.' He touched Kate's arm lightly. 'She's a frightened lady, it's there in every gesture.'

Kate nodded. 'I know.'

Stuart Duncan had known this too, that was why he had sent the note so willingly. 'What's stretching a point between friends?' he'd said.

'Well, this should help to turn that fear into something else.' Jimbo's eyes were very blue, very kind and very wise, and as he looked at her Kate felt the stirrings of something.

Ben called then. 'Come on, Jimbo, we haven't all day. Barbs is raring to go.'

61

★

Kate sat in an old armchair outside a wooden office set at the back of the hangar while Barbs lay face down on the tarpaulin curving her back like a banana, following Jimbo's movements. Veering between amusement and concern, Kate sipped coffee from the disposable cup Ben had produced. He sat on the arm of her chair whilst Tony, the other customer, mimicked the actions, concentration in every movement.

'Can we try that again?' Jimbo asked Barbs. The tarpaulin smelt of summer grass and picnics as she lay face down. The pain. The pain.

Jimbo's hand was on her shoulder. 'You OK, tiger?'

She lifted her head and curved her back again. 'Like this.' She should have taken more dope. Had Kate any on her?

'OK, relax now.' She did. 'We'll fall out of the aircraft, then we'll assume that position and fly.' Jimbo's hand was on her shoulder again. She summoned her strength, clambering to her feet without his help, avoiding Kate's eyes. No, damn it, she'd been right not to want the dulling of the senses that went with pain relief.

Tony and she stepped into their jump suits. Jimbo zipped her up the back. Barbs winked. Kate raised her eyebrows and laughed. Tony's was very tight, Barbs's wasn't. Nothing was tight any more.

She stepped into the harness. Jimbo adjusted it around her crotch, tum and shoulders. Again she winked. Again Kate laughed. They pulled on the skull caps, hitching the goggles on to the top of their heads.

They left Kate at the entrance to the hangar and walked to the waiting plane. It was very small. There was still very little wind. Tony was chattering. Nerves, Barbs knew. She had none; all she had was regret that this was not a solo dive because if it was she would not have opened her parachute – messy but effective, and how wonderful to die on the edge.

At the plane Barbs and Jimbo waited whilst Ben sat in the entrance to the berth, his legs apart, encouraging Tony to back up to him. 'Closer, closer. Come on, I'm not going to bite.'

'That's not what I'm afraid of,' Tony muttered.

Everyone laughed. Finally they were egg and spoon enough for Ben to clip Tony to him, and shuffle back into the plane.

Jimbo looked down at Barbs. 'Right, it's last in, first out. Now come on, no false modesty, got it?'

Barbs grinned up into that young face. He sprang into the open doorway and spread his legs, but as she backed she felt embarrassed, stupid, reluctant, and very sorry for this young man who had to be so intimate with a silly contaminated old trout. Finally she was close enough, and as she felt his warmth, as she heard the click, she also heard him say, 'This is an honour for me. I shall remember it as a high point.'

She could have wept. In another moment she felt his hands around her waist, felt herself lifted, and though the pain caught and held she was smiling. Even as she shuffled back into the tiny berth she was smiling. Even as the plane shuddered and roared and jarred, increasing its speed along the runway, and finally left the ground, she was smiling.

Ben had explained that he would call the altitude every thousand feet.

'One thousand.'

Jimbo sat with his arms around her, talking her, yet again, through the moves once the door opened.

'Two thousand.'

Though it wasn't talking, it was shouting with his mouth against her ear because the noise of the plane seemed not to have lessened once they were in the air.

'Three thousand.'

Jimbo talked of fear too, exploring his own when he began to skydive, calling it a person's greatest hazard, something waiting to ambush him, waiting to destroy his intelligence.

'Four thousand.'

Waiting to clog up the brain and prevent him from reaching infinity.

'Five thousand.'

'Fear is a danger to those performing alone. Fear is a nuisance, it doesn't aid us in any way. Worry is also a nuisance, since it opens the door to fear. Concern though, is something else. Concern is worry without fear. Concern helps you plan for a better result.'

Still his warm arms were around her, still his young legs lay alongside hers.

'Six thousand.'

Barbs allowed herself to lean back against him and sift through all that he had said, and strangely, at last, she felt the pieces which had been flying around in her mind since the diagnosis begin to

63

form a shape. At last someone's words were making sense of her emotional struggle.

'Seven thousand.'

Jimbo checked his watch which was really an altimeter.

'You OK, Tony?' Jimbo shouted against the roaring and rattling.

'Eight thousand.'

Tony nodded, his face taut and anxious. Barbs knew they went at nine thousand, and now excitement was building, and, in spite of what he'd said, fear. She couldn't help it, fear was coming in again and it was so bloody silly, because it would be a relief, wouldn't it? No, not with this boy. Anyway, there was still hope, wasn't there? Still hope that a miracle would happen, a cure could be found?

'Nine thousand.'

Last in, first out. The door was released by the pilot. The air roared in and past. Jimbo tapped her head, and shouted, 'Goggles down, and shuffle, Barbs. Now remember, after I've wrapped my legs around you, fall out when you're ready. But you don't have to go. It's your choice. Right to the last minute it's your choice, but whatever, smile for the camera.' Jimbo was laughing.

Camera? Barbs thought. But yes, there was one on the wing or somewhere like that.

He waited, exerting no pressure. She shuffled forward against the force of the wind. He came too. She forced her legs over the edge but they wanted to fly sideways with the wind. Jimbo's were either side, helping her. The wind was dragging at the skin on her face. Her hands were like claws. The earth was far down, it looked like a child's toy farm. So far down. She didn't want to go. She couldn't go, not falling down into nothing. The noise was terrible. The engine, the wind. Jimbo was crowing in her ear. She thought she heard him almost scream, 'We've got a cloud. God almighty, we've got a cloud. That is truly magnificent. It's your choice, Barbs. Your call.'

The ground was obscured by cloud. His legs were wrapped around her. She was crazy. Peter was right. Keith would have said the same. She was a fool. She couldn't. She looked down at the soft, tumbling, white-grey cloud.

Then it happened, a closing of the eyes, a step into nothing. Out and away from the plane into silence, Jimbo with her. She felt water droplets cooling her face and opened her eyes. Her goggles were misted. The wind cleared them. They were plummeting through soundless cloud, falling, falling, and it was like nothing she had ever known. It was peace, it was freedom, it was everything.

She felt a tap on her head and together with Jimbo she curved her back and there was some pain, but not too much. Suddenly they cleared the cloud and there were fields, and colour and beauty. They were flying, not falling, and it was as though she was non-existent. It was as though she had fled the confines of her body, and was everywhere and nowhere.

There were cattle grazing. A few sheep. The cloud they had fallen through cast a shadow over the land to her left. A river flowed. Cars travelled the roads, birds flew but it was all as nothing, insignificant. They were part of the past.

Another tap on the head. It startled her; of course, she hadn't fled the confines of anything. She was with Jimbo, blue-eyed, young and kind, and the parachute was about to be pulled. It was pulled. A slight jolt, slightly more pain. But not too much. A hauling up into the air. A suspension, a floating. Just the sun on her face, just timeless perfection, just all the minutes and hours and days of her life here and gone, and in their place, acceptance. At last there was acceptance.

Another tap. Soon they'd be down. It didn't matter. Nothing mattered. The trees were rushing, the grass. There was a van, a white one at the side of the landing field to take them back to reality. But reality wasn't the same. The ground was closer. There was no fear. There was concern.

She relaxed, she remembered her instructions. The ground met them. Jimbo took the jarring, taking her with him in his roll. She felt pain, but not too much. For a moment they lay there together, and then he was unclipping her and the parachute was being hauled in.

Still she lay there as he bundled it up. Kate was running from the van, but there was no hurry. No hurry any more. Jimbo was bending over her. 'You OK?'

She laughed into those blue eyes. 'I'm wonderful.'

'We know that, but are you OK?' He was laughing back at her, nodding as she nodded, reaching for the hand she offered him, hauling her to her feet. He said, 'Was that something, or was it? Give me a high five.'

She gave him a high five and he hugged her. 'You did good. You'll do good. You'll get to the end and you'll do it well.'

Kate was running across the grass, her shoulder bag banging against her thigh. She was out of breath when she reached them, her face flushed, gasping, 'Are you all right?'

'Never been better, blabbermouth,' Barbs said as Jimbo concentrated on the parachute.

That evening, early, Barbs lay in bed, exhausted but calm and tranquil as she had not been before. Yes, she could cope with this. Yes, the anger could go, and the fear. Her mind was clear tonight, there had been little need for pain relief somehow. Had a miracle happened? Hope stirred, then drifted. Probably not. She lay back and looked out at the night sky. She never drew her curtains, it was too claustrophobic. She needed the sky, and the stars, which tonight were bright.

She could almost feel the droplets of this afternoon on her face. Yes, without fear her mind was clear. She could go to the limit, and all the time she could be preparing. She checked her bedside cabinet drawer. Yes, the capsules were there, hidden beneath her diary. She could prepare, she had a choice.

She closed her eyes and began to doze, but then a harsh light flooded the room, jolting her awake. For a moment she was confused, frightened, but then she sat up, her stomach knotting, beating her knees with her fists. She'd told him. For God's sake, she'd damn well told him. She reached for her glasses, finding her way to the door, then to the alarm box. He had programmed the security light. She found the book of instructions on the windowsill, but couldn't work them out. She wanted to phone him, get him over, but that would mean waking Kate.

Stumbling back to her room, she closed the curtains and eased herself into bed, the pain worse. She lay there unable to sleep, fraught, distraught, but as dawn broke it seemed to absorb that light, and then she dreamed, and it was of floating through the air with a man's voice calmly telling her of the nature of fear, and when she woke she wished she had met someone like that, aeons ago.

But a deeper regret was for Kate, darling, placatory Kate who still had those aeons to live through with Peter, who had programmed the security light.

CHAPTER EIGHT

Peter waited in the lay-by – the same one he'd chosen to phone Alan from that night when John had informed them of the contents of the will. He kept the engine running, because it was a sight colder than it had been then. In fact, he wouldn't be surprised if there was a frost this evening, but then what could you expect on the first of December?

He checked his watch. Jan had said she would try to meet him at six fifteen, but that she might be late. She was, so far by thirty minutes. Perhaps Kate's replacement wasn't proving to be quite as efficient as Jan had thought? But surely she must be better than Kate, considering the state she had continued to get herself into. Bloody hell, these women. Since leaving the Medical Centre she'd had a week of pratting around with bugger all to do about the house, but it hadn't done any good – she was still up and down like a bloody yo-yo.

He twisted in his seat, looking behind him at the car that had drawn in. No, it wasn't Jan, probably just some couple snogging. He checked his watch again, wishing she'd get a move on because he'd only just realised that the battery of his phone was dead, and his secretary might have put calls through to the house, which was where he'd said he'd be. Bloody stupid of him to tell her that, but he hadn't thought it through properly. But he could put that one down to Alan.

None of it would matter if Kate was later in than him, but it would be a bit of a bummer otherwise, because there was no knowing what interpretation she'd put on it at the moment. He could hardly tell her that he'd been stuck in a lay-by for an hour, with his mistress.

He shook his head. It was all so darned complicated that sometimes he wondered if it was worth the candle. He lowered the window a fraction. The trouble was that no one had a sense of urgency about anything – not the buyer for the bungalow, who had twiddled his thumbs because the wife was ill, though at least they'd signed contracts now and would complete next week, and certainly not Kate, who'd wasted the last week instead of viewing the houses he'd sorted out for her in the West Country.

What went on in these women's heads? What the hell was the problem with repossessed properties? Thank God Jude had got behind the Fowey one, or he didn't think Kate would have agreed to view it – not that she'd phoned him this afternoon with an update; that would have been too bloody organised.

Then there was the Capo di Monte. Of course she hadn't come right out and accused him, but the suspicion was there as it had been over the hotel room. He stretched. The worry of it all was disturbing his sleep, for God's sake.

He'd even had to let Alan in on the larger overdraft, and the personal loan he'd taken out to cover the gambling losses, and what was the best arrangement the idiot could come up with? An interim payment of £10,000 on each to the bank by the end of November, which would take up the £20,000 they'd already metaphorically earmarked from the conveyancing balance for his 'pension arrears'. That had just left some fast talking to calm the other creditors.

What had happened then? Kate had only had the damned cheek to ask to see the figures on the pension arrears. He felt himself begin to sweat, in spite of the cold. Alan had agreed to a swift phone call to her, but nothing on paper, the wimp, and it had served the purpose, but would Alan leave it at that? Oh no, he'd phoned Peter earlier today on his mobile, which was probably why the damn thing had run down, sucked dry by his moaning. Sort the gambling out, and sort Kate out, had been the gist. Get her viewing properties if you're to dig yourself out of this particular pit.

Easier said than done with her in the state she was. Just when she seemed to settle down, she'd go off half cock again. She'd have to get something from the doc, that's all there was to it.

A car pulled in, the headlights flashed. Jan, and about bloody time. She opened her car door and hurried across. As she got into the passenger seat she passed him the backdated note he had asked her to write. He would put it in his mother's bureau at the bungalow. 'Well done, darling,' he said, placing it on the dashboard, kissing her. Her lips were cold. He slipped his hand inside her coat, her mouth opened beneath his. Jan stirred, and he ran his tongue round her lips.

Over her shoulder he checked the time. He shouldn't, but he needed something to relax him, for God's sake. 'Back seat,' he whispered. 'Please, I just can't resist you, you're the most important thing in my life, the thing that makes all the difference.'

'You always make me feel so loved,' she said.

He knew he did; it was what they all said. It was what Kate used to say.

That morning just after Peter left for work, Kate and Penny had found their way on to the M5 and headed towards Cornwall with the map and a list of estate agents' properties, including details of the only repossessed house which seemed suitable, or suitable to Jude and Peter, anyway. Would she actually view Journey's End, in Fowey, though? She hadn't decided, but that was because she couldn't decide about anything any more.

The will had made everything such a muddle. The surgery had torn at her, minute by minute, hour by hour, and long day by long day, and Barbs's letter had become worn from reading and folding, and the miracle was that she had got up at all every morning. Yes, she had got up, and she supposed she had functioned, just as she was doing this morning.

Beside her, as the windscreen wipers cleaned the drizzle from the window, Penny hissed, 'I really can't be a party to a speed offence of such magnitude. The flower ladies would be irretrievably shocked and I would be unsettled by the youth of the police. Though I suppose you'd be proud that this old heap was officially logged doing over ninety.'

Kate looked down: 95 miles per hour. She found a space, indicated and slipped from the overtaking lane into the middle one, keeping to a more respectable speed. All this would pass. It really would pass.

Half an hour before Plymouth they stopped for a coffee at a roadside café festooned with Christmas decorations and she half listened as Penny coerced herself into not feeling guilty about eating two mince pies while they checked the map against the list of properties Peter had presented yet again at the weekend.

Of course Jude was right, Kate thought, she should be grateful he was taking an interest, grateful he had not chosen to make her life a misery because Barbs had left her the bungalow. Of course she should, but she couldn't be, because she was the one with the terrible nightmares which left her with the heaviness of Barbs in her arms.

Penny said, 'So we're dealing with them sort of chronologically, are we – the closest first? That makes it Kingsand first, Fowey last.'

'If there's time.' Kate's voice was too harsh. She said again, more gently, 'If there's time.' She ignored Penny's glance, just as she had ignored her tentative kindness over recent weeks. She didn't deserve it.

Within an hour they had crossed the Tamar and reached the neighbouring seaside villages of Kingsand and Cawsand. Together they walked through the narrow streets, pulling up their collars against the wind. 'December's probably the best time to see it,' Penny said. 'We're not about to be seduced by sun and blue skies.'

Kate had forgotten her gloves, and her hands were already frozen. She blew on them.

'Where is this house?' Penny asked, the cold making her irritable.

There was no one to ask, so Kate used Penny as a windbreak while she found the estate agent's sheet. 'We need to go back the way we've come. It says it's a few steps from the sea, with parking.'

Penny headed off, yelling, 'Race you.' Kate stared after her. These last few weeks it had been all she could do to put one foot in front of the other, all she could do to perform the most simple tasks, making the beds, a cup of tea.

Penny turned, 'Come on, race you.' She beckoned Kate, her face alive with laughter. Suddenly, in spite of herself, Kate was running, harder and harder, all the way down the street, and as they leaned against the sea wall their blood was circulating again, and there was feeling in their extremities, and they were laughing. How strange, Kate had forgotten how her laugh sounded, how it felt as it rocketed up her chest, to her throat.

'How much is this one?' Penny asked as they looked at the neatly presented three-storied terraced house with the bay window. It was a window clouded by salt, but in the summer it would be clear, with views of the sea, the sound of which must fill the bedrooms at night.

Kate knew the details by heart, because each Sunday she had been made to look through the pick with Peter, made to listen as each week he amended the list according to which were still for sale, made to listen as he berated the slowness of the bungalow buyers, and the silly old bat who was sick. 'Cheap enough to give Peter this magical £20,000 balance which will get him out of the hole. Or it will be £20,000 if these particular vendors come down £5,000, which they usually do, don't they?'

The anxiety was back, her stomach knotting, her heart falling, tumbling, far in excess of the situation, and she wanted to be back in her life as it had been a year ago, two years ago.

'But what hole? I still don't understand.' Penny was staring at the houses either side and nudged Kate who withdrew, wanting her to be quiet, to leave her alone, for everyone to leave her alone. Penny was leaning into her, though, not letting her escape, hunting her down, chuntering on about the damn houses either side of the property which was for sale. 'Those are both in good condition, too, which is heartening. One's neighbours are of the utmost importance.'

A laugh was expected. It was given, but it died, and was not genuine anyway, and they both knew that. Kate made an effort. 'Quite, but one lives in hope of a change of personnel.' She wondered as she did every day how one could exist at two levels. Where did the words come from?

'What hole?' Penny repeated, linking arms, the wind whipping her hair across her face.

'Apparently he's been unable to pay into the personal pension for months and months, or is it years and years, because of Jude's uni, and the aftermath of Simon's PhD, and all sorts of other things that I can't remember. One way and another things have added up. The required amount is £20,000.'

'You've seen the figures?'

'Alan told me.'

When Kate had asked that question Peter had flounced from the room and Jude had shouted, 'For God's sake, Mother, Dad's told you that's what he needs so what are you stirring up trouble for? He's being exceptionally gracious about all this so get a grip, and while we're about it, do stop going on about the Capo di Monte. It was only a bit of china. Barbs probably gave it to someone.'

She had felt disgusted with herself, and ashamed, and wished she had some control over the words that leaped unbidden and fell at his feet, as it were.

'We ought to knock,' Penny was saying, dragging at her arm. For a moment Kate didn't know where she was and looked up and down the road in confusion, then rushed after Penny who was crossing the road. Rushed, because she didn't want to be alone. Rushed, because the wind and the sea were too noisy, too fierce.

Penny said, her hand out to stop her, 'Steady, hey, steady, my darling girl.'

Kate was too tired to answer, too tired to look round a house. As they reached the front door, she whispered, 'We're early.'

But Penny was already banging the painted knocker, saying over her shoulder, 'I'm used to arriving at awkward times and expecting admittance.' Then, more gently, 'Darling Kate, you shouldn't have gone on at work. You should have taken sick leave. I should have made you.'

The young woman who was opening the door had a baby on her hip and a wide smile. Mrs Hawkesworth was a naval wife. She was following the drum, she explained as she drew them into the terracotta hall. Paperchains looped across the ceiling. Christmas came earlier and earlier each year, Kate thought. 'I need a fairly quick sale, so that's why it's reasonably priced.'

Kate watched the baby, so wholesome, so fresh, just like hers had been long ago.

Kate walked around the house, and saw it as though through gauze. There was no balcony, no garden, and the parking wasn't on site but instead there was a lock-up at the edge of the village. She remembered: £20,000, that's what he needed. She asked the girl, 'How far can you drop?'

Mrs Hawkesworth said she couldn't. But they always said that, didn't they?

'Did you like it?' Penny asked as they returned to the car. Like? She didn't like or dislike anything any more. She just seemed to feel anger, or darkness, or tiredness, or nothing.

They viewed two more houses, but they were put to the bottom of the list, as Peter had said, because they were too far inland. It was Penny who insisted that they drive to Fowey, and she was quite right. They had time, and Mrs Hawkesworth might not come down, and Peter needed his £20,000. Yes, she was quite right, and besides, their appointment to view was at three, and it would be rude to leave Mr Henderson in the lurch, and anyway he would tell Peter, and then it would go on and on, and she would flare up and he would again say she needed treatment.

She turned left towards Fowey, and then took a right which brought them round the top of the town. Slowly they drove down through the delightful ancient unspoilt town, which was what the auctioneers' blurb called it, lying alongside a deep harbour. Down and down they went, winding their way eventually along the narrow main street, keeping the river on their right. Across the water was the village of Polruan, clinging to the steep cliff. There were still yachts anchored on the water, and tourists milling in the streets, or people with cameras anyway. 'I prefer this to Kingsand,' Penny said. 'It's more sheltered. I like the river, there's more going on, and look, within five minutes I bet you can walk to the mouth and along the coast.'

Kate said, 'Kingsand and Cawsand are closer for weekends.' It didn't matter what Jude or Peter or Penny said, she didn't want to buy here, and Mrs Hawkesworth would come down. She must come down, and all the time the thought of Peter's financial stress was nudging at her, and the sound of his voice, and her stomach was knotting too tight.

Outside the post office they had to wait behind a van which was unloading building materials and she clutched the steering wheel, and in spite of Penny's running commentary she wouldn't look out to the river where a huge ship was making for the open sea. 'What d'you bet it's carrying china clay?' Penny said.

73

The van driver waved his thanks as he climbed in, and moved off. 'You'll be defrocked if anyone hears you betting,' Kate's voice was calm. How could that be? They were approaching a car park and were about to swing into it, when they realised there was a barrier.

'Private car park,' Penny called. 'No punters allowed.'

They drove on. Again Kate said calmly, 'We'll go round again and park at the big one at the top of the town.' That way they'd miss their appointment, and it wouldn't be her fault. It would be fate.

There was a car park, however, which came into view as they reached the end of a row of waterfront houses. They pulled in, paid and displayed, and watched the Bodinnack car ferry on its way back to pick up the several cars that were queuing, just a stone's throw from them.

'Let's have a look then.' Penny took the folder from her, extracted the clipboard and read the details of the Fowey house. Number four, otherwise known as Journey's End, was to be auctioned, but the anticipated price was so low that it would give Peter his balance, and, in addition, enough funds to do it up.

Penny tapped the folder. 'For once I agree with Peter. Someone has got to buy these places, you know, and they could do with a bit of love to heal them. Rather you than some developer, Kate.'

Kate didn't want to love anything else. Love didn't heal. Her love didn't heal.

Penny set off along the narrow street, past a slipway leading down to the water where two swans glided serenely. She made Kate check which houses were holiday lets, and which were lived in permanently. 'Seems it's a pretty good mix,' Penny announced as they came to the end of the terrace. It was here that they found Journey's End, an end-of-terrace house, just beyond a property with a yellow front door called Zanadu. Even Penny fell silent as they stared at the rotting windows and the neglected, dingy whitewashed plasterwork, but when she noticed the bright red door which opened directly on to the street she squeezed Kate's arm. 'Lovely red door.'

Kate turned on her heel. 'We'll leave it.'

But Penny was holding her back. 'Hang on, the details say it has a view, so this is really the back. It could be stunning, absolutely wonderful. It could put Kingsand in the shade.'

Kate shook her off, and her voice was savage and came from somewhere she didn't recognise. 'I don't care if it's the eighth damned wonder, I'm telling you we'll leave it.'

Penny recoiled. What did Kate care? Because this old place had been in the process of renovation, you could tell from the door, and someone had to leave it, had to walk away from the view, from the dream. Let a developer do it up, heal it, she didn't care. 'Do you hear, I don't care,' she shouted at Penny, who was coming to her, who was holding her, pulling her close to her, hushing her, stroking her hair. 'I don't care, but it's not going to be me. This time I don't want to be the one to do it. It. It. It.'

Penny was rocking her. Her coat was rough. Kate's breath was warm and wet, the wool was too. She pressed her face into Penny's shoulder, pressed and pressed, biting her lip, making herself breathe slowly, slowly, slowly. Again and again. It was how she coped. Every day, it was how she coped.

There was a cough behind them. They turned. A young man stood there, embarrassed, a file in one hand and a key in the other. He smiled, looking from one to the other. 'Mrs Maxwell?'

Penny said, 'We're a bit behind, we can't wait.'

But he looked so like Simon. So young, and underneath, unsure. Kate motioned to Penny. 'It can't hurt to look, can it, Mr Henderson?' Her lips felt stiff, her skin wet. She dragged her hand across her mouth.

Penny squeezed her arm, whispering. 'Are you sure? My dear girl, you're exhausted enough.'

Once in Journey's End they stepped over the sad heap of junk mail and tried to ignore the dreary hall as they followed Mr Henderson into the downstairs study/bedroom. The window looked out on to the street and would need replacing. Some channels had been dug in the walls ready for rewiring, but not enough. Some plaster had been chipped off, but not replaced. Kate said nothing.

Penny held her arm, whispering, 'What's wrong, darling? What's really wrong? Barbs's death is affecting you more . . .'

'Than it should.' Kate's voice was too harsh, again.

'Than I had expected,' Penny finished. 'Is it Peter, he's pushing this house business too hard, isn't he, and I haven't helped?'

Kate said nothing. She had to be careful. All this must stop, or one day Penny would ask again, and she would tell her, and that wasn't fair on her friend. She walked past Mr Henderson who was trying to ignore the whispering. She climbed the painted, chipped stairs. It was so dark, so lacking in natural light that Mr Henderson flicked on his torch, overtook her and led the way to the landing.

The bathroom contained a Victorian bath. 'Stained beyond redemption,' Penny murmured. Kate laughed, because it was expected. The hand basin needed replacing, the lavatory was something neither woman cared to examine. Mr Henderson had ceased to give his running commentary, knowing when he was beaten.

He led the way back along the landing into the kitchen, which was a bare, decrepit shell with no cupboards, cooker or sink, just torn lino on the floor. There were the expected channels for rewiring, but not enough. There was a dirty, torn, pale blue blind at the window, with bright light streaming through the rents. Mr Henderson excused himself as he hurried past Kate and thrust aside the blind as though he was about to produce a rabbit, and in a way, he was, Kate thought, staring at the view of the river.

A river upon which the sun danced, warming the room, bringing it to life. A river upon which craft were bobbing, and over which birds were flying, and beyond which trees adorned the opposite bank, the opposite hill.

Oh yes, this had been someone's dream.

She said nothing, just turned and left, and opened another door, stepping into a sitting room which rose right up into the peak of the eaves, with rafters running down, and a window that stretched almost the height and width of the room. Behind her Penny gasped. Together they stood bathed in light, gazing at the wooded hill rising out of the river, and the cows grazing on the fields above it, and the blue sky above that. To the right was the river mouth, and to the left the Bodinnack ferry ploughing towards the far side. Kate turned. It was too beautiful and she must leave.

76

Mr Henderson dogged her footsteps out on to the landing, 'It was a sailmaker's loft and could be so very beautiful. All the windows overlooking the river have been replaced.' His hand was on the door of yet another room. 'This is the double bedroom.'

He opened the door into a room with a window overlooking the patch of garden, but Kate wasn't looking at that, or the channels for the rewiring, or the peeling wallpaper which revealed rotting plaster, or even the rotten window itself. She felt rooted to the bare boards as she stared at the four purple ornaments which had been placed on the windowsill. Purple.

Mr Henderson was still talking in the background, something about a flying freehold over part of Zanadu, something about it keeping the price down, but all she could see were the four purple ornaments.

Behind her Penny said softly, 'My God, Peter really wants you to have this, Kate. No wonder you're beside yourself, living with this sort of pressure.'

So she wasn't mad, or overreacting, or unreasonable. He'd been here, or sent someone here. How could he? How the hell could he?

Together the women left, hurrying down the stairs and out of the house, shaking Mr Henderson's hand, leaving him bewildered.

All the way home Penny chuntered, trying to talk it through, but even when she'd come to the conclusion that Peter was suffering from his mother's death too, and was getting things out of proportion, even when she'd worked out that he was desperate for Kate to agree to the repossessed house for financial reasons, ones that she could appreciate, she still couldn't condone the placing of those purple objects.

Kate said nothing. Her mouth wouldn't work, nor would her mind beyond keeping the car on the road, turning into the drive and switching off the engine in the glare of Peter's security light.

She couldn't speak to Penny, just let her friend kiss her then pushed her away, smiling tiredly when Penny asked yet again if she would be all right.

She walked to the front door, glad that she had left the inside lights on, and the radio. She dropped the map and the lists on the telephone table. The answer machine was flashing. She pressed it and listened as she hung up her coat. It was Peter's secretary saying that as his mobile was turned off she'd asked a Mr Murphy to try and contact him at home. 'I expect you're there by now,' she finished.

The answer machine noted the message time as six. It was seven thirty now.

Behind her the front door opened. Peter came towards her and kissed the air above her head. She stared up at his dark, handsome face.

'What?' he said.

Her mouth worked. It spat the words out. 'Where have you been? She thought you were at home. And how dare you put purple in the house? How dare you?'

It didn't matter that he was close, that he loomed over her, that his lips tightened. 'How dare you!' she screeched.

He brought the flowers from behind his back, throwing them on to the hall table. 'I was out buying these to welcome you home. It meant going to Safeway and I checked up on the bungalow on my way back. Here, do you want to see the receipt?'

He pulled it out and threw it at her, before pounding up the stairs. Kate clung to the banister, then sat on the stairs, rolling her head in her hands.

She was still there when he came down again. Still there with her head bursting. He sat beside her, slipping his arm around her, pulling her to him. She tried to move away but he held her firmly, talking to her all the while, just as Penny did, stroking her. He told her that she must rest, that she must get things into perspective, that otherwise she'd have to see someone. So he wasn't talking to her as Penny did. He was telling her. Yes, that was it; he always told her things, never asked.

But it wasn't about this she ranted, held tight in his arms, it was about purple ornaments, about repossessed houses.

Peter shook his head. 'I'll get Stuart Duncan round, just for a little chat, Kate. This is all going far too far.'

CHAPTER NINE

LATE JUNE

Barbs sat on the garden lounger, well supported by all the cushions Kate had stuffed behind and around her, as though she would protect her from the pain that way. Somehow she had, but it wasn't the cushions, it was the love, and being out of hospital after the operation last week – an operation designed to bring some relief, or so that young doctor had said. It was being here, in her home, the sunlight soft on her.

Kate was inside, threading the extension lead through the sitting room window. Barbs lifted her hand and made winding signs. Kate made an altogether different gesture in return. Barbs laughed. 'Now that wasn't nice. Hurry, hurry, these young men's balls wait for no one.'

'The umpire would have you turfed out of Wimbledon if he could hear.'

'You can't be serious.' Barbs grinned, easing herself against the cushions. She missed young McEnroe, though at the time she had wanted to smack his bottom.

Kate had set up the television beneath the lilac tree, taping the sides of a cardboard box to it to cut out the glare. Between Barbs and the other lounger was a table on which Kate had set a jug of iced Martini and a bowl of strawberries. These had been dusted with brown sugar, Barbs's absolute favourite. The sugar was dissolving. She lay back.

Behind her closed eyes she could see the red heat, could hear the sound of the breeze in the honeysuckle which trailed up the fence, could breathe in the healing scent, could rally the strength to hold the cocktail which Kate would shortly give her, to pluck a strawberry from the bowl, to perhaps eat it, or perhaps just pretend. But now, for a moment, she would just float.

It was the sound of the applause that drew her back. With a start.

How long? Quite long. Henman was a set up. She feared she had dribbled. She touched. No. Thank God.

Kate was on the other lounger. The breeze fumbling with her Indian cotton skirt, her eyes on the screen, her voice gentle as she said, 'He won't win without you, you know.'

Barbs nodded, her head heavy, taking a moment, summoning her reserves as Kate poured two Martinis. There was no ice left. Yes, it had been some time. She took the glass that Kate was offering. It was sticky where the jug had dripped. It was heavy. Her voice was cracked. She tried again. Yes, that was better. She said, 'I was alongside him at every moment.' Her voice wasn't tart enough. Kate smiled, nonetheless, careful to show nothing. Always so careful, beloved Kate. Darling, beloved Kate who was taking care to hide something else as well. Barbs pressed the glass to her cheek. 'Sticky but cool.'

'Make up your mind, you daft old thing. Sun or shade, that was the question. You chose sun.'

Kate was scrabbling under the table and came up with a straw hat. 'Look, I've even found a purple ribbon for it.'

Barbs laughed, really laughed and it didn't matter that it jarred her. 'If you think I'm putting that cow's dinner on my head you are very much mistaken.'

Kate tucked the hat away again. 'How rude you are about my taste. So, shall I move you to the shade?'

'Absolutely not, I was merely commenting. Now shut up, I almost missed that ace.'

As Henman won the point the court erupted and Barbs sipped her drink again. Tiny sips these days; savoured. Little things were such delights. Kate was offering her strawberries. Not yet. Food was just one step too far. But all this — she looked around at the tiny garden, at the television flickering, at Kate. All this was so delicious.

Her breathing was shallow. The effort was there. She hadn't noticed before how often one breathed. It wasn't something she had thought of. Now she had to.

Henman was serving, she watched. Another ace. The glass was heavier. She placed it beside the bowl of strawberries. She slept, just for a moment, for when she woke it was still his serve. Then she heard the score. No, several games had passed. How many? She concentrated. That many? Time did that, slipped away. Well, that was fine.

Barbs loved the sun on her face, on her hands. She turned to Kate. She had the aberration of a hat on, it cast her face into shadow. She was drawn. I'm so sorry, darling Kate. So very sorry, *she wanted to say again.* I should have said nothing. I should not have interfered.

For Kate had suspected Peter of an affair, and too many words of encouragement from Barbs had caused her to phone the hotel. Now Peter, metaphorically clutching the manager's letter between his teeth, was aglow with righteous indignation. Now Peter had Kate on the repentant run-around. Now whatever confidence there had been in that poor lass regarding her relationship was finally gone, and that was not fine. That was unbearable.

It had led Barbs to grip his suit lapel last night as he had bent to deliver his swift kiss. It had led her to grip even more firmly as he had tried to draw away and take the chair beside the bed. In a low voice, almost against his ear, she had said, 'It was my fault, I cast doubt in her mind.'

He had taken hold of her hand, unpeeling her fingers one by one before sitting down. He had nodded. 'You really should not let your mind give way, Mother.' There had been such anger, his and hers. 'You really should not cause so much trouble. We both have enough to do without this.' He had actually gestured down the length of her body.

This. This.

Henman won the match. Kate reached across and touched her arm. 'Well, I never did. The Brits are in with a chance but only because you were rooting for them.'

Barbs kept her smile. She shut her eyes but kept her smile, because she would not weep. She was damned if she would weep for all that Peter had taken from her with those words, all that he had taken from Kate. Or was it all that she had taken from Kate with her stupid advice? Now she was too hot. Now she was hurting. She turned her head away from Kate. Away from everything.

Kate came. She was stroking her hair, her thin, stupidly pink/purple rinsed hair, she was wiping her cheeks. 'We'll go in.'

Barbs shook her head. 'No, I have Sanchez to support.' She took the tissue from Kate's hand, trying to find a smile, trying to find a crispness to her voice.

Kate was still on her knees beside her, hiding her concern, hiding everything. Darling, beloved Kate.

Kate said, 'But he's American.'

'Maybe, but he has glorious legs.'

Kate grinned. 'You're a disgrace.' She returned to her seat.

'I'm sorry, Kate,' Barbs said quietly.

'No you're not, you'll have a poster up next.'

'I'm sorry,' Barbs repeated.

Kate stared at the television. 'Don't be. It was me. I lost it.'

'For everything. Sorry for everything.'

'Shut up, Barbs. Lie back and think of England, not Sanchez's legs. We want Henman in the semi-finals at the very least.'

CHAPTER TEN

Two days after Kate and Penny had been to Fowey Kate held the door open for Alan and Peter as they lugged Barbs's bureau into the sitting room at the Old Vicarage. It was all that was left of the furniture, after the rest had been included in the sale. Apparently, Peter had explained yesterday, the buyers' own was needed for some son who was setting up house out of the blue, and of course, Kate wouldn't want to lose the sale after the dithering that had gone on already.

Dr Stuart Duncan was with her at the time, doing his best to persuade her to try a course of anti-depressants. She had refused Stuart, and agreed with Peter. Anything for the sake of peace.

Alan was bending his back, not his knees, silly man. Worse, he was twisting as they eased the bureau into position in the alcove to the left of the fireplace, where they usually put the Christmas tree. That was now positioned to the left of the patio doors, though the lights still weren't working. It was all too early really, just the third of December, but it had been something for her to do. A trail of pine needles showed its passage. Similar pine needles were caught in both men's sweaters. The cards were done, the presents bought, and if she heard any more tinkling seasonal muzak she would go stark staring mad, or was it madder? That's what they all seemed to think, wasn't it?

The bureau didn't go, actually. It was painted a sort of dull pink, had been for years. Had that been a try-out for the purple stage? Kate remembered that Barbs had often talked of stripping back down to the wood. Was it oak? Perhaps she should have a go, it would get her into practice for what was to come.

Peter was dusting off his hands. Alan was rubbing his back. 'Time for a gin, I think, don't you, Alan?' Peter said, fingering the dull gilt drawer handles. 'Wonder what's in here?'

Kate said, as she made for the dining room, 'I thought you'd been through it already.'

'Only the business bit in the top.'

There was plenty of gin. She'd been to the supermarket to restock. The tonic was in the fridge. There was no lemon, but there was ice. She poured three hefty measures. The ice clinked as she carried them through on a tray.

Peter had one drawer out on the beige rug in front of the wood burner, whilst Alan sat on the sofa with another balanced across his knees. Just one remained.

She placed a gin on the table near Alan, another on the hearth for Peter. 'Watch the ice doesn't melt.'

She took her own across to the other sofa, watching the men. They were like children rediscovering long-lost toys. Alan was laughing and holding up a crayon drawing. On it was the legend: 'Peter Maxwell. 6 and ¾'. Peter scurried across on his hands and knees, taking it from his friend. 'Good God.'

He rummaged further. There was a folder with more of his early work. Another with his school reports. She watched as he read, watched as he grew thoughtful. 'You see, she did care deeply,' she said and couldn't keep the edge from her voice.

He stared up at her, but his mind was elsewhere, and for that moment he looked vulnerable, young, almost the Peter Maxwell who was once aged 6 and ¾. Almost the devastatingly popular Peter Maxwell she had met whilst he was at university and she at nursing school, the Peter Maxwell who had sat on the steps leading to the main door of the hospital in that first November, tugging at her skirt and insisting he would stay until he froze, until he was taken in as an emergency hypothermia case, unless she agreed to a date. She had, of course, agreed and her friends had almost fainted with jealousy for the next ten months, until it was confirmed that she was pregnant. Because her periods were irregular she hadn't realised, and it was too late for an abortion. Some weeks before Peter had asked her to marry him. She had said she would release him, but he had stuck by her. She sipped her gin.

Alan blew the dust off another old folder. School photographs. In those she could see Jude, and a little of Simon. She could also see the lines of strain and tiredness on the present-day Peter far more clearly, against the unformed Peter Maxwell.

She ran her finger round the rim of the glass. Well, at least the prospect of a balance of £20,000 was looking good, if the auction went to plan.

Peter was smiling at her. 'Come on, there's another drawer. How about doing a bit of work . . .'

He just managed to stop himself saying, for a change. But perhaps she was imagining it.

She put down the gin. 'It's her correspondence drawer,' she said dully. 'That's all.'

'Never mind, we should go through everything.'

The drawer was packed with bulging buff envelopes. Back at the sofa she balanced it on her knees as Alan was doing. Each envelope was labelled *Correspondence,* and dated. Peter was back at his post by the fire, rooting through old leaflets, and out-of-date offers, heaping them into a pile.

'I'll fetch a bin bag,' Kate said, about to move the drawer off her knees.

'No,' Peter waved her back. 'I'll go, you relax and get on.'

Again that kindness. That disarming kindness. Why? Was it guilt? For Barbs, for the purple objects, for the figurine? She clasped her hands. No, she had promised herself and Stuart this would stop, promised Penny, for they were right – how could he have got there when you really stopped and thought about it? And his denials were so vehement. But he hadn't been at work, had he? She said, 'They're under the sink.'

As he passed he touched her shoulder. She flinched away.

She read through letters of condolence on the death of Keith, of congratulations on the birth of the first grandson, on the birth of the first granddaughter, of sympathy for Kate's two miscarriages, and Barbs's worry about Kate's health. Kate hadn't known that anyone had been upset besides her. She wished she had. She would have felt less alone, less foolish at the tears, the loss, the strange dreams of raging seas that snatched her existing children and left her searching endlessly. 'Jungian,' Stuart Duncan had said. 'Classic for this sort of "unseen" loss.' The dreams had stopped at that rational explanation. Peter had been pleased, because he had been almost as exhausted as she after night after night of her thrashing about, and had almost messed up a project as a result.

In another Penny had written in reply to Barbs's pleasure at her ordination, and concern at Kate's problems with Jude. She stopped. It seemed intrusive to be reading letters penned by those she knew. She stopped and sipped her drink, catching Peter's eye as he glanced across, the half-full black bin bag at his feet. 'Anything interesting?'

'Letters to Barbs and Keith. You might like to read a few. There's one about the miscarriages.'

He looked blank. He'd forgotten, obviously. She said, 'I've got to more recent ones, from people I know.'

Peter leaned forward, interested. 'Oh, anyone I know?'

'Penny.'

'Ah.'

Alan called out, 'Here's you in your birthday suit, a vast improvement on today.'

Peter took no notice, though Kate was looking at the photograph Alan held up. 'We'll keep all that stuff, Alan. Jude's home any day and Simon might be here for Christmas. They'd *love* it.' Yes, she sounded almost normal.

Peter was dragging the bin bag across to her. He sat beside her. 'Come on, we've got to go through the lot.'

'But as I've said, it's only personal stuff.'

He said, grimly patient, 'My love, it might look like that, but Mother's more than likely to have misfiled something. We don't want to miss anything important, do we? Or I certainly don't.'

There it was, real normality, the tense put-down. It was almost a relief. She sat back as he grabbed two full envelopes and worked his way through both. There was one left. She knew he was waiting for her to begin and so she did. In it were letters to Barbs in the final stages of her illness. On Barbs's bad days it was Kate who had placed them in the envelope. She knew most of the contents, and gave them a cursory glance, but then one held her attention. It was from Jan, thanking Barbs for the Capo di Monte figurine, insisting that she had done nothing to deserve it, that the few visits she had managed were her absolute pleasure.

Kate felt so hot she thought she would pass out. Her heart

was beating so fast she thought she would cease to breathe. It was like last time. It was like the hotel manager's letter. All that fuss, all the pathetic, paranoid chasing in her head. She folded and refolded the letter, pressing the seams. So hot, really so hot.

Finally, reluctantly, she handed the letter to Peter. 'I'm so sorry,' she said, as he read it.

Alan was watching her watching Peter. Peter handed her back the letter, then patted her hand. 'Don't worry, it's all just been a bit much for you. Once you're busy with the let you'll get things sorted out, get things into perspective. That's what the Doc told you, wasn't it, so perhaps you'll finally accept it, from me, if not him.'

She should be grateful he was so reasonable. She folded the letter and returned it to the envelope. Her hands were shaking and she really did think she might be losing her mind.

Two days later Kate sat in the back of the car as Peter and John talked in the front. Peter was tail-gating all the way down to Plymouth, and then on into Cornwall, and she was the only one who seemed to mind. The auction sale started at 6.00 pm but Journey's End was third on the list, so they had plenty of time. Outside the sky was clear, the stars were bright and normally she would have felt Christmassy.

Peter overtook a car weighed down by a laden roof rack, still talking to John. 'Just wish I could have done a deal and not have this bloody auction nonsense to go through. Ben Aspers thought he might be able to persuade Henderson's lot to arrange a private sale, but no such luck, and neither was he prepared to bring the hammer down a bit smartish. Straw behind their ears, that's the trouble with these yokels.' He pulled in sharply to avoid oncoming traffic.

'For someone who hasn't even seen it, you want it very much.' Kate pressed her lips together. But it was too late, she'd spoken her thoughts aloud, horribly loud.

'For God's sake, Kate, it's only a business thing. I don't need to see it, I just need to listen to those who have, and the surveyor's pronounced it sound. I've done the work of ringing round the local builders and found the cheapest one for you. McTravers can start work once everything's signed and sealed.

I mean, what more do you want, a red bow?'

'Well, I have seen it, and I don't want it.' There it was, loud and clear, and she should have kept it inside her head.

Theirs was the only car on the road. The headlights were picking up the high hedges. Suddenly Peter drew into a passing place, braking. Gravel spun beneath the wheels. He turned round. 'Fine, it's your money. Your decision. We'll wait until the spring, miss a season while we sort it out. I assume you won't mind getting Stuart Duncan to give your replacement her cards. I assume you won't mind going back into that world.' His voice was heavy with meaning. 'Because you realise you'll have to do something to help me out of the financial hole that is swallowing me up. Me, not you. A hole that I've dug because of our children. Anyway, I doubt we'll get it. It's too good a buy. It's just too good to happen to us.' She heard the shake in his voice. John was staring out of the window.

She said quietly, 'It's just the principle.' She could see the Fowey house, the purple shell, the obelisk, the bowl, the perfect sphere.

Peter said, 'I can't afford principles. I have to complete Jude's education, I have to . . .' Still there was that shake in his voice. He was staring at her.

She hated him, hated that voice, hated herself, hated Barbs for giving her the damn house, for making her stick with the bequest, for making things a million times worse, for dying, for getting ill, for everything.

The auction sale was held at a hotel. They sat on velvet-covered upright chairs. Number one had gone for a great deal of money, and number two looked to go that way too. Kate relaxed, wishing she had not said anything, not exposed herself, because it looked as though it had been unnecessary.

The hammer came down on the figure of £150,000. Peter looked worried and conferred with John. She heard the word under-bidder. She heard, 'Calm down.'

She looked through the details again, then around at the other people in the room. There weren't many. Perhaps it was too close to Christmas. Perhaps repossessions and what they meant affected people more at this time of year. Perhaps she was not the only spineless one.

The three of them each had the particulars; the photo, the words. The property is freehold. Vacant possession on completion. Not true. It already was vacant, work suspended, the dream finished.

The auctioneers were changing. A plump, slightly balding man in a dark suit was taking the gavel from the older man. Peter wriggled in his seat, whispering to John.

The auctioneer said, 'Good evening, ladies and gentlemen.' There was a murmur in reply. He was fiddling with the tape recorder in front of him. 'So sorry, just turning the tape.' He did so, then took up his pen. It looked like a silver Parker, like Barbs's. Barbs had used violet ink in her last two years. It was that pen she had used to write her last letter.

The auctioneer was talking them through the particulars. She followed them on the sheet. He clarified that there was a flying freehold, that was to say, part of the property extended over another property. She saw John and Peter exchange a look, and nod.

'What does that mean?' she asked, vaguely remembering Henderson's reference to it.

'It's less attractive because there's a potential for problems. For instance, if the walls need attention, the downstairs owner might not agree to contribute to the work. It puts people off.'

The auctioneer was peering round the room. '£35,000 then, ladies and gentlemen.'

She saw John's hand lift from his knee in a gesture. Wait.

A pause. 'Let's try £30,000 then,' the auctioneer said wearily.

But it was down to £25,000 before someone to their left started the bidding.

The bidding went up in thousands, but sluggishly, and she wished it would leap and bound as the others had before and leave them far behind. It was hot in here, her hands were clammy. Peter was wiping his on his trousers. The walls were a dark red flock. There were discreet wall lights, dark framed paintings, and a smell of coffee coming from somewhere. The bidding had slowed almost to a halt. Still John held up his hand.

Then John's hand signalled 'go'. Peter opened his mouth. She gripped his arm and hissed, 'It's my house, I'll do it.'

89

He was stunned. People were looking. Who cared? Peter did.

'A new bid to my right.' It was her. The bidding took off again, in a flurry to begin with, then slowing again. Ben Aspers had discovered the reserve figure, the amount the building society needed to realise, and they had passed it, so whoever made the greatest bid would get it, but Kate was near their ceiling. Soon it would go beyond. Soon Journey's End could not be theirs.

The under-bidder was a florid Toad of Toad Hall man in a check suit, or was she the under-bidder? Either way he looked bored. The auctioneer was looking round. 'Let's try another £250.'

Another bidder came in and gave that amount. Peter was looking at her. She lifted her hand to a further £250. She was almost beyond her ceiling. Please, please, she begged. Just a little more.

Toad called, 'Go on then.'

Relieved, Kate waited until the auctioneer practically begged, but still the new bidder did not come in. At last she nodded. Toad reciprocated. She was nearly out of it. Very nearly out of it.

She nodded again. It was her last offer, she could go no higher. It would go to someone else. She could make an offer on some inland property, some good clean buy, and his stupid purple things would have been wasted.

She sat back, exhausted. Peter was staring round the room, and now she realised that Toad had said nothing, that the auctioneer was bringing down his gavel. Bang. He was looking at her, but it was Peter giving their name.

The auctioneer leaned over the podium, giving his sheet of paper to a woman in a dark navy suit. John and Peter were leaving. She followed, squeezing past people who swung to one side to let them through. She followed them through to the office. They all sat down opposite the woman in the navy suit. Her hair was rigid with hairspray, her lipstick immaculate. Kate knew that hers had been chewed off.

She watched as John unscrewed his pen, wrote out a firm's cheque for the ten per cent deposit. She took the pen when he handed it to her and signed the form the woman had filled in.

'It's brief but binding,' John advised her.

She nodded, handing back the pen. She had ink on her finger. She rubbed it. John was nodding to the woman, who reminded them that they had twenty-eight days in which to pay. 'Then it's yours, before if the paperwork is completed.'

Peter was already rising, his hand was out. The woman shook it, she shook Kate's. Would she have ink on her now? John followed them from the room. They had a drink in the hotel bar, a bottle of champagne, as John told them that everything could be rushed through, and McTravers might be able to begin work before Christmas. Peter only had two glasses because he was driving. She had three and she slept fitfully on the return journey, and not at all that night.

CHAPTER ELEVEN

THE PREVIOUS SEPTEMBER

The leaves were falling past the window. Soon they would pile up, sodden, in the corner of the small garden. The patio slabs would be green with slime by the spring, but it would be someone else who had to clean those up. Barbs smiled faintly to herself; so there were some perks to popping your clogs.

She moved slightly on the pillows. Not that it would be Peter sweeping them up, he'd have sold the bungalow long before then. She wished she could leave the property to Kate, but that would leave her at the mercy of an outraged Peter, and he was already too empowered by the false accusation. But Barbs wouldn't think of that, it disturbed her hard-won equanimity.

Jan, who had popped in and was sitting there like a shop window dummy, noticed her restless hands. 'Can I do anything?'

Shove off, and take your platitudes with you, Barbs thought, not wanting to make conversation. From the affront on the woman's face Barbs knew she had spoken aloud. She knew she should apologise, make good, but life was too short and she didn't like this woman. Jan settled back in her chair, shifting slightly when Kate brought a tray of coffee, making a move to take the red mug. Kate said quietly, 'Not that one.'

Jan picked up the one with Mr Happy blazoned across it. It was chipped. She drank carefully from the other side as Kate explained quietly that Barbs liked a shot of brandy in the red mug at this time of day; it was a ritual. She placed it on the bedside table.

Barbs watched through almost closed lids as Jan checked her watch. It was only ten o'clock, hours before the sun went over the yardarm. Barbs waited. Sure enough, Jan said, 'Is that wise?'

Kate settled herself on the opposite side of the bed to Jan and said gently, 'Absolutely.'

Barbs was satisfied to see that perfectly made-up mouth tighten.

Barbs had never been able to stand women who hid behind layers of muck. Why didn't they just say, bugger the lot of you, and let the world see them as they were? She was pleased Kate had asserted herself. Again Barbs moved restlessly, angry with herself, hurt for Kate. Guilty, guilty.

Jan watched her agitation but had the sense to say nothing. Good, because it was bad enough that the Medical Centre had taken it upon themselves to play a sort of visiting musical chairs while Kate rushed around making them coffee. Though Stuart was always welcome, the lovely Stuart. Barbs hoped the coffee wasn't very hot, and the woman had a gullet like a drain. Maybe then she'd go, not that she'd come very often, thank the Lord.

Jan was saying in a loud whisper, leaning over the bed, 'I gather from Stuart that pain control needs to be stepped up. It'll be the drip from Friday, won't it?'

Kate frowned warningly. Barbs already knew this, because that Stuart had a voice like a foghorn. A drip which would pinion her to the bed. Or was she wrong, could you get up and move? Probably only if you dragged the damned apparatus around like a ball and chain. Well, bugger that for a game of marbles, she'd fight it, but then she felt her eyes closing, her thoughts escaping, drifting, flying.

Later, when she woke, the evening had set in and it seemed too early for the dusk, too early for that damned security light to come on. Peter had set it on the timer after she'd complained about it coming on and off like a yo-yo whenever anyone approached. She'd meant him to turn it off altogether, but he'd insisted that it made him feel better if his two girls were protected. She and Kate had decided on compromise and switched it off the moment he left each evening.

Her coffee had gone. Of course it had. So had another day. But it didn't matter. All had been done, that needed to be. 'Except for Yellowstone, and Australia,' she murmured. Her mouth was dry.

There was a rustle from the chest of drawers opposite the window. It was Kate. Of course it was Kate. She was always there, even though Stuart had coordinated a team of additional helpers to fill the gaps. She liked the Macmillan one, she wasn't patronising, or jolly hockey sticks, and how are we today, dear?

Kate was by her side now, holding a cool glass of water to her lips. How did she always manage to produce cool water? She sipped. 'Come on, you can do better than that, you old trout. If it was brandy you'd have the whole beaker down you.' Barbs sipped several times, then shook her head.

Kate would accept that. Kate only ever pushed so far. She had a good instinct. She'd said that to Peter. 'Your wife has a good instinct, so have I. I hope you're not telling porkies about that hotel.' It was the second time she'd brought it up, but it was like toothache, it was nagging at her.

In response he had been like the hospital doctors, all highfalutin, and every second word was unnecessarily long. The end result was the same too. The recipient left feeling two inches high.

Kate must have left and come back, for now she brought scrambled eggs. Barbs ate just a little, and drank the tea, just a little, and listened as Kate read out Jude's latest letter from Greece. It gave her arrival date and time, Saturday week. Fine. The drip was this Friday.

She touched Kate's arm as her daughter-in-law passed over the photographs Jude had sent. 'You will go to Yellowstone for me.'

Kate had long ago stopped replying, 'You'll be driving those bears up the wall yourself.'

'One day,' she replied.

'We've had some fun.' It was a statement.

'We have indeed, though I will never go white water rafting again as long as I live.' Kate shuddered.

'Neither will I.' Barbs nodded sagely. Both women laughed, but then they often laughed. Why not?

At seven thirty they watched Coronation Street on the television set up in the bedroom. They didn't bother with any lights because of the security blast from the garden. If Kate hadn't boobed over the hotel would she just have turned it off and damn the consequences? At eight they heard the front door. Barbs stolidly watched the adverts. Kate straightened the bedclothes. Barbs snapped, 'Are you expecting matron?'

Kate winked. 'Perhaps.' Again they laughed.

The door opened. 'Sounds fun, what have I missed?' Peter waved towards his mother, kissed the air above Kate. He slung his mac over the back of the chair where Jan had been sitting, leaned over and kissed Barbs. His nose was cold, and, she fancied, a little wet. She did hope not.

'Nothing. We've saved you lasagne,' Kate said.

94

'That'll be great. I'll be out shortly.'

It was the same old routine. His father had been the same. Why had she gone on with it for so long? A proper place setting, even at lunch. Did they think they had staff? Well, they had, of course; her. Bad rates of pay. Trouble was you forgot there was another way to live. She was sliding away into the blurred, timeless world which enclosed her more and more often. She came to with a start. Peter was coughing. Damn, only five minutes had elapsed, another twenty-five to go.

He came to see her when he wasn't travelling. Thirty minutes he spent with her, on the dot. Then he ate, then he was gone. And with his going Kate dowsed the infernal light and blessed darkness came, and the stars shone, and she escaped into peace. Just Kate and her. Kate in the truckle bed. A bed Kate swore had its good points. Was that because it was single?

Barbs came to again. She must stop this. He was innocent. He was outraged. It would all settle down – but to what? To meals at table, to Kate just one pace behind instead of two?

He was reading the Financial Times by the light of the bedside lamp. In the top drawer beneath the lamp his father's leftover morphine was kept. A drip indeed. She'd been kept on a lead for too much of her life to die tethered to anything or anyone. Each day she checked that the bottle was there. Each day, while the carers were busy, she tested that these daft old hands could cope with that damned lid.

Had any child failed to remove it? Of course not. They had the knack of these newfangled things. It was like the video machine that only Jude could programme, apart from Peter of course. Still, no need to worry soon.

Again she jerked awake. His mobile phone was ringing. Well, not ringing but tootling in that sort of musical way. She couldn't be bothered to look. It was Alan again. They seemed joined at the hip. She'd never liked Alan, he was a wide boy with the morals of an alleycat. He'd been like that even at school. Poor faded little wife. Did he still have her?

She half opened her eyes. Peter had dragged the covers as he stood up. He was moving away, his shoulders hunched. He still did that, then. He was a great huncher. She'd given up telling him it gave you headaches. 'No, go on,' she heard him say softly. What was it about whispers that made you listen?

He was smiling out of the window, nodding. Then he frowned. 'Yes, I know, she's been dipping into her shares far too much with this stupid list of hers. There's really only her insurance left, and that's nominal, but the bungalow will sort everything out.' His voice was lower still, his shoulders even more hunched, and he was walking towards the far corner. Barbs stopped breathing, needing to listen. 'No, there's been no more trouble. The letter sorted things out. It's Mother's fault, she stirs things, you know. In a way it'll be a blessing when she's . . .' He nodded. 'Yes, I know.' She could hold her breath no longer. She gasped, panting. He didn't notice. Again she held it.

'She's fine, came with me to Sweden, separate flights after the last scare.' Again a pause. 'Of course we had a good time. Now she's in the flat she's another who can't do enough. But I warn you, Alan, make it a habit to butter up any and all hotel managers.' He laughed.

Barbs heard the slam of the kitchen door. It would be Kate coming back. She yawned, opening her eyes, staring at Peter's chair, acting surprised, looking around the room, finding him. Finding the little shit, wanting to strangle him.

Kate entered. Peter smiled at her, beckoning her over, holding out the phone to her. 'It's Alan, phoning to see how Mother is. D'you want a word? What about you, Mother?'

Kate took the phone, chatted for a moment or two. 'She's fine, just the same old dollop.' She raised her eyebrows at Barbs, who waved the phone away, making a sleepy signal. 'But tired. She sends her best, Alan. Love to April. Thank her for dropping round the flowers. Sorry I wasn't here, I'd just nipped to the chemist. Tell her we'll have a bite sometime.'

Barbs was watching Peter, and it was like watching Keith. The same bouncing on the balls of their feet, the same half smile, and as she watched recognition dawned. So, Keith had not only been a bully, but a womanising bastard, like her son. All those years of loyalty which she had mistaken for love had been wasted. All those years. Her eyes were closing, her mind was slowing . . . All those years. But then she snapped back. She already knew that, stupid fool. Already knew that she could have made more of them. But women too. Women too . . .

Peter's lasagne was ready, his thirty minutes were up, and the room seemed cleaner when he left. In the dining room Kate would *be sitting with him, listening to his day, ministering to his needs as Barbs had done. She stared out at the illuminated garden. The bloody leaves were still coming down.*

CHAPTER TWELVE

It was the evening of 23 December and to all intents and purposes Peter was still at the firm's do. Well, what the eye didn't see ... He thought of them all still in the office, underneath those ghastly streamers whilst he was relaxing back into his parents' sofa, smiling at how well the best bits of their furniture fitted into his other home.

Even the old dining table looked as though it belonged down the far end of the room, and went well with the sideboard he'd bought with the proceeds of the sale of bits that hadn't suited. He called to Jan, 'Smells good. I only nibbled at the nibbles, so I'm ready for the fatted calf.' She laughed.

The flickering of the flame-effect gas fire was comfortable. Christmas cards stood on the mantelpiece, others were strung on red or green ribbons and brightened all the walls. He walked across to examine those hanging on the wall to his left. He recognised the one from the surgery. It had been sent to Kate as well.

For a moment he looked at it, his gin in his hand, not knowing what he was feeling. Then, suddenly anxious, he checked whether Jan had used Sellotape to attach it to the wall. No, drawing pins. Well, that was all right. He didn't want to have to make good that sort of mess. In the corner, by the patio windows that led to the small balcony, was a white artificial tree with flashing lights. God, he couldn't stand them.

He called, 'Any way of cutting out the flashing?'

'What flashing?'

He sipped his drink. What other flashing was there, for God's sake? 'The tree.'

Jan came to the door, wiping her hands on her apron, her face anxious. 'I didn't realise you didn't like them. I'm so sorry. I'll just turn them off.' He watched the movement of her hips beneath her red silk dress as she hurried to the plug. Bending, she flicked the switch.

'Stay right there,' he ordered, putting his drink on the mantelpiece, knocking cards over and off.

He moved swiftly to her. Her thighs were trembling with the strain of holding the position. With one hand he cupped her breast, with the other he followed the line of her back, her buttocks, that trembling thigh, probing lightly, stroking, probing again, and as he did so the trembling increased, along with his own excitement, and he wanted to take her, there and then.

'The meal,' she whispered.

Damn the meal, but then he sighed and pulled her to her feet, holding her against him, smelling the cooking in her hair. Well, he was hungry, after all, and they had all evening.

Whilst she resumed work in the kitchen he flicked from channel to channel. At least now there was a place for the remote. At his mother's it could have been anywhere and it had been quicker just to get up and deal with the television direct.

Slowly he finished his gin, loosening his tie. There was only one wardrobe but Jan had left hanging space for him, and two drawers. She had also bought him two shirts and a pair of trousers. At first sight he had felt suffocated but then it had seemed like a good idea. It was like playing house. Playing. But he wouldn't change tonight, that could be a New Year thing, another celebration.

'Are you ready to carve?'

It was his first Christmas with a girlfriend, and it was fun, he decided as he sharpened the carving knife. Carefully he ran his thumb down the blade. He would be doing this in two days' time, only then Kate, Simon and Jude, together with Rob and Penny, would be chattering away, not looking, noticing, or admiring as Jan was doing now.

He smiled at her. 'Thank you for all of this.' His gesture encompassed the table and the decorations.

Sitting opposite, her eyes never left him as he carved. There was a flickering candle between them. He could smell the wax. It was in a sort of holly and silver nest. There were another two at either end of the table. The old oak table was gleaming in their light. And there were no crackers containing those appalling paper hats. It really was time Kate stopped that particular ritual, but the kids protested that it wouldn't be the same without them. Perhaps that summed up what was wrong. Too much boring nonsense, not enough moving with the times.

The table mats were Jan's, and they were tatty. Peter smiled to himself; she would be pleased with those he had bought her, and she had been very pleased with the Chablis, which was in the cooler to the left of him. Did she realise just how fine it was? He must drop it into the conversation.

He carved paper-thin breast, and some ham. The kids liked it thick. Well, maybe he should let them have it this year. There were chipolatas. There was nut loaf for Jan, and bread sauce, there were sprouts mixed with almonds, which looked interesting, but sprouts gave him wind and that was the last thing he wanted this evening. Jan said as she took the plate he handed her, 'I never know how to keep everything hot.'

As he helped himself to carrots and sweet potatoes he said, 'We have a heat tray.'

There was a silence. Jan stared down at her meal. He reached across and took her hand, lifting it to his lips. 'We'll buy one too, shall we? Now, a happy Christmas, and a wonderful New Year.'

'It will be, won't it?' It was a question. He saw the anxiety in her face, the longing.

He moved along swiftly. 'Busy, of course. Lots to do, and I'm going to need to concentrate but, yes. It will be. Now, let's eat.'

Though it was delicious he ate sparingly, shaking his head at the thought of the turkey the day after tomorrow, and he knew he'd end up feeling as he had in the early days of his marriage when he and Kate had shared Christmas between the two sets of parents, having lunch with one, and dinner with the other. They'd hardly been able to move on Boxing Day. They'd have to sort it out next year, or if he was no longer with Jan, with whoever was sitting opposite.

He lifted his glass. 'Well done, my darling.' As she leaned forward and lifted her glass he saw the swelling of her braless breasts. They were so firm, the nipples so pink. They were as breasts should be. As Kate's had once been. Back then she'd been fun, but then the kids had come. He looked over to the

Medical Centre card. So what could she expect?

But it was Jan now who was reaching for him, taking his hand, forcing him to drop his knife, kissing his palm, running her tongue the length of his fingers, laughing softly, giving him back his hand, and it was she who reached for her glass, saying, 'To us.'

He nodded, his hand wet from her mouth. Her bare foot was now moving on his thigh, higher, higher. It reached him, felt his hardness, pressed, withdrew. Pressed, withdrew, slid down his thigh, then back again. His hand was drying. He closed his eyes, reached beneath the table, caught her foot, brought it back to him, moved it. He could hardly breathe. She pulled away. He tried to keep her, but was glad that she wouldn't stay, for it would all have been over too quickly.

He could eat nothing more. Neither could she. She took the plates, brushing past him on the way to the kitchen. He gulped his wine, smiling, seeing his image in his mother's mirror, the high colour, the half closed eyes. Life was good. He found his zip, drew it down, adjusted his clothing.

She brought in the pudding, aflame with brandy. She placed it between them, handed him the serving knife. She sat and her foot was back again. He watched her eyes widen. He felt that foot, bare flesh on his bare hot flesh. He sank the knife into the dark, soft moistness. His breathing was fast, his heart too. He pushed the plate towards her and always their eyes were locked. He served himself. The brandy flames had died, the artificial flames were flickering. There was only the sound of their breathing, only the sound of her sliding now beneath the table, only the sensation of her finding him.

Later they lay together before the fire, naked, satiated, the debris of the meal forgotten on the dining table, and then she spoiled it by saying, 'It could be like this every night.'

He kissed her neck, ignoring the remark, because it wouldn't be. It would be boring; it would be the television, married friends, work, her cellulite, her sagging breasts, her relations. Real life, that's what it would be.

She stroked his hair but this part always bored him. He wanted to get sorted out, or go to sleep, one or the other. He lifted himself on to his elbow, slapping her thigh lightly. 'Come on, shower and clothes on, or you'll be in bed with a chill for

Christmas, and then what would your mother say?'

'That's what it could be like if we were together. Bed all Christmas.'

He kissed her. It saved finding an answer. They showered together. He liked her new bath towels. The ones at the vicarage were getting a bit thin. He dressed, smoothed his hair, wiping the steam from the mirror. Behind him Jan was pulling on her silk dress. It was creased. She looked as though she had been dragged through a hedge backwards. Well, she had, more or less. He felt a hardening and thought of something else, anything else, because there wasn't time for a re-run now. 'Coffee?' he said. She smiled, and left.

By the time he reached the sitting room the coffee was in the cafetière on the small table. Beside it were two porcelain coffee cups and saucers. She certainly had some nice stuff. He watched Jan pick up the fallen cards and return them to their place, and her eyes met his in the mirror. 'They're from my friends, but they could be from our friends.'

'One day they will be,' he lied, breaking eye contact, pouring two coffees, drinking his while he stood.

'But why not now? You said it's over. You said she doesn't care about you, or you her. You said it's a marriage in name only, that you've agreed to stay together for the children. You said . . .' She had turned to him, her back was to the mirror and her hair was all fuzzy, like Jude's had been when she was a baby.

He stopped her with a finger placed against her lips. 'Shh. One day, just believe that. One day. Right now you know that I have commitments, there's Jude. Now, I've a gift, several gifts . . .' He put down the cup and strode to the hallway where he had left the packages the girl in the department store had wrapped for him. Surreptitiously he checked his watch, he wanted to be off by eleven.

Back in the room Jan was holding out a new expanding briefcase, tied with a red bow. He was thrilled. It was just what he needed. He could always tell Kate he'd won it in the office raffle. Yes, that's what he could do, he thought, as Jan explained that it could double as an overnight bag. Did she think he didn't realise that? Why did women have to spell everything out? He put his gifts for her on the sofa, and as she unwrapped them he checked his watch again.

She liked the table mats, the napkins and the pepper mill but he sensed her disappointment. It irritated him but he was careful not to show it as he gestured around the room. 'Oh, Jan, I'm so sorry, but I just couldn't do anything else this year. It's all stretching me, and I thought you'd realise the Capo di Monte was for Christmas too.'

'Please, of course I realised.'

But he could tell she hadn't, and he wished he'd thought of saying it earlier, but it had only just come to him. He dragged his hand through his hair. 'Jan, when I didn't get any money for the furniture, when I didn't get Mother's house . . .' He could hear the strain in his voice, and emphasised it.

She came to him immediately. 'Please, darling. Please don't. Let me help. I can pay more rent.'

He held her close. 'I wouldn't hear of it. I've told you, I want to look after you, it's just that this Christmas . . . You do understand? I'm just so sorry, so very sorry.'

He managed to get his voice to shake. She was holding him. 'You need a break, that's what you need.'

'I wish,' his longing was heartfelt.

He could see the clock. For God's sake, she knew the score, she knew he was married, that there were children, that his mother had just died. What the hell did she want, bells on it? For the first time he seriously wondered if it was time to get out. Jan moved against him. But no, not yet. His arms tightened around her.

Alan didn't think she'd go when the time came, but she would. After all, there was no proof anywhere that this current relationship was anything other than a landlord–tenant situation, because she hadn't been the one to witness the remortgage, that had been some business chum.

He also had a rent book he could produce with all her payments noted, payments which went through a separate business account he'd set up, payments which might be less than the going rate but which were nonetheless legal. If there was any sticking on her part, or threats, he'd simply evict her. Alan would back him up and if Kate came to hear of it, Alan would speak up then as well.

Again she moved against him. He looked at the clock. Her

hands were on his neck. Had he time? No, best to get out while the going was good. He eased free from her, kissing her forehead. 'Have a good time at your mother's. I'll phone.'

She looked tired. For a moment he felt something tug at him. He touched her face. She said, 'Are you sure?'

'Of course. I'll be missing you so much, how could I not? Now, I'm going down to Fowey to check on the builder's progress on the twenty-seventh.'

'With Kate?'

He avoided her eyes, feeling uncomfortable, and then resentful that he should. Of course with Kate – did she expect him to take the milkman? He nodded, gathering up his mac and two briefcases. 'I have to, it *is* technically her property. Look, darling, why not phone me on the mobile at midday on the twenty-eighth. I'll say I've been called to the office and we could have two nights together.' He knew that would be worth more than a load of expensive presents to her and get her on side again.

Jan hugged him and was ecstatic. 'You really do love me, don't you?'

'Yes,' he replied, and perhaps he did, for now.

As he drove away he pushed in a tape of Joplin. It was eleven twenty. Jude would be home by now, and maybe Simon too. Wasn't his plane due in this afternoon? The thought didn't thrill him. He was a cocky little bugger and seemed to be flying up the ladder much faster than Peter had ever done. He'd be at the top before he was forty, and Peter wasn't sure if he'd ever make it himself now. He wound down the window slightly, needing the cold air. He was pretty sure he wasn't over the limit, but he was tired. Then he grinned, remembering the meal, her foot, and the hour that had followed.

He was home by midnight. In the glare from the security light he took the red ribbon off the briefcase, stuffing it into his pocket before carrying both briefcases into the house. Jude came roaring down the stairs. 'Good party, Dad?'

He hugged her, raised his eyebrows at Kate and Simon who came out of the kitchen. 'Oh, tiring. You know what these firm's do's are like.'

CHAPTER THIRTEEN

Kate, driving back from the Christmas morning service, diverted at the T-junction, turning left instead of right. Jude yelped, 'Mum, for heaven's sake, where are you going?'

Beside Kate Simon murmured, 'Insane, I should think, in the face of your whingeing.'

Kate flashed him a look, and said to Jude, 'I had a sudden need to see Barbs's bungalow, and say hello.' She could sense Jude rolling her eyes. 'And that's enough of that, enough of the quarrelling altogether, you two. It's the season of goodwill.'

Jude grumbled, 'As though we could miss that fact. Midnight service, morning service, anyone would think we're Born Agains.'

Kate was turning left into Ellesmere Road. Acacia Avenue was second left. 'For goodness' sake, Jude, what else would you have been doing?'

Immediately she realised that was a mistake, for Jude said, grimly patient, 'Sleeping, opening presents, you know, the normal things we used to do before Penny got promoted to full fancy dress.'

Kate said nothing. She didn't want to pursue a conversation which had been running along similar lines for the last couple of years. Beside her Simon was shaking. She knew it was with laughter, and if she looked at him she would catch it, she always did. In the past, when Peter had sent Simon from the room until he could control himself, she knew he had wanted to banish her as well. She was so glad Simon was here.

Now she was turning left into Barbs's road. She slowed to a snail's pace. She had wanted to dye a sheet purple and use it as the Christmas tablecloth, but it hadn't seemed worth Peter's mutters. She half wished she had now.

She stopped outside, staring at the house, dropping the gear into neutral, letting the engine idle. Simon wound down his window, propping his elbow on the sill. 'No one there, from the look of it.'

Jude snapped, 'There is next door, though, the net's lifting.'

'And so it was and always will be,' Simon intoned. Suddenly all three of them were laughing.

'Come on, Mum,' Jude said at last. 'The turkey will be falling off the bone and he's not going to be able to carve it into slivers.'

Kate lifted her eyes to the rear-view mirror in surprise. There had been a note of censure in her daughter's voice, almost distaste, but for Peter, not Kate. Jude caught her eye, and flushed. She said, 'Well come on, they'll think we're a load of nutters just sitting here.' The antagonism was back.

Simon though, had put up his hand. 'Hang on, if there is no one here we could go and look in, see how they've rearranged Barbs's furniture.'

Kate had been thinking in tandem, and her hand moved to the door. She wanted to see if somehow Barbs's presence was there, because Christmas had miraculously calmed her. Or perhaps it wasn't Christmas, perhaps it was having her children around her. Or was it that a New Year was coming? Or simply that she wasn't having to go into the Medical Centre. There, the thought didn't even make her shudder.

Whatever it was, everything was improving; the nightmares were not every night. There were days when the sun was metaphorically shining, and the awful heavy darkness lifted. Each day it was easier to leave her bed, to go from minute to minute, hour to hour, day to day, not looking backwards, or forwards. Just taking one step at a time, as she had always advised her patients. Nursey had healed herself. She smiled slightly.

Jude was slapping Simon's headrest. 'If we peer in looking for ghosts they'll *know* we're a load of nutters. Come on, we'll be late, Mum. This is stupid. Dad's home alone and any minute Penny and Tom will be there and Dad'll have to look after them as well as sharpen the blessed knife so he'll get tense. Why do you have to do this, wind everyone up, make everything such a mess?'

'Do you have to be objectionable all the time?' Simon was swinging round. 'You're supposed to be an adult, so put a sock in it.'

'Oh, that's right, just turn up when you feel like it and start telling me how to behave when you know nothing of what's . . .'

'Be quiet, both of you.' Kate put the car into gear. 'The turkey's on target for firm flesh, Jude, and we'll be back before Penny and Tom. I warned them I'd be taking the scenic route.' As she drove away she took one last look at the bungalow. It wasn't Barbs's any more.

She switched from Radio Two to One. She half heard her children singing along. Music was a great unifier, but also a great excluder – of generations. But Barbs had even swallowed up that gulf in the last two years, and never missed *Top of the Pops*, or *TFI Friday*. She smiled. Dearest Barbs.

Back home they waited for Penny and Tom to arrive before opening their presents, but Johnny, their son, had trouble phoning home from Australia, so the Maxwells were two glasses of wine along the way before they arrived. Penny was in mufti, and Tom in the three-ply sweater Penny had suddenly decided to knit him, though the ladies of the Bible reading group had to take over when she reached the armholes. Peter passed a beer to Tom. 'Where's Johnny off to next?'

'Some wineries near Margaret River, in Western Australia.'

Peter nodded with pleasure. 'Some good wines coming out of there, right now.'

Simon was passing the presents from beneath the tree. Peter's to Kate was an electric screwdriver, and Simon's an electric drill. She brandished both at them. 'Next time I lose it they can make a film about me. Massacre down Vicarage Street.' She caught Jude's eye and they both smiled.

Simon continued the distribution whilst she slipped to the kitchen where Penny joined her, a glass of wine in either hand. Together they manoeuvred the turkey on to the huge serving dish. 'This looks as though we're performing some undignified medical procedure,' Penny panted, removing the carving fork from the turkey's backside.

'It's not nearly as entertaining as you losing count of the purl and plain. It looks good, incidentally, and almost fits.'

As Kate drained the sprout water into the gravy, Penny

leaned back against the sink and sipped her Chablis. Kate gestured her to one side, and put the pan in to soak. 'You could swill that out.'

As Penny did so, Kate scattered almonds on the sprouts, something Peter had suggested. Along with the briefcase he'd won at the firm's raffle, he'd also won a cookbook, but had passed it on to one of the typists, or did you call them administrative assistants these days? Anyway, the typist had read this offering to the assembled congregation.

The meal went well. Peter carved the turkey more quickly than usual, and the slices were thick. Simon met her glance, as surprised as she. Penny and Kate wanted the name of the cookbook on the strength of the sprouts, but Peter couldn't remember, and toasted the cook. It was something he did every year, though this was the first occasion on which he had actually worn his paper hat. It was red.

Jude's was purple, and she had flushed with pleasure when it had whizzed out of the cracker. 'Good old Barbs,' she had said, sliding it on over her newly permed hair. Kate liked it with the kinks, and now told her so for the hundredth time.

Everyone laughed as Simon said, 'She's got to the repeating stage, no more porter for that woman.'

Though everyone protested that they really couldn't manage Christmas pudding, Kate carried it in flaming nonetheless, and placed it before Peter. He 'carved' this as well but as he cut into it he seemed preoccupied, slow. Simon shouted at Tom, 'No more porter for that man.' Tom took up the chant. Peter looked up and it was as though he knew a secret, as though he was looking down on them from a great height. Was this the patriarchal male surveying his flock, Kate wondered, her thoughts gloriously slowed by alcohol.

But as her hat slipped off her head yet again Peter clicked back to them with a loud bellow of a laugh that took them all by surprise. 'I love Christmas pudding,' he said. 'It has hidden depths.'

'No, only old sixpences,' Jude crowed.

'Five pence pieces, actually,' Kate grinned, her lips clumsy. Lord, she really must have nothing more to drink. The laughter went on. It went on even when they were playing Monopoly after the brandy. OK, so she had no self-control, she told Simon, who said that was the way to do it, let it all hang loose.

It went on late into the evening when they gathered in the sitting room with cups of tea and pieces of cake and Kate could hear nothing but the happiness of her friends and family and felt it herself.

The weather was dry in Fowey when Peter and Kate arrived on the afternoon of 27 December. Simon had flown back the previous evening, and Jude had nipped up to London to stay that night with university friends. The bed and breakfast was welcoming, and their room overlooked the river. Peter stood there, his hands in the pockets of the olive cords she had bought him for Christmas. The ripples were reflected on the ceiling. Kate unpacked, and then stood beside him. He said, 'It's certainly a good view.'

'Yes, it is.'

He said, 'Told you it would be a good investment to buy here.'

He moved to his briefcase and took out the plans for the high-ceilinged room he had been working on all Boxing Day. 'McTravers will meet us there. Did I tell you he's already put in several days' work, and is prepared to carry on over the Christmas period, a near miracle in the building trade?'

He had told her, several times. Did he want a red star? She stared out across the water. Christmas was fading, and the sun with it. She breathed slowly. Come on, minute by minute, hour by hour, that's all it takes.

'I phoned last night. He's sub-contracted the windows and they're in, and an access door to the garden at the end of the landing, though no staircase yet.' Peter slapped her on the behind. 'It's good to be away, to be free of life for a couple of days. Come on, then. Let's go and see your property.'

There was no edge to his voice, just a sort of suppressed good humour, and he even put his arm around her as they walked through the town, stopping halfway up the short angled hill by the post office, looking through the gap at the river again. He said, 'We're going to have no trouble attracting someone to . . . attracting lots of someones,' he laughed. 'I mean, tourists are here now, for goodness' sake, even though

109

it's the dead of winter. So I'm sure we can set up a really good letting proposition.'

He was right, there were people strolling past, and the car park had been almost full. He sighed with satisfaction, urging her on. 'Can't wait to see what stage the men are at.' They walked towards Journey's End and she found herself digging her hands hard into the pockets of her fleece and felt her stomach knotting, and now it was all back, the darkness, the panic.

Mr McTravers was on site, and there was scaffolding along the end wall with a young lad working there. There were planks heaped untidily in the small stretch of garden. He met them in the small room at the bottom in overalls dusted with white. He shook hands. His were callused and huge. He addressed Peter, not Kate.

She stared up at the house, then made herself walk inside and up the stairs, along the landing into the room, *that* room, a room that smelt of fresh plaster now. They were gone, there was nothing on the windowsill. Of course not – how could there be when a new hardwood double-glazed window had been fitted? Instead of Peter's purple tempters there were plaster splashes from where the walls had been made good around the window frame. Brown-pink plaster against old whitewash.

She touched the plaster, it still felt damp. Of course it would be. There was no heating to dry it, no sun. She leaned her head on the cold pane, moving only when she heard their voices on the stairs. When they entered she was kicking at the plaster blobs which were stuck to the bare boards.

'Don't you worry about that, Mrs Maxwell, it'll come off with a bit of a scrape.'

'Once we've got carpets down it won't show anyway,' Peter said, peering past her and down at the garden. 'We're leaving the staircase to last, aren't we, Mr McTravers?'

She said, 'They were here.' She was pointing to the sill.

Peter looked blank. Mr McTravers looked puzzled, then nodded, holding up a finger. 'Got 'em under the dustsheets in that main room. Nice little bibelots.'

In the raftered main room there were dustsheets over a workman's bench in the corner. She pulled it off as though she was Paul Daniels. 'These,' she said.

But Peter was looking at the view. 'This is stunning.' He was tapping his roll of plans against his leg. There was real admiration in his voice.

'These,' she repeated, but even before he turned to look she felt foolish. What did it matter any more? She'd bought the place, they were here, work was under way. She let the dustsheet drop but not before he had caught sight of the purple objects. He waved his hand towards them, and towards her.

'Oh, not this again. For God's sake, Kate, I don't know what you're fussing about, they're just kids' things left behind, that's all. Nothing to do with me.' This last he said quietly, glancing quickly at McTravers, not wanting him to hear. Not wanting him to know that his wife was a shrew, or barking mad, Kate thought.

Mr McTravers was taking the plans from Peter and together they eyed up the high room, checking where the joists would go for the ceiling, and looking again at where to split the window.

But they weren't kids' things. They were beautiful works of art.

She went to the window, pressing her forehead against it, wanting the cool of glass to freeze her mind, but it hadn't worked in the smaller bedroom, so why should it work here? It didn't. Her stupid, chaotic mind went on spinning out of control, imagining things, suspecting things, regretting and whingeing about things when she had thought she was better.

She opened her eyes. There were small craft sailing towards the sea, their sails full. They were escaping, they were being cleansed by the power of the wind.

McTravers said from beside her, 'Bit of a sailor, are you?'

She straightened. Behind her Peter barked a laugh. 'Anything but. My wife likes to watch but if she sets foot on board she has to head for the nearest bucket.'

She murmured, 'Goodness, Mr McTravers, you never saw my lips move when I answered your question.'

Peter sighed. 'So, we're back to this, are we?'

She hated herself, hated him. They weren't children's bits and pieces, they were works of art.

They stayed at Journey's End, growing cold. When darkness fell McTravers and Peter continued to plan by the light of the builder's strong torch. At seven Kate and Peter ate in a pub.

111

There were other tourists, and that was what she and Peter were. Yes, they'd bought a house, but it was not a home. They ate turkey pie. It was not a success. 'I'll grow feathers soon,' Peter said.

'Then you should have chosen the fish. Gills are in this year.' She watched as he toyed with the menu. Had he just picked up any four purple objects? Had he sent his secretary out for them? Or had he got the bloody builder to do it?

He was checking his watch. It was only eight thirty but holidays meant sex. 'Another drink?' she suggested.

He shook his head. 'Early night.' It was as though he was offering a child the chocolate buttons off the Christmas tree.

Back at the bed and breakfast the landlady met them in the hall. She offered coffee but Peter, his arm guiding Kate towards the stairs, said, 'How kind, but it's been a busy day.'

'Full English breakfast in the morning?' the landlady called after them.

'Wonderful, we'll have an appetite.' Peter squeezed Kate, then pushed her ahead of him into the bedroom.

He showered before her and she undressed in the dark, slipping on the lightweight dressing gown that packed into nothing. She didn't admire the view. She did nothing but sit on the side of the bed and listen to his humming, to his teeth cleaning, his gargling. He emerged from the en suite bathroom naked. She hurried into the remains of his steam, showered, fiddled about, sneaked into the bedroom. He was in the bed, his breathing even. He was asleep.

Relieved, she carefully lifted the bedclothes, slid under and then his hands were round her naked breasts. They felt cold against her skin. He pulled her round. She thought of the list of thank you letters she had to write. His hands were all over her. Hers remained still. 'What's wrong?' he asked, hurt. Here in the dark she touched his face. Here in the bed he was hers. It was how they spoke, she supposed. It was what made them man and wife, it was here that children were conceived, that comfort was given, sometimes.

She willed herself to feel something, making herself concentrate, move outside herself, watch these two bodies in the bed, and slowly it worked as it usually did, but this time the lovemaking became harsh, and it was she who led it, and he who followed. It was she who was on top, dictating his orgasm, he who lay helpless, his breathing fast, asking her, begging her. It was she who said no, not yet.

It was she who rolled off suddenly, leaving him unfinished. It was she who then pulled him on to her, holding him too tight, forcing him to alter his pace, and for what seemed like hours this wordless battle was fought, and it was only when she saw the excitement, the pleasure in his face that she let him come. Ashamed, surprised, disgusted, wanting it over, feeling cold and clammy again. But he lay on top of her, panting, laughing into her neck. Surely he knew she hated that, but had she ever told him? No, it would spoil his moment. He whispered, 'Fowey suits you.'

Nothing suited her. She was a mess. He withdrew. There was nothing good about that bit. He went to the bathroom, and then she too. There was nothing good about that bit either. But at least he would sleep now. Would she, or would the nightmares be back, along with everything else?

They didn't come back, because she lay awake until the dawn came up, and even the brimming light over the water couldn't end the loneliness that she felt. A loneliness that continued over breakfast; two rashers, two chipolatas, one egg, one fried bread, a million fat cells to clog all available arteries. But loneliness was part of the grieving process she would have to go through. It was what everyone went through, and if Penny told her that again she would murder her.

She took a gulp of coffee. But then she was good at murder. She looked anywhere but at Peter, cold suddenly. It was back. She had let it back. Simon should be here, telling her, as he had told Jude, that she was an obnoxious whinger.

It was as they were taking the path that led along the coast that his mobile phone rang. He cursed, putting a finger in one ear, turning his back to Kate and the wind. 'What, is there no one else?' A pause. 'Damn it.' He looked across at Kate. He seemed to hesitate. For a moment she thought he'd refuse. He said, turning away from the wind again, 'Look, Mike, it's very difficult. I really don't think . . .' Another pause. 'OK, OK, you can count on me. Tell him to get better quickly. Hang on, you'd better speak to my wife, she might think I'm running off with another woman.'

He held the phone out to her. She shook her head, but wanting all the same to snatch the phone.

He came to her, putting his arms around her, pulling her close. 'I really didn't want this to happen,' he said, and it sounded as though he meant it.

He held her even tighter for a moment, and then they retraced their steps without speaking. Now she could leave this place, before the darkness grew more intense. Soon she'd be home and she would find a decorator who would paint, and furniture that Peter could bring down. That's why it was back. That's why. Because she was down here, because she had stepped inside the house, which was someone's dream, a house she didn't want to heal. A house she wanted nothing to do with.

To her right the sea was whipping into white peaks. The wind was cold. Peter said, 'Why not stay on until tomorrow as planned, keep an eye on McTravers? You could get the train back, I'm sure Penny would collect you from the station. It would give you time to sort out a cheaper place, maybe even set up camp at Journey's End.'

'Camp?'

'We haven't really organised the ins and outs. You'll have to be down here during the week, won't you, and you'll want to keep expenses to a minimum while you do it up.'

They were heading into town. She said nothing. They were level with the path that ran down to the Polruan passenger ferry embarkation point. Still she said nothing. They were walking on. Houses lined both sides of the road. They walked until they were at the bed and breakfast.

Camp, in that damp house with no electricity and running water the only service? Camp in a house once owned by someone with a dream? Sleep on the truckle bed, which had been at the foot of Barbs's bed?

The landlady smiled at them. Peter said, 'I have to return immediately, a project crisis. Kate, what about you?'

Kate said, somehow finding words, somehow forcing them out. 'I'll come with you. I can't leave Jude on her own so soon after Christmas.' She sounded rational.

Whilst they packed he lectured on the advisability of hands-on project management. She said, as calmly as she could, 'My family is also my project. McTravers has a mobile phone. I will

114

keep him on the boil. My plan is to come down when Jude leaves. My plan is to find a bed and breakfast, perhaps this one.' Her voice was shaking. It wasn't anger, not really. It was the realisation that she had to be here, a fact which had been lost in the chaos she had been living through, in the echoes of the past she had been fighting, in the stupid trivia of purple objects she had been obsessed by.

She wanted him to say, 'There's no need, I'll take control.' After all, that was what he always did. But he just picked up her weekend case. 'We'll offer to pay half of tomorrow night but no more.'

She was staring at the river, the damn and blasted river. He walked from the room. Above the river the winter sky was busy with billowing clouds, just as the airfield had been. She wasn't like Barbs; brave and bold. She made mistakes, she panicked, and she hated the dark, and there was no electricity at Journey's End.

He called her from the hall. She hurried down, grabbing his arm, wanting to shout, 'No, I can't.' Instead she whispered, 'No, we'll pay the full whack.' He frowned, shaking his head. She insisted, saying, 'It's peanuts, and I'm going to have to stay in this town, find someone to deal with the cleaning when the season starts, so we can't have bad feeling. I'll need friendly faces.' She was calm, firm. How?

He nodded his approval. 'Good thinking, Batman.'

She couldn't return his grin, or laugh at his stupid joke. Instead she stared at the tourist brochures neatly arranged on the hall table whilst he paid, and all the time her stomach was churning, because if they'd bought one of the inland cottages it would have been a clean purchase, just the letting to arrange. She was stupid and weak.

And how dare he lie about the purple things, how bloody dare he?

They rowed about these all the way home, and carried on when they arrived, and she thought that she'd never seen him so angry, or so dismissive. But she didn't care. This time she was so sick and angry she didn't care when he stormed out, telling her he would be back in two days and by then he hoped she'd be in control.

115

CHAPTER FOURTEEN

Penny sat in Kate's kitchen picking at the debris of the Danish pastries and sipping the last of the painfully ground coffee, grumbling, 'Why the hell you don't just buy an electric grinder I simply do not know.'

Kate patted the manual grinder she had bought herself in the January sales. 'It gives me a bit of peace, because while I'm turning the handle I can't do anything else, or hear anything else.'

'That's all very well, but it's a bit much having to do your own when you're asked round for a quick cup.'

'I never said quick,' Kate smiled, quite normally.

Penny laughed. 'Nor you did, and I'm not sure that I like the recovered and together you. It was better when you were pathetic and in a tizz; and slung me an instant.' Then she patted the letter that lay between them. 'What on earth are you going to do about this?'

Kate reread it, keeping the smile somehow. It was from the double glazing sub-contractor. 'I'll have to phone McTravers.' Her stomach knotted, just as it had when she opened the letter this morning, or should she say, knotted further, and there was nothing she could do to prevent it, because suddenly Fowey was here, in front of her.

Fowey, which since her return she had shut from her mind, and just held on, somehow, letting no one guess at the effort. Fowey, which was back again, clamouring for her attention, and she was no longer the calm Kate who had picked her way around Jude and Peter as they bonded ever closer over the decorating plans and quotes, the letting schedules and cheap ways of marketing.

'What do you think, Mum?' Jude had asked.

'Excellent.' It was what she had decided to say to everything. To the coving prices, the assembly pack furniture price list. To

116

the foam-back ghastliness Peter hunted out at the huge carpet warehouse, a ghastliness which swirled so much it would disguise all manner of dirt brought in on the soles of shoes, and in addition would fit the cost he had scheduled. He hadn't bought it yet, but that day would come, and she was grateful, because the less it involved her the better.

Each day he called McTravers, and at least twice a week he repeated that it needed one of them on site right now. And she replied, as she always did, 'When Jude goes back.'

Jude said, 'For goodness' sake, I'm not a child.'

Well, now it was the third week of January, Peter had gone to Czechoslovakia on a business trip, and Jude was back at university, together with her plants which they had lugged upstairs properly in pallets. This time there was no one clocking them in, no parents standing about looking strained. Instead they were depositing their offspring and making a run for it, which was precisely what the offspring wanted.

Before Kate drove away, though, Jude came running out, gesturing for her to wind down the window. 'For goodness' sake, Mum, now I'm not there to do it take some of the load, get on with the decorating, because the quotes were far too much. And show some enthusiasm about the property when Dad gets back.'

She hadn't waited for a reply, just flounced off.

Kate had packed her grip last night. Yes, she could decorate. Of course she could. She had booked a room at the bed and breakfast, comforting herself with the thought that at least in Fowey she wouldn't have to show enthusiasm; she could just strip down the woodwork, slap on the paint, get some furniture somewhere down there, working into the evening now the rewiring was done. She would include Journey's End in a holiday letting brochure and get home again, and she would cope. Kate Maxwell would cope, and soon she would even be able to look at Peter again.

An hour ago, though, this letter had arrived, almost at the same time as Penny, who had nipped across for a coffee before Kate left. Carlton's, the double glazing sub-contractor, was writing to say the balance of their invoice had not been settled. It had been agreed as half payment before, the rest on completion. The 'rest' was what was missing. The 'rest' should have come from McTravers's Stage One payment. The knot tightened.

McTravers liked 'hands-on' control, and Peter had appreciated those sentiments. McTravers had moreover been the only builder prepared to cut short his Christmas break, and the least they could have done was to have been down there with him, he would say. Yes, she could just hear it now, and she felt sick. She took the plates to the sink.

'When I reached McTravers on the mobile he said he put a cheque in the post to Carlton's yesterday. The post can't have been delivered yet. I've arranged to meet McTravers when I get there. He says work is on schedule, the ceiling is done, the kitchen fitted, and the bathroom plumbing and all electrical work due for completion tomorrow.' Her hands felt as though they were trembling, but looking down she saw they weren't. Why had she brought the plates to the sink?

Penny elbowed her aside and stacked them in the dishwasher, then she put her arm around her. 'Come on, you senile old fool, I'd be nervous, especially if I had to do it on my own. And as for the cheque, I bet it's all fine. I bet by now Carlton's are happily ripping open the envelope and the rest of the work is up to schedule. Just think of the coving you have to put up, the magnolia you have to splash about, and in no time you'll be back.' Suddenly her voice was not as cheerful, or as confident. 'Phone Carlton's again, Kate.'

'You've forgotten the self-assembly furniture with never enough screws.' Kate was working at two levels again, trying to distract Penny.

'Phone Carlton's, Kate.'

Kate did. The post had come. There was no cheque. She told the man at Carlton's she would have it sorted by the end of the day. He said that he hoped so, because he'd been round to Fowey and there was no sign of McTravers, no sign of much being done, of much having been done.

Penny was leading her through to the hall, her voice fierce. 'Call me if McTravers has done a bunk. Oh Lord, Kate, do you think he has? Shall I come with you? But there's hospital visiting. Shall I come tomorrow, but there's . . . Kate, promise me you'll call.'

Kate stood by her grip. She had rolled up Peter's plans and

118

they were lying on the top. Penny said, 'Promise me.'

She decided to take the camp bed. Not the truckle bed, not the one she'd slept in . . . She'd take the camp bed just in case. Because if it was going pear-shaped she'd need every spare penny she could find. There, she sounded calm, normal, but why shouldn't she when all along she had known that something like this would happen? Because things went wrong when you had done something terrible.

She drove, foot hard down. The camping lamp, camping stove, mugs, plates, and Uncle Tom Cobbly rattled in the cardboard box. She stopped west of Plymouth for a coffee, and to use the phone. McTravers's mobile was turned off. Perhaps he was halfway up a ladder and didn't need any distraction.

She returned to the car and made herself repeat that she wouldn't be away for more than a few days. If McTravers had fled, Peter would have known, someone would have known, and she must push the encroaching chaos back. Far, far back.

She crossed the Tamar and headed between the rolling hills, turning up the radio, pushing it all back behind Ken Bruce, behind the battle the wipers were waging against the rain which was pouring down.

She fiddled with the air vent, trying to direct it on to her side window which was mugging up, wiping it with her sleeve again and again because this wasn't Peter's smear-free zone. This was her car, and she didn't have to peer through a tiny area of windscreen until the blower cleared it. This was her car, and everything would be fine.

It was only as she turned left at the mini roundabout after Liskeard that she slashed the sound to pianissimo. 'Now that's power,' she said aloud, but she couldn't make herself smile. She parked near the Bodinnack ferry. The rain had lessened, but not by much. She pulled up the hood of her cagoule, tying it toggle-tight against the wind which was sending an empty Diet Coke can clattering through the spaces reserved for boats and trailers. There were none, of course. But in the season . . .

She opened the car door, stepping out into the wet coldness of this place which she had never wanted to be involved with. She slung her bag over her shoulder, dug her hands into her pockets and struggled head down towards Journey's End.

Once into the shelter of the narrow street she was able to walk upright, but the rain still stung her cheeks. She dug into her bag for her microscopic umbrella, but even before she reached it the force of the wind changed her mind.

There was no one in the street, no sign of life in the houses she passed, but when she paused for respite, turning her back and huddling in a doorway, she heard a radio from the depths. For a moment she waited, breathing deeply, not wanting to go on, feeling the dragging in her body, the fragmenting of her mind, the awful shaking that kept coming and receding. She took one more breath and stepped out again, quicker now, then made herself run head down past the bus shelter and slipway where no swans flaunted themselves today.

She slowed to a walk. It wouldn't do to look flushed and in disarray when bearding McTravers. Because perhaps he was there. She looked ahead to the distant house. There was no sign of life, no ladders, no scaffolding. But there wouldn't be – the windows were done, the repointing too. He would be inside. She was walking much slower now, not wanting to arrive. But of course she did, and now she stepped into the road and peered up at the lifeless windows. She moved forward, cupping her hands against the hall window. She saw nothing. And there was no sound.

She tapped on the door, then banged again and again. Nothing. She should have phoned from the car park – he'd be in the back, and couldn't hear over the radio. All builders had radios. But there was no sound. She banged harder, harder. Her fist hurt. She stopped, letting her hand drop. Had McTravers's van been in the car park? She couldn't think. She checked her watch: 1.45. Lunch. That was it. He was at lunch.

'Need help?' For a moment she couldn't work out where the voice was coming from. 'Need help?' The voice was louder. To her left she saw a hand waving briefly from Zanadu's doorway, the flat over which they had a flying freehold.

Head bent, she walked the few paces to the yellow door, which opened wider. An elderly man in frayed slippers and knee-worn cords pulled her inside, shutting the door quickly. It seemed so quiet suddenly. Kate stood dripping on the mat whilst he gestured towards her cagoule. 'Do take it off.' His dentures slipped, but his smile reached his eyes, and it was this

120

smile that cut through everything, stopping it all dead, making her see her surroundings again, drawing her back from where she'd been.

The hall was narrow, and halfway along a marble-topped dresser stood against the wall, with a Tiffany table lamp throwing its soft light on old prints. The wallpaper was a warm red. At the end of the hall a door was opening slowly and a plump lady with her hair in rollers peered out. 'In trouble?'

Kate pushed her hood off her head. 'Not much.' The man gestured towards her cagoule again. She shook her head. 'I can't stop. You see, I'm your new neighbour, Kate Maxwell. I've come down for a progress report from the builder. In fact, I'm down to keep a bit of an eye on things. I do hope he hasn't been too noisy.' She sounded quite normal, didn't she?

The woman was patting her rollers. 'No noise at all. Forgive these. We're off to Tenerife tomorrow. There's a fire in here. Why not sit?'

Kate shook her head. Again she strove to sound normal, calm, merely curious. 'You haven't seen the builder today?'

The man looked at his wife, and then at her. 'Not for days. Nor heard. Not for weeks. Not since the windows, and the walls. That's all he did. Thank you for doing our pointing.'

Kate shook her head. 'Please, it was nothing.'

It had been something though, to Peter. But she had insisted that neighbours were important, neighbours could warn you of tenant problems. 'Call it PR.' He'd agreed. But that wasn't important. Nothing had been done for weeks. She was shivering. She hadn't noticed that. The water had run into her pockets. Her tissues were wet. She found one in her bag instead. 'We phoned him daily.'

'Mobile?'

Mutely she nodded.

The elderly man said, 'There you are. You can say you're here, but you're somewhere else instead.'

His wife was a picture of concern. Kate looked away from her. 'I know.'

She reached for the latch. 'I know,' she repeated.

Outside again, she fitted her key into the lock, her lock, but someone else's dream. She turned the key. She pushed the

121

door; it stuck, then opened. Inside it was dark and cold and damp. Get storage heaters, the Glovers had said as she held the door open, letting their heat out. For Ted and Mary Glover were the names of the dear, sweet neighbours who seemed almost as upset as she.

She climbed the stairs, feeling her way. Was this how those who had owned it, those who had cut the channels, had felt their way? She stopped. Was it really dark or was her personal darkness all back, really back? She gripped the banister hard, harder.

She felt her way along the landing and into the high-raftered room. Here it was light. Here she could walk to the huge window. A window that had not been halved. A room without a lowered ceiling. 'Get storage heaters.' But before heaters came power. And before power came rewiring. And before rewiring came McTravers. McTravers and his mobile. I know, she thought, of course I know what phoning a mobile means.

She rested her head on the window. It was so cold against her forehead. It was so cold in the room, which smelt of plaster. Damn you, McTravers. Damn you, Barbs. Damn you, you stupid silly woman, but this time she meant herself. Of course she knew what a mobile meant. She had always known, but what could she prove? And if she could prove anything, should she? Because she knew that Jude found something with her father that she couldn't with Kate.

The pub the Glovers had suggested had a roaring fire in the grate and not many customers. Behind the bar a large man of about the Glovers' age was washing glasses, a tea towel slung over his shoulder. Dandruff? Don't think about it. She ordered a dry cider and a pasty and took them to the seat nearest the fire. The rain had come through her so-called waterproofs. She steamed.

'He'll know of someone,' they'd said. 'So sad about the other owner. He could turn his hand to anything and had such plans.'

It was a veritable speech, and made everything worse. The pasty warmed her, the cider did very little. Perhaps she should have had brandy? She stared at the flames, leaning back as the barman arrived to put on more logs. Sparks rose. Her mind grappled, panicked, sorted. She'd have to camp, in the house of the man who could turn his hand to anything. She stopped. Yes, she'd camp. She'd find an electrician, a plasterer to make good the walls, a plumber, someone to put up the ceiling. On and on it went. A log fell forward. Automatically she reached for the poker, but the barman was there again, saying, 'Don't you fret.'

'I'm not fretting,' she snapped.

He looked at her, his eyes startled beneath bushy grey eyebrows. She put up her hand. 'I'm so sorry.'

He shook his head. 'No matter.' He had grey sideboards which met his cropped beard. He rolled the log back and replaced the poker. His hands were the size of hams, hard and work worn. There was not a sign of dandruff on the navy sweater.

'Sorry,' she said again.

As he passed her, he squeezed her shoulder briefly, not pausing but carrying on to the bar, calling back, 'It's forgotten. Would you like coffee?'

'If it's no trouble.' She checked the time: two thirty, she should be doing something. She forced her mind to work. What money was left after the first stage payment to McTravers? Take away from that the cheque she would deliver personally to Carlton's this afternoon. But perhaps she could find McTravers, make him pay. It would calm Peter, it would sort out everything. She had his address, after all. She reached for her bag, but the paperwork was in the briefcase, which was in the car. She'd go to him later. But what if he wasn't there? Or what if he was, but laughed in her face? Then Peter would come. Peter, who would shout. Peter who wanted to be accessible. Peter who was in her nightmares.

The barman brought her coffee. She said, 'I came down to see McTravers, the builder. Somehow I always pick the wrong weather.' So normal, so calm.

The barman leaned towards the fire, bracing his hand against the beam. The flames lit his weather-beaten face, a face gouged by deep lines, but one that was open and friendly. 'You'd have picked the wrong builder too, if you got hold of that one. But no fear of that, I reckon. I heard tell he's gone off to Saudi, just last night. He's been dodging about for a month or more getting enough cash together to set up some job or other over there. I gather he has some pretty good references – dodgy, no doubt. I bet he's been raking in the first stage money, and then going on to the next sucker.' He stopped and looked more closely at her.

Kate reached for the pre-packed cup of cream, trying to peel back the paper, looking at it far too carefully. Defeated, she put it down and drank her coffee black. The barman was still there. Now her gaze was steady enough to meet his. She nodded at the unspoken question, but even with the taste of coffee still so fresh, her mouth felt too dry to talk.

'You weren't to know,' he muttered sympathetically. 'Left you with a lot to do, has he?'

She swallowed. 'A bit. A lot. It's my fault. The whole thing.'

He was looking at her curiously.

She remembered where she was. She remembered that she must be calm. She said, 'I should have been on site. Stupid, I'm so stupid.'

He reached for her cup. 'Another?'

She shook her head, standing, shaking out her cagoule. 'I must get on.'

He was making for the bar and now, as she prepared to leave, she realised that she hadn't paid. The flagstoned floor was uneven, but not badly so. The bill was ridiculously reasonable, and as she returned her purse to her bag, she knew that everything from now on would have to be the same.

The barman was polishing glasses. 'So, where are you at?'

She wasn't sure what he meant.

'How much has he done?' the barman asked.

The words came amazingly easily. 'The windows and the pointing. I rang yesterday. He said there was someone coming to finish the rewiring tomorrow . . .' She stopped, and said in a small voice, 'Perhaps he meant he was just beginning.'

The barman smiled noncommittally. They both knew she was being absurd.

'Perhaps he did.' In the corner three old men were taking for ever to drink their pints; outside the wind and rain were making their presence felt. The barman said, 'But if he doesn't turn up, Isaac would help out.'

'Isaac?'

'He helps some evenings here. Very handy. Has to be in his line. I'll talk to him, if you like, and then you let us know if he's needed. Where'll you be?'

She rubbed her arms, feeling cold again, though nothing in the heat of the fire had changed. 'Camping at the house.'

He raised his eyebrows, those great, strong, bushy eyebrows, which made his hazel eyes look darker than they really were. Hers were hazel, and Simon's, but they looked it. 'Here?'

'Journey's End.'

But he had begun nodding before she spoke, though all he said was, 'Well, you let us know.'

She phoned Penny from the car park phone box, keeping her voice light, telling her that it would be OK, that there was someone belonging to the pub who could do things if the electrician didn't come in the morning. That if she camped instead of paying out money on bed and board she could undo some of the damage, that she wouldn't tell Peter until she'd sorted something out, that she'd also get a mobile phone, like everybody else.

'You're sure you're all right? Shall I try and come?'

'No, keep an eye on the rest of your flock.' But she wanted her, wanted someone, anyone to be here with her.

Penny laughed. 'Someone else went after the lost sheep; I could too.'

Kate said goodnight and put the phone down. A lost sheep? Was that the sum of her?

She cancelled the bed and breakfast and hauled the cardboard boxes with her camping gear to and from the house, and then the decorating equipment, until, with the light fading as four o'clock drew closer, she finally shut herself in with the dark.

She set up her bed in a corner of the raftered room, the lightest room. Hastily she lit the gas lamp, and although its light didn't reach into the rafters its spluttering and hissing was another sound to keep her company. Drawn to the window, she watched as dusk settled. It was still raining. Tonight the stars would be hidden but Barbs would have shrugged and said that they'd be more glorious for the wait.

She turned. McTravers had created the archway through to the kitchen and blocked off the door that had opened on to the landing. So at least that was something. In the corner were the old windows propped against the wall, and in front of them a dust cloth under which was probably the workman's bench. She checked. So, at least her stage payment had bought her that. On it were the four purple ornaments. For a moment she froze, then raised her hand, but it was heavy, so heavy. Bloody men, so clever with their ploys. So damned clever that they didn't even check out the builder, so damned clever that . . .

A banging on the front door startled her. She let her hand drop. McTravers? The electrician? She held the gas lamp high as she went down the stairs, calling out, 'I'm coming, don't go, I'm coming.'

The door jammed for a moment, then opened with a rush. A man of about her age stood there, his eyes a vivid blue even in the gaslight. For a moment the image of the skydiving master flashed into her mind, and then just as quickly it was gone. He was hugging something wrapped in a black bin bag which the wind and rain were worrying. Kate said quietly, though she knew the answer, 'Are you the electrician?'

He shook his head, concerned. 'I'm afraid not, but I bringeth heat.' He glanced up at the rain, and then at her. 'If I can come in?'

She barred his way. 'I'm sorry, I don't understand.'

He said, 'After what you've been through today, I don't blame you. It's just that Joe worked out that if you had no wiring, then you had no heat, and if you're camping . . .'

'Joe?'

He shook his head. 'I'm Isaac. Joe sent me down from the pub with this paraffin heater and a can of fuel, both of which I shall drop unless I get it up those stairs and set up within the next thirty seconds. Rain makes everything so damned slippery.'

He was shouldering past her, leading the way. She shut the door. It seemed quiet again. She turned. He was climbing the stairs, going up into the dark. He had brought her heat. Joe had sent him. She wasn't alone. She tried her voice. 'Wait, let me light your way.' Calm and normal.

But he was at the top, calling, 'Which room is base camp?'

'The rafter-dome,' she called.

'Good one.' He laughed softly as he went ahead.

She was at the top of the stairs by now and followed along behind, her lantern throwing a little light. He opened the door, the right door, and put down the heater a couple of yards from her camp bed. There was a rustle as he pulled the bin bag free. He was wearing an old yellow waterproof and his hood was still up. He was patting his pockets. 'Knew I'd forget something.'

'Matches?' she queried, reaching into the pockets of her jeans. Water was dripping off his hands and his waterproof and forming puddles on the floor. It didn't matter. What was there to spoil?

He took the matches, smiling at her, nodding to the lamp. 'Missed your vocation, eh? The lady with the lamp.'

He crouched down, busying himself with the heater. She watched him raise the wick, trim it, lower it with crisp, efficient movements, then finally light it. He settled the glass over the flame which burned blue. He shut the front with a snap, and stood. He was about six inches taller than her, but not intimidating as some men were.

She realised she was still holding the lamp up. He took it from her. 'Where would you like it?'

She pointed towards the upturned cardboard box by the bed. She should make him tea, ask him to sit, but there was only the camp bed. He rested the lamp carefully on the box. 'Joe said that there's a room available at the pub.'

Again he turned towards her. With his back to the light she couldn't see the colour of his eyes, and anyway, really, he looked nothing like the skydiving master. With that Barbs disappeared as quickly as she'd come, and if he'd asked Kate now if she was a lady with the lamp she'd have said yes. Because that would be normal.

She shook her head, 'That's kind. He's kind. But I need to recover a bit of financial ground. I'm going out to pay Carlton's at seven. He's busy until then. I'm not sure what he's doing. But that's what he said. Seven.' She must stop talking.

Isaac was looking around the room. 'What about the rest, you know, the electricity, plumbing, decorating?'

'Decorating is my job. It'll do me good. Everyone says . . .' No, she must stop talking.

He was walking to the corner where the remnants of the

127

murky day picked out the purple ornaments. He touched them. 'These should be back in the window.'

Kate stared. Now it was he who must stop talking, because those were Peter's. 'Those,' she had told Peter, 'are yours.'

'I beg your pardon,' she said.

But by now he was walking out of the room. From the landing he called, 'Putting them in a window is an old Feng Shui trick to counteract the number four, which is not a good number. Perhaps that's why Journey's End is always known by its name.' He poked his head around the door. 'Put them back, there's a good girl. Anyone who is prepared to camp out while they're doing up a place deserves good luck. I'll check with you in the morning to see if McTravers's electrician has miraculously materialised. You'll want to be ready for the season, I expect, and I'm fast and I'm cheap – but don't take me on trust, ask someone. It pays to be careful, you know.'

She was following his words, all his words, the ones about the purple objects too, grabbing them, pinning them to the board that was her mind, rearranging them until they made sense. He was along the landing. He was descending the stairs. He was at the bottom. She moved now, rushing out, calling down, the words horribly high, 'I didn't hire McTravers. It was my husband.' But the door had slammed.

It wasn't until she returned from Carlton's well after seven thirty that she let herself look at the words pinned on the board in her mind. Each one seemed huge. Each one was clear, and Peter loomed over everything because the purple objects were not his.

With the dawn the rain ceased, though the sky was still watery and grey. Gulls called and flew across the estuary. The paraffin heater had caused condensation which trickled down the windows. Her anger at Peter should have trickled away like this. She had no grounds, not any more.

He was merely a businessman. A businessman with a mobile phone. He was not someone who crept into houses and tempted wives with purple objects. He was not someone who understood medical matters, and as the sun seemed about to break through, she at last made herself be quiet.

After a mug of tea she made herself check his plans, his schedules. She must concentrate on getting this right. It was her job for now. It would be good for her, get her back to normal. But no thinking. She'd been doing far too much of that, thank you very much, Barbs. So put a sock in it. Yes, that sounded normal.

She cut a slice of bread, but she had no butter or margarine. She could sort that out later. She turned off the paraffin heater. Refilled it. Relit it. She'd never done that before, but she'd watched Isaac. That's all it had taken, just one lesson. She could do this. All of this. She looked around the room. Yes, she could.

She went to the four purple ornaments, picked them up. They *were* beautiful. She carried them through to the window and placed them carefully. She would need luck, Isaac was right. But who was Isaac? She checked herself. Fewer questions. There had to be fewer questions. But it was the answer she had arrived at during the night that kept coming back to her, and she couldn't understand why someone who had lost their dream should care about the new owner.

But then, perhaps she was wrong. Perhaps as in everything else she was wrong.

CHAPTER FIFTEEN

LATE SEPTEMBER

Barbs knew she was being petulant, but why not, when life had stopped, before it had stopped?

She turned restlessly, away from the security light. The damned drip seemed as though it were trying to tug her back into oblivion, but not yet, my fine friend. The trouble was that on this side she had Peter to look at. What the hell was he reading? Why did he come in the evening? If he came in the morning she and Kate could get him over and done with, and feel released for the rest of the day.

She looked towards the television. Was it time for Coronation Street? *No, silly old bat, that had just finished.*

She moved her legs, knowing that she'd lost the thread. Dying was different from post-op wooziness, which knew where it was going. Dying was a clawing up to a different light, a clawing out of something, into the unknown. There she was again, snatching at fragments of profundity, apparently incredibly wise, but was it the drugs? Should she have taken some mind-stretching substance years ago, worn flowers in her hair and let the world benefit from her insights?

Peter turned the page. The cover was glossy, bright. On it were machines. Computers. Glossy and bright wasn't biodegradable, didn't he know that? Or had a way been found? It seemed important for her to know. She tried to ask, but her lips were too dry. On reflection she was glad because she didn't want to invite a lecture. And how he loved to tell; patiently as though the questioner was several sandwiches short of a picnic.

Why was she so mad? So crazy, angry and mad? Because dying put you on the periphery. It distanced you, it gave you the time to listen, to observe, to think, to become wise just when it was all too late. Strange that, a veritable bugger, but when you were in the midst of life there were just too many trees.

Peter was running his finger from his nose to his lip, just as he had always done. It was another ghastly habit, but he never listened. He should. For everyone's sake he should. She'd tried with him, of course she had. For years she'd said, amongst other things, many other things. 'Now Peter, don't fiddle, it doesn't look nice.' Very recently she'd said one of those other things too: 'No, Peter, that's no way to speak to Kate; she is your equal.'

He'd said, still wounded and betrayed, 'She didn't trust me, Mother.'

She'd been cautious, and hadn't revealed what she knew. 'She was right not to in the early days of your marriage.'

'Oh I see, you've been talking. I'm impressed by her loyalty.' He could be such a sharp little shit, and before you knew it you were apologising again. Having made it worse for Kate, of course. That was the trouble, she'd become wise in her head, but still the words came out and did no good.

She eased herself a little, turning back to the light, trying to ignore the IV drip. It was colourless, relentless. She should be grateful for its power but it signalled the end of herself as her own person, the end of life, before the end had arrived. For a moment she wanted to cry, but she was slipping away, just for a moment, slip sliding away, spinning, pirouetting . . .

She woke and Peter was still there, so it really had been a moment. He'd come fifteen minutes ago. Could she somehow sleep through the rest? But that was typical of her, wasn't it, to sleep through things. Just take the first forty-eight years of her married life – how dare she try to talk to him about his behaviour when it was she who had established the precedent of bully and victim for him to witness? Crikey Moses, she hadn't even fought free at the end, it was Keith's death that had released her.

Why had she not done more? Because she was scared of life, life alone? Yes, but that wasn't the whole of it. Perhaps it was because she just hadn't realised what her life could be. She smiled. Yes, that was it. She just didn't realise what it could be, and of what she was capable. But she'd had his money to show her that after he died. So economic equality was the key? Not necessarily. Without it you still have a right to be treated with respect. You have a right to live the life you should live, to explore just who you are. Respect; yes, that was the word. You have a right to the respect of others, and to respect yourself.

131

'What was that, Mother?' Peter said the words too loudly, too clearly. He thought dying meant all your faculties were down the swanny. He was peering over his magazine. She pretended to be asleep. The pages turned again.

So, in the summer, courtesy of her pushing, Kate had tried to beard him and been balked, and was now expected to follow his lead with even greater alacrity. And so she did, and in the doing was diminished. Again Barbs moved restlessly.

The dying should have special gifts, they should be able to wave wands, work magic. But they couldn't, and their words of hard-won wisdom came out as bollocks. Anyway, it was Kate's life, she must run it as she saw fit. But Peter was her son, and she had made him.

She moved her hand on the covers. She could almost see the ridges of her ribs. She was working up to drifting again. It was like a hot flush, no control but you knew it was coming.

What was that? She was jerked back. What was that?

It was like one of those computer games. It had stopped.

'Hello?' It was Peter's voice. She snatched a look. His phone. Of course, his phone. She should know that. It was always going. It had gone the other night, when. . . No point in thinking of that.

They had different ringing tones, some musical, some strident, all annoying, especially on trains. People shouted into them in trains, and on the street, forcing you to listen to their conversations, forcing you to invade their privacy, know too much about them. She felt the bitterness rising. Could Kate really not understand how truly mobile they really were? But Kate wouldn't talk about it any more. Indeed, there had been a dramatic flourish to end the last effort, which had quite upset Barbs.

'What would I have done if it had been true? Jude has nailed her colours to the mast – she is defensive of him, she loves him.'

'She's embarking on her own life. You have a right to yours. Don't use it as an excuse.' Barbs had thought that line had a perfect sense to it.

'It will all settle. We've so many years invested, so much history. We have two kids, we'll get back to normal. You don't just throw marriage away.'

'You are back to normal.' She had thought that was full of sense too.

'Oh Barbs, it's never been as bad as this, the circumstances are *exceptional. It will improve.'*

'When has it been good?' She'd liked that too.

'Often.'

Barbs supposed it had, and perhaps it could be again, as long as Kate knew her place. She had said that aloud. It was this that had led to the dramatic flourish, a veritable door bang. Barbs had been pleased, really. It showed that there was spirit, if it could be tapped. Then, astonishingly, and very loudly, she had wept for all the years that Kate would be lonely, having sex because it made him feel better, having dinner parties because it was expected, being half of an empty whole. She had wept, also, for all her own empty years.

Should she have told her about the phone call? But what proof was there? Who was the other woman? He'd only wriggle free again.

Should she speak to him once more? If she did he'd be a million times worse.

She flicked a look as he muttered to Alan, for that was who it was. Peter had better be careful to cut him off sharpish or he'd be chattering away, a hostage in this room for more than the allotted time. Would he then turn into a frog? Probably not, you had to be a prince in the first place.

He lowered his voice even more, getting up and moving across to the chest of drawers. Did he never learn? But why should he when he didn't know she'd tuned in the last time? He was dialling. More whispers. Half of her wanted to hear, half of her didn't. She wished it was the usual business call, the showing-off 'I'm an indispensible manager' call. But whispers meant something else. Whispers meant something dangerous.

She'd asked Stuart why her hearing had become so acute when the rest of her was crumbling. He'd said it was because she was a nosey old crone who'd go to heaven on a broomstick. She'd said his post-scrum face would never get past St Peter, so what was he so pleased about.

'No, I'm in the room with her, but she can't hear at the best of times and now she's asleep.' It was quite a loud whisper, a careless whisper. 'It's the drip, but then I needn't tell you that.' Who was it? Her?

She heard his soft laugh, and knew it was a woman. 'I'm fine, bearing up. It can't be long now. It'll be a kindess for her really. Thank you for coming to see her.'

133

At this Barbs moved. Who? Who?

He saw. 'Must go.' He slapped the phone shut, and slipped it into his pocket.

Kate popped her head in the door, saw Barbs asleep, and called softly to Peter. 'Your meal's about ready. How is she?'

Barbs knew she'd be nodding her head towards the bed, her heart in her eyes, eyes which were large and long-lashed. Barbs had taken to examining Kate's face because there was so little time left. She wanted to take the image of her beauty into the sky with her. Dearest, darling Kate. It was this person, and this person alone that made dying hard for Barbs.

Whilst Peter ate Barbs lay thinking, demanding that the drugs leave her mind clear. She knew he would be back to say farewell, just in case she died in the night. He'd been doing that all week. How disappointing the mornings must have been.

Carefully she edged herself towards the bedside cabinet, opening the drawer, checking that the pills were still there. But where else would they have gone to since this morning? Each day she checked, each day she made sure she could press and turned that damn top, though as the week had passed she'd decided it would not be her opening the lid after all.

She caught sight of herself in the mirror, all hollow eyes and sunken cheeks. It was as well she'd be long gone by Hallowe'en or she'd have earned all sorts of treats.

Yes, it all dovetailed rather well, actually. Jude would be back tomorrow evening. She just had to remind herself of her script. She had to summon the strength to speak loudly and clearly. She had to make this work, these words work, this action work. She had to make sure that Kate not only saw Peter for what he was, but that she came to realise her own strength. She wanted the balance rectified, she wanted an anger to be born, an anger which would lead to growth and resolution, either within the marriage, or outside it.

She was panting, struggling for breath. She calmed. She breathed slowly. She had used her last week to prepare for this moment; the sacrifice of her independence. But what did it matter really?

He popped his head round the door at nine on the dot. She summoned him in. Surprised, he almost checked his watch, but some remnant of courtesy prevailed.

He sat. Barbs sought his hand, found him. She felt his withdrawal. She held him, but not too tight. She must not appear capable of strength. All week she had made her hands appear weaker than they were.

Kate would come soon, to see why the routine had changed. She did, her face concerned.

'I need to talk to my son about something that need not concern you, Kate. Perhaps you would wait outside the door. Don't go far.'

'Something's happened, you're not well?' Kate approached the bed.

'No, just leave.' The asperity in her voice upset Kate, but she would survive.

When Kate had gone Barbs said, 'I'm dying, Peter.'

Peter nodded. She could almost see him thinking, that's why we're all here, isn't it, you old fool. She struggled to sit just a little straighter, but it was too much. She needed her strength for her voice. 'This is a great moment in my life, the last one. I have a right to choreograph it as I wish, do you agree?' Well done, good and strong, and not too many puffs and pants.

Guardedly Peter nodded. 'Within reason.'

Oh God, always the non-committer. She said emphatically, 'Dying is a part of life. I want a good death, at a time of my choosing, with those I love around me.'

She heard movement outside the door. Of course Kate would hear, that was the whole point, but she must stay outside. She must not intrude.

She did not.

'I saved capsules. They're in the drawer. Your father's morphine. My hands, these stupid hands.' She lifted them. 'Arthritis, such a pig. I can't open that top myself. I want someone to do it, to hold me, to be with me.'

Peter was staring at her, appalled. He pulled away and she let him go. He sat back in his chair. 'Mother, don't be absurd. The drip is helping, you have little pain.'

She shook her head. What did he know about pain? 'It isn't the pain, it's the fact that I have no dignity, and will have even less soon. I can do so little for myself, tied to this thing. I didn't want to be tied and dependent ever again.' Her voice quivered. Tears were running down her cheeks. This was not in the script. Her voice must be strong. It must carry.

135

'Mother, please.'

She understood his discomfort. People asked how she was. She told them what they wanted to hear. Now she was saying it as it was, safe in the knowledge that he would refuse her.

She said, the tears still falling, and they signalled the end of the Barbs who had developed enough to wear purple, 'Please, I want to die soon, and I need help.'

'Mother, it's against the law. You're nearly there – what do a few more days matter?'

'Peter, it would be an act of charity and courage.'

'It's outrageous. How can you ask this of your child?'

'It's because you're my child that I ask. Who else can I turn to on something like this? Help me, Peter. Please.'

'Look, Mother, I have to go. I have a trip to Sweden tomorrow, things to prepare. We'll talk when I get back. This is just a bad time for you, a bad day. You'll feel better in the morning.' He was standing up, leaning over her, kissing her cheek. He'd be able to taste the salt, he'd be able to smell the talcum powder which she hoped disguised the smell of illness and decay.

She reached up, touched his face. He was her son, after all. 'I love you, Peter.' And she did, she just didn't like him. 'I wish, how I wish, I didn't have to ask this of you, but I do ask it.'

He pulled away. 'Believe me, you'll feel better in the morning.'

He was distressed. He didn't look round. She said goodbye to his back. She'd never see him again. She hoped he would grow up one day. She hoped that he would become the son she and Keith should have created. Yes, it was her fault, their fault, but it was also his. He should have been kind, he should have counted the blessing of having Kate.

She wanted to call him back, but it was done now. For she could hear him outside the door, hear him ranting, hear Kate calming him. She could hear what he then said to her.

Poor, dearest, darling Kate. Yes, she would take the role Barbs had manoeuvred her into. Yes, she would be manipulated by the Maxwells yet again, and on a grander scale than ever before. But it was for a good cause. Would St Peter accept that? Well, he damn well should, because medical interference had made her life last this long. Why couldn't it shorten it as well?

Tomorrow she would get the solicitor over while Kate was lurching round the supermarket and the home help was here. The *will would be rewritten. It would make him madder, make for a stronger catalyst, one which would make Kate think, reassess, redress the balance.*

But would Kate assist her to die, kill her, just as Peter, ranting outside the door, had inferred she should?

Oh yes, she would, out of love. For her, or Peter? Probably both. Either way, she would do it. She would resent it, fight it, but do it. But first Barbs would make sure that damned security light was turned off and she could see the stars.

CHAPTER SIXTEEN

The mobile phone lay on the passenger seat. The salesman had been kind, and only began to shift from foot to foot when he had to go through the various tariff options for a third time, but Kate must get it right. Every penny counted at the moment, and would for the next three months. She'd thought about doing without a phone, particularly as reception wasn't good unless she was in the upstairs rooms, but apart from anything else the flat beneath was empty from tonight.

She used to keep a hammer under the pillow when Peter was away, to ward off attackers long enough to get to the bedside phone. She blushed at the thought as she changed the Metro down for a bend. And blushed further at the thought that she was still afraid.

She glanced warily at the phone, hoping it wouldn't ring. What had he said – 'Press the OK button when someone calls'? But of course it wouldn't ring, no one knew her number. She took the Fowey turn at the roundabout. She'd phone Penny later, and get her to leave her number for Peter. He wouldn't be back from Czechoslovakia until Friday, which would give her time to get Plan B underway before she spoke to him.

If only she could decide on Plan B.

Back in Fowey there was plenty of room in the car park, and as she hurried back to Journey's End she tried to keep all hope damped down. Of course McTravers's electrician wouldn't have turned up – but she couldn't help clamping her jaw when this proved to be true.

Opening the gleaming red door, she saw a note on the floor. It was from Isaac. *Remember, if you need an electrician, I'm at Joe's.*

She folded it, and again, staring at nothing in particular. Plan B. But why would someone who'd had their house repossessed want anything to do with the new owner? How could they bear to be a hired help in what should by rights still be theirs? Was he the previous owner, anyway?

Check, he'd said.

She sidestepped to Ted and Mary Glovers' door. They answered her knock promptly, and from the suitcases lined up in the hall, and the coats they wore she could see why. 'Just off,' Ted said, smiling.

Kate nodded. 'Have fun.'

Mary cocked her head. 'Need help?'

Kate explained about Isaac's offer to help. 'Is he good?' she queried.

Ted nodded. 'He's good. Has to be able to turn his hand to anything in his line.'

Kate waited but nothing more was forthcoming. 'So, what's his connection to Journey's End?'

'Bought it, lost it. Sad, but he's good. Sails, that's what he does.'

'Ah.' A sail maker, who had bought an old sail-making loft. Yes, there wouldn't be much money in that, he'd have to diversify into other areas. 'So, if he offered to help me you'd think it a good idea?'

'For you both. Nice for him to get it finished, to see how it could have been.'

It was another speech, and Kate was moved. 'Have fun,' she repeated, leaving them to wait for their taxi, which passed her as she walked slowly to the pub.

Joe was polishing glasses behind the bar. Had he moved from there since yesterday? Kate smiled. A smile was easy. A laugh was harder. She handed him the chocolates she had bought in St Austell. 'Thank you for the loan of the heater. It was very kind. Once I've sorted out the wiring I can get storage heaters in and let you have it back. Or do you need it sooner?' She was suddenly anxious that she had presumed too much.

The eyebrows were doing their usual dance. 'You can have it till the cows come home, m'dear. I don't use it.' He was picking at the Cellophane around the chocolates. 'We'll have a coffee and one of these, just so long as you don't pick the Turkish delight. And thank you kindly. It's a nice thought. And milk chocolate too. Can't stand the dark stuff.' She took the stool he indicated, just opposite him. There were the same three men in the corner, but this time the coffee he slid across the bar was in a mug, and already had milk in.

'Don't want you fiddling with those edges again, do we?'

Kate laughed. Yes, it was harder, and no matter how she tried, it sounded false. Because it was. She cradled the mug, resting her elbows on the bar. The horse brasses on the beams reflected the flickering of the flames. She said, 'I've a problem. Isaac offered to help me with the rewiring, the Glovers say he's good, but how can I expect that of him, after he lost the house?' So normal.

For an answer Joe raised his eyebrows towards the doorway. Isaac stood there, holding a crate of cider. 'You're not expecting anything, though, so I'll help. I'm not a fragile flower, you know, who's in mourning for a building, but I appreciate the sentiments.'

He carried through the case of cider and dumped it at the end of the bar, eyeing their coffees. 'Well, don't strain yourself, Joe, whatever you do. I mean, I've only lugged this lot fifty yards and I can quite understand if a step backwards, and the pouring of a coffee, is just a bit too much for you.'

Joe laughed, and busied himself. Isaac came and sat next to her, undoing his waterproof as he did so. He was so close that she could smell . . . something. For a moment she wasn't sure what, but then realised it was sawdust. There were even bits of it on his navy sweater. Their shoulders were almost touching. Too close. Far too close. She angled herself away.

He rubbed his hands together. They were calloused, and weatherworn, but they would be. His knees would hurt too, isn't that what they said? All that kneeling over the sails. But would odd-jobbing really equip you properly for rewiring?

It was as though he read her thoughts. 'Well done, you checked up on me. I've just bumped into the Glovers.' It appeared he had met Ted and Mary as they pulled away in their taxi.

'Tell her I've magic fingers, Joe.' He was leaning back on the stool, sitting astride it, his legs powerful beneath his jeans. He lifted his cup and drank, his eyes laughing at her over the rim.

Joe said, handing him the chocolates, 'I've got magic fingers, Joe.' As Isaac took the Brazil nut Joe murmured to Kate, 'Go on, he's itching to stick his oar in, and it'll give him a break

140

from Molly. And after all, he's already done some of it, hasn't he? Did the surveyor pick up any boo-boos with the roof, the front windows, the positioning of the cable runs?'

Kate had almost finished her coffee, and now drank down to the dregs. No, he hadn't, and if none of them found it strange for Isaac to work on something that was once his, why should she? She pressed her hand to her forehead.

Behind her the fire was spitting. Damp wood? In the corner the three old men were chatting inaudibly, and beside her Isaac was murmuring softly to Joe something about Sanders wanting to return another crate, but of wine this time. Apparently the party had ended early with the return of the wife.

Kate swirled the dregs round and round. Good for Mrs Sanders. Well, OK. What else could she do? But how much to pay, how to approach it? Isaac said quietly, as Joe was writing out some sort of invoice over by the till. 'I'm reasonable, just five pounds an hour. Pay me at the end of the week, after the work is done, then there's no fear of you getting into another McTravers situation.'

At that remark she looked away, not wanting to see the superior expression she knew would be there.

'I only work until three at the latest. I like to get back to Molly,' he said.

She liked the sound of that. Poor Mrs Sanders, lucky Molly. Joe was taking her mug. 'Don't worry, he's a fast worker.' He laughed and winked. The three men in the corner guffawed.

She edged further away, but Isaac was swinging himself round and off the stool. His jacket snagged on her shoulder bag, but he didn't notice. It freed itself as he turned back a little, shaking his head, saying quietly, 'Take no notice. I'll get my tools and meet you at the flat.' He stared at her, then as she dropped her eyes he touched her arm. 'There's no need to worry, you're quite safe.'

She walked back to the flat alone. She opened the door, alone, climbed the stairs, alone. She wanted to be at home with Penny grizzling about the coffee grinder, the central heating ticking away, and Bertie peeing beneath the *leylandii*.

Kate put on an extra sweater and did the unforgivable by moving the paraffin heater without first turning it off. But hey, the world didn't end. Her own bitterness shocked her. Gently she settled it down near the rafter-dome door, the one Peter's schedule said she must strip first. She gathered up the paint stripper and scraper because she'd never got on with a blow lamp. To sand old paint was unwise as it almost certainly contained lead. There, she was calmer again.

She liked wood. It was warm, mellow and homely and had been the one point she had stuck on with Peter and Judy. They had just wanted her to cover the chips with a quick coat of magnolia. She applied the stripper, hoping that there weren't millions of layers. It wasn't long before her hand was aching, but that would pass.

Soon the wood was revealed, just as she remembered the sawdust on his sweater. She hoped he wouldn't be splitting his time between here and another job, and what about his sails? There, her mind was working, normally.

Just then Isaac knocked, and as she tugged at the front door she realised that at one time he must have had a key, but now he was pointing to the top and bottom of the door, where there were signs of wear on the paint. For a moment he set down the stepladder he was carrying. 'It's swollen more than I thought it would in the damp. I should have left it to season just a while longer, plus it's dropped, and probably needs a bit shaved off the bottom.'

She led the way up the stairs, her mind still on the key. Of course she could change the locks. But how? It would seem so obvious, so dreadfully rude, neurotic. Not normal.

'Shall I do the door?' Isaac was saying.

'The door?' she repeated, her mind still on the key. 'Oh, no. I'd rather we did the electrics first. I think that's the priority.'

He grinned. 'Good, hoped you'd say that. Door hanging is a pig of a job.'

They were in the rafter-dome now, and Isaac was making his way into the kitchen, his tool bag clinking. 'Thought I'd get on in here, and work clockwise, if you get my drift.' He was still in jeans and his navy sweater. Peter had clothes for every occasion. There was never a scrap of sawdust on him, and he never smelt of anything but Old Spice, and for the first time for ages the familiarity of her husband had an appeal.

She stood in the doorway and surreptitiously checked her watch. She needn't have worried because Isaac was bent, head down, writing something in a notebook which he propped up the kitchen windowsill. 'I've clocked an eleven thirty start, OK? Just so we know what's what.'

'OK.' She waved vaguely to the door. 'I'll be here, or rather the other side. You know, if you need anything.'

The door this side was only half finished, but if she continued with it she'd have to talk, find everyday words, everyday thoughts . . . He smiled at her. 'Fine.'

It was dark on the landing, and she had to open the door to gain enough light and to get to the edges, but Isaac worked solidly anyway, not speaking, just chipping out more grooves, running cables, edging past her as he came through the doorway, and on up the ladder into the loft, drilling holes through all the ceilings, and along the rafters in the large room for the cables to feed through.

Each time he passed there was the smell of wood, or was it her imagination? Because paint stripper should have drowned even the most powerful of smells.

When she had finished she tackled the door into the lower study/bedroom. She had to work with the front door open to give her light, and though it had seemed mild on her walk to the pub, the wind that whistled in was anything but.

She needed another sweater but that would mean digging about in her case in front of Isaac who, from the sounds of it, had moved into the rafter-dome again. She pulled up the collar of her shirt. Vests were the thing. Maybe she could drive into St Austell and pick up a few thermal ones. Her hands were so cold they felt stiff. Yes, and some fingerless gloves. See, her mind was working properly.

Isaac's touch on her shoulder made her jump. He had put the camping lamp on the stairs behind her. 'Thought you could do with this, then we could put the peg in the hole, and we'd both be warmer. And I've a flask of coffee upstairs, if you fancy one?'

He was closing the front door firmly. She shook her head, examining her brush. 'Sorry, I didn't think. No, no coffee, I want to get on.'

He nodded. 'I *can* do both.'

She flushed, looking up at him. 'I didn't mean that.' But perhaps she had? 'Really, I . . .' She was speaking to his back as he ran up the stairs. She'd like a coffee, but now it was out of the question. She continued working, but there was another tap on her shoulder and Isaac gave her a plastic mug half filled with steaming coffee without saying anything, and again retreated.

She sat on the bottom step. The coffee tasted just as it had so many years ago, when her parents had taken late holidays on cold Cornish beaches where beach huts were on the point of being dismantled for the winter. Her mother would wrap her up in her own cardigan, and pour the two of them coffee whilst her father read his paper in the car, alone. He liked peace and quiet. Her mother preferred coffee because tea seemed to change its nature completely once it got 'even the sniff of a flask'. Dear Mum. How she must have frozen.

Kate drained her mug, staring at the dregs. She had forgotten that beach, that wind, the scent of her mother's cardigan.

After another two hours the door was done, back and front. Upstairs there was the sound of movement. It must be lunchtime. She wasn't hungry but she must live by the routine, the routine that made her feel normal.

She would go and make a sandwich of Marmite, as usual. She took her brushes with her, climbing the stairs slowly. So tired. Always so tired. On the landing she heard Isaac in the loft. Normal people would offer the same to him, wouldn't they? After all, he'd given her a coffee. But how could she? She had no margarine, and a dry sandwich wasn't what you offered people. Perhaps he'd already eaten his own?

She rinsed the mug and brushes in the bathroom, locked the door and had a pee. The whole room smelt damp. The bath must stay, as it was Victorian, but the basin was awful, and as for the lino . . . While she washed her hands Isaac tried the door.

'Ooops, sorry,' he called.

She dried her hands, wondering if she should call out, *Won't be a moment*. Was he queuing outside?

Tentatively she opened the door but he was back in the loft. She carried her brushes through to the rafter-dome where she stopped quite still, confused for a moment by the brightness.

Out there, in the world, the sun had swept aside the suffocating cloud layer and burst brightness into the room, and on the raftered ceiling was the reflection of the river's ripples, just as it had been on the day she had viewed, but forgotten.

In this room it was warm, and as though she had stepped into somewhere else, somewhere infused with energy, warmth and light, a place which was quite stunningly beautiful. Across the river the branches of the trees moved gently. Slightly to the right cattle grazed in a small meadow. A small craft put-putted past with an elderly couple in it, and two Spar carrier bags perched in the prow. Slowly she walked to the window, lifting her face to the sun, feeling the heat. It seemed to seep into her, slowly, deeply. She dropped the brushes. They lay at her feet.

When she looked at the river again the small boat had disappeared. She turned, her breathing easier, her stomach less knotted, her shoulders less tight. Now the sun was on her back, and she rested against the window, just for a moment because she could hear movement above the kitchen, and now she thought of the Marmite sandwiches. She looked at her watch. She saw the brushes. They must be put away.

She did so.

Her guest must be fed. But was he a guest? It didn't matter. He should be fed if he had watered her. Yes, that was nice and normal. She found her bag. She called up into the loft space, 'You provided the coffee, have lunch on me.'

There was a scrabbling, then Isaac's dirty face appeared in the loft opening. 'A sandwich would be great.' He coughed slightly. 'I should have sorted it out up here when I bought the place, or at least before I lost it. I'm glad it's me up here, getting filthy. It makes me feel embarrassed.'

He really did look it, and vulnerable, somehow, so she called back, as she headed down the stairs, 'Oh, I don't know, you could do a soft shoe shuffle this evening and bring the punters into Joe's in their hundreds.'

'Politically incorrect to black up, my dear Mrs Maxwell.' But he was laughing.

She smiled. A laugh was harder.

In Spar she found pâté, soya margarine, salad, rolls, cheese. She picked up a tin of black olives from the delicatessen. What else did she usually have? Dressing for the salad. But what would she put the salad in, and could she serve the dressing in its bottle? Well, she had to, and the salad must go straight on to the plates, since she only had two. Napkins? Yes, perhaps she should. Peter always insisted.

Back at Journey's End she washed the lettuce in the bathroom sink. Her fingers were cold. She laid out the two plates with equal portions of everything, including two rolls each. What about seats?

She placed her pillow opposite the camp bed, and a cardboard box upside down between them, with the plates upon it. Isaac was still in the loft, running cable down into the other bedroom, or so it sounded. She checked. Yes, there was the cable waggling about. Find the cable, and you find the man. Penny would like that. She smiled and somehow it seemed easier.

She called up into the loft, 'Lunch when you're ready.'

She stared at the food, not hungry. But then she wasn't, ever, now. She picked up a piece of tomato because it was what she used to do. She caught the pips which fell and sucked them from her hand.

'Hey, I thought you meant a sandwich.' Isaac was right behind her, staring down. 'You didn't have to. I mean, honestly, a sandwich.' He was embarrassed, and now so was she.

They ate in silence, he on the pillow, she on the bed. But this wasn't normal, so she asked about Joe. Kate pretended more interest than she felt, and Isaac provided more details than were necessary about Joe's ownership of the pub and past life as a marketing director at a brewery. At last they were finished and she hurried back to the safety of work.

She was sanding the lower banister when he called for her advice on the power points, asking how many for each room. She hadn't thought. What did the schedule say? She hurried up the stairs, finding the relevant column on the beautifully executed broadsheet. 'Two,' she called up the loft space to him.

'Singles or doubles?' It sounded as though he had screws in his mouth or something.

'Doubles, I should think.'

'Plastic or brass effect? Brass would give a bit of class, to

146

match the stripped doors. I like those. You're not painting them are you?'

'No.'

'Wood is a good warm finish. But brass sockets cost more, and after the McTravers fiasco . . .'

She hesitated, her stomach knotting. So, like Peter, he would bring everything back to that.

He said, 'If it's a letting property some argue that cheap will do, but quality induces greater care from the tenants.'

She must breathe, she must take her time, she must not let herself slide down. After a moment she said, 'How much more dosh?' There, so normal.

'The brochures are in my tool kit, along with a price list. Pour us both another cup of coffee while you're there, will you? I'll be down any second.'

She found the price list and was estimating the cost when she heard his feet on the ladder. She hurried to find the flask, but he was there before her, fumbling in the tool bag, his back to her, saying, 'No worries, I'll do it. You just sort out the important stuff.' She stiffened, knowing there had been sarcasm in his voice, wanting him out of her house, wanting . . .

But it had been his house. She was here, in his house.

He turned, the flask in his hand, squatting beside her, pouring half a cup each. 'It won't be very hot, I'm afraid, but it hits the spot. What do you think?'

He handed her the mug she had used before. She sipped. 'It's lovely.' She saw him smile, and knew he had meant 'plastic or brass'. And she didn't care that it had been his house, didn't care that . . . She snapped, 'Actually, it's half cold.'

'Actually, it's half hot.' He stared at her, his voice firm.

It was she who dropped her eyes first. It was she who said, 'Things get to me. I'm a bit on edge, I'm sorry.' But she wasn't, not really, because he had no right to his superiority, to his Olympian height. He had no bloody right. Neither he nor Peter had any right. All she wanted was to get this place sorted, finished and not have to accommodate another bloody person while she was doing it, not have to tread on eggshells because that person had lost the flat she had bought at a knockdown price, not have to feel uncomfortable and guilty even though she was, and anyway the coffee *was* appalling.

147

He was drinking his whilst he made a drama out of studying the prices, and ignoring her. She stalked to the bathroom and poured the coffee away, rinsing the mug, stalking back, putting it on the floor next to his tool kit. He still squatted, tapping the brochure, looking at that, not her. 'I'd like to get these first thing tomorrow. I can borrow Joe's van. But if you need more time to think, that's fine by me.'

'Brass. Two doubles for each room, plus the light switches.' She snatched the brochure from his hand, flicking through it. 'This design.' She showed him. 'I expect you'll need money up front?' The moment she said it, she knew she'd been stupid. So stupid. She said, 'So why don't I come with you, then I can pay for them myself.'

Isaac was getting to his feet, and he was laughing. Not out loud, but it was there, in his eyes. She hurried on, 'Or better still, I'll go and get them and bring them back for you.' Then I don't have to sit in a car with you, she wanted to shout.

He just looked at her, and there was no laughter any more, just concern, and that was worse. He said, his hand out to her, 'Let's start again, shall we? I've got on your wick, though I don't know how, but if I've offended you, I'm sorry. If I've taken over, I'm sorry. I just want to help but you seem to see it as something else . . .'

'But why?' she heard herself say, because she didn't know what she did see. 'That's what I don't understand. Why do you want to help?'

He bent down and picked up his tool bag. 'I need the money, and I know how big a job this is for one person, and I think you've got balls to camp down here and just get on with it, that's why. But there are others who can help, if it makes you feel uncomfortable having me around. It shouldn't, though, because I'm glad I haven't the worry of it any more. On the other hand I don't like leaving a job half finished, especially one like this, one that ought to look good.'

He wasn't moving from the spot. The sun was highlighting his enthusiasm, it was etching in the deep lines running from his eyes. He wasn't handsome, but the mobility of his face made him so. Perhaps he hadn't been patronising, perhaps it was her. Of course it was her.

Still he just stood. There was more dust than sawdust on his sweater, and bits of what looked like bird's nest. He saw her looking. 'You need insulation up there. Sorry, I didn't get round to it. I was going to save the treat of fiddling with fibreglass until the very end, then I could itch in peace.'

She turned from him to the river. The sun was still out, the ripples still flickering. It seemed so quiet. He said, 'Fresh start, have we cleared the decks?'

What other option had she? She had to tell Peter about McTravers. She had to have the work underway before she did so. She had to shake the hand this man was offering. But she must repeat what she had said: 'I'll take you to the electrical shop.'

His smile was gentle. She took no notice of this because the decks might be cleared but there'd be no more money up front for anyone, any more. Or no quarter given since he seemed determined to use nautical terms, and certainly not to him, because at no time had he mentioned his wife in all of this. What the hell was she feeling as he worked here, in what had been their home? Her anger surprised her. She wanted to take it out and look at it, turn it over in her hand, but then it slipped from her.

'Tomorrow morning,' he said, heading for the stairs. 'I'll come here, eight thirty sharp.'

'Nine sharp,' she called after him.

He laughed. 'Right you are.'

She checked her watch and came out on to the landing, calling to him just before he shut the front door behind him. 'Tell Molly I'm sorry I'm sending you home late. It's ten past three.'

'Don't worry, I wrote the time in the notebook while you were beating the mug to death in the bathroom. The last ten minutes have been terms and conditions time.'

'Tell Molly I'm sorry anyway.'

'Oh, Molly can wait.' He was trying to shut the door. It jammed, he tugged. It slammed.

The anger was back now. It wasn't in her hand any more. It was spilling out and around. It wouldn't let her stand still. Molly can wait. Always the wives could wait, stand in line, be trodden on. It drove her to her tool bag, to her electric screwdriver. She found her DIY handbook. She had an hour of daylight, and the privacy to put on as many sweaters as she pleased, so please help me get the front door off its hinges, Penny's boss. Help me shave off the swollen wood, and put on the primer coat before bedtime. Please, please, please, let Molly shout at him for being late. Let his electrics be better than his door fitting. Let me sleep tonight, because I'm exhausted, and the Glovers have gone, and there's this great darkness which keeps nudging at me, and my feet are so cold, and my hands, and everywhere is damp.

CHAPTER SEVENTEEN

Kate was in a barrel which was tumbling out of control down the street, a cobbled street. It was dark, she was cold, bruised, she was crying out, beating against the sides. She was sick, giddy, nothing stayed still, everything was chaos. She tried to breathe. Tried to find another cry for help, but the sound of the barrel against the cobbles was drowning her, dragging her down, tossing her this way and that. She woke, sweating, exhausted, freezing, but the banging continued. And now there was shouting. 'Mrs Maxwell, are you all right? Come on, open up.'

Again the banging. She stared up at the rafters, her heart beating too fast. What the hell . . .? Then she remembered, and swung out of bed, staring at the clock. Nine thirty. How could she?

She stumbled, shivering, into bra, pants, a shirt, jeans, all of which felt damp, fumbling with the buttons of her shirt, her fingers too cold to function properly. She forced her feet, sockless, into her trainers. Bang, bang. She did up her zip as she ran down the stairs calling, 'I'm coming.' She reached for the latch, dashing her fingers through her hair. Swinging open the door, she stepped well back as he walked in, not wanting to breathe morning breath all over him.

His face was the picture of concern. 'I was worried.'

She didn't care about that, because of Molly, the Molly who could wait. She hurried up the stairs, heading for the bathroom. 'I was up late redoing your peg. Give me five minutes.' She shut the door firmly, washing in bitterly cold water. As she brushed her teeth and rolled on deodorant she peered into the mirror she had propped on the edge of the bath. She looked like a disintegrating bird's nest. Was this just today's look or had she been like it for weeks? She realised that she hadn't noticed.

She dragged a brush through her hair, easing her shoulder. The door had been a pig to rehang and she had ended up trying to read the book, take the weight of the door, and juggle with a manual screwdriver – because of course there was no electricity. But by two in the morning she had done it, and having gone so far it seemed absurd not to put on the primer, but then she had to wait for that to dry. Forced to leave the door ajar she had taken up position just behind it, making a cocoon of the pillow and the sleeping bag, and had fallen asleep until God knows what time.

But whatever time it was it had been even colder. The primer had been dry, though, and the door was a perfect fit, so she had crawled to the camp bed and known nothing else until the banging which had dragged her from the dream. A dream which had not been of Barbs, for once, so it didn't matter. A dream which hadn't drained her as all those other nights had done.

She stretched, noticing the cracks in the ceiling for the first time. For a moment she paused, looking around. Everything seemed clearer this morning. She dropped her arms. They no longer felt like lead.

'Mrs Maxwell.'

She grabbed her phone, her bag and her car keys from the cardboard box beside the bed, and swept up her jacket. The paraffin heater had already burned out. She glanced through the huge window. The grey cloud layer was back in place but it didn't seem as thick or as dark. She almost ran down the stairs to where Isaac was sitting on the bottom step. He sprang to his feet to let her pass, saying, 'You've done a brilliant job.'

She knew she had. She most certainly had. Isaac was holding open the front door, embarrassed, rueful. He still smelt of wood. He still wore the yellow waterproof, and the navy sweater, but this one was slightly different – no cable – and clean. Of course, if he wore overalls Molly wouldn't have to be hand-washing the other as he swanned off to the day job. For a moment she thought of telling him but instead stepped out smartly in the direction of the car park, nodding as she heard the clean click of the door shutting behind her, nodding again, this time with relief, as she realised Isaac had no key, or he would have used it this morning.

152

Once away from Fowey Isaac directed her to the electrical shop, though it was more of a shack, she thought, tucked away down a back street, and a good few miles away. As she drew the Metro into the car park, trying to avoid the potholes, he said, 'Don't be put off.'

But she was. For a moment she faltered. She parked, reaching over the back seat for her handbag, but Isaac had done the same. They both drew back. 'I'll get it, you lock your door,' she said.

Inside the shack a paraffin stove was burning. In the corner stood a forlorn Christmas tree. Kate had planted hers in the garden. One day one would take, if there was any justice in the world. Justice. For a long moment Kate stood quite still. But then Isaac was taking her elbow, urging her on. 'Don't be put off.'

At the counter Isaac pressed a shrill bell set into a counter loaded with boxes spilling out fuse wire, fuses, light bulbs. He said, 'It really isn't as bad as it looks.'

He pressed the bell again. The noise was a relief. It slammed shut the gates of memory. It jerked at the tiredness which was reclaiming her, which made the Christmas tree merge indistinguishably into the rest of the room. It jerked at it, but only for a moment, then on it came.

She heard movement behind the beaded curtain that divided front of house from the rest. 'Get us a coffee, if you have any pity, Alfie,' Isaac shouted, 'and then come and serve some paying customers.'

The beads rustled, and a bald man with a huge beard poked his head through. 'Bloody hell, Isaac, you're back again. I heard a rumour but thought you'd sailed off into the sunset.' He saw Kate and raised his eyebrows. 'Two coffees then, is it?' He disappeared, but within a moment was swishing through the curtain, a tray of steaming mugs in his hand. He shoved the boxes aside, making way for the tray. No one took sugar, though it was there in its packet, a dessertspoon sticking out. There was also a saucer with biscuits. Kate had no appetite.

He was a big man with a surprisingly limp handshake, though his eyes were shrewd. He appeared to be weighing Kate up, or was it her requirements, which Isaac was rattling off? She forced herself to listen closely, to stay with the present.

153

Alfie pulled a face, but Isaac just grinned. 'Cut the performance, we're late as it is. Bit of a timekeeping problem.'

She stared at Isaac. Oh yes, he just had to, didn't he? It was hot suddenly. Far too hot. She undid her jacket, wanting to be out in the cool air. But now Alfie was saying, 'All in stock. You've got this idiot doing the work, have you, Mrs Maxwell? Well, you could do worse. He's fixed more things than you or I in all sorts of rather nasty corners of the world, not to mention Molly. Yep, I suppose you could do worse.'

As he spoke he took the pencil from behind his ear and made a list of the costings but it was still too hot. She put down her mug, breathing deeply. Alfie coughed. She caught the look he exchanged with Isaac. 'Did you catch that, Mrs Maxwell?' he asked.

In that glance she saw Peter. Alfie showed her the total, tapping his pencil.

Peter tapped his fingers.

She stared at the figures, but the pencil was still there, up and down, up and down, until she could stand it no longer and said far too loudly, far too harshly, 'We'll expect a discount for cash.'

The pencil stopped. Isaac turned, his waterproof catching her arm. He dragged his hand through his thick curly hair. 'We will indeed.' Again there was that shared look.

She rephrased, '*I'll* expect a discount for cash.'

Alfie looked embarrassed. Isaac replaced his coffee mug on the tray. Alfie consulted his figures. 'Ten per cent enough?'

Isaac said, his voice noncommittal, 'Fifteen's what you usually give me, you old rogue, so let's not change the habits of a lifetime.'

Alfie pulled at his beard with his huge pale hand and grinned. 'Done.'

There was a flutter of beads as he disappeared into the back, whistling as he did whatever he had to do. Kate and Isaac stood side by side saying nothing, staring at the posters, the till, the empty mugs, the shelves, as though nothing had ever been so absorbing. He would be expecting her to apologise, and to say thank you for bucking up the discount. She should. She couldn't.

Their silence wasn't broken until Alfie came back through

the doorway, setting off the strips again, and tried to put the boxes he was balancing on to the counter. The inevitable happened and there was a burst of 'Steady,' 'Let me help,' and far too many hands not making light work.

Alfie shouted, flapping his hands at them, 'Bugger off and let me manage.'

Instantly Kate backed away, but Isaac grabbed her arm. 'Don't let the bad-tempered old fool frighten you off, he's always like this.'

Alfie was stacking the boxes neatly, and suddenly he grinned at Kate. 'Another coffee?'

She shook her head. Alfie said, 'I suppose you're going on to view the auction, are you? Ideal for furnishing a holiday cottage, and then you can see what you can pick up and sell on, Isaac.' He didn't give either of them a chance to reply but rattled on as he stabbed out figures on his calculator. 'So, my old mate, you must be refitting Molly if you're not actually swanning about on her. Where to next time?'

Beside her Isaac scratched his head and gave Kate a sideways glance. Refitting Molly? She didn't understand until Isaac started talking about replacing the fuel injector, the rods, main bearings and piston rings while Alfie found two boxes for their sockets and switches.

She said quietly, 'I'll pay that bill now.' Isaac was picking up the boxes as she counted out the notes, then the change. Neither she nor Isaac looked at one another as they made for the door.

Alfie repeated, 'So where *are* you off to, you antisocial slob?'

Isaac called over his shoulder, 'Just round the world again, if I can raise the necessary. I've been commissioned to write an account, but that won't fund it all, so yes, it would be good to go to the auction.' Still they didn't look at one another as they walked to the car, or as she opened the boot and he arranged the boxes. She pushed it shut. It seemed so heavy.

Isaac grabbed hold of her arm, for the second time today. She shook free as the words tumbled out, pushing past her mind which was saying, Shut up. Shut up. 'It must have amused you to let me go on thinking you were rushing off to your wife.'

155

Isaac bit his lip, but the deepening of the lines running from his eyes gave him away. 'No, not really. But you were in such a sulk I thought it would be death by scraper if I tried to put you right about anything.'

She was walking to the driver's seat. She unlocked her door, got in the car, opened his door. 'Just get in.'

He did so, and sat beside her all in a bundle of yellow waterproofs. He said as she started the engine, 'Can we start again, clear the—'

'Decks,' she cut in quietly. The steering wheel was heavy in her hands. 'So, you're not a sail maker after all?'

He looked puzzled and shook his head. 'I never said I was.'

He hadn't; she had assumed that was what the Glovers had meant. He hadn't told her Molly was his wife. It was what she had assumed. She assumed things but that's what she did. It was all getting muddled again, all flying around in her head, and her shoulder ached from rehanging a door, which had probably dropped again by now and would jam again. Of course it would.

She drove out of the car park. Was all this supposed to do her good? What had Barbs been thinking of? What the hell had she been thinking of when she'd done . . .

Frantically she put her foot down, and took the corner too fast. 'Furniture. I need furniture,' she garbled. 'I was going to get new, and self-assembly, but auction stuff would be cheaper.'

She knew he was looking at her strangely, but she kept her eyes on the road. He gave her directions, his voice measured and calm. Gradually her hands ceased to sweat, her clutch control improved, and she concentrated on keeping the windscreen clear, because a drizzle had begun to fall that was neither heavy enough to make it worth the wipers' while nor light enough to dispense with them altogether. Yes, she must concentrate on that.

At the retail park she let him lead the way towards the huge warehouse-type building. He ignored the swing doors which led to a smart reception area and darted instead straight into the auction room. A lad wearing a dark green apron and with more optimism than testosterone judging from the straggly little moustache he was sporting stood behind a counter. He gave them a perfectory glance, then did a double take and beamed. 'Hey, Isaac, great to see you. How's tricks?'

Isaac leaned casually against the counter, shaking the lad's hand, asking after his mother, his sailing dinghy, the stuff in today. The lad nodded. 'A few things that could bring a bit, once they're done up.' He laughed. 'But no tennis balls. You'll need them for the headsail rigging, isn't that right, laced on to the stays above and below the spreaders?'

'And why?' asked Isaac gently.

'To prevent chafing.'

'Well done. So, how about coming out with me when it's time to give her a test run?'

The boy was nodding eagerly. 'Please. So when are you off again?'

Kate had been following their conversation, and now she listened more intently. Isaac said, 'When I've finished helping Mrs Maxwell.'

She should feel relieved, but she felt nothing, just tired. She moved towards some wardrobes, waiting as a dealer examined a mahogany one closely. He made a note in his pad, checking the number again. She remembered Toad at the house auction. She turned, trying to locate Isaac. Did he really not mind? Momentarily her stomach tightened, her mind sharpened. Should she line up alternative tradesmen? What if he couldn't stand it and sailed away?

She reached out, tugging at a wardrobe door, making her mind shut down. The door jammed. Did everything jam around here? A final pull. It opened. There were musty old books heaped inside. Isaac's voice was close. 'Those will be a separate job lot.'

Why did men have to *tell* you all the time. She could see the lot number, couldn't she? 'I've been to an auction before,' she snapped, walking on.

He called softly. 'I know you have.'

She stopped. But she hadn't meant . . .

Isaac was examining an old tea trolley, lot number 234, which stood next to the wardrobe. He was running the trolley backwards and forwards on its casters, when an older man in a green apron carrying a clipboard called from behind a marble-topped washstand, 'So, how's Clara getting on with the house?'

From where he squatted Isaac said quietly, 'She's not, she did a bunk with George.'

The older man hesitated, shocked, then said quietly, 'Sorry, my old mate.' Isaac was getting to his feet as Kate headed for the next row. Out of the corner of her eye she saw the two men talking, the old man patting Isaac's shoulder.

Drifting down the second row she stopped by a glass-fronted cupboard. The wood of the scalloped sectioning shelves was damaged, but in its prime it must have been rather attractive. Isaac was at her elbow again, enthusiasm quickening his voice, 'I like the way the curves are repeated on the glass, but it could be much better if it was also echoed on the glass at the back. I just love it – so full of life, such fun, so exuberant. Art Deco, you know?'

She didn't, and she said so, wanting to do something for him. He was standing too close again as he talked fluently about the Egyptian influence, the strong colours, the strong simple lines incorporating angles and curves. 'That's what's so great about the sales. You can buy this stuff,' he waved his arms around the room, 'and do it up. A bit of masking tape here and there, a bit of sanding. You just need to decide on a theme, really.'

This was what Peter had said to his mother, because there had been no theme in the bungalow. She had bought what she liked when she saw it, and added it to the sober core she had transferred from the family home. Why the new owners wanted Barbs's furniture she would never know, because for them there wasn't the bonus of memories of Barbs in every piece. But she didn't want memories, not now.

'A theme?' she repeated desperately.

Isaac pointed to an old pine wardrobe. 'You could mask off the doors, paint it, oh I don't know, perhaps a brilliant blue. Or cut a shape with a jigsaw, stick it on, make it Art Deco. Make it fun. You know, bright. A statement. Something fresh, something different. Journey's End can take it. Dirt cheap, too.'

They pressed back against the cupboard to allow several people past, but Barbs was still here. 'That's what you're going to do with the stuff you buy, is it?' she asked, struggling to hold on to the present, to the hum of conversation all around, to the

158

clearing sky she could see through the high windows.

'There's no need for me to create a theme, I'm just buying to sell.' He lifted his hand, acknowledging a salute from someone he knew, someone who was lifting his hand to his mouth, and mouthing, 'Time for a quick one?' It was the height of normality. It helped her.

Beside her, Isaac was shaking his head at his friend, saying to her instead, 'Have you seen anything that strikes your fancy?'

She had seen nothing that he could know about, but how could she explain that? 'I'm just getting my bearings,' she said, her voice too quiet, too flat. He was concerned, but she shook her head as he gestured to the coffee sign. Instead she started again, writing numbers down, whilst he did the same, including the trolley, explaining that he would do it up.

'Art Deco?'

'No, with a nod towards Feng Shui, balancing the energies through the use of colour.'

'Feng Shui?' she asked. Hadn't he said something about Feng Shui before, when he was talking about the purple ornaments? She'd been too distracted to take it in then. She wrote down the pine wardrobe, which had a sticking door. After all, if she could sort out a front door, she could sort this, and suddenly she felt better, suddenly it seemed brighter. The sun must have come out.

'The maintenance of harmony and balance using colour and design. Living at sea for months at a time with just your navel for company makes you feel that everything has a natural balance.'

'A balance?' She was writing down the lot number for a pine chest of drawers.

He pulled out the drawers. 'Don't go higher than twenty pounds. The universe, the earth, people, all in balance. Nothing happens without consequence to something else.'

Well, she didn't need Feng Shui to tell her that, and what was he, some kind of nutter? She almost laughed, and was astonished at herself.

He had moved along to a bookcase. 'You must think you're employing a nutter,' he said. It wasn't a question, but he was laughing too.

She shrugged, smiling. 'A bit, maybe, but everyone needs something, especially when—' She stopped in time. Clara had gone, but he didn't need reminding yet again this morning. Just as she didn't, but everywhere she went . . . Was it the same for him?

He was squatting again, this time by an oak drop-leaf table. But then something else he had said struck her. 'Just your navel for company? Don't you have a crew?'

'Not even for the short trips, unless young Brian comes.' He indicated the lad he had spoken to when they came in. 'Though Clara came once.' He stood, pointing down at the table. 'You might like one of these. They can fold against the wall, but opened out will take at least six.'

The surface was ringed by too many mugs, but she could always sand it down, if she wanted to. But she didn't. Tables like these reminded her of winter, and Sunday high tea with celery in a pint glass, fresh brown bread which gave her hiccups, and made her father apoplectic with irritation, and her mother a nervous wreck as she tried to placate him and pretend nothing was wrong. She reached out and touched it. She had forgotten about that, too.

Isaac was taking her arm, moving her along. 'Never buy if *you* don't like it. There's no rush, they have a sale every week.'

They arrived back at Journey's End at midday, parking as usual in the car park, and walking together towards the house, each carrying one of Alfie's boxes. As she unlocked the door she asked, 'Have you any red paint left?'

'Well, Clara took a lot with her,' Isaac said. 'But I can remember the colour. I'll pick some up, or a good enough match anyway.'

The door opened easily. She needed to say something to draw him away from Clara. She said, 'Why red? Does it bow to the gods or something?'

They were in the hall and he was opening and shutting the door. 'Facing the way it is it should be white, but red is associated with warmth and happiness so it seemed a better idea.' He finally shut the door. 'You know, this really is very impressive.' He loped ahead of her up the stairs.

They put the boxes in the kitchen, then he pulled off his

waterproof and threw it on to the trestle and sheets which remained in the corner. He said, 'So, you make a habit of this, do you?'

She was searching through her box over by the camp bed, trying to find the scraper and paint stripper. 'This?'

His voice was distanced as he moved to the kitchen. 'Hanging doors.'

She put on rubber gloves, and Peter's old shirt she'd worn to do the door, then started brushing stripper on to the rafter-dome door, starting at the handle and working up. 'I've only decorated before, but the manual was good. It was a Christmas present from my friend Penny.'

She was struggling to reach the top of the door, and there was no answer from Isaac for a moment, but then he was there behind her, taking the brush, reaching the corner easily, returning it to her, saying – and again he was too close – 'That really is *very* impressive, then.' His blue eyes were almost violet and they were as alive as his face.

As he returned to the kitchen she picked and probed his tone for sarcasm but there had been none. Perhaps there never had. Perhaps that too she had assumed.

They broke for lunch at two o'clock. This time Isaac produced sandwiches. 'My turn, pâté and salad. Got them at the auction rooms. They're usually good.'

Again they sat opposite one another, she on the camp bed, he on the pillow, but this time it was easier. This time he ate with gusto, talking animatedly, with his mouth full. He poured half cups of coffee for them both from his flask. He grinned, holding up his mug. 'Cheers, to cleared decks.'

The sun was streaming in through the window, the sky was blue. She laughed, suddenly happy, and it was as though a window had opened inside her. 'To cleared decks,' she agreed, raising her mug to him.

She sipped, watching the gulls dipping and gliding, and then asked, 'Don't you get lonely, out there all alone? Aren't you scared?'

Replacing his mug of coffee on the upturned cardboard box, he uncrossed his legs and hugged his knees. The pillow had puffed out either side, his bite mark was in the sandwich he held. He wiped his mouth with the back of his hand; she did

161

the same. 'Alone isn't the same as lonely. Lonely is what Clara was because she loved me in a way I didn't love her. I tried, but you just can't make yourself feel what isn't there, so she found herself George. Now she's happy, and good luck to her. As for fear; it's a hazard, it overcomes your intelligence. It's a nuisance, it messes up your brain. It's like doubt or worry. Concern's all right. Concern is facing up to the reality of the situation. Concern without worry, that's what I aim for.'

She swilled her coffee round and round, delving back, knowing she had heard this before, but when?

He took a great bite from his sandwich.

'Do you achieve it?'

Lettuce was hanging from his mouth. He pushed it in, then saw her watching, and grinned. 'I suppose I do, most of the time. But what goes out of the window are social graces.' He twitched his little finger in the air and took a minuscule bite. This time she took his humour at face value, not looking for hidden meanings, or making the assumption that he was mocking her. This time she laughed, and it was a real laugh.

They finished the coffee and sandwiches. She washed both mugs in the icy bathroom, then hurried into the kitchen to put them into his tool kit before scraping the softened paint from the door, struggling to match his words with the echo that was niggling on the periphery of her mind.

As the afternoon wore on she opened the window to allow the fumes to escape. A small craft was putt-putting away from the mouth of the river towards Golant. The Bodinnack ferry was still toiling backwards and forwards, cars driving on and off. She called, 'It really is a very popular place.'

He shouted from the kitchen where the small radio he'd brought was producing tinny music. 'Good investment on your part.'

What could she say to that? But she needed to say nothing, because Isaac continued, 'It really is. It should do you proud.'

She knew enough about regret to recognise it in another and returned to her door, saying nothing. Again, as she stretched to reach the right-hand corner, he was there, taking the scraper from her, reaching those parts she couldn't, handing it back, returning to the kitchen. 'Is your middle name lager?' she called.

His laugh was gleeful. 'Got it in one.'

She found herself smiling and singing quietly to the radio, and it seemed no time at all before she had to move from the rafter-dome to the bathroom. Here it was gloomy and dark, and she knew that this was the room that would have a white door to go with the decreed magnolia walls, and there must be some sort of a mirror to reflect the measly light, and white tiles. For warmth the taps must be brass.

At three Isaac called from the kitchen. 'Molly calls, so I'm off, but I've taken out of the equation the hour at the auction view. You'll just owe me for the rest. It suited me to be there.'

She met him at the entrance to the kitchen. Behind him she could see that he had run the cable down to the cooker point which he had placed on the wall, sideways to the view. She had wanted it beside the window, overlooking the river. Why have a view and ignore it?

He saw her face and followed her line of sight, concerned. 'I'm sorry, didn't you want it there?' He stepped back into the kitchen. 'It's just that my markings were still up and so I thought that must suit you. I should have asked. I'm so sorry.' He was putting his tool bag down, bending over it. 'I'll just . . .'

She was shaking her head, tapping his shoulder. 'No, that's fine. I was just surprised it was done. It seems so quick. Yes, that's absolutely fine.'

He looked up at her, his face intent, his eyes searching hers. She smiled, stepping back. 'It really is.' Because it was. What did it matter? She wasn't going to live here. That's what she'd tell Peter. After all, this way you could have a working surface either side; it was much more sensible. Yes, she'd tell him that too.

'It really is fine.' He was relaxing, she could see that he accepted she was telling the truth.

He packed his tool bag again, then stood up. 'If you're sure. And is it OK to take that hour out, or do you reckon it was more?' He was easing past her, heading for his waterproof.

'Less,' she said. 'Definitely less. Look, I needed to be there too, so just forget about it.' She was smoothing down Peter's shirt, embarrassed to be talking money.

He shrugged into his waterproof in spite of the sun, which was still bright. He came into the kitchen again, scribbled in his book, then showed it to her. 'Compromise. We'll meet in the middle. I've taken out half an hour.'

She shook her head. 'It really doesn't matter.'

But he was putting the book back on the windowsill, and again edged past her. Each time there was the smell of sawdust. 'It really does matter, to me,' he said, whistling as he headed for the stairs. 'Now we can get a bit of work in before our first number comes up at the sale tomorrow, so shall I be here at eight thirty, or nine a.m., and will I need a battering ram?'

She laughed again. A real laugh. 'I'll be up and about by eight thirty.'

He was at the bottom of the stairs. 'Is that a promise?'

'Just shut the door after you. You can now, you know.'

Again his laugh was gleeful.

CHAPTER EIGHTEEN

Kate swept into the drive and sagged with relief as the harsh security light snapped on, welcoming her back to civilisation, and central heating. She switched off the engine and opened the door, hoping to hear Bertie declaring his lavatorial intentions, but there was silence. What did it matter? She was home and she'd survived her first week.

Scooping up her grip and the fish and chips she'd picked up from Martock, she hurried in and shut the front door behind her, feeling the warmth of her house, reaching for the light switch, flicking it, absorbing the luxury of electricity, leaning back against the door, closing her eyes.

Gradually her shoulder muscles relaxed, gradually she heard the faint rumbling of the boiler, the ticking of the hall clock. Gradually she felt the heat of the fish and chips. Damn. She almost ran into the kitchen. Again that flick of the switch, the huff of the gas oven, the pile of plates in the cupboard. Cupboards! The miracle that was modern living. With the fish and chips tucked into the oven, she unzipped her grip and piled her clothes into the washing machine. A washing machine! She made tea. A kettle!

Carrying her mug into the hallway she checked through the mail – mostly bills – and activated the answering machine, listening with half an ear as she viewed the sitting room, the dining room; all so beautiful, all so warm, all so civilised. She phoned Stuart and Elaine Duncan, putting off the mid-week invitation to dinner, a coffee morning, and all the others, but assuring them that soon she and Peter would be back into their social routine, his travelling permitting.

She took her steaming tea into their en suite bathroom, running the water, pouring in bubble bath, watching it fill far too high and too hot as she stripped, sinking into it, hardly daring to believe she was here.

She lay there until the water lost the sting of its heat, and her tea was cold. She could do nothing about the tea, but with her toe she wrenched out the plug, let the water level drop, then let the water suck the peg back into its hole. Plug, she corrected herself. She then ran in more hot water.

It was only when her fingers resembled prunes and she heard the slam of the front door that she heaved herself from the water, feeling almost light-headed. Hurriedly drying herself, she reaching for her towelling wrap just as Peter entered the bedroom.

He looked tired as he tossed his grip and expanding briefcase on to the bed.

She smiled at him. When should she tell him about McTravers? Her stomach flipped. She kept the smile. He kissed the air above her head. She leaned forward, resting her head on his shoulder. She wanted arms around her. They came. The cold still clung to him. She smelt the remnants of his Old Spice. He patted her ·shoulder and moved away, tearing off his tie and unbuttoning his shirt, then disappeared into the bathroom. 'God, I'm bushed. What's for dinner?' he called.

'Martock's best,' she called back. She slipped into beige jeans, beige shirt, moccasins. Here there was no need for warmth-inducing layers, for socks, for fingerless gloves which she had found in a shop in St Austell.

In the kitchen she dug out an attractive platter and put it to warm. It probably wouldn't help but he'd lose his appetite soon enough anyway, once she told him of McTravers. Leaning back against the sink she rubbed on hand cream. She hadn't had bath wrinkles like this since she was a teenager and prone to long periods of introspection, to the accompaniment of whatever was on the tranny.

She laid the table in the dining room, wishing she'd put a nice hock in the fridge to blur his edges. As he came down the stairs in his green cords and deep blue shirt he queried, 'Martock's best?' He was flicking through the mail on the telephone table as she crossed into the kitchen. She should have thought to buy chicken instead – she could have tarted that up and he would have been none the wiser.

She rubbed her forehead, then arranged the fish on the

platter, putting the processed peas in a separate bowl as he entered. He carried his Filofax, and his folded schedule and plans of Journey's End. She felt sick. He saw the fish and chips. 'God almighty, you've got to be joking.'

'I was a bit pushed, a bit tired.'

He slammed the bills down. 'Well, that's the story of my life, so now you know how I feel. Or do you? You know I don't like grease.'

'These aren't greasy.' She slipped the baking tin into the sink, disguising the fat beneath the running tap.

'Well, at least let's have soup. This is our first evening together for a week.'

She fished cream of mushroom out of the cupboard and heated it for a moment in the microwave, watching it rotate as though nothing had ever been as fascinating. Don't ask how McTravers is getting on, please don't ask that, not yet. She should have phoned him, of course. That's what he'd say. There was no answer to that. She should. She hadn't.

They sat opposite one another at the gleaming dining room table. The soup met with half-hearted approval, and the bread rolls she'd brought from Fowey were squashed. He pulled them into bite-sized pieces. He spread the butter so thickly his arteries would go into orgasmic shock. She noticed how plump his hands were, though plump was a marketing term for fat. Plump and pale.

Her own soup tasted like the tins she had been heating over the camping stove. She was unable to finish.

'How . . .?' he began, but she interrupted.

'How was your week? Did the meeting go well? You were where? In Sweden or Czechoslovakia?'

He looked up, his last spoonful halfway to his mouth. 'It went well, and it was Prague.'

'I've always wanted to go.'

She knew he would spend the next five minutes explaining why wives couldn't.

This he did whilst she cleared the plates and brought the fish, nodding understandingly all the time, in the correct places, because it was a well-known path.

She served his fish. It looked marginally better because she had found some limp parsley in the salad drawer at the bottom

167

of the fridge. He laboriously peeled off the batter and made a production of eating the savaged cod. He ignored the peas entirely, nodding towards the chips. 'These are a recipe for a heart attack.'

She said nothing about the butter, forcing herself to eat every last scrap on her plate before laying her knife and fork neatly together, at an angle. It was only then that she looked at him. 'I have some . . .'

It was his turn to interrupt her. 'How is McTravers getting on, still on schedule?'

He had some fish on his chin. She looked away. 'That's what I was about to say. Work is a little behind but there's no need to worry because I've laid on someone else.' It was what she had rehearsed endlessly, and it sounded pretty good.

He had been dabbing at his face with his napkin but now all movement stopped. 'You've what?' As she explained he threw the napkin to the table, but at least the fish on his chin had disappeared. She thought of this, not the awful tumbling in her stomach, the thudding in her head as he ranted and raged, finally almost screaming at her. 'For God's sake, do I have to do everything? Projects are all about managing, about being there, and builders are notorious. I *advised* you to get down, though far be it from me to *tell* you.'

He was right, apart from the bit about advising, not telling. He was right, and she shouldn't be feeling that she could kill him. The silver-plated candlesticks left to her by her mother were gleaming on the sideboard. Poor Mum, she had thought they were solid. It was what she had been told by Kate's father when he brought them home for their twenty-fifth wedding anniversary. This too she had forgotten.

Peter was thumping the table. 'Why the hell didn't you tell me? And who is this Isaac bloke?'

She folded her napkin again and again, very carefully, and as carefully she said, 'He's been recommended, and I pay him at the end of the week, when the work is done. That way we won't lose money as *you* did with McTravers.' Now she looked up at him, and she knew she shouldn't be shouting, but she couldn't stop. 'I'm also collecting furniture from auction sales because you have sold Barbs's stuff. I'm also camping with a lamp, a bloody canvas bed and a cooking stove, and yes, we're on schedule.' She felt suddenly very tired. 'Well, more or less on schedule.'

He reared back in his chair like some hysterical Othello. 'Oh, yes, and more or less on schedule is bloody magnificent, is it? And if you think you can offload the blame of this on to me, you can think again. I was only trying to help, but would you do your bit? Would you take responsibility for *your* house?'

'Responsibility.' She was on her feet, shaking, seeing nothing but his fat – yes, fat – white finger stabbing the table. 'Responsibility. Don't you talk to me about responsibility. What about Barbs . . .'

Now he too was standing. 'For God's sake, do you have to drag in everything? This has nothing to do with my mother, except for the fact that she chose to leave you the bloody house, and even then you can't sort yourself out enough to do the job she told you to do. I've had to set it up for you, and Christ, haven't I enough to do?' He was shaking his Filofax at her, his plans had fallen to the floor.

She leaned on the table, anything to disguise the trembling. 'You took over, for God's sake. I didn't want that damn house in the first place.' Her voice was an ugly shriek.

'Oh, and I saw you stopping me. I saw you finding some-where better.' There was spittle on his lip, she felt it on her face. The phone began to ring. She was panting, her throat was sore. He was right. She sat down, exhausted. He was right and she was hysterical, crazy, and she thought she had moved on from that.

He swept from the table into the hall. The phone stopped. She heard his voice, heard his laugh devoid of amusement. There was a smear of grease on her plate, and a green stain where the peas had been. He returned. 'It's Jude.' He picked up his plans, refolded them, set them neatly underneath his Filofax.

In the hall she flicked on *all* the lights, took a deep breath and picked up the receiver. 'Hi,' her voice was hoarse.

Jude said, 'Oh God, Mum, what the hell have you done now? Why didn't you do as he said in the first place?'

Kate said, 'Not now, Jude.'

'Yes, now. I didn't need you to be with me. I've grown up, for God's sake, and it's time you did the same. Why don't you just . . .'

'I think that you are probably the rudest eighteen-year-old I have ever come across.' Kate didn't have the energy to raise her voice, or even to put the phone down, though she wanted to do both.

Now Jude was saying, 'I'm sorry, Mum, but you've got to try and hack this, you've got to get a grip, you've got to stay down there, for God's sake, and see it through.' Now Jude was talking to someone else, her voice muffled but clear enough to make it evident she was holding everyone up. 'I've got to go, Mum,' she said.

'You go,' Kate agreed, 'please go.' Before I say something dreadful, she thought. Before I crack and say something shocking, something that can't be forgiven, that is coming up into my mouth. Before I say, bugger off, and never phone me again.

'Don't be like that,' Jude said. But Kate summoned the energy to put the phone down, took several deep breaths and went to the kitchen, not the dining room. She filled the kettle and found the camomile tea bags, putting two into the mug, instead of the usual one.

She must go to bed, to her nice, warm, comfortable bed. Her hands were still shaking. The wrinkles had gone, but the roughness of the last week remained. The kettle boiled. She poured it into the mug. Outside Bertie was barking. It must be nine. She glanced at the clock. It was, and she couldn't bear the person Kate Maxwell had become.

'I'm sorry, I'm just tired and worried.' Peter spoke from the doorway. She replaced the kettle. For a moment she couldn't believe the apology she had heard, and so she just did nothing. The boiler thudded into action again. She tried to stop the tears, the stupid, loud, snuffling tears, dragging her hand across her eyes again and again. She tried and tried to stop and now his arms were round her, turning her to him, holding her, and she wanted him to take her pain away, to soothe her, but it was he . . .

She was making his shirt wet, and any minute now he would tell her she was being hysterical, any minute he would tell her to take control of herself. She groped for the tissue in her jeans pocket, half laughing as she pulled back and wiped her face, not looking at him. 'I was making a drink.'

170

'I can see that.' His voice wasn't sharp; he was half smiling, his eyes full of worry, and irritation.

She reached out and touched his arm, feeling a terrible sadness filling her, a regret for all that was happening to them, all that had happened. 'I'm sorry, and thank you.'

He nodded. She said, 'Would you like a drink?'

'Coffee, I've got to work.'

'Will instant do?'

'Fine, whatever.' He had taken her usual place at the sink, leaning back, his arms folded. As well as looking plump he looked tired and strained, and she was a bitch. Of course she was a bitch. She could go to bed, but he had to work.

She said, 'You're right, I should have stayed.'

He shrugged, taking the coffee from her, sipping it, moving slightly as she put the camomile bags in the compost bin beneath the sink. 'What's done is done, but talk me through what progress you *have* made.'

She explained the door stripping, the auction sales, the wiring. He nodded. 'So the doors are finished, and the wiring will be next week?'

'I haven't quite finished stripping, I was diverted by the front door.' The moment she said it she knew it was a mistake.

'The front door?' He was watching her over the rim of his mug.

She explained and watched the exasperation build. His voice was measured, overly patient. 'Who put it up like that in the first place?'

She could lie of course. She said, 'Isaac.'

He was slowly shaking his head, his lips pursing. 'So this is the man who comes recommended, is it? Not only is he clueless enough to have a house repossessed but he happily puts in a naff door. Oh yes, you've obviously made a wise choice of workman, or does he blame his tools?'

She heard herself gabbling, 'His girlfriend was in charge of doing the place up, but she did a runner while he was away.'

'Away?' Peter had put the coffee down on the drainer, and was back to arm folding. 'So he's a weekender? Things just get better and better. Tell me, is he some sort of whizz kid who's taken a week off to help a woman from the sticks? I mean, have you thought this through at all?'

171

Kate could see the wet patch on his shirt. Nothing held still for long enough; not a moment of regret, not a raging argument, not a train of thought. She picked up her mug. She was going to bed. He stepped forward, his hand held up as though she was a wayward truck. 'Well?'

'Of course I've thought it through, and he isn't a whizz kid. He's into . . .' She hesitated. 'Into boats.'

'What, builds them?' He was too close. Everyone stood too close.

She shook her head. 'No, he sails. You know, long distances, alone.'

At this he turned towards the window, throwing up his hands. 'Oh, bloody marvellous, a beach bum, and this equips him to do up my mother's house.'

Very slowly, very loudly she said, 'It equips him to do up *my* house.' The silence was profound. She tried again. 'He's done all sorts to finance his trips, both before he sets sail, and when he puts into land. He's done electrics, carpentry, decorating, plumbing, he's even shovelled coal and worked on building sites, because his writing doesn't cover it all. He was just telling me yesterday . . .'

Peter's laugh silenced her. 'Ah, so I can sleep sound in my bed knowing that someone who can use a pen is running cable in our, I'm so sorry, *your* house. Kate, I'm only worried about your well-being, can't you understand that? I mean, is that so unreasonable?'

'Well, stop . . .' She walked to the door. He had to stop shouting. She had to stop shouting or her head would explode. 'I know, and I'm keeping an eye on everything, and we will meet the deadline, and it will be all right. I promise it will be all right.' With each step of the stairs she thought, It must be all right. Isaac has to be all right. It sounds so crazy. The whole thing sounds so crazy. Peter's right, it's completely crazy, and when it's over he'll stop shouting, and I'll stop shouting, and my head will clear.

CHAPTER NINETEEN

Journey's End seemed bleaker and colder still on Monday morning. Kate had left the Old Vicarage at 6.00 am and had a good run down, determined to be there early, the employer greeting the employee with sandpaper in her hand, sweat on her brow, and the doors showing distinct signs of progress.

When he still hadn't arrived by ten she slumped on the camp bed, holding her hand up to the paraffin heater. It was McTravers all over again, and what was she going to do now, what was Peter going to do? There were cable ends sticking out of the walls, there was no ceiling in here, the plastering needed to be finished.

She rubbed her stomach, trying to ease it, watching a passing container ship, delivering china clay to God knows where. Her toes were numb. She paced up and down, up and down. She needed to think. She couldn't. She stared down at the floor, the paint-flecked bare boards and then at the kitchen. At the power point on the wrong wall. Suddenly the anger was there, roaring again. She kicked out at the bed. It slid across the floor, hurting her toe. She rubbed it. The anger fled.

She collected the bed and returned it to its rightful position, picked up the phone, started to dial Penny's number, stopped. What good was that? Instead she picked up the DIY book and located electricity in the index. She found the pages. The diagrams should have made things clear to a five-year-old. She obviously had the mental age of four and three-quarters. She read through again, following the arrows with her finger.

She turned to the section on plastering. Yes, perhaps she could do that if she artexed over it to disguise the mess.

A quick look at Peter's plans, then back to the index. More flicking of pages. No, she couldn't do the ceiling. The joists would need two of them.

She returned to the doors and tried to think, but she couldn't get past the panic, and soon she was fighting tears, fighting and fighting them, because they served no useful purpose, they never made anything better. They didn't come.

When the rafter-dome doors were as smooth as silk she dusted off her hands and found her keys. She'd try the local electricity board – they'd have an electrician they could recommend. She was on her way downstairs, her bag over her shoulder, when there was a sharp knock.

It was Isaac, grinning at her apologetically, his yellow waterproofs gleaming in the sun, which she had failed to notice. He spread his hands. 'Sorry, had to check some nearly new storage heaters which Alfie's got hold of.' He noticed her bag and jacket. 'Oh,' he stepped to one side, 'I'll tell you when you get back.' He swept a courtly gesture.

She could have slapped him. Instead she turned and marched back up the stairs. 'I was going to find an officially recommended electrician.' She slammed the door of the rafter-dome behind her, dropped her bag on the bed and covered her face with her hands. No tears. No.

There was a tentative knock on the door. She dragged her hair back from her face, dug her hands in her pockets and turned, finding her voice. 'Oh, just come in, for God's sake.'

As he entered she was shrugging into her body-warmer. He shifted from foot to foot in the doorway, his tool bag in his hand. She patted her pockets for sandpaper. His face was concerned, the lines around his eyes deeper. He put out his hand, then dropped it to his side. 'Look, I'm sorry. I would have rung but I haven't got your number, and I wanted to stake an interest in the heaters before the old devil moved them on. You can't go on like this.' He nodded towards the paraffin heater. 'The bed'll be damp after the weekend. It's just not on.'

'That's not the problem.' Her voice was crisp. 'The problem is getting this place up and running. The problem is knowing what the hell is going on.' She fished a pen out of her bag, tore a page out of her diary and wrote down her mobile number. He had walked into the kitchen and was removing his jacket. She followed and put the scrap of paper on the windowsill. He reached across and picked it up, along with his time book. Again there was that smell of sawdust. She stepped back, out

174

of his way, leaning against the wall because there was no sink. She'd been rude.

He was checking his watch which he wore on the inside of his wrist, and wrote the time. She said magnanimously, 'You should note the time you left for Alfie's.'

He nodded. 'I just have.'

Rebuffed, she moved out into the rafter-dome. 'When do you think the electrics will be finished?'

'A couple of days.' He was right behind her. Whatever had happened to personal space? She crossed her arms and moved away. When she turned she saw he had in fact been busy with the light switch. He looked over at her. 'There's just the outside light to do now.'

'Outside light?' she queried. 'Was that in the spec.?'

He shook his head, staring into the workings of the switch. 'It would be a good idea, but it's up to you, of course. You're the boss.' This time there was an edge.

She ignored it because she deserved it. 'I suppose it would light the way for the tenants.'

'Attracts good chi too.'

Oh, God. She gave her consent, then waved up at the rafters. 'I suppose we should have put the ceiling in first, but I imagine you could make provision by running the cable through from the loft space at the side, and fix it when we've put the joists up.' It sounded as though she knew what she was talking about, and it should, because that was what she had just read in the book.

There was no answer, and when she looked back at him he was standing with his hands on his hips, a perplexed expression on his face. She stalled, doubtful suddenly. This time it was she who was tentative. 'I'm sorry, am I ahead of myself? I assumed you were here for the duration, till the bitter end. I thought you were going to stay on the job until it was done. Oh, I'm sorry.' She shut her eyes. This was just . . .

'Hey,' he was here beside her. He had taken her arm. She opened her eyes and saw his concern, again. It was in his voice too, as he said, 'Hey, yes, I'm going to get it finished. I said I would, though perhaps you should make sure that you're satisfied with the electrics first. If everything fuses, just get rid of me.' He was smiling. 'It's just that I've been meaning to talk to you about this room. It's so beautifully proportioned it seems a crime to section it off. You'll be shortening the window, too, cutting down the light and the ambience. Have you ever considered keeping it as it is?'

He was still holding her arm. She moved away, appreciating how Barbs must have felt when people visited and took her hand uninvited.

'Just look,' he urged. 'The proportions, the light . . .'

'It'd be difficult to heat, and the plans . . .'

His gestures were impatient. 'Yes, but the views, the light between the rafters . . . And it's tall enough to take a platform bed. You could put one here.' He was pointing to the north wall opposite the window, drawing it in the air, and then he paused, and it was as though a light had gone out. He shrugged and half laughed. 'Well, maybe you're right, a ceiling is the sensible course.'

He returned to the kitchen, and Kate patted her pockets for the sandpaper again, but all the time she was sizing up the room, trying to imagine the ceiling, then a platform bed. But the plans were drawn up, and Peter would be angry.

What sort of a platform bed?

Heating *would* be a problem.

She glanced towards the kitchen, folding the sandpaper, unfolding it. Isaac was singing quietly to the radio. She left the room and sat on the stairs, working on the newell post by the light of the gas lamp, sanding the paint the stripper had missed, concentrating on that, not registering the ringing of her phone until Isaac called her.

'Right.' She began to get up.

He called again, 'Stay there, I'll bring it.'

She waited. It was still trilling when Isaac ran down the stairs, handing it to her, then running back up. He was lithe; light on his feet and hardly made a sound. She thought of the skydiving master again, but that meant Barbs, so she pressed the button. Penny or Peter? 'Kate, thought I'd check in to make sure this one's back on site.'

'Of course, Peter, why wouldn't he be?' Her stomach was already churning.

'No need to take that tone.'

She knew there wasn't, but it just happened when he took

176

that tone. 'Sorry,' she said.

'Anyway, just checking. Call me if you have a problem. Take care now.'

She switched him off.

Over half-full cups of coffee at eleven, provided by Isaac, they discussed the merits of Alfie's storage heaters, and the number needed, which brought them back to the rafter-dome.

Isaac calculated that with the ceiling in place they could get away with a large one on one wall, and two medium on the other. She wrote it down, while he calculated the price. He also calculated the price of the joists, the time taken, the wages for the extra pair of hands that would be needed. It came to the same as McTravers's estimate. To cut the cost Isaac offered to take less pay, and maybe Joe would too, for he was to be their labourer. Kate wouldn't allow that. By eleven thirty the coffee was barely drunk, and quite cold.

All the time the reflection of the water was playing on the raftered eaves, and the sun streamed in and the cows grazed on the top of the hill opposite, and the clouds scudded across the sky in full panorama.

Isaac turned round the paper he'd been scribbling on so she could see better. 'I've cut a few corners, what do you think?'

She looked at the latest figures, then back at the view, then up at the rafters, then at the north wall. Isaac's face was expressionless. Could he tell what she was thinking? He always seemed to. She said awkwardly, feeling her way, 'If we had a platform bed in here it would give us space for an additional two tenants. This living area would remain?' This time it was she sweeping her arm around the room. 'So too, the view, the ambience. We could advertise it as a four adult, two children let, if we put bunk beds in the study bedroom. We could emphasise the character of the place and even put a sofa bed under the platform, providing another double bed.' Isaac was nodding slowly. She saw his excitement. 'I could tell Peter that we've saved that.' She tapped the sheet of paper. 'He'd then come back with the extra cost of heating, so I could explain that we can ask more per week with the extra bed space.'

Now she was ticking the points off on her fingers. 'I've seen bunk bed instructions in my DIY book. They seem easy enough.'

Isaac was fidgeting on the pillow, holding his mug between two hands, grinning broadly. He sipped, pulled a face, put down the mug.

'Has Alfie got three of the largest storage heaters?'

Isaac was uncertain for a moment. 'I'd have to call him.'

'Fine, use my phone. And the bed, how do we go about getting one of those?' She dragged her hand through her hair. 'That's a point, it could cost a fortune.' She put up her hand. 'Let's just hang on a minute.'

But Isaac was shaking his head. 'Problem solved, I commissioned one before I went to sea. I put something down, and should have paid the rest later. Made me feel bad when I couldn't. Harry's still got it, half finished. You could get it if you stump up the balance that's owing. It could kill two birds with one stone, be good for you both. I've felt very bad about leaving him in the lurch.'

She moved the sheet of paper up and down, up and down, brought to a sudden halt. She didn't look at him, or at the ripples on the ceiling, or the cows, but at the paper. She rubbed her forehead, then looked out at the view. Another ship was passing. There was a man with a peaked cap in the wheelhouse. They both waited, both watched. When it was gone out of sight Isaac said, 'Look, you don't even know what the design of the bed is, so how can you make a decision?'

With a few quick strokes he drew it. It was stainless steel, clean and clear curved lines. 'Art Deco,' she murmured. Again she moved the paper up and down. In the double bedroom there was auction furniture that they were going to tart up as Art Deco. But what was wrong with that, when she liked the style? The bed would be appropriate, in accordance with the theme, and she would get it cheap.

He said, 'I'm not sure how far he's got with it, but if you didn't like the shape, perhaps he can adapt it to something else.'

He was getting to his feet, collecting the mugs and taking them to the bathroom. She let him. Outside, the sky was clouding over. Inside the paraffin heater was on low.

She left the rafter-dome and returned to the newell post, immersing herself in the mindless activity of fine-sanding the wood, trying to concentrate on that, not on his excitement, the plans that had once been his, the sense that she was being used.

Exasperated, she let the sandpaper fall to the paint-spattered bare wooden stairs, rubbing her eyes, forgetting all about the dust covering her fingers, blinking to try and remove it. Damn, damn. But then Isaac called from the landing. 'I'm sorry to keep on, but Alfie needs a yes or no on the heaters. I really want to get on with them, and I also need to whack up a wall heater in the bathroom, and something in the kitchen. Keeping you lit and warm must be a priority. Alfie's heard of some kitchen units, including a sink, that are coming out of a mate's kitchen. They'll only go in a skip, so let's grab them. In a couple of weeks you'll have enough mod cons to make it seem like paradise, and all the time we'll be lopping great chunks off the cost.'

She wiped her hands, aware of him standing above her, knowing she was sitting like a dying swan in a sputtering gas spotlight. 'We can't put heaters on the wall without decorating first.' She was only stalling.

'Fine,' his voice was patient. 'We'll get paint for the rafter-dome tomorrow. You can get those two walls done. We can't decorate the kitchen until it's finished because tiles have to go up, though security glass is what I was going to use. It's different, and cheaper, and the tenants won't mind. We can't decorate the bathroom until we've sorted that out either. I can take those heaters up and down easily, so there's no problem there. We just need a decision from you.' He turned his wrist, checking the time. 'In five minutes, I'm afraid.'

He disappeared. Tenants, and money, she thought, scrambling to the safety of common sense at last; that was the bottom line, so did it matter whose design they worked to, whose schedule? Just so long as they arrived at the end in time. This was just a project, not a home, so what was wrong with letting someone see what they would have created. Yes, what *was* wrong with that, especially when the Maxwells were the ones who had bought up those hopes cheaply and whose real home was waiting in the wings?

Besides, it was this man who had taken on board that her bed was damp, and that she needed to be warm, and that this was no way for anyone to live.

★

On Tuesday they set off for the DIY store in Joe's van. In the back Joe's extension ladder was rattling about, and his rollers and trays. 'He's so kind,' Kate said above the noise.

Isaac agreed, 'Yes, but I think it's partly because Clara stayed at the pub once the kitchen had been ripped out, and the wiring declared defunct. She was supposed to be keeping up with the mortgage repayments with money I sent and getting on with the electrics, but instead she was keeping up with George. Joe thinks he should have done something.'

'Should he?'

'No one can do anything except the people concerned. Even then you have to rely on the truth being told.'

For a moment she was quiet, then she murmured before she could stop herself, 'How do you recognise the truth?'

His gaze was too penetrating. She fiddled with her safety belt whilst he changed gear for the hill. The van brushed the high banks. She groped for something else and found it. 'Did you say Clara was doing the electrics, or supposed to be?'

'Oh yes, she learned a lot when we took passage down the west coast of South America, odd-jobbing along the way.'

At the DIY store he headed for the screws and Lord knows what, whilst she steered for the magnolia paint, but was distracted by the gloss shelves. She might as well pick up a can of red gloss as none had come via Isaac. His voice startled her. 'That's the one. Sorry, I said I'd sort it, didn't I? I couldn't find it, must have chucked it away when I allowed myself the post Clara tantrum.'

He reached over her for the smallest tin, tossing it up and catching it. 'Won't need to do the whole door since you sorted it so neatly. I really *was* impressed.' All she felt was irritation. After all, if Clara was capable of handling the rewiring, praise for rehanging a door was just patronising. She moved the trolley forwards, heading for the magnolia, but he held her back. 'The only downside to amalgamating the living room with a platform bed is that you are mixing up the two uses, so we have to work a little harder at mixing and matching the five elements. If you decide to keep the curves of the platform the chi will travel well. It doesn't like corners.'

'Does anyone? They're as bad as crusts,' she murmured, shaking her head and sneaking a sideways look at this man who seemed so normal in other ways. If solo sailing could be called normal.

He didn't hear because he was busy reaching for a colour chart which he opened with his usual quick, fluent movements. 'Yellow is good.'

Magnolia is better, she thought. Several tins of the same, and no waste. He turned to her. 'It just seems sensible to try, if we can, to turn the luck of the place around. Yellow attracts brightness and honour. And apart from anything else, it's a damn nice colour.' For a moment he seemed vulnerable.

Yellow it was. 'And why not stencil with a light green and blue which are appropriate for east-facing rooms? I know it's south-east, but what's a degree or two between friends? It should enhance health, family life harmony . . .'

'Fine, blue and green it is.' So it went on, with the children's room white for purity but because it was a yang colour they needed some yin. She chose red. He thought maybe not, but how about turquoise which corresponded to the north-east and represented learning?

'Of course it does. How have we lived so long without it?' Jude's room was a soggy green, a colour which depressed Kate but which seemed to stimulate her daughter, though according to its position, Isaac said, there were others more suitable.

'Enough,' she ordered, cutting him short, but smiling as she did so.

Isaac ran his hand through his hair, groaning quietly. 'Peg in the hole immediately. Clara found me irritating too, but out there, the elements take on a different meaning. It's hard to leave them behind.'

What did it matter? The colours would jell, the tenants would come and at least he would see it complete. But when they came to the bathroom she nearly changed her mind, since the combination of flushing water which seemed destined to gush all wealth away with it and north-west aspect which ideally required the colour of grey was such an appalling concept that she was adamant. 'Oh come on, I won't have grey.'

'Don't blame you.' Isaac was tapping the chart. 'How about a mixture of blues, pale with deeper tones?'

181

She raised her eyebrows and waited. He laughed. 'It'll keep the water moving and encourage good cash flow.'

'You leave me no choice – blue it is.' He added it to the collection in the trolley. The kitchen was to be white, for purity again, and because it is associated with the element of metal and was therefore in harmony with the stove. It was at this point that Kate switched off, and decided that it would be a miracle if men in white coats weren't waiting on the dock for him when he returned.

Just before they left the paint department she darted back and bought two huge cans of white emulsion, and chose a sponge. Isaac waited, and this time it was his eyebrows that were raised. 'Those high walls will look much better sponged, and I don't give a monkey's what yang says to yin, or if chi has a problem with this.'

She waved him aside and took the trolley, pushing on ahead of him, but heard his laugh, and his comment: 'Sponging will be fine. It'll look great. Won't affect things at all – yin and yang will still be pleased and the chi ecstatic.'

She shared her thoughts on the men in white coats. He was still laughing as they loaded the van.

On the way back to Fowey they diverted as planned to pick up the kitchen units from Alfie's. The car park looked as sad as ever, but not as sad as the units which were stacked in the garage. Kate's heart sank as Isaac picked over them, grinning and humming, assuring her that they'd be great once they were stripped down and repainted.

'White?' she cut in.

He looked up at her, smiling. 'With new handles.'

'Let me guess – red?'

He shook his head. 'Too hot for a kitchen. Purple. It's associated with the south-east.'

The game was over for her because Barbs was back.

They stacked the units and the sink in the van and returned, pretty much in silence. Isaac left at 3.00 pm. She worked on, propping up the ladder against the wall, filling all the cracks for as long as natural light would allow. Then she returned to sanding the doors, and completing the skirting boards. By eleven she was exhausted. She brushed her hands off, thought about eating, but decided against it.

The bed was still damp but she slept almost immediately, then woke at two, frozen, with her head full of Barbs, of the past. For the rest of the night she tossed and turned and paced, because the force of it all was ferocious, sucking her back down, and it was as though she'd never risen above it, even for a minute.

The moment the day dawned she was up. She brewed tea on the camping stove, she washed in the cold yin-full bathroom, she sanded down the cracks, sweeping the walls with the broom that Joe had lent them. 'Does that man have an Aladdin's cave?' she asked.

'No, just a big heart,' Isaac murmured, finishing up the wiring for the rafter-dome. By ten he was gathering up his tools to complete the outside light.

'Say hello to chi for me,' she called to his departing back, glad to be alone and to be allowed to drop the façade, to rest her head in her hands for a moment, just a moment, before resuming the preparation of the walls.

She worked until midday, by which time Isaac was installing the kitchen wall heater he had brought in from Alfie's that morning. 'Put your time in the book,' she remembered to say.

'I have.'

'Put Joe's petrol, too.'

'I have.'

She poured paint into the tray, sponging yellow on to the walls, watching the paint run down her hand to her wrist, seeing it dripping on to Peter's shirt. Suddenly she couldn't bear to wear it. She tore it off, found a sweatshirt of her own, and worked until one o'clock.

By then the sun was heating the room, and the sweat was trickling down her back, and her head was throbbing from the fumes, in spite of the open window. She prepared thick cheese sandwiches while Isaac poured two half mugs of coffee. She carried hers to the bed, but instead of heading to the pillow Isaac slipped on his waterproof saying, 'Time for a breath of fresh air. The fumes, you know. You should too.'

'Maybe I will.'

He waited expectantly. She hadn't meant now, with him.

She looked at the sponge, but she had washed it out, and it

would wait for her. To protest would be tiring. It would be rude.

She sighed, leaving her bread and cheese untouched. 'Mustn't be long. I don't like leaving a wall in the middle.' She didn't mind leaving her lunch, though.

'It'll still be there when you get back.' He held the door open. She picked up her cagoule and did not bother to reply.

They walked through the town. The sun cast long shadows. She should talk. She should beat these shadows away, the shadows that were stalking her, probing, hurting.

She tried the weather, the gulls, the national news. His replies were monosyllabic, almost reluctant. She balled her hands into fists. He must help. He could read minds, he knew about balance. He should help. He should talk, about anything, everything. He should batter her with questions, drag out answers, anything to keep her sane.

He was digging about in his pockets, and then she saw why, as he took his cling-film wrapped sandwiches from his pocket, and ate as he walked. He offered her some. She shook her head. He sighed, rewrapped the cling film and put it back in his pocket. 'You're right, but as I said, my social graces tend to desert me. Penalty of the job.'

She didn't care if he ate.

They were almost at the end of the esplanade. The wind was catching them now, but it was far stronger as they made their way out of the town and round the headland.

Barbs had loved the sea, and her ashes had been scattered in the wind.

But no. All that must not come back and so Kate talked and talked until her throat was dry, and as they brushed between two gorse bushes she moved from EuroStar to his solo sailing. 'It must be dangerous, all this circumnavigating alone?'

His answer was as delayed as all had been so far but eventually he replied, 'I suppose there's a concept that solo sailing is bold and adventurous.'

He was looking at her, and at last it was as though those blue eyes were picking through her mind. He would help. He would talk, distract. She searched the sea behind him. It was rough, the white tops were whipping and running towards shore.

But he said nothing.

184

There was so much to do. They'd blown the fumes away, hadn't they? She would turn back.

He answered her question at last. 'No, it's not that dangerous. It's just a question of finding the right alternative. You know, one plan is never enough, you need two to cover most of the angles. And you need to be wary. Passage down any coast is far more wearying and potentially dangerous than crossing the ocean, because there's so much to account for and second guess.' He quickened his pace, his head down, his hands in his pockets.

So, he didn't really read minds and therefore he couldn't help. No one could help.

She didn't move. He stopped, walked back a few paces, and said, 'A break is essential. Don't feel guilty. You have a right to time for yourself.' The wind was pulling at his yellow waterproof, tugging at his hair, but he seemed impervious, lifting his head, closing his eyes slightly.

She said, 'I must get back.'

He looked at her, smiling gently, and she turned away. He said, 'Listen.' He held up his hand. She was confused. Listen? To what? She looked around. There was just the gorse, the hummocked grass, the sea roaring in, and in the distance a fishing boat like the one she had watched with Barbs, and now it was darker still.

She whispered, 'What?'

'Just listen. Take some time to stand and stare, and listen. Take some time to think.'

She stared at him, furious now, because Barbs wanted her to think, and Barbs wanted too much. Too much of her, always too damned much. She shouted, 'I can think while I work, that's what women do, Isaac. It's men who can only do one thing at a time, and sometimes they can't even do that. Not even one thing.' She stopped. There was just the sound of the wind.

'Better?' he asked.

'I'm going back.'

He just stood calmly, then nodded. 'OK; I'll be along soon.'

He didn't even notice her going, and she felt as though she was stumbling and staggering along, with the wind behind her. At last she was back, at last she was unlocking the door, taking up the sponge, working ferociously now, driven by a great energy, hardly hearing him knock. When she did she wanted to ignore him, wanted to be alone because he had not helped her, and for some stupid reason she had thought he would.

She walked slowly down the stairs and hesitated for a moment, her hand on the lock. He knocked again. She opened the door. He stood, his collar up. She left him there, hurrying back to the rafter-dome, back to the ladder. He didn't run up the stairs as he usually did, nor did he bound into the room. Instead he came and stood quietly by the ladder, waiting.

At last she stopped, her wrist aching. He said, 'I thought a walk would help you. I thought it would chase the shadows from your eyes. I thought you needed to see the vastness of the sea. I thought you needed someone with you while you faced whatever it is that is tearing at you, more than usually today.'

He walked quietly downstairs, and worked in the study bedroom until it was three, and then he left. All they said to one another was goodbye.

That night she did not sleep again.

The next day they walked together. Why not? She asked him a little about his sailing, he asked her about her home, her family, her life, but when he asked about her job he took her silence as a need for peace as again the wind tore at them once they rounded the headland. From then on neither spoke. But arriving at the bay they collected pebbles to place in bowls in the living room. 'Yin, yang, or chi?' she asked.

'Just because they're nice.'

She nodded. Above them the gulls were wheeling, the surf was rushing quietly over the sand, the seaweed was glinting, the brine was thick in the air. She drew in great lungfuls; she stared at the clouds.

They walked back, their pockets heavy with the pebbles, and as they entered Fowey again they were discussing the need for sleep, the self-steering gear, the fact that he slept in snatches during the day whilst at sea, and was alert at night. There was another long silence when she asked why he sailed single-handed. She waited, she was learning. He said at last, 'My mother was a free spirit, a bohemian, I suppose. She thought that in order to live life honestly and to the full we have to know

186

the best and worst of ourselves, and then we can face it in others. I suppose I sailed alone to begin with to understand myself, and I continue because I am content with what I've found.'

He laughed and added, 'Perhaps, too, because I'm paid to write books about it. And because I enjoy life in Fowey when I'm home. And because . . .'

She held up her hands in surrender.

That night, though Barbs, and also Peter, tore at her it was not as much, and above them both she heard the sea, and the wind, and faced towering waves and bottomless troughs and fought them all, and sometimes she won. At least sometimes she won.

By Thursday evening the two walls were finished. Isaac had been filling in time by stripping some of the kitchen units. He wanted to get the kitchen set up so that she could have some civilised catering on hand.

On Friday they switched arenas, and it was Isaac working in the rafter-dome while she attacked the units, and since there was no painting, there was no need for a walk, and since it was pouring with rain they said it was a blessing, and since Isaac was racing against time to get the heaters connected and installed he ate while he worked, and so did she. At 3.00 pm she called through to him from the kitchen. 'Come on, knocking off time.'

He shook his head. 'I want to get these up and running before I leave, then come Monday, everything will be looking better for you.'

He didn't leave until 4.00 pm, and as he had arrived at eight he looked tired. More importantly the daylight had gone and he'd have to rely on artificial light while he worked on Molly. She paid him, in cash as usual, but put in an extra £20. He took it out and returned it, folding her hand over the note. 'No need, we're friends.'

She felt warmed. Friends. Yes, that sounded good.

Instead she gave him the tennis balls she had tracked down in the cupboard under the stairs at the Old Vicarage, and which she had been meaning to pass over ever since she had arrived on Monday. 'For the chafing,' she explained. He peered into the Safeway carrier bag and said nothing, but as he looked up she remembered where she had heard about the conquering of fear. It was what the skydiving master had said to Barbs, and it was what Barbs had told her, in her turn.

On the journey home the phone rang when she was half an hour into Devon. She pulled in and answered. It was Peter. She tensed. He said, 'Just to say that fish and chips are fine, if you want to bring some home. Sorry I was such a grouch last week.'

She was so amazed she had to get him to repeat it. She replied, 'Well, I bought chicken breasts and a bit of pâté at the Spar; it won't take me a moment.'

The traffic was heavy, and her car seemed to shift as each vehicle passed. The line was breaking up. She leaned forward, a hand to her other ear. Peter was saying, 'No, no, leave that for tomorrow, you've done more than enough today. Tell you what, phone me from the fish and chip shop and I'll put plates in to warm.'

Again she was amazed. 'Are you sure?' Then, 'Are you home?'

'Any minute now,' he said. 'I'm knackered, it's the end of a busy week and I thought we could do with a night in together.'

The line was breaking up completely. She cut the connection and drove on, trying to absorb this about turn from her husband, and it was as she left the M5 at the Taunton turn-off that it occurred to her that Peter was scrabbling through his emotions just as much as she, that he too was trying to come to terms with all that had passed. After all, if she, as the daughter-in-law, was in chaos, then he, as the son, must be in the same state, and she felt ashamed that she had forgotten this.

CHAPTER TWENTY

Peter stood in the kitchen doorway holding a tray with two steaming mugs of coffee, working out the approximate time of Kate's arrival. Jan called down, 'What are you doing, picking the coffee beans?'

He shut the door quietly behind him, then shook his head at his stupidity. Did he think Kate could hear, or maybe Penny, or that disgusting dog of hers? He opened and shut it, this time with a bang. He hurried upstairs, wishing he had worn his robe rather than the towel he had knotted around his waist. It was too cold for this sort of heroics.

In the bedroom Jan was leaning back against the pillows, her full, taut breasts on open display. In spite of just having spent an hour in bed with her, he felt excitement rising again as he approached the bed. She smiled, seeing the movement behind the towel. 'I don't need coffee,' she murmured, pushing down the bedclothes. She had a damn good body.

He put the tray on the bedside table, wishing he had had the foresight to hide the Wallace and Gromit alarm clock that Simon had given Kate. He'd never liked that sort of gimmicky humour, and now it brought his son to mind, and his family, but Jan's hand was slipping up beneath the towel, teasing his thighs, rising higher, higher. He felt his breath constrict. He pressed his knees against the bed. Higher, higher. Her fingers were there. He closed his eyes. God Almighty.

Now she was pressed against him, those breasts so warm, her mouth so wet on his. The towel was being pulled undone. He wouldn't look, he liked it this way, the not knowing, the surprise. She was sliding down his body, surely she was almost there. He groaned as her tongue found him. He held her head against him, but she was moving up, kissing his belly, his chest. His hands found her breasts, and still his eyes were shut, as together they fell on to the bed, and he was on top of her, and in her.

He looked down at her swollen mouth, her eyes so full of love, of longing. Soon she would whisper, 'Please.' She always did. But instead, as she had done just an hour ago, she called his name, loudly, fiercely. He silenced her with his mouth as he had done before. Stupid bitch, did she think he didn't understand? The knowledge made him powerful, made his thrusts deeper, made it possible for him to climax for the second time, groaning deep in his throat as she sobbed his name, quietly this time.

For a moment he rested his full weight on her, exhausted, their sweat mingling, her arms holding him tightly. He hated this bit; the tears he knew would flow, the meaningful whispers, the 'if onlys', the 'whens', the 'why can'ts'. Again he stopped her mouth before rolling off, staring at the ceiling. It really did need redecorating. And those tennis rackets should be under the stairs, not slung up there. Was that Simon? Must have been, he'd borrowed them when he came for Barbs's funeral.

He shut his eyes.

Next to him Jan was nuzzling his neck. Why did women do this? Hadn't she had enough? He checked Wallace and Gromit. Plenty of time, but Jan didn't know that, for he knew she was hoping they'd be discovered. He moved slightly. She clung. For a moment he let her, he even held her as tightly, but all the time the rackets were annoying him. He'd be bloody glad when this Fowey business was sorted and Kate could get this place up and running as it should be. He'd had to take the Swedes to that French place, which meant he couldn't drink, or hardly a drop.

Jan was whispering, 'I miss you, I hope you didn't mind me phoning today. I just couldn't last another minute without you.'

He levered himself up on the pillows. 'Course not, it was a good idea.' It was a bloody awful idea, actually. Except, having said that, there was a certain excitement in doing it here, though little danger in fact.

He hadn't even bothered to shut the curtains of their back bedroom, certain that Penny was doing her rounds at the hospital, Tom was at work, the conifers which divided the house from the road blocked the view opposite, and he knew more or less exactly now when Kate would be coming home. He smiled at Jan, patting her buttocks. 'It was great, you're great, and you know I feel the same.'

She was kissing his chest, which he also found post-coitally irritating, so he reached for the mugs. The coffee was only marginally warm, but he wasn't tiptoeing around getting his feet cold on the kitchen tiles again, and besides, she really must be gone in about fifteen minutes. By then he'd have had more than enough.

'Here, get yourself up and have a slurp.' Reluctantly Jan sat, taking the coffee and looking round the room. 'You don't still sleep with her, do you?'

'Of course not. I've told you, it's a marriage in name only.'

'Where do you sleep then?'

He stared at her. 'Well, I mean, I do sleep here, I just don't sleep with her.'

Jan looked away from him, her eyes filling. He took a sip of his coffee, knowing he had to be careful, knowing there was a chance he might need her. He said, 'Jan darling, hang in there. It won't be long.'

He took another sip. It was disgusting, but it saved him talking. Next to him Jan was staring round the room. 'I'd do it differently. You're right, Kate has no imagination. Poor darling, I can see why you're so frustrated.'

He let her talk, nodding at appropriate points, bored beyond endurance, because he hadn't built all this up to let half of it go. He was a family man, that's how he was seen, and besides, he loved his kids, and Kate was all right, or would be, once she had settled down. It was all to do with her age, of course, on top of everything else. Still, as long as there weren't too many scenes like last weekend. Bloody hell, she really got above herself. He looked at Jan. This evening's little diversion was no more than Kate deserved after all that bloody fuss.

His coffee was finished. He put the mug on the tray, and took Jan's from her. 'You use the bathroom first.'

He watched her pout, and touched her cheek. 'Quickly now, I have a lot of work to catch up on, the work I put aside when I took your irresistible phone call.' He kissed her, but his mind was already on the work he really did have to do. As she walked to the bathroom he watched her. There was no spare flesh on

191

her, her skin was taut, and for a moment he wondered what it would be like with her in this bed every night, waking to her in the morning. As quickly he dismissed it. Bollocks. Nothing stayed that good – there'd be nappies and PMT, more school fees, and then the menopause.

He checked the clock again. Kate hadn't phoned from the chippie yet, and it would be a miracle if she'd covered that many miles by now anyway. He leaned forward, wishing Jan would hurry up. At that moment she came out of the bathroom and he took her place at the bidet, only to hear his phone ringing.

He towelled himself quickly, shouting, 'I'll get it.' Christ, if she took it into her head to answer it he'd bloody well kill her. Jan was at the dressing table, combing her hair, ignoring the phone, but listening as he answered it.

It wasn't Kate, but Alan, who said without preamble, 'I tried your office, but I guess you're going through those figures I sent.'

Peter nodded, running his hand through his hair. Come on, for God's sake. He checked the clock again. Kate could be trying to get through. 'Make it sharp, Alan, I've got to run in a minute.'

Bloody hell, Jan was standing at the window. Penny could be back by now. Alan said, 'You're taking it calmly.'

'Don't I always, and why not? I've got it covered.' Peter had moved to the window and was putting his arm around Jan's waist, pulling her to him as though he wanted one more snog, backing to the bed as Alan talked, trying to ignore the knot of tension that had gripped him, the tension that had given him a headache when he'd received the figures.

'Look, I'll get back to you, OK.'

After he and Jan had remade the bed with clean sheets he bunged the others in the washing machine, but it was she who got it going. These things were just a mystery to him. He could tell she liked being in Kate's kitchen, but already he was hastening her out of the door, checking quickly that there was still no sign of life from next door. There was none.

He turned off the security light, hurried Jan into the car and backed out quickly. She slid her hand on to his thigh. 'You still haven't said if you can get away for a break next week. I

192

thought we could get a last-minute deal?'

He roared off, heading to the car park where they had left her car. God almighty, the last thing on his mind was a holiday when Alan was panicking yet again about the debts, because on top of everything he really had had to make good his pension contributions.

He shut out Jan's voice as he changed down for the long rising bend, trying to get things sorted in his mind, but why did the guy go over and over things the way he did?

OK, he'd spent out a bit too much on Jan, and then there was Marjorie, who had been good while she lasted, but anyway, if that last bet had paid off . . . Well, he didn't want to think about the ten thousand he'd dropped. He must have been drunk.

He loosened his tie, and undid his top button. Hell, come April they'd have income from the lets, and then in October they'd be up and running, and what a bloody blessing the McTravers debacle had been. Camping without heat, light or hot water would jaundice anyone against a property, and it was bloody nonsense for Alan to be throwing up the possibility of Kate not wanting to sell when the time came. Besides, did he think Peter Maxwell wouldn't already have covered that remote possibility?

After he had been through it a couple of times he felt calm, and in control again, until, abruptly, panic snatched at him. Where had he put Alan's figures? Christ, not still in the kitchen? He relaxed. No, in his study, top drawer, now locked.

But he'd have to tell the silly prat to stop sending his little missives. OK, it was only to cover himself, and show that he had warned Peter of the worst-case scenario, but increasingly it appeared that he had no balls and that wasn't what anyone needed in an accountant. He eased himself in his seat. Jan was still prattling on about Tenerife but he let it run over him. Peter's father had always said as much about Alan and he'd been right.

Suddenly Peter was drenched with a longing for his father. God, he missed him. He'd always been there to talk to, someone who had pointed out the pros and cons, and possible alternatives. So calm, so together. He'd handled his life just as Peter wanted to handle his.

And the women! But they'd never seemed to hassle him as Jan was doing. Or had they? Perhaps his father had hidden that from him, not wanting to worry him. Peter's eyes filled. His father would never have lost his marbles like his mother, and roared all over the country making a damned fool of himself and spending more than he should, or influencing his daughter-in-law into the bargain. What's more he'd never have diverted the family assets, never have asked the impossible from him. He found he was clenching the steering wheel, cold sweat running down the centre of his back. Jan was saying, 'We could go to Tenerife, it's always warm.'

He wanted to yell at her to shut the hell up but instead he made himself concentrate on changing gear, finding a gap at the roundabout, accelerating into it and then out on to the straight. By the time they drew into the car park he was back in control, mentally flicking through his diary, working out what meetings could be moved to make a week away possible, a week in which he could do the groundwork, as he was sure his father would have done.

Outside it was sheeting down, and the wind was almost rocking the car as he said, 'You've talked me into it. See what you can drum up on Ceefax.'

Jan was staring as though she couldn't believe her ears, then she threw herself at him. 'I love you, Peter, so much.'

He held her. 'I love you more than you can know,' he replied, smelling the shampoo on her hair, but thinking of Alan's wail of protest when the Canary Isles entered the equation. 'A necessary expense, a back-up, an alternative to Plan A,' he'd say, but no more than that.

CHAPTER TWENTY-ONE

By eleven on Wednesday the skies had cleared and Kate, standing at the very top of the stepladder and stencilling at the apex of the rafters, paused, blowing her hair upwards, easing her shoulders. It was so warm with the heaters, so gloriously warm, and for one mad moment she wanted to sing along with Radio Two, which was churning out Roy Orbison.

As Isaac passed through the rafter-dome he said, 'I really liked this guy. Did a fair bit of smooching to him around Glastonbury.'

Well, so had she, come to that, but her smooching had been in Camberley where she had lived, pre-Peter but post parental divorce, after twenty-five years of marriage. She and her mother had lived in a tiny flat. It was a shifting, uncertain time with ghastly visits from her father, drink sodden and confused, and terribly vulnerable. 'Marry a man who is in control of himself,' her mother had said. 'One who is focused and knows where he is going.'

It was her parents that Peter had made a point of blaming for her lack of trust when the hotel fiasco had occurred. But as Barbs had said, Peter was in the habit of making a great many points. She laughed, overreached, and quickly steadied herself against the wall. Isaac's voice broke through, 'I'll hang on to the ladder while you finish that bit. You really are taking a bit of a chance.' Looking down she saw that he was holding it. Thank God she wasn't wearing a skirt.

She moved the stencil along, pressing home the sticky tape, dipping first one brush and then the other into the soft green and blue paint cans hung over her arm like some weird twin handbag, then along again until she had to climb down the ladder and wait while Isaac moved it, as he insisted on doing. Then it was back up again, and how much easier everything seemed without layers of clothes.

Heat, how had she survived without it? She sang along with Chris Rea as she peeled off the final ridge stencil and began to work downwards. 'It's OK now, Isaac, and I really can move the ladder myself.' She peered over her arm, catching sight of the river as she did so. Although the sky was grey the light was catching the varnished decks of a yacht sailing out to sea. For a moment she watched, absorbing the sense of gleaming light.

'You all right?' Isaac called, still gripping the ladder, his head back, watching her. He had a blob of her paint on his hair. How could she mention that little fact?

'Fine, but you're not. I've anointed you but presumably you'll see that as auspicious, as I'm working on the east wall.'

His hand flashed to his hair, finding the paint. He examined his fingers, then laughed up at her. 'I shall consider myself blessed.' For a moment the Dive Master was there, an unsettling flash, but the next the ladder was wobbling as she ventured down.

She gestured him away. 'Well, go and feel blessed putting that other storage heater up.'

He salaamed her, and made his way to the door. She moved to the window and followed the yacht as it tacked to the mouth of the river. 'You know,' she said, 'we could save more money by ditching the idea of carpeting, and sand and varnish the floor instead. What's more it would look really good, sort of appropriate, especially overlooking the river, *and* with the platform bed; a ship's bridge effect.' The cans of paint were dragging on her arm and she rested them on the window ledge. 'The boards are perfectly good but we'd need to fill the cracks.'

There was silence from Isaac and for a moment she thought he had gone, but looking up she saw that he was watching the yacht, a thoughtful expression on his face. Was he wishing he was aboard? She moved the ladder so that it was at a better angle to the sloping wall, before retrieving the paint, but Isaac still stood.

No one else she knew could be so still. It was as though he merged with his surroundings, as though he just relaxed into them. Just watching made her feel quieter, somehow.

As she climbed back up the ladder he turned away from the window and in his turn, examined the floor. 'Varnish is a killer, slippery. Some Hooray Henry even varnished his hatch covers

196

before inviting several of us on board, and it darn well hurt. Mark you, it could have been a carefully laid plot.' He winced at the memory.

She stuck the stencil in place, annoyed. She hadn't asked for his opinion, had she? But he was still there, his hands on his hips, looking up at her, whistling silently. Hadn't he any work to do? She painted, conscious all the time that he was there. Eventually he said, 'The alternative is to varnish the areas that will be safely covered by furniture and paint a design on the floor . . .'

'Oh God, not some weird Feng Shui protection?'

He laughed, a great roaring laugh, and she knew that if she looked down he would still be standing with his hands on his hips, and his face would be alive. She painted on. 'No, you've an Art Deco theme, follow that. I can get hold of some non-slip paint that I use for Molly's decks, or if you don't like the colours we can mix some sand into a colour of your choice. We could pick up some rugs from the auction and you can go off into the night, safe in the knowledge that you are not going to be sued for a broken ankle.' The last little bit he had said as a sort of chant as he made for the door, leaving her to think it through.

She painted on grimly, moving the ladder every so often, but all the time the idea was growing, and a design was forming, and he was right. To be sued was not the idea of this at all. She grinned at the thought of Peter's face if she was served with any such papers.

They took their sandwiches with them on their lunchtime walk, sitting on a rock to eat them, using an old hawthorn tree, gnarled and bent by the wind, as a shelter. Kate was worried about the noise of bare boards for the Glovers. 'No problem,' Isaac assured her. 'When the Glovers moved in they insulated their ceilings.'

'Are you sure?'

He munched his crust. 'Quite. I asked them.'

She wrapped up her crumbs in the cling film and put it in her pocket. 'But we'd have to hire a sander, and think of the dust, when I've just decorated, and there are the heaters.'

Isaac slapped his hands together before wiping them on his handkerchief. He got to his feet, shaking his trousers free of

197

crumbs. 'The cost of hire, plus paint and varnish, is still much cheaper than the cost of carpet and underlay and so on. We can cover the heater and seal your beautiful walls. Joe's got loads of polythene.'

Isaac was leading the way back. Kate followed, glad that he was taking the brunt of the wind. She smiled. 'Of course he has.'

Isaac grinned in return. 'We can pick the sander up tomorrow in Joe's van, but those sanders are heavy varmints to use, they have a habit of running away with you.'

'Life does,' she agreed.

The wind was dragging at their coats again. Above a seagull was wheeling and dipping. Ahead of her, Isaac stopped, looking suddenly tired. 'Too true.'

She was alongside him now. Above the gull called, then seemed to stall, as though beaten to a standstill by the force of the wind. Isaac moved on, silent. She kept pace. 'My mother-in-law died. She left me the money to buy Journey's End, to give me thinking time. I'm just so sorry . . .'

His hand was on her arm, though neither slowed. 'Look, I've told you I don't mind. You have no idea how good it feels just to be working on it. There's a sort of balance to it. The money I'm earning is going towards the next trip, and I'm earning the money by sorting out the house. Don't you see the symmetry, the payment of dues?'

She supposed she did, but why had she mentioned Barbs? Now it was all back, rushing at her as though carried by this damned wind, all the darkness, all the sadness, when it had seemed to be leaving her in peace at last.

He said, as they re-entered Fowey, 'I almost died once. A freak wave flipped Molly over, I kept going down. Stupid, didn't have my line on. Well, I fought, of course, but when it seemed hopeless I had no desire to hang on. There was just a calm, easy acceptance, almost a welcoming of death. I suppose it gave me an acceptance of everything, a respect for everything . . .'

Her voice was harsh as she interrupted him. 'I nursed my mother-in-law, it's my job. I . . .'

She stopped. Into the silence as they left the esplanade Isaac said softly, 'So, you really are the lady with the lamp?'

'Not any more.' Her voice was crisp. 'I'm a painter and decorator.' She could hear the bitterness. It was ugly.

She closed her lips, increasing her speed, wanting to be alone, but he remained alongside, and his voice was heavy with sympathy when he said, 'You must have felt so helpless.'

'I *was* helpless. No feel about it.' Her voice wasn't harsh any more, it was fractured, weak.

He touched her arm, 'I'm so sorry.'

She shrugged away from him.

That night she prepared for bed, sliding into her sleeping bag, forgetting to be grateful that it felt dry and warm, braced instead for a return to the weight of Barbs in her arms, the feel of the capsules, the sound of Peter's refusal, his expectation of her involvement, the roaring seas, the terrible, endless awfulness of it all.

At dawn, though, she woke laughing, and her night had been full of Barbs, but a different Barbs, one that had walked with Kate and the children, one that had swung her handbag at the geese who had charged at them out of a farmyard without once missing a beat of the anecdote she was telling. It was a handbag that had turned into a can of paint, a farmyard that had become the rafter-dome, but above it all had been the sound of their laughter.

At eight thirty Isaac hooted. She hurried down and out, slamming the front door behind her. He was waiting in Joe's van, and the frown line that was between his eyes eased and disappeared as she chatted. She led the way into the hire shop and did a discount deal, and wondered how this sort of thing could ever have made her nervous.

Together they carried the sander into the back of the van. Together they carried it up the stairs when they arrived back at Journey's End, but it was to be her job, she announced to Isaac. He seemed about to argue, but then said nothing, just smiled before dashing down ahead of her to the van which he'd left with its engine running, nicely blocking the road.

Whilst he toted up a huge roll of polythene into the rafter-dome she delivered the van to the car park to save taking it back just yet via the one-way system. When she returned he was scampering up and down the ladder, which she held this time, until both walls were sealed with polythene. It was polythene which smelt like a groundsheet, and musty summer days were brought flooding back, days spent on camping holidays as a student nurse, with pre-Peter friends, days she had forgotten. Long, endless days of burgeoning confidence, lecture notes, and exuberant fun.

She opened the windows wide, and checked that the filling between the boards she had done last night was smooth and firm. She plugged in the sander, expecting him to give instructions; to offer to do it for her; to at least stand and witness her mistakes. He merely handed her goggles, ear protectors and mask, with the warning, 'Keep it moving or it'll sand you through to the Glovers' flat, or even Australia. If you've had enough, give me a yell. I'm finishing the storage heaters and starting on the bunk beds.'

With that he was off. She shut all the doors before switching on. For a moment she thought her arms were being wrenched from their sockets as it skidded away from her with a loud screeching roar she could hear through the protectors. She fought, using just her arms. It wasn't enough and she almost overbalanced. Panicked, she switched off, panting, braced to tell Isaac everything was all right when he asked what the hell was going on. He didn't.

She began again and this time she used her body as a counterweight. Slowly she came to terms with it. Slowly she took control, keeping it moving, but not too fast, not too slow, slowly she adjusted to the noise, and the sawdust, and her sweat beneath the mask, and the ache in her shoulders, and the vibration in her hands which went up her arms to the roof of her mouth.

By lunchtime her goggles were plastered with dust, her hair was thick with it, her clothes disguised by it, but half the floor was done, and there were no great dips, just a few minor ones.

She switched off, removed her ear protectors, her goggles, the mask. The relief was glorious and Isaac's knock when it came seemed far away, though his nod of approval was only to be expected, she told him, through the haze of dust. He laughed, then coughed. Holding the back of his hand to his mouth, squinting, he said, 'Come on, fresh air.'

They walked briskly, and neither talked. They stopped at the same boulder, sheltered behind the same hawthorn. Was that the same seagull, she wondered? Isaac wouldn't let her throw him her crust. 'You'll encourage him to pester.'

She ate it instead, but still she felt hungry. Gradually her ears were clearing. She held her nose and blew. He said, 'Diving gets me the same way.'

'Diving. Would skydiving?' she asked, and couldn't understand herself. Why bring it up? Why rake it over?

He shrugged. 'Don't know, my world's down there.' He gestured to the sea which was almost as blue as his eyes today. Beside her he shifted his weight, pointing to the gull. 'Ask him,' he laughed.

She stared up at the gull, and the clouds galloping behind, and heard herself say, 'Barbs skydived. She had a list of things she wanted to do before she died. She did most of them. She was seventy when she did it.' Yes, she could hear herself saying these things, but why the hell was she doing so? Now she was sweeping on, and it was as though she was jumping off a diving board into a pool, and the words were rushing out of her as though released from a dam. 'And she white-water rafted, and abseiled. And wore purple.' She recited 'Warning', standing up, shouting it at the gull. It seemed very quiet when she had finished and she wondered if she had gone quite mad, but it was as though she had suddenly wanted the world to know how wonderful that woman had been. How totally, utterly wonderful.

Isaac was still sitting on the boulder, just watching her. 'What's left on the list?' It was as though he really wanted to know, as though nothing bizarre had just happened, as though she had just done something extremely normal.

'Yellowstone Park.' This time it was she watching him closely. He nodded. '*You* won't need a cloak. *You* can just go.'

A cloak, what was he talking about? He was sitting back crossing his arms, smiling quietly. She thought for a long moment. Of course she could just go. She'd use the income from the flat. Of course she could. She had the whole of the summer. Somehow that had eluded her, somehow the future had disappeared.

The gull was wheeling lower and lower. She watched it as she'd watched Barbs, but it didn't come to earth as Barbs had, softly cushioned by the skydiving master. She turned to tell

Isaac. He was still watching her. Something moved inside her.

She looked away quickly. He said, 'The adrenaline rush from the sander has gone, and it's time we got back.' He checked his watch. 'We don't want to pay for another day's hire, do we?'

He joined her on the path. They walked together. She said, 'You can have longer. You haven't had your hour.'

He shook his head, 'No time today, other priorities. So, you see, you've rubbed off on me.'

This hung in the air.

Isaac took a turn sanding, until three, when she took over. Later on he came back to Journey's End to collect the sander in order to return it, and left Joe's Dyson vacuum cleaner. That evening she finished the edges with her Black and Decker before vacuuming up the dust, and creeping downstairs into the small bedroom where she had set up her camp bed. All around were sawn two by two lengths of wood, sawn slats, Isaac's bag of screws. In the corner heaped one on top of the other were partly sanded down chests of drawers they'd bought at auction.

She slept soundly, and the smell of wood was the only reason that she dreamed of navy sweaters dusted with sawdust, and skydive masters who cushioned her fall.

They spent the first hour of the next day drawing her floor design on graph paper, and she decided that she would incorporate the lines of the platform bed design. She then watched as Isaac measured up the room and transferred the design to the floor, helping once she understood his method. They worked through lunch by tacit agreement, talking little, and today there was a distance between them, a careful courtesy, and it was amazing how much time they gained. Perhaps she wouldn't walk again. It seemed sensible.

Isaac disappeared at two to collect some varnish and paint from the store that kept Molly sparkling and bright. He'd get a better deal if he went alone, he explained. She was relieved and sandpapered the furniture in the small bedroom, rubbing it down until her hands ached, trying to imagine how it would look with the cut-outs glued and pinned to the front, and picked out in the bold turquoise they had talked of. This was to mirror the bold curving turquoise of the bottom half of the wall.

At his knock she let him in and reached for the varnish, fumbling with the metal handle as he tried to detach himself. They laughed, their fingers entangled. She was a fool. He let her lead the way up the stairs.

They vacuumed again, then went over the floor on their knees, with a damp cloth, each taking one side, meeting in the middle. She backed to the landing, peering along the surface of the floor from the doorway. It was as free of bits as they were going to get it.

Isaac was backing towards her in his turn. She moved to one side. He rose, handing her his cloth. 'I'll get on with the bunks. OK?'

He didn't wait for an answer, but walked in that silent way of his to the stairs. The windows were wide open in the rafter-dome, the sun was out. The floor was quite dry in half an hour. She took the can of varnish, poured some on to her cloth and starting stroking the varnish on to the boards, backing away from the door, using even, steady sweeps, working quickly, her rubber gloves taking the brunt, her fingers sticking to one another.

She accommodated the area to be painted, and ran the varnish up to the skirting boards, backing, backing until she reached the window. Only then, when she was trapped, did she realise what she had done.

'Oh bugger.' She scratched her head, marooned on her island of bare boards. The varnish stuck her hair to her fingers. 'Oh damn.' Somewhere she could hear a phone ringing. It was hers. It was in the downstairs bedroom. Isaac would bring it. 'Oh bloody hell.' She crouched, the cloth in her hand, the metal can at her side, waiting for his inevitable arrival, her inevitable discovery. There was a knock, the sound of the phone ringing, louder now, a tentative call. 'I've got your phone for you. Can I open the door?'

'Why not?' she said. 'There's no chance you'll get in my way.'

The handle turned, the door opened. Isaac stood there looking at her, then at the expanse of varnish that led to her. The phone was still ringing. He held it out to her, quite serious, horribly serious, ferociously serious.

'Answer it for me,' she snapped. 'Tell whoever it is, I'm tied up, and I'll phone back.' But please let it not be Peter, she prayed.

He pressed the button. 'Hello.' There was a pause. He said, 'Yes, you have the right number. Mrs Maxwell is rather tied up at the moment. She can't quite get to the phone.' He was starting to laugh.

For God's sake.

He tried again. 'She's asked me to tell you she'll phone back, when she's free.' He was laughing again, his hand over the mouthpiece, looking at her helplessly, holding out the phone, then putting it to his ear again, nodding.

How the hell could you hear a nod, but she could feel her own laughter coming, and now it was here, exploding out of her, and she threw her hands in the air, and just walked across the varnish. Taking the phone from him, she walked into the hall, and heard Stuart Duncan's voice saying, 'Hello, hello.'

It was always hard to get reception in Fowey and today was no exception. 'It's me, Stuart. I was a little tied up.' She heard Isaac laughing again and tried not to herself.

Stuart wanted her to stand in for Jan. Apparently she had had to change her leave date at the last minute to take advantage of a good holiday offer on Ceefax, and as she had been a bit out of sorts lately the practice wanted to let her go, if they possibly could. The flight was tomorrow, but a bank nurse wasn't available until Wednesday. 'Any chance of you covering until then?'

Suddenly there was nothing funny any more. Wednesday? But they were due to start the bathroom on Monday, and how could Isaac if she wasn't here? It was the middle of February already, the schedule . . .

He said, 'Oh go on, I'll suck your toes, I'll buy you Milk Tray . . .'

'Calm down,' she said, smiling reluctantly.

'Please, for me. I'd really like to work with you again.'

The line was so bad as to be almost incomprehensible. Her mind raced. It would be extra dosh, and Jan wouldn't be there, and nice Mrs Murphy would, and the others, and anyway, it would mean she could pay Isaac something towards the platform bed without dipping into the renovation money.

'Please,' he repeated. 'I'll never call you an old tart again. There, what can I say to better that?'

And anyway, Peter would be pleased if she was keeping her hand in at the surgery. It'd make him less annoyed when he realised that she'd diverted from his schedule, altered the plans . . . But she didn't want to think of that. 'OK, but never calling me an old tart again isn't enough. I shall expect you to approach at all times on bended knees. When do I start?'

'Tomorrow morning's emergency surgery at the latest, tonight's at the earliest. Bollocks to the bended knees.'

'Fine. Tonight then.'

'I owe you.'

'You most certainly do. Big time, double time, in fact.' He laughed. She said, 'I mean it.'

He was surprised. So was she.

He agreed. She felt satisfied, powerful as she switched him off.

Isaac was working his way backwards towards the door as he stroked out her footprints. For a moment she watched, then checked her watch, running downstairs to the study/bedroom, stepping over the wood lengths, throwing her stuff into her grip before emerging and calling up the stairs. 'I've got to go. I won't be back until Wednesday so Molly's in for a treat.'

There was a silence, then Isaac emerged, a rag in one hand. He peered over the banisters. 'Wednesday?'

She raised her eyebrows. 'I'm doing my lady of the lamp bit.' When he didn't understand she explained the situation.

He sighed. 'Hell, that's a shame. It'll put us right back. It'll be the end of next week before your masterpiece of a rafter-dome is finished, and there's the bathroom . . . Oh well, can't be helped, but on the other hand . . .' He stopped.

She moved from foot to foot, checking her watch, her mind keeping up with his. She chewed her lip. Isaac interrupted her, 'I could always . . .' He stopped. 'Perhaps not.'

'What are you thinking?'

She wanted to go, before he presented her with the answer that they both knew was the only solution to keeping on schedule, but it was one she didn't want to hear.

'Go on, we don't want you in a pile by the side of the road.' He was turning away.

She picked up her bag, then hesitated. He was running his hand through his hair, and so now he'd have tangles too.

He turned back to her. 'It's just that if you're not here, I could turn the water off and blast through, and finish the bathroom completely, and maybe even put us ahead of schedule.'

She knew it would, and that she was more likely to be able to present Peter with a fait accompli, one that came in within budget, one that would reduce his reaction. But she'd have to leave a key. It meant he'd be alone in the house, like McTravers, it'd mean ... Well, what would it mean? He wasn't McTravers, was he?

He was calling down to her. 'Go on, I'll work on Molly as much as I can this weekend, then I can put in a bit of extra time when you get down. Maybe we can drag Joe in on it. Hang on, I'll just grab my tools.' He groaned. 'Damn, they're in the kitchen. Oh hell. Never mind, I can borrow what I need from Joe.' He was whistling as he half ran down the stairs, wiping his hands with the cloth.

He darted behind her, tidied the wood lengths and emerged with his waterproof. He held the door open for her. As she went through, he said, 'Drive carefully.' There was no irritation, no pressure from him, nothing that made her stomach knot and made her feel as though she should have done something else.

He shut the door behind them, smiled at her, and headed towards Joe's. For a moment she watched, then, her mind made up, she groped in her bag. She wavered again. He was already thirty yards down the road, still whistling. But of course he wouldn't walk away. Joe wouldn't let him, and after all, the Glovers had recommended him. And why not let him be alone in her house – what was she worried about?

She called, 'Isaac, for heaven's sake come back and take the key, then you can get your tools when the floor's dry. If you feel like it you might finish the non-slip painting, or maybe get on with the bathroom, but don't wear yourself out, and make sure you note your hours down.'

He was trotting back, his coat swinging. He reached her, took the key. 'Are you sure?'

No, she wasn't. 'If I'm getting double time, so should you,

for Saturday and Sunday anyway. I have to go,' she said, turning away from him and running for the car in case she changed her mind. And if he wasn't here when she returned she'd find someone else, and change the locks. There, all quite simple, really.

CHAPTER TWENTY-TWO

Kate drove into the Old Vicarage drive too fast, but she had cut it very fine and she left the engine running as she dashed into the house, and up the stairs, into the bathroom for a quick wash, into the bedroom for a quick change into her uniform. She had filled out and it fitted again. She twirled in front of the mirror. In fact she had curves. She blessed the ladder, the walks, the sandwiches, whatever had wrought the miracle, then dashed back down the stairs, out to the humming car.

Penny's lights were on. She checked her watch. Five thirty. Soon Bertie would be on early evening *leylandii* patrol. She backed into the street. She had left the sitting room lights on, which would bug Peter but it would welcome her back after surgery.

The Medical Centre car park was filling but Jan's place was almost more sacrosanct than the doctors' so there was no problem there. As she locked her car she checked to see who, besides Stuart, was on duty. Sydney and Claire. That was nice. She liked them. She dropped her keys into her bag, then wished she hadn't. She must, simply must, remember to use the side pocket or she'd spend her life groping about as she had done this afternoon.

She was walking to the entrance, and knew that she was filling her head with trivia, because she didn't want to be here. She didn't want to have to cope, not just with the patients, but with herself. Damn Stuart. Damn Jan and Ceefax. Where had she gone, anyway? She snatched a quick look at the sky. Well, somewhere where the sun shone, that was for sure. Kate was glad she wouldn't have to witness 'the tan', glad that by then she'd be back in her jeans, smelling of varnish, or sawdust, trying to put this and the memories she feared it would regurgitate back where they belonged.

Arranging her smile, she pushed open the glass door into the

208

already crowded waiting room. She had forgotten the stuffy smell, the buzz of conversation, the hushed cries of the children as they grew restless in the Wendy house.

Mrs Murphy was there, opposite the doctors' board which buzzed and flashed for the next patient. The nurses still didn't have one? Good, Jan had been blocked on that then. She saw Mrs Beard, who waved, as did Mrs Murphy. Kate's smile was genuine now.

Brenda the receptionist winked and grinned, holding out a stack of patients' notes, almost miming, à la Les Dawson, 'Great to see you. Catch up over coffee when bedlam is ended.' Was her boy still driving her mad with his monosyllabic fourteen-year-old grunts? Brenda's hair had changed to a deep auburn frizz. How life went on.

Stuart buzzed. Mrs Beard was up off the blocks and hooking her number over the wrought-iron peg in one easy, practised movement. One day she really would have something wrong with her. Would she be delighted or dismayed?

Kate followed her down the corridor as far as the nurses' clinic. She opened the door, bracing herself, then entered, clutching the notes far too tightly. For a moment she stood, trying to get the breath deep into her lungs, ready to push away whatever came. But nothing did.

She looked around at the disposable packets of everything, the glinting, impersonal cleanliness. The room had been decorated, but it didn't smell like Journey's End, just of antiseptic, and it seemed smaller, unthreatening, irrelevant. She dropped the notes on to the examining couch and peeled off her coat, anxious to start, anxious to leave, just as she had done before Barbs. She waited. Barbs. She said it aloud. Barbs. There. Still nothing.

Still nothing as Mrs Murphy came in, her hem sagging, her coat smelling of bonfires, her legs still ulcerating but according to the notes this was now due in the main to hardening of the arteries. Kate dressed her leg, chatting easily, touching her shoulder when she was finished, listening to that tired, uncomplaining voice telling her of Dr Duncan's kindness in getting her to a specialist, of the tests they were going to do, of the long words which she didn't understand.

Quietly Kate explained the procedures, repeating them a

second and third time until she was sure that Mrs Murphy understood. Only then did she see her to the waiting room, and pick up the next patient.

Still nothing by the end of surgery, just a job well done, a coffee with the staff, a quick word about Mrs Murphy with Stuart Duncan as they walked to their cars. He held her door open as he used to, looking at her intently, saying, 'You look so well, better than I've seen you, ever, I think. You're strong, sharp, and I'm poorer, but it's bloody brilliant to have you back. Just like old times.'

'It's great to be back.' But it wasn't. It was just a job. One she had left. One she didn't want to return to. One that didn't interest her any more. It was as simple as that.

She drove home. Peter's car still wasn't in the drive. Penny's lights were on, and she hooted to let her know she was back. They'd arranged supper tomorrow night, just the four of them. Penny wanted to be brought up to speed on Journey's End. Kate put the car in the garage and let herself in through the kitchen door. She could do with being brought up to speed herself and wished she had left the mobile with Isaac, then she could contact him, get an update. But a mobile proved nothing.

She dropped her bag on to the table, staring at the clock. She ran the tap, filled a pint glass, drank it, all of it. She wanted a walk to blow away the surgery, but there was no brisk sea breeze to do that here. She leaned against the sink. There was just the ticking of the central heating timer, not even Bertie barking in the distance.

Restlessly she cleaned the sink, and the draining board, though there was no need because Mrs Anderson had been here before her. She checked the sitting room, the dining room. There were newspapers neatly folded on the table, unread. So, was he still away? She'd thought he was due back on Thursday evening.

She checked the mail, the answering machine and there he was, in Sweden still, but bound for Czechoslovakia where he had a meeting set up for first thing Monday, and a million others for the rest of the week, and maybe the week after. He'd phone her on her mobile. He'd tried earlier, but she was engaged.

She made herself cheese on toast and watched the television, but the chair seemed too soft, the gardening show boring – but that was crazy, because Titchmarsh was her hero. She flicked through the newspaper. She phoned Penny, putting off supper tomorrow. 'Peter's held up. Come for lunch instead?'

'No, you must still come to supper here.'

She was in bed by ten, but tossed and turned because it hadn't been just the chair that was too soft. She woke when Wallace suggested to Gromit that they see what was on the radio. She stared at the ceiling, wondering where she was, listening for the gulls, the wind, the river. But she wasn't at Journey's End.

It seemed stuffy. She rolled over, staring at the floral curtains, the soft, restrained, cosy decor. She showered, made a quick coffee and headed out to the Medical Centre for the Saturday morning emergency surgery. Rather than go home afterwards she went into town, cruising the clothes shops, but there was nothing. She drove into Crewkerne and tried the antique shops, then drove towards Beaminster. At Drimpton Antiques she bought an Art Deco inkwell; clear glass with a black lid.

She phoned Penny. 'I'm off to Branscombe. Does the vicar feel like sandwiches and an afternoon off?'

The vicar did, and what's more she made the sandwiches while Kate drove home and picked her up. As they headed for Branscombe, Kate heard about parish business and the hapless church warden who had pleaded compassionate visiting as an excuse for parking on a single yellow line. It had not been successful and the church warden's language had been inappropriate, and had continued to be so all week.

At Branscombe the café was shut and Penny grizzled about the lack of a coffee, but Kate merely pulled up the collar of her coat and set off up the hill, enjoying the pull in her legs and the wind which buffeted them until they reached the shelter of the woods. Now Penny fell silent, and it was Kate who said, 'In the spring the violets will come again. Life goes on.'

Penny tucked her arm in hers. 'Dearest Kate.'

Kate smiled. 'Race you to the top.'

She ran up the shallow steps which had been cut through the woods, then left at the top, on into the open where the wind caught her, fought her, tearing at her hair and coat. She turned her back to it, waiting for Penny to join her which she did eventually, wheezing, bent over, groaning and grouching, eventually straightening and shaking her head. 'You're too fit. You're too well. It's a disgrace and I'm so glad I could kiss you.'

With that, she did, and together they stood at the top of the cliff, shading their eyes from the wind, staring out across the sea, both talking of Barbs, all of Barbs; the good, the bad, and the ugly, as Kate said.

That evening Kate changed into cream trousers and a silk blouse and tried the Art Deco inkwell in the dining room, the sitting room, the hall, the bedroom, but finally had to admit that it suited nowhere. She wrapped it in tissue paper and then in her washed and dried jeans before putting it in her grip. She'd put it on the Art Deco cabinet they'd bought at that first sale, and as it was black it would look good, and bring success, and . . . She shook her head. God almighty, she was getting as bad as him.

She checked her watch. Should she ring Joe? He'd know how things were going. But would it seem like checking up? Even as she was thinking the phone rang. It was Peter. The connection was bad, but good enough. 'Who's with you?' she asked.

She heard the impatience in his reply, but she hadn't meant that. He said, 'No one, and if you think it's fun sitting in a hotel room which is just . . .'

She'd heard it a million times before and this time her impatience matched his. She cut in, 'I just wondered how work was going?'

'Fine, how's yours? It must be strange being back.'

She rubbed her forehead. How did he know? She said slowly, 'Back?'

His voice was stronger now, as the line cleared. 'Back? At home, after all the camping, and finding an empty house.'

She shook her head, exasperated that she was back to jumping at shadows. 'Well, it's stranger than that. I'm working at the surgery.'

'You're what?' His surprise was loud and clear.

212

She explained and could almost hear his cogs turning over. 'So,' he said slowly. 'How are you?'

'Fine, absolutely fine.' Her voice was brisk, already irritated because she knew his next comment would be one of relief.

Instead he said, quietly, 'It's your well-being I'm concerned about, you must remember that.'

She did remember it, all through supper with Tom and Penny, all through the coffee afterwards and the laughter and the questions about the rafter-dome, and her replies which were of necessity vague and brief, because Penny might discuss it with Peter before she could. And she didn't want to bring on a case of apoplexy until it was finished.

Tom walked her to her door, kissing her cheek in the bright harshness of the security light. 'It's a shame you'll never live at Journey's End, because I think it's found a place in your life, and that would have pleased Barbs.'

Kate smiled, because she had covered that one. 'There are the winter periods.'

Tom patted her arm, took her key and unlocked the door for her. 'I thought Peter said you were going to target writers, artists, photographers, that sort of thing, out of season.'

'I can keep some dates free. I *will* keep some free. I haven't worked this hard to turn it over to other people completely. You should see the river, Tom. The town, the sea, the narrow streets, the life, even in winter, and the walks.'

Tom was laughing. 'Yes, I think we heard a bit about its astounding merits over the pizza. I'm assuming you'll let us have a discounted week.'

'Assumptions are a mistake,' she said, stepping into the hall. Again he laughed. The answer machine was blinking. She dumped her handbag next to the phone, her finger poised over the play button. She looked at Tom. 'Twenty per cent, and that's the best you'll get out of me. Now go home to the parson and confess your penny-pinching ways.'

Tom closed the door. There were two messages. One was from Isaac with a progress report. He hated machines and this was clear from his awkward, brief message. 'Isaac to Mrs Maxwell. I'm on target. The house is safe. No water where it shouldn't be. Alfie's got hold of a cheap new kettle, toaster, that sort of thing if you want them. That's it, then. Er, goodbye.'

She smiled. It was nice to know that sometimes the laid-back self-possession could be thrown.

Simon had also phoned. She rang him back. They talked about her stint at the surgery and about Journey's End. Simon said, 'Changing the schedule? What's this, rebellion in the camp? Go for it, Mum.'

'It's just a response to the situation as it's unfolded. It just happened.' She couldn't quite remember how, after the wine she had drunk tonight.

'It's too late for him to alter things now anyway, if you're going to hit the season, especially if he's up to his neck in meetings abroad.'

She played with the address book. He really was right, and she found herself smiling. 'And thanks for your drill, couldn't have done without it.' She told him of varnishing herself into a corner, of Alfie's offer of a kettle, and toaster, of his Aladdin's cave.

'Off the back of a lorry?'

'Who knows?'

'On second thoughts, don't try and find out.' Simon laughed.

'I won't.'

'You'll buy them then?'

'And an iron.'

'So the next attachment you'll need is a file, for sawing through the bars.'

They were both laughing as he signed off.

Sunday seemed to drag in spite of going to church and listening to the sermon, the bare bones of which Penny had run past her on the way back from Branscombe, and which centred on compassion. In the afternoon she walked for miles, but the fields seemed tame, the light wasn't the same and she regretted the next two days at the surgery.

She refused Penny's offer of a Sunday roast dinner, and Stuart Duncan's also. She couldn't settle, didn't want to have to perform, didn't want to ... She moved away from the phone. No, there was no need to phone Joe. Sunday evening was busy in the pub, and besides, Isaac was on target.

She tried to picture the rafter-dome floor, the bathroom with a new lavatory and basin. She checked her watch. She could drive down now, as Peter wasn't here. Why hadn't she thought of that earlier? She dashed for her keys, then stopped. How stupid – it would be almost midnight by the time she arrived. If she'd wanted to do that she should have gone yesterday, after morning surgery.

She paced the hall then flopped into an armchair, flicking on the television. Nothing. She picked up a paperback and put it down. She read the papers, nothing. She checked her watch. Only nine thirty. Should she phone Joe?

She was on her way to the hall when the phone rang. It was Jude. Kate had let her know that she would be home for a few days and had thought she might ring, but that once she found out that her father was absent it would be short and sweet.

But it wasn't, and soon Kate was joking abut Alfie's kettles, and Mrs Beard, and Stuart who had yet to suck her toes. They talked about Simon, about Penny, about Jude's essays, about Journey's End being on schedule, though Kate didn't explain whose schedule.

They talked briefly about the pressures of the business world today, but only briefly. For once they had a normal conversation and when her daughter said, 'I must go, take care, Mum,' Kate felt that university might be swinging a few changes.

She lingered by the phone. Her bag was still there containing Joe's number. It was still relatively early. Isaac would be there, and the bar not too busy. She could respond to his message, get an update. It wouldn't look like checking up.

She phoned. 'Hi, Joe.'

Joe recognised her voice immediately and was concerned. 'Kate, everything all right?' From the way he spoke she could tell that it had been a typically liquid Sunday evening.

'Fine.' But that had been the question she had wanted to ask him, or rather Isaac. She said, 'Is Isaac there?'

Joe sounded surprised. 'No way, he's still at the house. Floor's done. Right beauty it is, popped me head in this afternoon. It's going to be quite something, Kate, with the platform bed and all. Now the water's off and he's hard at the bathroom. I took him a few sarnies, and he's brewed up some soup on your little stove. That's all right, isn't it?' She heard him gulp his beer.

215

'Of course.'

'Be an idea to get a microwave off Alfie when he gets the cooker. Not for now, for later. Emmets like them, or tourists, to you.'

'Emmets will do,' she laughed. The floor was done. It looked good. Excitement gripped her. 'Do I want to know where Alfie gets these things?'

Joe guffawed. ' 'Spect they're sound enough.' It wasn't really an answer and they both knew it.

'So, when will he be back?'

'Who, Alfie?'

She shook her head. 'No, Isaac.'

'I don't think he will be, until the job's done. He wants it civilised for you, he's like that, though I think, meself, it's because he feels guilty.'

'Guilty? What the hell has he done? I thought everything was all right. He phoned and left a message saying there was no water where there shouldn't be.' Her voice was rising, all excitement forgotten. She *knew* she shouldn't have left him to it. It wasn't as though she didn't know what chaos-managing from a distance brought. Didn't she ever learn? And she had left her key . . .

'No, not like that. Guilty in himself, that's what he's working through, I think. Feels bad because Clara wanted him to sell up Molly to give them the wherewithal to get it straight together. He didn't love her enough for that, not nearly enough. He feels bad about Clara, bad about you struggling with the mess he left. He's embarrassed, and I know it's been worrying him, though he never looks as though he's got anything going on in that bonce of his.'

For a moment Kate was quiet, then she said, 'That's absurd, it's we who should feel that. Anyway, we bought it as seen.'

There was laughter in the background. Things were hotting up in the pub. She could picture Joe shrugging, and those great hands of his making the receiver look like a toy, and the pint glass a thimble. 'Ah well,' he said, and again he gulped. Now he'd be smacking his lips. 'It's swings and roundabouts, and the best thing is that you've given him the chance to see it as he always knew it could be, and he's grateful for that. He's a good man, you know. You should have met his mother. Crikey, good as gold, and fun. Why, I remember . . .'

He was on the way to being maudlin. Kate said quietly, 'Thanks, Joe. I'll be back on Wednesday. Tell him not to work too hard.'

Joe said. 'Oh? Oh right, but he won't charge double, don't you fret.'

That was not what she'd meant, but Joe was saying, 'Bye now, then.' The line went dead. It was not yet ten. Usually she'd still be stripping or sanding, rescheduling, filling cracks, standing at the window, watching the river, or trying to make out the cows in the meadow opposite, or making tea, drinking it from the plastic mug, daring herself to wash in the cold bathroom.

She dragged out the vacuum and worked for an hour, doing stuff that didn't need doing, then she tried to relax, but the restlessness wouldn't leave her, and it was only as she finally showered and sank into the bed that she admitted that she was missing *her* house, and wondering if Isaac really was as good and sensitive as he seemed and as Joe thought.

On Monday they were busy and Monica, the full-timer who had taken her place, spent some time trying to tell Kate how Jan organised this, that or the other, until Kate told her that for now, they'd do it Kate Maxwell's way. It couldn't be said that a friendly working relationship was the result but it certainly made for a surgery that ticked over efficiently until clocking off time had come and gone, taking Monica with it.

As Kate reached for her coat Stuart stuck his head around the door, 'I don't know whether this will cast you down, or lift you up, my dear Mrs Maxwell, but a bank nurse has appeared like a puff of smoke, and can take over tomorrow morning, if you wish.'

She wished. Stuart Duncan grinned. 'I'm sure that a discount on a week at Journey's End will be available for a dearly beloved colleague?'

'Twenty per cent, and don't tell Peter.'

He grinned, coming right into the room and kissing her. 'Can't wait. I feel I know it, every nook and cranny.'

'Have I been going on?'

'Absolutely, but I forgive Fowey everything, if it does for me

217

what it's done for you. Haven't seen such roses in cheeks for a long while.'

She drove home too fast. She flung clothes into her grip, and phoned Joe, warning him that she was on her way. 'Bloody hell,' he said. 'Don't think it's quite ready. That's a bummer, he wanted it all done.'

She told him she'd wait until the morning, and after that the evening didn't seem so bad.

CHAPTER TWENTY-THREE

'Tenerife can be relied upon for good weather, even in February, just as our company can be relied upon to give you a wonderful time. Cheers.' The package tour rep. waved a leaflet at them and raised her glass of sangria, even though it was only ten in the morning.

Peter shifted uncomfortably in his chair in the darkened bar which reminded him of an old tart without make-up. Jan squeezed his hand encouragingly, and leaned against him. She had found a wedding ring from somewhere. All around were tourists, some with children, all in summer gear. It was tasteless enough to have suited Barbs. He, of course, wore taupe slacks and a neutral short-sleeved shirt.

Again Peter glanced at Jan. Did she really enjoy this? Well, he wasn't used to it. Not to this Butlins fiasco, not to a crowded plane with his knees up round his bloody ears, and a trolley of drinks that took its time arriving, and wasn't free. She squeezed his hand again as the rep., her smile working overtime, extolled the virtues of a coach tour of the island. 'We could go on that,' Jan whispered excitedly.

We bloody well couldn't, he decided, not even to keep the relationship going for another – what was it? He mentally ticked the months off until October. But then again, surely he wouldn't need . . .

He sipped the sangria, unsurprised to find it mainly fruit juice. He'd already tossed the paper umbrella on to the marble-veneered table and wanted to follow suit with the orange peel, but didn't, hoping this wasn't the height of things to come for the next week, or maybe two. Automatically he patted his breast pocket. His credit card company had upped his limit but he hadn't shared that with Alan, who was edgy enough after that second acrimonious meeting with the bank manager.

Peter shifted again but with anger this time. What a damned

sanctimonious little jerk that Jackson was. 'That's all very well, Peter, but Journey's End is Mrs Maxwell's property, and unless we arrange it with her, we can't consider it as security for these mounting debts.' He'd even steepled his hands, for God's sake, and he couldn't have been much more than thirty; wet behind the ears, and far too bloody big for his boots.

Alan had taken his time coming in on that poncy remark, but once he'd finally launched into his spiel it sounded possible, all of it. It was only after, as Alan downed a double Scotch at the first pub they came to, that he gave an impression of a deflated balloon.

It wasn't just Peter's affairs that were worrying him, of course. He had a lot of clients who were sliding down various poles. 'That's what comes of living on credit, taking it to the hilt,' he'd said. But hell, if his oldest client and mate was keeping cool, covering all angles, it wasn't too much to ask that the professional did too.

Jan was nudging him enquiringly. What had he missed? He nodded and smiled. 'Great, I'll do this on my card.' Well, it was the line of least resistance and he must keep her sweet. Besides, she was up and weaving her way round the tables towards the rep., and those shorts she was wearing were certainly a pretty good shop window for her arse.

Later though, as they lay by the pool, Peter stayed firmly beneath the umbrella as she pointed out the route the coach would take in the guide she had bought at a small shop just outside the hotel. He smiled and nodded again, rubbing on more factor twenty-five. He had to keep the tanning down though he wasn't unduly fussed, since he'd tell Kate about the facilities expected of the best hotels, whether in Czecho-slovakia or Timbuktu. Surely even she had heard of sun beds. But, on second thoughts, maybe he'd better confirm that there was such a facility. He reached for his mobile, then relaxed. Kate wouldn't check, not again, ever.

He offered the tube of sun protection to Jan, wondering if he could smooth it over her breasts, here, in public. She swung round, sitting up, reaching forward to kiss him, her breasts touching his chest, her mouth open, her tongue brushing his lips, then sliding deep into his mouth, before withdrawing, leaving him breathless.

She sat, her elbows on her knees, assessing the result, and giggled. He wished she wouldn't.

She rolled over on to her front, saying, 'Please, darling, but use mine, not the sun block. After Stuart Duncan's remark about sex, sun and sangria, I want a really good tan.'

Peter squeezed factor twelve on to his palm and smoothed on the sun cream, spreading it out over her shoulder blades, bending and kissing the small of her back, feeling the tightening of her skin, seeing the clutch of her buttocks. He ran his hands down the backs of her thighs. She relaxed, wanting him, spreading her legs slightly. He wished they were alone, wished that a damned kid wasn't learning to dive just two yards away, wished half the population of middle England weren't gathered here for a cheap winter break. But not so cheap when you were paying for two.

He kissed her again, tasting the sun cream before sitting up and slapping her backside lightly. 'There, you'd better do the rest or I'll get arrested.'

He sat back in the shade, staring around. The bougainvillaea was vibrant against the whitewashed walls that enclosed the hotel grounds. It was only when walking back from the mall lugging two huge plastic bottles of mineral water after their arrival last night that he'd seen the wall from the other side; the unpainted breeze blocks, the waste land in which the hotel was set, the discarded building materials.

God, he hoped Journey's End was going to be ready by Easter. Well, it just bloody well had to be. He glanced at the mobile. He wanted to phone, wanted a progress report, but that would set Jan off. He picked up the *Telegraph* just as a child ran past, her towel streaming from her shoulders like a cloak. For a moment he was distracted. It was how Jude had worn hers.

There was a splash, a loud shout from the father of the boy learning to dive a few yards to his left. 'That's right!' Peter peered over the top of the home news page. The boy was in the water, spluttering and gasping, wiping the water from his eyes, pulling at his nose, then making his way to the side using a dire crawl. 'Put your face into the water, Matt,' his father called.

Matt did and his speed immediately improved. He stroked to the edge where his father was waiting, his hand reaching down. The boy took it, grinning. 'Better?'

221

'I should say so.' The father was in tight swimming trunks, his top was tanned, his legs were white. A builder probably. The man pulled Matt out of the water as though he weighed next to nothing. 'Had enough?'

Matt hadn't and lined up to go in again. He looked about the same age Simon had been when he learned, seven or so. Mark you, Simon hadn't been very good, ever.

Peter's father had tried to improve his style, and for a moment Peter saw the two divided by a generation, standing on the edge of the villa pool they had all taken together about fifteen years ago. Barbs had come out to watch and spoiled it all, by nagging, 'Keith, don't be so hard on the boy, please.' This had set Kate off when she returned from the market. Women just didn't understand that boys had to be toughened up, it was for their own good. Simon was the living proof – just look where he was now.

When he'd reiterated this to Barbs a few weeks before she died she'd said dryly, 'America.' She'd snorted too. Good God, where had she picked up all this attitude?

Jan was pushing herself up into a sitting position, her face alive and happy. There were slat marks across her breasts, those glorious, pink-nippled breasts. Kate wouldn't go topless, but perhaps it was a blessing. He'd said that she shouldn't have breast-fed for so long, and had been proved right, though looking round the pool he wondered if it was just a mid-life thing, since there seemed to be an awful lot of low-slung jobs around.

A waiter was making his way round the pool, a tray held high. Peter had ordered a light beer, and a Martini for Jan. He thought he could spot them amongst the clutter of glasses on the tray. Jan was adjusting her sun bed into a sitting position, and sweat was trickling between her breasts like rain down a window. He wanted to trace it with his finger. Instead he returned to home news, but the girl with the cloak was back, and running around their sun beds.

Out of the corner of his eye he watched Jan watching her. Jan was thirty-five, she had five years to go, she'd said last time they'd been in bed together. He'd brought condoms with him, just in case she'd stopped taking the pill. He turned to the sports page. 'Why?' she'd asked last night, when he'd stopped

222

the proceedings to put one of the wretched things on his John Thomas.

'I've been reading an article,' he'd said. 'I couldn't bear to transmit anything to you. I mean, though Kate and I live our own lives now, I've a feeling she put herself around in the past, and who knows what she's up to in Fowey.'

She'd swallowed it, because then she'd asked how he could bear to be so loyal to such a wife. 'For the children,' he'd said.

It had been a mistake. Not only had he been so put off that John Thomas shut down the shop, but it had raised the biological clock again. A clock that ticked louder every bloody hour, it seemed, and now she was watching the girl who shouldn't be running around them with her cloak, but over there, driving her own parents mad.

The waiter arrived with their drinks. The girl stood and stared. Peter glared behind Jan's back. The girl poked her tongue out. Bemused, Jan turned to Peter, who was fishing for his wallet as though nothing had occurred, satisfied because the girl was running back to her parents, shouting, 'I want a drink, Mum.'

The waiter put the drinks on the table, and the bill, which Peter checked. He smiled in satisfaction. He liked to calculate the cost correctly. He handed over the necessary pesetas, and the tip. It was the obligatory tip he resented, always had. The waiter left. Peter lifted his glass to Jan. 'Cheers.' She reached for hers, the gold-plated bracelet he had bought her on the plane sitting nicely on her wrist. They clinked glasses, then she sat back, trying to find the girl again. Irritated, Peter returned to his newspaper. This was normally when he'd back out of a relationship quicker than a dose of salts, but hell, not yet.

He wasn't reading the paper, he was just staring. Maybe Alan was right, and the flat had been a stupid idea, but no, it wasn't the flat that had been the mistake – it was not second-guessing his mother correctly. The thought disturbed him as it had begun to do increasingly, because if he had not correctly estimated the last wishes of his mother, what about Kate? Surely she wouldn't stand out against him? Surely not.

Lunch was taken at the pool bar; another drink each, and a light salad, then a brief swim. Their towels had reserved their sun beds and they lay side by side, hand in hand, he in the shade, she in the sun, but then her fingers found his armpit and ran down his chest, stopping at his belly button. He liked lying on his back, his belly dropped away and made him feel slimmer. Her fingers were gentle, they slipped beneath his waistband and out again, and up to his chest, and he had to turn on his side, because her fingers were not the only thing that was up.

His lids felt heavy, and hers too, from the look of them. They smiled at one another. He took hold of her hand, kissing each fingertip, thinking of work, of his second in command, of Kate, anything to let things subside for the walk inside.

At last. Now he sucked her middle finger. 'Bed,' he murmured.

She nodded. 'I thought you'd never ask.'

They left their towels, slipping shorts and tops on, before strolling hand in hand past the palms in pots, and people on sun beds, one of whom called to Jan, 'Hi, Jan, off for a siesta?' The tone was suggestive.

'Just to the shops,' Peter called back, not liking that sort of familiarity.

There was a bark of laughter and a giggle from Jan. Peter quickened his pace and the cool of the interior of the hotel was very acceptable, a quiet relief. Jan was still giggling as they entered the lifts. He wanted to slap her, but instead he pulled her hard against him as the doors shut, his hand inside her top. He kneaded her breasts, kissed her mouth. There, that'd shut her up. Only then did he press the button, but when he turned back she was still smiling. He sighed. 'What the hell is so damn funny?'

She pressed herself against him, her hands on his buttocks. 'There are no shops open until three. Everyone knows that.'

In their bedroom he shut the door behind him, grabbed her, stripped her clothes from her, there in the hallway. She looked alarmed. Well, at least he'd wiped the smile off her face. He held her at arm's length, staring at her, seeing the lines between her eyes, the crinkles at the corners, seeing one or two grey hairs. Oh yes, she was definitely past her sell-by.

He threw his mobile phone way over on to the bed, then kissed her deeply, pressing her against him, harder and harder, thinking of Marjorie, not her. She struggled, 'Peter, your belt.'

It was pressing into her, was it? Well, what a calamity. He loosened his hold, but did not let go. 'You shouldn't be so desirable,' he murmured, passion thickening his voice. She giggled. He tried to ignore it. He kissed her breasts and then the imprint of his belt, and his passion surged again.

He knelt, not feeling the cold hardness of the tiles, his face between her thighs, his tongue finding her. She gasped. Her fingers were in his hair, pressing him harder against her, then pulling him back, then against her again. Then she was pulling him up by the hair. He always let her do this, because he liked the pain. She led him to the bed, only one hand on his head, the other down there, not on him, but her, just as he liked.

They did not pull the curtains. Let the bloody world see. He knelt beside her, watching her work on herself, listening as she cried out, moving back as she reached for him, waiting for her to beg, which she would do. Which she always did. It was a game that Kate wouldn't play, so what else did she expect, but this?

'Please, please.' Her hands were reaching for him. He smiled and only now did he go to her, bearing down on her, entering her, leaving her, hearing her beg again, entering her again. He could taste the sun cream, the sweat, the perfume, his own beer. For hours they played, or so it seemed, and at last he came, at last they lay separate but together, free of sheets, hearing the noise of the pool at an acceptable distance, watching the gentle wafting of the net inner curtain.

He let her come nearer, let her lay her head on his shoulder, let her play with his nipple though all he wanted was her attention. Lazily he tried to reach his watch on the bedside cabinet. He couldn't. He tried again, almost dislodging her. Again he failed. He kissed the top of her head. 'Ups a daisy, just for a moment.'

She obliged. He checked the time. She watched. He put the watch in the drawer, sinking back on the pillows, gathering her up, holding her tight, then releasing her. He said, 'When you visited Barbs, did you ever see the medicine bottle in her bedside drawer?' Had he kept it casual, whilst making an impression?

Jan moved next to him, lifting her head from his shoulder,

225

looking at him, then relaxing back. 'No, what medicine bottle?'

He jerked his head towards the cabinet. 'My father's morphine capsules, the ones he didn't use, and no one ever threw away. I asked Kate to, when I realised they were there, but she said they were important to Barbs. Poor old Barbs.'

Jan was idly brushing her hair back from her face. Was she listening? She'd better bloody be.

Peter reached for that hand, kissing the palm, and each finger, saying thoughtfully, 'I wonder if I'll be the same?'

Jan brought his hand to her mouth, kissing his fingers as he had kissed hers. 'The same?' she asked.

'Arthritic. Poor old Barbs, she was helpless by the end, lost all strength, couldn't grip a thing. Don't you remember?'

Jan laid his hand over her breast. He could feel her heart. Her voice was sympathetic, 'Poor darling, it was a gruelling period. I can't bear to think of Mum ever going. Come on, let's put it behind us, it's not good to be thinking about these things.'

Quite frankly, he couldn't give a shit about her mother. What he wanted was for her to very much think about it. Was that too much to ask?

She was leaning over him, kissing him, but no tongue, thank God. Then she was gone, and into the shower, but he had seven days, perhaps more. It would be enough.

That evening they danced after dinner, and he watched the waiters watching her, and the husbands who should know better, and in the softer light, and with make-up, the lines were gone and she looked as good as he'd thought her at the surgery party a year ago, when it had all begun. He ordered champagne. They sat together, her hand on his thigh, and when it arrived in the ice bucket he toasted her, and kissed her. Eat your hearts out, he beamed to the men who hadn't got her, and that night they were too far gone to make love, and in the morning his head was throbbing, and so was hers, from the look of her.

At eight they joined the queue for breakfast and Peter was all right as long as no one spoke to him; to emphasise the point he buried his head in the same *Daily Telegraph*. The coach which would show them the island was due to pick them up at eight thirty, but how long did it take to eat a dry roll, a pat of odd butter and drink a grey cup of coffee which Jan brought him from a machine set in the middle of the room?

Too long, it seemed, because Jan checked her watch and was up on her feet, telling him to bring the roll with him. *Telling* him. He sat quite still as she hurried towards the lobby, not even looking to see if he was following. Eventually he did, knowing the coach would not be there because they were never on time. But it was, though the queue which led to the tour rep and her clipboard was slow moving, and Jan still had three people in front of her.

Peter strolled towards her, saying loudly before he reached her, 'There was no need to rush. You really must stay calm.'

For a moment there was an expression similar to that which Kate sometimes showed, but then it was gone, and Jan's smile was warm as she drew him close. 'I'm just excited, darling.'

Her excitement paled when the tour rep. read out, 'Jan Seymour and Peter Maxwell?'

Subdued, Jan led the way on to the bus, her floral skirt lifting slightly in the breeze, her thin strappy sandals and red toenails already looking good against her burgeoning tan. Peter felt a pang of sympathy for her. Had she really thought it would be assumed they were married to one another? If she had, she shouldn't have signed up for this God-awful coach with a loud-mouthed clipboard girl, and what about the reception desk which held their passports?

They sat together over a wheel, which was unfortunate, but at least Jan was not Kate, and had no need of acupressure bracelets and a large dose of Sturgeron. Instead her excitement was infectious as they headed north to Mount Teide which dominated the volcanic landscape. Jan took photographs until Peter told her that they'd be too blurred to be any good.

They stopped at a small whitewashed hacienda-type coffee house, and queued again, but at least the coffee was good, though they had to share their table with another couple, who hailed from Middlesex. Jan explained that she and Peter had dashed away for a few days, taking a break from the decorating. He joined in the game, using the magnolia/white colour scheme of Journey's End, whilst she talked up his mother's furniture.

He was laughing quietly as they resumed their seats on the coach, but she was muted. By the time they reached the 'old town' of Puerto de la Cruz Jan had begun, in a whispered whinge, to talk of settling down, of turning the dream into a reality, and he was gentle with her, patient.

The coach stopped and he hushed her only when they filed down the steps, out into the midday sun which was harsh and bright. He reached for his hat and sun block. Her lips tightened and she walked away from the coach whilst he turned back to the rep. They'd already been told what time to be here for the return trip, but he always checked.

He also checked his watch. Three hours. Fine. Time for lunch and a wander. He'd buy her a present, of course. There were some duty-free shops, apparently, and his very good friend Visa would bear the brunt. He caught up with Jan as she waited to cross the road with half the coach contingent. He took her hand. She tried to pull away, but not with any great determination. He kissed her cheek.

It was the talk of Journey's End that had done it, because she wanted that sort of effort put into the flat, their flat. She wanted to be living there, her future intact, her belly swelling. Well, it wasn't going to happen, but as long as she thought it would . . .

They ate calamari, washing it down with cool lagers before walking through the narrow streets, dodging from awning to awning, window-shopping. At one he insisted that Jan choose a ring, knowing that such a gift, such a symbol, would swing it. She found a sapphire, in red gold. It fitted, and looked good as she examined it in the light of the doorway. The shopkeeper placed it in a velvet-lined box and presented it to Jan. Peter took it instead, paying with Visa, gesturing Jan out ahead of him. He looked both ways and saw a bougainvillaea tumbling down the wall opposite a drinking fountain. He grabbed Jan, hurrying her to it, and there he took the box from his pocket, opened it, and placed the ring on her wedding finger.

Her gasp was audible to those around, her cry of joy intense as she flung her arms around him. A man in a garish short-sleeved shirt and shorts stopped and asked if they'd like him to take a photo of them with their own camera, to record the event. He was from Birmingham. Peter shook his head. 'We'll sort that out, thank you.'

228

The man nodded, and moved on. There were to be no photographs of the two of them together. He was daft, but not that bloody daft. Jan linked her arm in his, and he let her talk, let her plan, let her think what the hell she liked, his only dictum being that it would all take time. This, at last, she accepted, along with his sun block, along with the call from the phone box to Kate on their return to the hotel because he wanted a progress update. Instead he nearly blew it, by asking what it was like to be back. But all the time Jan's hands were in his pockets, and her body was pressing up against his, her mouth was on his neck, and then his lips.

He hurried the call, hurried back to their room, eager for happy hour and half-price drinks, but eager for this too. Again it was as they were lying there that he spoke of the past, deliberately, baldly, in a way that she would remember. 'My mother asked me to kill her, you know, when she was ready.'

Beside him Jan stiffened, turning to him sharply, astonished and appalled. For a moment she stared, then she said, 'I don't want to hear this, Peter, I really don't. I don't want to know . . .'

He pressed his finger against her mouth. 'Do you really think I would do something like that? For heaven's sake, her pain was being controlled and there was no need. It was just a wild impulse on her part, I'm sure. Some sort of an insurance in case things got worse. It was her hands, you see, that damned arthritis as I've said, took her independence. There's no way she could have unscrewed that cap herself, or even held the glass, but you would have noticed that. The thing is, I'm pretty sure . . .' He stopped, began again. 'Well, not sure. I can't bring myself to think it.'

For a moment Jan looked at him. 'What are you trying to say?'

He shook his head, getting up, pacing. Outside music was playing, people were singing in the distance. At the bar below others were talking. There was a great burst of laughter. He came to her, taking her hand, kissing her ring. 'That's why I asked you about the morphine. You see, after her death I found the bottle. It was still in the bedside drawer but it was empty. I suppose I wondered if, as a nurse, you had found it and thrown them away, because if *you* didn't . . . You see, Kate would have done anything for Barbs, but perhaps she just threw them away. But then, wouldn't she have thrown the bottle too? Then again, there was the will, the *new* will. I sometimes wonder if *she* decided Barbs had to . . .'

He stopped and let the thought linger, just long enough, then shook his head firmly. 'But I shouldn't have mentioned it. It's just that it's been going round and round in my mind.' He broke off, as though distressed. 'This isn't fair, I shouldn't be loading this on to you.' He kissed her hands again, fingering the ring. His voice firm, he said as though reaching a decision, 'No, it's all nonsense. Forget I ever said anything, darling. I know how you feel about assisted suicide.'

'Murder,' Jan said flatly.

'No,' he shook his head. 'We both know Kate, she'd never have done anything like that, but then, I didn't think . . .' He looked at the packets of condoms.

There was another burst of laughter from outside. Jan ignored it. He could see her trying to grasp all he had said, and so he kissed her, pulling her to him, talking of the bigger flat they would one day buy, dragging her away from the possibilities he had just planted, and away from the weakened hands, and the screw-top medicine bottle, but knowing that it wouldn't be forgotten, knowing it could be accessed should it be necessary to exert pressure on Kate to sell the property. Knowing that if pressure failed the perpetrator of a murder could not gain for six years from their crime. But it wouldn't come to that, there was no way it would come to that, and anyway, there was only fifteen minutes of happy hour left.

'Come on,' he said. 'Last one dressed is a cissy.'

CHAPTER TWENTY-FOUR

As Kate drove across the Tamar into Cornwall the light seemed to change. It became brighter, as it had done millions of years ago when she was a very young child and her father promised her 6d if she saw the sea before he or Mum did. That was her father pre-work pressure, pre-redundancy, pre-booze. But she hadn't time to think of any of that now and she pushed the car to go just a little faster.

She had left the Old Vicarage at seven thirty, eager to be away, to see progress, to stretch her legs along the coast, to hear the gulls and breathe in the ozone. She urged the car on faster still.

Soon she was approaching Fowey, threading through the high-banked lanes which in a few weeks would burgeon with primroses, violets, and probably daffodils. She slowed. Yes, the daffodils were already coming out. She found herself singing loudly to Whitney Houston's 'Bodyguard'. Not quite making the high notes, but what the hell.

At nine thirty she parked as usual in the car park, and paid and displayed. Cars were being ferried across, the cows were grazing, the air was the same. For a moment she stared at the river, feeling that she had been away for months. She set off towards Journey's End, forcing herself not to break into a run, but when it came in sight she sprinted, her grip banging against her leg, her small backpack bumping.

Now she saw the outside light on at Journey's End, lights on in the Glovers'. How had the Canaries been? She should stop, knock, and ask, but instead she was groping for her spare key in her cagoule pocket. The red door was gleaming. Should she knock? Damn it, it was her own home. She inserted the key. But perhaps she *should* warn him. She knocked, turned the key, entered, calling, 'I'm home.'

As she shut the door she saw that a brass safety chain had

been fitted. She touched it, then slid it into its slot. Isaac's voice startled her, seeming very loud. 'Thought it a good idea as you'd let me have the key. There's always the niggle that maybe someone could make a copy and come calling without an invitation.' He was leaning over the banister, in yet another navy sweater, a wide grin lighting his face, making his eyes seem even more blue.

She brushed her hair back and laughed as she headed up the stairs towards him. 'Hey, never entered my mind.'

'Well, it should, if you go leaving your key with an odd bod.'

He was walking ahead of her towards the rafter-dome. The door was shut. He stopped, seemed to take a deep breath before turning to her, his hand on the door. Now that she was close she was shocked to see how tired and drawn he looked, though his smile was still reflected in those eyes. 'Ready?'

She nodded, smiling nervously. He flung the door wide, and as always it was like walking into a world full of light, but this time it stopped her dead in her tracks. The floor was as per her design; the colours, the myriad yellows, the deeper ochre, the lighter cream, the swoops of the shapes, the gleam of the peripheral varnish. But it wasn't just this that rooted her to the spot, it was the platform bed which had been erected, and stood gleaming, and was quite utterly wonderful.

For a moment she said nothing, just stared. Isaac stood close, as usual. She didn't mind. She was used to him. She whispered, 'It's wonderful. Just so wonderful.'

He pointed her to the stainless steel ladder set against the wall. She climbed up. There was a stainless steel balustrade all around the platform, its curves suiting the room to perfection. On the base of the platform Isaac had laid floorboards which were varnished, though she could feel the non-slip sand. He had also laid down a double mattress. On it he'd set up her sleeping bag.

'The sofa, when you get one, can go beneath.'

Silently she walked to the balustrade, looking down at the river, across at the cows, up at the ripples reflected on the ceiling, seeing the crossed bamboo on the beams. She laughed down at him. 'So, tell me.'

'To neutralise the sha the beams carry. Sha can cause . . .'

'Don't tell me.'

He did, standing at the epicentre of the design, and now she knew she would be protected from headaches, confused thinking, and career and financial problems.

'Well, that's nice to know.'

He was laughing too, and she had forgotten how he could boom out to fill every space. 'Like it?' he said.

From here the design on the floor looked even better. It was all so much a whole, so exciting, so different. She ran her hands along the stainless steel balustrade. 'What about metal on a north wall?'

'No probs, just wouldn't do it on an easterly one.'

'Of course you wouldn't.'

He was still looking up at her, and now neither were laughing, neither were smiling. She said quietly, 'I love it, and I thank you.'

For a moment longer he held her gaze, then nodded. 'You're very welcome.' He dug his hands deep into his pockets, and the movement broke the moment, and now a large ship, high in the water, glided into sight on its way to fill up with china clay and broke it still further.

Impulsively she waved to the skipper, bridge to bridge. Of course he didn't see, but who cared.

Isaac said, 'The mattress is sprung in individual pockets. Better for your back, especially at your great age, Alfie says.'

She groaned down at him. 'Oh, one of Alfie's. What with the kettle, the toaster, an iron . . .' She laughed. 'Am I to expect police knocking at my door in the near future?'

He grinned. 'I would stand between you and them, never fear.'

'While Alfie disposes of the items.'

'Something like that.' They were laughing again as she turned back to view the platform. It was warm with the rising heat, it was tranquil. It would do. More than do, and though she didn't subscribe to Isaac's little yin, yang and bumps a daisy, she could well understand why some might believe that if a soul took it upon itself to leave the body during sleep it would want to return to this cocoon of colour, and peace.

She descended the ladder. Isaac was there to steady her, though even with her backpack still on, it was unnecessary. She jumped the last two rungs, then remembered the Glovers and winced. Isaac shook his head. 'They'll be unpacking, and it'll be muted. As I said, I sorted that before I lost the place.'

'Does being at sea give you second sight or something?'

He smiled gently. 'I don't need it with you. You're transparent, always thinking of the worst scenario, always thinking of cause and effect, always . . .'

'All right,' she cut him off, suddenly irritated. She didn't need another person telling her she was neurotic. She stooped and touched the floor paint, feeling the sand in it. 'How do you know how much sand to use?'

'Experience.'

She pictured the chest of drawers against the east wall, the cabinet against the west, chairs here and there, the sofa, as he had said, beneath the platform. Then they'd need rugs, and some wardrobes set in the corners, diagonally. She had been playing with a design last night, and maybe bookshelves and a window seat, in one unit.

A yacht was making its way out to sea using its engine. The sky was clearing. It should be a good day. Isaac was watching too, but as he dragged his fingers through his hair she was reminded of the hours he had put in. 'You must have worked so hard,' she said. 'We can tackle the bathroom when you've had a day off. I've things I can be getting on with today, and I'll give you a hand tomorrow. Go on, go and get some sleep, please.'

She wasn't disappointed that the bathroom wasn't done, how could she be? She was just completely thrilled with what had been achieved. The yacht was almost level with the pedestrian ferry point, and suddenly she thought of Clara. 'Poor Clara,' she said slowly, slipping off her backpack, crouching, fumbling for the flask of coffee she had brought. 'It's so sad she won't see this.'

Isaac's reply was thoughtful. 'I hadn't thought of that, but I'll write.'

She was pouring two mugs of coffee and looked up, surprised. He came and took the mug she held out. 'You're still in touch?'

He sipped the coffee. 'Oh yes, they're anchored off Magaluf, ready to zoo-watch when the season starts, in between earning a bit of money. George hankers after a bacon and eggs café on the Costa del Sol eventually.' He was expressionless.

She stood, easing her knees, sipping her coffee. It wasn't very hot, and she apologised. He waved that aside. 'Do you mind?' she asked.

He laughed. 'What, the fact that he's going to start a café? I think I can live with that.' Yes, she rather thought he might be able to.

'No,' she went on, digging, wishing she wasn't, but being driven to see if Joe had been right, and he didn't care. 'Do you mind keeping in touch, being informed of her life?'

He drained his mug before going through to the kitchen and washing it out. He wiped it on the kitchen roll they used instead of tea towels, calling back, 'Absolutely not. You only mind if you're in love. Besides, she's so happy and that's really good. With us there was too much strain, too much of that "feeling better now, dear?" sex. You know, when you've done your bit so they'll sleep, grateful that you can stop feeling so darn sad, so lonely. Wishing you could be what they want.'

She stared at her coffee, wishing again that she hadn't intruded, that he hadn't answered, because she had thought she was the only one in the world to feel like that.

Isaac was back in the doorway, ready to throw the plastic mug to her. She caught it one handed. He grinned. 'Getting better every day. Anyway,' he gestured around the room, 'will your husband like it when he sees your idea brought to life?'

She busied herself putting his mug away. 'Heavens, yes.' He would, once he knew of the extra money it would bring. He would, if they finished on schedule and it was too late to change anything. But they'd have to get on, and Isaac wouldn't be here much this week, as he'd need to make up time on Molly.

It was her turn to wash her mug, but Isaac blocked the doorway. 'Try the bathroom.' He was grinning.

'The bathroom?' For a moment she didn't understand, and then slowly as he continued to grin, and she saw the suppressed excitement, she gripped his arm. 'Surely you didn't have time, not with all this?'

He shrugged, trying to appear nonchalant, but failing dismally. 'Actually yes, with the help of Joe and the three stooges who gave up their perches and beers for an afternoon, all for the price of one of your smiles, and several rounds of the hard stuff on you, and a trip out on Molly from me before I disappear over the horizon.'

She shut her eyes for a moment, moved. Joe hadn't mentioned it. He had spoken only of Isaac's efforts, but of course someone had to help put up the bed. She viewed the room again. What could she say? 'Thank you,' she managed. His hand covered hers.

'We wanted you to have a bit more comfort. It's gone on long enough.'

His hand was warm, hard and warm. She could hear him breathing, feel his body heat. He was too close. For God's sake, he always got too close. She stepped back, snatching her hand away, busying herself by moving her backpack to the corner before making for the bathroom. He wasn't following. Well, a good thing too.

She paused for a moment outside the door, imagining her pristine white, magnolia, ideas waiting for her. Slowly she entered.

For a moment she stood appalled. For a further moment she could not believe what she was seeing. She felt very cold, her hand felt clumsy on the door handle. Where was the light, airy room, the welcoming, relaxing . . . ? But he was coming. She had somehow to arrange her face. She had to loosen her grip on the door, and try to hold her shoulders straight. She had to step further into the room.

'Well?' he said.

Well, indeed. He had used a pale blue and turquoise as a background colour for the walls, together with navy blue. He had stripped the floor, varnished it, painted a design in that same blue, and a darker one, but there was green and red in it as well. Just behind her he was saying, 'I know we decided on blues to keep the water moving to encourage good cash flow, but there's so much yin I felt you had to have all the help you could get.' He was pointing at the green dragon, the white tiger, the black tortoise he had painted on three of the walls.

She felt sick, angry. She fought to keep her voice level, delighted, appreciative as the walls threatened to close over her, those walls with those things which leaped out at you the moment you opened the door. 'The dragon's on the,' she worked it out, 'east wall, the tiger on the west, the tortoise on the north?' she asked calmly, averting her eyes from the huge painted beasts.

'I was worried I'd gone too far. Joe thought I had, so I reduced them in size.' Reduced them? Good God, how big had they been?

'They're all extra protection for you. In Chinese lore, of course, the dragons and tigers are the hills and mountains arranged in a particular way for maximum protection. I couldn't move the mountains to Mohammed, so this was the next best thing.'

He was pointing out the tiles, a job lot from Alfie. There they were, a nice clear white. The bath had been buffed up and fitted with new brass taps; its feet were blackened. The basin and lavatory were nice. She flushed the system. There were white chrysanthemums on the sill. She touched the petals. 'And these?'

'They just seemed right for you.'

She was stalling, knowing that when the house was finished and he was gone, beating up the river in Molly, she could simply cover the walls with magnolia, bring some light into it, cover the floor with lino or cheap carpet. If he returned and was hurt she could say the clients had objected, or caused damage, something. Anything.

She buried her face in the blooms, gradually feeling calmer, but not yet calm enough. He said, 'I know you wanted a sanded floor in here too, so I thought we'd better keep the non-slip theme. The white tiles are the light shade which is best for a bathroom, the blue, well, I've just explained . . .' He trailed off. 'You're very quiet.' He shuffled. 'I also thought that you could . . .'

She turned, beaming, interrupting him, 'I'm just totally amazed, and moved. How on earth did you do so much? No wonder you look exhausted.' She touched his arm quickly. 'Thank you. Thank you all.' He was examining her too closely, so she said again, and there was no doubting her sincerity, 'I am so moved.' Again she turned, sweeping her arm around in a grand gesture. 'Gosh, so many surprises, after a long drive. I don't know, I feel quite blitzed.'

He said nothing, just switched the light on. It seemed marginally more cheerful, a little lighter, and she prattled on

237

about the floor, then the cupboard, the heated towel rail. He said, 'I picked it up from . . .'

'Alfie,' she finished, laughing.

He was brightening up now, pointing out the blower heater on the wall, and the shower attachment he had rigged for the bath. He drew the shower curtain with a swish. Pale blue. Well, that could stay, though personally she hated their clamminess. She lifted her hand to push it back. The phone rang. It was in her backpack, which was in the rafter-dome, which was in the house that Kate had bought, she chanted to herself as she hurried through, with money from Barbs, who had . . .

She snatched it up. The sun was on the river, the ripples were on the ceiling, the light was beaming in. Yes, she could easily run a few layers of magnolia over the walls, and no one would be any the wiser. She was smiling as she said, 'Hello?'

Penny and Jude would be here in half an hour. Kate had tried to sound delighted and from Penny's reaction she had obviously managed, so perhaps the stage was missing its greatest asset, or the world its greatest teller of porkies.

Apparently Jude had hoped to surprise her mother by taking her out to lunch during her last day at the surgery, and instead had found her gone, so Penny had thought it a great idea to drive them both down and 'do' lunch in Fowey instead, and have a look at progress so far.

'Damn and blast,' Kate said again, as she returned the phone to the backpack.

Behind her Isaac said, 'Visitors?'

She nodded. 'The esteemed Revd Penny and my less esteemed, except in her own eyes, daughter.'

'Is that a problem?' He was collecting his tools from the kitchen and scooping up his yellow waterproof. Of course it was a bloody problem, because the schedule was shot to hell, the design of the place would be rumbled, and the bathroom was an outrageous disaster.

He waited, one hand on the door. Again his tiredness leaped at her, and she hated herself. She smiled. 'No, no problem. I just wanted to show them the completely finished article, but there's loads to impress them as it is, and that's thanks to you.'

'Plus Joe, and the lads and . . .'

'Alfie,' she finished for him, following him out to the landing, leaning over the banister. 'But mainly you.'

He opened the front door. 'Oh, your key's on the kitchen windowsill. I'm going to get my head down for a bit, but I'll nip back later so we can get on with the rest. Or at least I can if you're tied up. I must finish the bunk beds or we'll get behind.'

He was gone before she could tell him to leave it until he'd caught up with Molly, because she didn't want Jude being rude, didn't want her throwing tantrums about the bathroom, the rafter-dome, didn't want Penny here either, and she particularly didn't want Peter down, hot on the heels of Jude's report, or not until she could make good the mess.

It was her backpack she kicked across the floor as the camp bed wasn't available. As she did so the phone rang. For heaven's sake. She walked slowly to reclaim it, hearing Peter's voice. Good God, he wasn't coming too? Thankfully not, but a vicar was and she must stop blaspheming.

He had left Sweden and was in Czechoslovakia and thinking of using the sun bed in the hotel. She made the right noises while she eyed the window. They'd need some form of blind to filter out the heat of the summer sun. She'd make a note of it in a moment. 'Try goggles,' she said.

'How's progress?'

'Good. The bathroom plumbing is completed, the sitting room is nearly there, and I've found a way of increasing the rental by creating extra bed space.'

'I was going to talk to you about that. I've been thinking that we could have a bed settee in the sitting room so it could pass as a flat for six people.'

'Great minds think alike.'

'Oh, so you've thought of it too.'

'More or less, but I think I can do something that will bring in even more by creating a permanent bed space and leaving room for a sofa bed. I'll think more about it, but do you agree in principle?'

'Of course I damn well do. It'll bump it up to eight possible tenants, won't it? Just don't decrease the appeal for people. What'll you do, split the sitting room? Anyway, you won't start until I've Oked it, will you.' It wasn't a question, and the line was crackling. Good old Fowey.

She said, 'Must go, bad line. Lots to do. Put sun block on. And of course, don't overwork, or will you be having your meetings in your bikinis, goggles and all?'

She broke the connection on his irritated reply. A sun bed? My God, life was tough at the top.

By the time she heard the expected knock Kate had taken so many deep breaths she had worked herself into a state of near hyperventilation. She took one more, then hurried down the stairs, calling, 'I'm on my way.'

'Can't wait, I'll batter it down.'

'Don't you dare, you'll put us further behind schedule.' There, that would warn them that things weren't quite as Jude would expect. But she should have told Jude, should have told Peter, because now it was all going to come out. Damn, damn. She opened the door.

Penny was wearing her 'let's go out for the day' gear. Anorak, polo neck and jeans; as far away from the dog collar image as possible. She grinned and hugged Kate. 'Hey, this has . . .' She was looking over Kate's shoulder into the hall. 'Oh, I thought this was finished? Well, it's certainly on the way to looking good. I like the stripped stairs.'

Kate was searching for Jude. Penny released her, stepping past, examining the newell post and the study/bedroom door. 'Oh, Jude's picking up some chewing gum from the Spar. She said my driving had taken care of a packet that she expected to last the day. That daughter of yours has a low pain threshold. She kept on about safety features in cars needing a bit of help by way of careful driving.'

Kate laughed and left the door on the latch, switching on the hall lights. Penny approved of the inset fittings, and seemed to be picturing the ambient lighting that Kate was describing. 'So you'll get those lamps from the auction sale too?' Penny asked as they climbed the stairs.

'Yes, Isaac says they come up very frequently, and they do seem to. It just hasn't been the right time to buy – storage is the problem, as you can see from the kids' room, especially when you're trying to build the bunk beds, and generally work around things.'

She was rambling on, but they were outside the rafter-dome

240

door. Instead of ushering Penny through she steered her along to the second bedroom, which was still in all its pre-decorated glory. Penny noted the rewiring, and listened intently to the decorating plans, liking the idea of the stencilling and sponging which Kate had failed to mention in all her talk of Fowey. Kate ran her hand through her hair. 'Well, as you work on a place your ideas change a bit. Sometimes they change a lot.' She knew she sounded nervous, and that Penny was picking up on it, looking at her intently, before putting her arm around her.

'Hey, it's going to be great. Come on, let's see the rest.'

This time it was Penny who led the way on to the landing again, and Penny who headed to the bathroom. Kate called sharply, 'No, let's do the rafter-dome first.'

They did and Penny gaped as she opened the door to the sunlight streaming in across the floor. It was also lighting up the yellow sponged walls, and the subtle stencilling. She stepped in further, speechlessly absorbing everything. 'It's the most wonderful room,' she said at last. 'It's absolute heaven.'

Kate had positioned herself at the window, looking at the craft, at the cows grazing, and the gulls flying, and she felt her shoulders relaxing, and a smile forming. She murmured, coming across to the centre of the room, 'Isaac suggested the non-slip paint. He has his own recipe – so much sand to so much paint. The bed was originally his and I liked the curves, they fitted in with the Art Deco theme. It gives us the potential for more rent, too, of course. We're going to echo the curves in the way we paint the walls in the downstairs room, and in the furniture we're doing up there.'

She was pulling Penny towards the kitchen, explaining how Isaac had carried through the Art Deco effect to this room, and as she did so Penny's increasing interest was clear. Kate warmed to her theme, hesitating only when Penny broke in, 'But you wanted the cooker over there.' She was pointing to the wall overlooking the river.

'Isaac had already run the cable down before I noticed, and it seemed easier to let it stay, and perhaps he was right. Though we still have to sort out the actual cooker. Alfie hasn't delivered on that yet.'

Penny laughed. 'So the Black Maria arrives shortly after.'

Kate squeezed her arm. 'Probably. But seriously, I won't buy unless it's kosher.'

Penny was moving out of the kitchen. Kate let her walk across to the view, let her stand and stare, let her repeat, 'This is heaven.'

She waited another moment, before taking yet another deep breath and saying, 'Now the bathroom.'

Perhaps she was wrong. Perhaps it was good.

She led the way, opening the door slowly, hoping that a gradual unveiling would soften the blow. It didn't. Penny stared around the room, and then at her, aghast. 'It's bloody awful.'

Kate ran her hand through her hair again, shrugging defensively, feeling annoyed. It was all right for her to say it, but . . . 'I know, but the basics are OK; the basin and the tiles and so on. I'll just splash on several coats of magnolia at the end of the proceedings, and he'll never know. It was a surprise for me, you see, so how could I spoil it? He didn't just want me to have hot water, he wanted me to be protected.' She pointed helplessly to the dragon.

Penny said carefully, her arm slipping through Kate's, 'Nice thought, but perhaps you could have said something. You have a right, it's your property, after . . .'

Jude voice startled them. 'How could you, Mum, how bloody well could you?' They spun round. Jude stood just behind them, glaring at her mother, lifting her hands high as though in despair.

Penny held tight to Kate. 'That's the point, the builder did it, and as your mother said, the basics are fine, and so were the motives, and . . .'

'Oh for God's sake, shut up, Penny.' Jude stalked from them into the rafter-dome. Kate, stunned by her daughter's rudeness, put her hand out to Penny, but Penny was already heading after Jude. Kate followed. As she entered Jude shouted at her, 'So, this is all according to the plan, is it, like the bathroom? Well I don't think so.'

'Will you behave yourself,' Kate said, finding her voice at last.

Jude just stared, wrenching at the multicoloured knitted scarf which was slung loosely round her neck, pulling it free,

242

stuffing it in the pocket of her duffel coat. 'The motives were good, the basics are fine? Well, what about the schedule I was slogging over with Dad? What about that then?'

Kate felt exhausted suddenly, and cold. Very cold. She just looked at her daughter, not wanting her here, not wanting either of them here in her world. Not wanting them assessing her home.

Penny came close, very close, whispering, 'You really could have said something, about the cooker, and the bathroom.'

Kate kept her eyes on Jude, who was still challenging her, hands on her hips, one Doc Marten on the design, one on the varnished boards. Penny repeated the whisper. Her breath was too hot, too moist. Kate moved slightly, saying, defensively again, 'He worked so hard, they all did, and I suppose it was giving him the chance to see it happen. It must be dreadful, to have your ideas come to nothing . . .'

Penny's voice was still quiet as she said, 'You do not have to take responsibility for everyone else's happiness. You do not always have to placate.'

Kate moved further away still. Why did everyone have to come so close? She said. 'I like the rafter-dome. I like . . .' She stopped, aware that her voice was becoming horribly loud.

Penny flashed a look at Jude, who was approaching, and shouting at her mother, 'That's utter rubbish. If it's what *you* wanted it wouldn't be so bad, but because it's what the bloody builder wanted you go along with it. When will you—'

Penny roared, cutting off Jude in her turn. 'Don't you dare speak to your mother in that way.' It was a voice that could quell a playgroup with ease, and now seemed to ricochet around Journey's End. In the silence Kate felt she could feel the walls waiting, the river too. Penny patted her pocket. 'You two could do with a little time to yourselves, and the Ivy Club could do with some pasties to get their gnashers round. It will bring the blessed sound of comparative silence to the cribbage squabbles.' She raised her eyebrows at Jude. 'Now, do you suggest the Spar?'

There was no reply and Kate just brushed the question aside. Penny nodded. 'Fine, I might be some little while. Be good, Jude.'

She hurried off, leaving them to their sinking ship. Kate

243

wanted to call after her, but did not. Jude didn't even wait for the sound of the front door closing, but launched into her, coming close, too close. This time Kate was ready, forcing her daughter to listen, insisting that though Journey's End was nothing like the plans, it was better, it was what she wanted, and whose property was it after all?

Again Jude shouted, 'What utter rubbish. No one can want a bathroom like that, and when have you ever been interested in Art Deco? No, you've let yourself be taken over again.'

Again? Kate backed as Jude came even nearer, nose to nose, her face contorted, too much like her father for comfort, and she was still shouting. 'Do you really think I wanted to spend hours messing about with those damned plans?' It wasn't a question for she tore on. 'No, it just kept him sweet for you, it kept him interested, kept him coming home, kept him propping you up. And what happens? You just give in to someone else, so now Dad'll have cause to gripe, and if he just goes off, what happens to you?'

Jude lifted her hands, her voice breaking. 'What the hell happens to you?' It was almost a whisper.

Kate reached for her, trying to catch up, hang on to the words, some of which were loud and clear and far too vivid, some of which were blurred, and without sense. Jude shook her off. There was a banging at the door. Neither of them moved. Another bang, then the sound of the door opening, Isaac calling, 'Hello, hello, anyone there? Did you know the door was unlocked, Kate?'

He'd never called her Kate before.

Jude moved. She was on the landing, calling down. 'Yes, we're not complete imbeciles, we did know my mother's door was unlocked, and I suppose you must be the builder? Well, I feel I know you, having been here just five minutes.'

Kate shouted, 'Jude, how dare you?'

'Oh, I dare, Mother, because I've looked at you not daring for God knows how many years.'

'I'll come back later,' Isaac called. There was the sound of the door shutting.

Kate was on the landing, staring at Jude. 'What on earth do you mean?' She couldn't keep up, she didn't know where all this had come from. 'What do you mean?' She was shouting it, almost screaming, taking hold of Jude's arm.

Jude walked away, back into the rafter-dome, standing near the river, subdued now. 'I'm tired of it, Mum. I'm tired of the burden of keeping things OK for you. Dad's a womanising shit and you let him be, and it's me that has to keep the whole thing afloat so he doesn't take off over the horizon doing whatever . . . Well, never mind that, but leaving you stranded, and what do you do to help me, or yourself? A big fat zero. When Grandma left you the house I thought that you might just swing it, might stand on your own two feet, get strong, get sorted, let me live my life. But oh no, you buy the house Dad wants, you let him draw up the plans, and just bitch, every so often. Just enough for him to justify what he does with all those evenings, all those . . . You hand everything to him on a plate, Mum, and I can't do any more for you.' She gestured around the room. 'You'll always seek out people who'll control you, and I can't take the burden of it any more.'

She didn't look at her mother as she passed on her way to the door. She just said, 'Tell Penny I'll be by the car.'

CHAPTER TWENTY-FIVE

Isaac returned at 5.00 pm. He knocked, once, twice, then again. Kate didn't want to move from the corner of the rafter-dome where she'd been sitting, hunched over her knees, but she knew she must.

Slowly she rose, slowly she walked on cramped legs to the stairs, slowly she descended, waiting for a moment at the bottom. He knocked again. Just go away, she thought, like Jude has, Penny has. Just go.

Of course he didn't. He knocked again, also called, and she could hear the concern. So, did he think they'd talked her into changing everything back, did he think that he wouldn't see the completion of his dream? Well, he was right.

She opened the door as far as the chain would allow. 'I don't like the bathroom. It's not what I want. Do you understand? It's not what I want.' Her voice was quiet. She felt sick. She'd felt sick since Jude had left. She'd felt sick when she'd sent Penny away.

Isaac spoke through the gap, coming too close. Why did people do that? She retreated until she was flat against the wall, until she could go no further. The wall was cold, but gave her support. She wanted to sink to the floor, to hug her knees, until she felt better, until the clamouring in her head ceased.

Isaac pressed further into the gap, reaching for her. 'Kate, let me in. Please, you're not well.'

'I'm perfectly well, I just don't like the bathroom.'

For a moment he said nothing, but then she watched him rest his forehead on the door. Such a tragedy, was it? He looked up. 'But why didn't you tell me? That's all you had to do. I'm so sorry, I told you I get carried away. You can paint it over as you like and they'll still protect you.'

'And the rafter-dome? And the kitchen? What about the plans, their plans?'

He was startled. 'What plans, whose plans? You said there were none, you said . . .'

'Shut up. Just shut up. You planned it. You'd even cleared up the noise problem for the Glovers. You planned this all along. You manipulated me, just like . . .' She stopped.

'Just like?' He'd stepped back. At last. Now, though, she could see all his face. It was so still. The blue seemed to have gone from his eyes, the life from his whole body. So hard to lose a dream, then, Isaac? Well, some you win, some you don't, some . . .

She stopped herself, feeling her mind slipping, almost sideways, just as it had been doing up in the rafter-dome; slipping sideways and down, everything tumbling down.

'Just leave me alone,' she said, pushing herself from the wall, pushing the door shut. 'Just leave me alone.' It was her turn to rest her forehead on the door.

That afternoon she drove to the DIY store and picked up a can of magnolia and sufficient white tile imitation linoleum. That evening she covered the dragon, tiger, and tortoise with a layer of paint, then another. She didn't protect the floor but let the paint splatter, let it seep from the sodden roller down her hand to her arm, her arm which was aching. It was an ache which spread to her shoulder and her back, and her neck.

The phone rang, twice. She didn't answer. There was no one she wanted to speak to.

At midnight she stopped, washing out the roller in the basin; Isaac's basin. Washing it and washing it until the water ran clear. Only then did she lie down, but not on the platform bed. She lay instead in the room where he had been making the bunk beds until the smell of sawn wood drove her to drag the camp bed into the hall, and all the time she fought the jumble of words, and thoughts, and memories which chased away all the aches. A jumble which had no sense, which came at her large and loud, and receded small and weak.

In the morning she bathed and hated the magnolia, hated the smell of it and the sight of it. But the tiger, the dragon, and the tortoise were gone. She boiled the kettle for coffee. She made toast. It tasted of paint. Her wrist ached, her shoulder, her back, her neck. She stared out of the window at the meadow, and the river, and the ferry. Everything seemed the same. Just as everything had seemed the same the moment after Barbs had died.

She had laid her mother-in-law down. She had eased her shoulders but the ache had not gone. She had stood at the window, looking out at the small garden, at the pile of leaves that were the same as the day before, at the blackbird that always came, and that morning came again. Everything had been the same, but everything had been different.

Now Kate reached forward and took the book from the windowsill, the book in which Isaac wrote his hours. She totalled them, collected anything and everything that was his and threw it into the boot of the car before driving to the cash machine. She drew out sufficient. Then she drove to the DIY store. She chose paint: yellow, blue, lilac, purple, red, and then white eggshell. From the specialist shelf she chose silver, pewter and copper. She bought new rollers, new brushes, and masking tape. Lots of masking tape, and a spirit level, and a four-foot piece of two by two.

She returned to Fowey and carried her purchases back to *her* house. *Her* house. She found a cardboard box in the small study/bedroom where there was still the smell of sawn wood. She packed the box with one set of brushes, a roller, and all the other small things Joe had lent. She put Isaac's pay into an envelope. She stayed squatting for a moment. It was dark here, like a cave. For a moment she closed her eyes, but Barbs was there; the weight of her. Jude's voice was there; the anger of her.

She struggled to the pub with the box. The gulls were calling, the wind was blowing, the sky was blue with light cloud. How strange, when it seemed so dark. She pushed open the door. She didn't care if Isaac was there. He wasn't.

Joe smiled. 'You OK?' He was concerned. The fire burned. The three old boozers were in their corner. They called a greeting. She returned it.

She thanked Joe for the loan of everything, explaining that she would return the ladder later, if she may.

'You may.' Joe's voice was neutral. She handed him Isaac's envelope, and his stuff. Joe shook his head. 'He's with Molly. Take it yourself.'

She left it on the bar, saying, 'His pay's in cash, as usual. Thank him.' She turned and left. Outside the sky was still blue, the clouds were still moving, the gulls calling, the wind blowing. But none of it touched her, because her world was inside her head, making no sense. All that did was her house. *Her* house, which needed her. Which must be finished.

She attacked the bathroom again, working until the small hours. Using the level, the two by two, and the masking tape to facilitate her design. But sticking the masking tape to her sweater first to take off the edge, as Isaac had told her to do. He was right, it peeled back off the wall effortlessly.

She slept little, just a couple of hours, and when she did she dreamed of Barbs, and Peter, and Simon, and Jude, and they were all taking bits of her, shouting and tearing at her, pulling, pushing while Penny stood, dressed in black, and tigers and dragons and tortoises scrambled towards them, and the noise of them all grew and grew until she struggled out of the darkness, groping for the light, brushing away the tears that were streaming down her face.

She resumed work long before dawn, spraying the bathroom cabinet silver outside in the small garden, then moving inside to the bathroom, using the masking tape on the mirror and painting an Art Deco design between the strips. When the paint was dry she peeled off the tape and stood back. It had worked. It looked good. She hung it and stood back. Yes, it worked. The same design was mirrored on the wall. Art Deco lived again.

Now she took the red and yellow and incorporated a Clarice Cliff style feature above the mirror. It made a whole.

With the dawn she moved on to the other walls, working solidly, ignoring the phone, getting it right. Do you hear, getting it right, she said to herself again and again, because this was what *she* wanted.

By midnight her hand was shaking. She had stopped for drinks only; tea. She slept. The dream was the same. She woke, groping towards the lamp. She struggled up the stairs towards the kitchen, her sleeping bag clutched around her, trailing like some princess's train. The rafter-dome was lit by the moon, a fierce bright moon. She stood by the window, watching the

249

water, leaning her head on the cold, cold pane, and slowly her mind stilled, her thoughts emptied, drained away, and now there was nothing. Just a great tiredness. A great, huge, dragging exhaustion.

The balustrade of the bed gleamed. She reached the ladder, climbed it, sank on to the mattress, dragged the sleeping bag over her, and in the warmth of the storage heaters she slept.

She woke at midday to a ringing phone. She ignored it and slept again, beneath the angled bamboo, in *her* bed, in *her* rafter-dome. She woke again to see the moon out. She slept, and all of it was dreamless until the following dawn, when she woke to ripples on the ceiling, a ship passing, and the gulls calling, and the phone ringing.

She stretched, her mouth dry, her stomach empty. She was hungry, so hungry. She rolled over and out of bed, climbing down the ladder, padding across to her backpack in her bare feet. The floorboards were smooth, the painted design rough.

It was Jude on the phone. 'At last, I was going to come down. I'm so sorry, Mum. Forget what I—'

Kate cut across her calmly. 'I'm thinking. That's what you wanted, and you were right. So leave me to think. Thanks, Jude.' She switched her off.

Jude must have rung Penny, for the phone rang as she devoured piece after piece of toast, standing by the kitchen window, watching the shoppers heading home with Spar carrier bags full of the week's fare. 'I've been so worried,' Penny gabbled.

'Don't be.' Kate's voice was muffled by toast. 'I'm keeping the cooker where Isaac suggested. He was right, and *I* like it there. I've changed the bathroom. It's Art Deco and bows to Feng Shui through the colours. It's as I want. I'm also thinking. It's what we all want, isn't it?' She switched her off too.

When she had drunk her third cup of coffee she rang Peter's office. His secretary didn't recognise her, but why should she? Kate always rang his mobile. His secretary asked who was calling. Kate said she was speaking on behalf of a contact in Czechoslovakia, and needed to be put in touch urgently to arrange a meeting.

The girl said, 'Mr Maxwell is out of the country at the moment, though I know he is due to be in Czechoslovakia in a few days' time. May I take your number and ask him to phone you?'

Kate said, girl to girl, 'My boss wants to contact him direct, you know what they're like. Can I reach him this week?'

The girl laughed slightly. 'God, yes, they do like this man to man thing, don't they? But he's on leave. Can't be disturbed sort of thing.'

By the beginning of the next week Kate had built the diagonal wardrobes in the two corners of the rafter-dome, closely following directions in her DIY book. If she didn't panic it proved more than possible, though she found the MDF heavier than she'd thought, and the hinges took several attempts. But hell, if she'd rehung the front door, what were these? She had painted a matching design on both doors, and these mirrored the curves and straight lines of the platform bed.

Each day she walked, and had an energy which startled her. Each day she thought, and it was as though pieces were clicking into place. There was still not a coherent picture, still not a decision, but it was coming. Something was coming and though there was an ache, though there was anger and bitterness, she slept at night and noticed the blue of the sky, the strength of the wind, the way the shadows leaped over the meadows in the morning.

She was working on the study/bedroom, painting it the palest of blue on top of the turquoise beneath when the phone rang. It startled her, because no one had interrupted her sojourn since Penny's call.

It was Peter. His voice was harsh, and burst into her house like some savage interloper. He said, 'Where the hell are you?'

'In my house. There's a season coming. Journey's End is in the brochure, so I've no time to waste.'

'But it's Saturday.'

'You were away.' The phone was sticky from the paint. She wiped it with a piece of kitchen roll, missing his reply. She put it to her ear again. 'Say that again.'

'Oh, for God's sake, Kate, are you going deaf as well?'

'As well as stupid, do you mean?' She felt totally detached. She imagined him taking a deep breath, as though he was communing with a congenital idiot.

251

'No, I mean, I'm always home on Saturday, from a business trip.'

She nodded, bored with him. 'It wasn't certain though, was it?'

'Well, are you coming home?'

I am home, she wanted to say, but couldn't be bothered. She switched him off and tucked him in the bathroom, on the lid of the lavatory where she couldn't hear his ringing until she was ready, and right now, she wasn't. She had a room to finish.

She painted until the two colours met in a great swooping line evocative of the sea. This room was not Art Deco. This room was for children, and would be fun, though that wasn't to say Art Deco was not. Tomorrow she would paint in ships, and leave space for their names, and each child that stayed could write in their preference.

The knock on the door when it came was brutishly loud. Peter's voice was loud also. 'Kate, Kate.'

Balanced on the ladder, Kate checked her watch, not surprised, not unsurprised. Two and a quarter hours. He'd pushed it, and no doubt made life a misery for everyone in his path. She put the can of paint on the top step, unhurriedly wiping the pale blue emulsion from her hands. They were steady, her shoulders relaxed, and how he drove was no longer her responsibility. Neither did she have to accompany him, or assume guilt for his actions. She no longer had to stifle resentment. There was none.

The banging had continued. She made her way down the ladder. She opened the door. His hand was raised, and was as tanned as his face. He wore his anorak and huddled against the chill factor of the wind, but he would feel cold, wouldn't he, fresh from those climes. He shouldered in, glaring at her. 'What the hell's the matter with you now, Kate? I hadn't finished talking to you.'

'I had nothing more to say, though,' she said, standing to one side as he stepped in, uninvited.

She shut the door behind him. He stared at the chest of drawers she had dragged into the hall whilst she decorated, and the pieces of the bunk bed left by Isaac and which she hadn't yet put together, but would. 'For God's sake,' he muttered. 'This was scheduled to be finished by now.'

She gestured to the stairs. 'Do go up. You'll need a coffee before you head back.'

He barged up the stairs, her remark lost on him. He went into the rafter-dome. She supposed she had to follow, but it was extremely irritating, because she wanted to finish the gloss paint of the door by five. She checked her watch. Well, there was still time.

She was halfway up the stairs when she heard the bellow. She didn't alter pace, but merely made a note of the pieces of paint she had missed when she'd stripped and sanded the balusters. She noticed them every day, and this evening she really *must* do something about them. She joined Peter in the rafter-dome.

He was standing in the kitchen doorway, looking from the kitchen to the platform bed, spluttering, 'You've gone insane. That's it, totally insane.' She'd never actually seen anyone splutter before.

She spread her arms. 'Isn't it heavenly.' It wasn't a question. She moved to the window to better survey the room. The only blot was Peter, but then he wouldn't be staying.

He lifted his hands in resignation, but then the spluttering got the better of him again. 'Insane, do you hear me. Nothing's as it should be. This isn't going to appeal to a tenant, let alone a buyer.'

She barely listened, just waited for him to finish, crossing her arms and leaning back against the wall. 'This is the extra bedroom. You agreed in principle, not that it matters.'

He was poking at the floor with his Hush Puppies. 'We'll have a lawsuit when someone slips and breaks their bloody neck.'

She shook her head. 'Not so. Isaac mixed up some non-slip paint. Of course, he won't share his recipe, his sand to paint ratio . . .'

'Just shut the fuck up.'

She did, looking at him dispassionately. He really was an objectionable man. Whatever did all these silly girls see in him? What had she seen in him?

'Talking of fuck,' she said, 'how was Czechoslovakia?'

The spluttering stopped, just like that. How extraordinary. He shrugged, taken aback. Then he reared up as she supposed he thought he should. 'Oh God, back on that, are we? Back on the old suspicions. What are you trying to do, distract me from all this mess? And what's more, I don't care for your language.'

He was back in the kitchen, then stalking through to the bathroom, where there was another bellow. She followed. 'Art Deco,' she said calmly. 'I've decided I like it.'

His hands were on his hips. 'It's that man, isn't it, that bloody sailor who's been helping you. You've let yourself be swayed. God, you're so stupid, Kate. I mean, who the hell is going to want this?'

She walked to the mirror, touching the silver design. 'Isaac painted a dragon, tiger and tortoise on these walls. I didn't like them. I told him and am now working alone.' Her voice was regretful, and something twisted inside her, something hurt, as almost nothing else had hurt. She faced Peter. 'I tried magnolia, as the plans suggested. I didn't like that either and now I've discovered what it is I do want. Pretty much as Barbs intended, I suppose.'

He was fiddling with the shower curtain, looking again at the designs, finally shrugging. 'I suppose this is all right. At least it's got a theme, and there is the extra bed space in the other room.' He hurried past her, making his way back to the landing, peering down into the hall on his way to the rafter-dome. When she arrived he was climbing the ladder.

She watched, and now there was tension, an awful panic, a sense of suffocation. Sweat broke out on her forehead, on her back, her shoulders had braced. She didn't want him up there, didn't want him near her bed. She called, 'No, Peter, come down. I want you to go, now.'

He stopped as he was about to step on to the platform, stunned. 'What?' The sun highlighted his tan. His nose was seriously overdone.

'Come down.' It was an order. He stared up at the ceiling as though he thought there was danger. 'Why?'

'Just come down.'

He did, slowly, looking at her all the time. When he reached the ground he dusted his hands, though there was no need, her ladder was spotless. But when he'd gone she'd wipe it down. 'It's time you went,' she said.

'What the hell are you talking about?' He was coming

254

towards her, not understanding.

She held out her hand to stop him. He kept coming. He took her arms, shaking her. 'What the hell are you talking about? It's time I went after I've driven all the way down to check on this, on you. What the hell do you mean?'

She let him shake her for a moment longer, then pulled away, moving to the door, holding it open. 'I need to get on. When I've finished I'll come back, and we'll talk.'

He didn't move, just shoved his hands in his pockets and thrust his head forward. 'About what, more of your fantasies?'

She didn't move either, but her grip on the door was too tight, and it was difficult to speak calmly, to hold back. Just so damn difficult, because it was all building now, hurting her chest, her throat. But she would be calm. Just for a moment longer, somehow.

'About your expected arrival in Czechoslovakia next week, about the leave you took last week. About my plans, my future, about Journey's End, which is mine, after all. Something you seem to forget with monotonous regularity, but then, that's my fault, I've allowed that, colluded if you like in the whole unequal set-up that is our appalling, empty marriage.'

There was a terrible silence. She could actually feel her heart pounding and a rushing in her head.

'Oh God, what book have you been reading now? Is it still this communication rubbish?'

It was no longer enough to grip the door. He was just too smug, too sure. The hammer was lying by the wardrobe door. It was heavy, but then hammers are, and it flew through the air effortlessly, rather like a demented Catherine wheel. It missed Peter, but she probably hadn't really been aiming for him. The sound of the glass smashing was appalling, and the turn of speed Peter showed as he dived to the kitchen impressive for his age and condition.

The sun was glinting on the shards, some of which had fallen inside. She hoped the Glovers weren't alarmed, hoped that no swan or duck had been beneath. She walked over to the window, looked down. No, it all seemed clear.

Peter emerged from the kitchen. His voice was hoarse as he said, 'You need treatment.'

She picked up a shard and turned. She hadn't realised that

255

someone with a tan could turn pale. She said, 'I won't hurt you, you're quite safe, but please get out of my house. I will be home next weekend by which time this will be finished, and I will know exactly what I am doing.'

He adjusted his collar, not sure whether to approach her or not. She shook her head. 'Better not, Peter. Just go.'

He did, taking the stairs two at a time. She watched him from the landing. He opened the door, then yelled back at her, 'Just you remember this is my house. It was bought with money you should never have had, so don't you try any nonsense. Just come home and we'll try to forget all about it.'

She still held the shard, and there was the rushing in her head again. Was he just terribly stupid, or was it arrogance, complacency, his never imagining that she could live without him, that she could walk away? If so, again, that was her fault, because it was what she had led him to expect. So she had to be clear, very clear. She had to make him understand, now that she understood herself.

She said, 'This house was brought with money left to me by your mother, whom you might recollect you left me to kill. I did it because I loved her, and I thought I loved you. I also did it because it was expected. I'm glad I agreed, Peter, for Barbs's sake. But I am not so glad that I assumed your responsibility, that I took on your guilt, that I let you get away with it, just as I've always let you get away with everything. You see, I didn't think I was worth anything else. I thought I had to earn my place in your life, and repay you for the great service you did me by giving our child a name.' She checked the bitterness, looking from him to the shard, laying it down and dusting her hands. 'I let you dominate me. Barbs gave me Journey's End to enable me to think. I have thought, and you have just underlined my decision. You're a creep and a coward and a philanderer, Peter, and I will be coming home, but just to pick up my things, do you hear? It's over. From this minute on, it's over. And don't slam the door when you go.'

She was too late. He did, of course.

Peter drove like a madman over the Tamar bridge. It had taken this long just to stop banging the steering wheel every few seconds. How dare she? How bloody dare she? And how had

256

she found out? Leave him! Of course she wouldn't. He'd phone later, smooth it over.

His hands were shaking, though, and his mouth was dry. When the phone rang he snatched it up. 'Kate?'

It was Alan and there was no preamble. 'Are you insane? You've missed yet another mortgage payment.'

'I needed the spare.'

'You need your head examined. All this for Miss Hot Pants, I suppose?'

Peter threw the phone on the passenger seat, wiping his forehead. He really didn't need this, not now. He really didn't need any of this, it was all unravelling, just coming apart. He was coming up fast on the car in front. He indicated, swung out. There was a blast from a horn to the right. He swung back, letting the guy who was already overtaking him shoot past, making himself take his time, dropping further and further from the car in front until he saw a Little Chef sign coming up. He pulled in, parked, and sat a moment. A coffee would help.

He had one, sitting in the no smoking area. He had another. He felt sick as he paid, and walked uncertainly to the car. She didn't mean it. Of course she didn't. She had children to consider. She was his family. He had no one else. She couldn't do this to him, and besides, what would he tell them at work? What would he tell the Swedes who expected to come to the house? He sat in the driver's seat, stabbing out her mobile number. She answered. He said, 'Come home, Kate. Let's sort this out, start again.'

'I've made my decision. I feel nothing for you except contempt, and a little pity. Pretty much what I feel about myself, I suppose. I don't want anything from you, Peter, I'll just keep Journey's End, and collect a few personal items. As I said, I'll be back next Friday evening. I'll . . .' He cut her off.

It took him all night to come to his own decision but it wasn't until Monday morning that he phoned DS Ben Meadowes to lodge a complaint against Kate, but only because she'd driven him to it. He had to have that house, because everything was going wrong, and his head was splitting, and none of this was fair.

CHAPTER TWENTY-SIX

Kate swept up the glass as the breeze funnelled through the jagged hole and the skipper on the bridge of a passing ship stared. She lifted her hands and shrugged. He appeared to commiserate, before turning back to see his own baby safely out to sea. Kate swept the area pristine clean. The floor was undamaged, the varnish and painted design unmarred. She leaned on the broom, Joe's broom, satisfied, totally and utterly satisfied.

She found the purple dress she had chosen from Barbs's wardrobe, ironed it, and hung it in the bathroom for now.

She found her cagoule and slipped to the Spar, buying pâté and crispbreads. She already had a tin of black olives. She would buy wine from Joe, but first she must see the Glovers. She didn't hurry; scampering and scurrying were things of the past. She knocked on the yellow door. After a count of ten it opened; Ted always took that long. He gestured her in, smiling gently. 'Was it worth it? The hammer throw.'

Kate laughed ruefully, her carrier bag banging against the hall table. She waved to Mary who was standing at the kitchen doorway. 'Definitely, but I'm sorry if I alarmed you, I . . .'

Mary shook her head. 'To begin with, but we saw him leave, and heard your voice so knew all was well. It is, isn't it?' It was the longest speech she'd ever made to Kate and there was genuine concern in her eyes, and in Ted's.

'Oh yes, all is well. He won't be back. But I'm sorry to have worried you.'

'We're friends, and that what friends do, worry.'

Kate refused tea and scones, and phoned Penny and Jude on her return to the rafter-dome, explaining fully, hearing quiet acceptance and support from Penny, and relief from Jude. She then wrote to Simon.

It took another hour to finish the study/bedroom and wash

her brushes. She measured up the hole in the window of the rafter-dome, which was back to being an ice-box. A sheet of polythene would temporarily solve the problem. She replaced the measuring tape, took a J-cloth from beneath the sink and anti-bacterial cleaner and dealt with the platform ladder, and the balustrade, and anywhere that he had been. She rang the 24 hours a day, seven days a week glazier. He would be round tomorrow.

Finally she showered, and dressed in purple, checking herself in the full-length mirror on the back of the corner wardrobe in the rafter-dome. Barbs would approve. Kate grinned, smoothing the skirt which clung, as she had not allowed the shower curtain to. She slipped on black heels, which weren't quite right, but you couldn't win 'em all. She dug the carrier bag out of the fridge, slipped in two plates, two sets of cutlery, two glasses and a corkscrew, remembering at the last moment to tuck the window measurements into her cagoule pocket, and remembering also to make sure that the outside and hall lights were left on to welcome her home.

In the pub Joe was wiping the ashtrays as he watched the football results, his tea towel over his shoulder. He turned at the sound of the door, his face noncommittal when he saw Kate. She smiled. It was not returned. The three stooges were still in the corner. Did they never leave? They returned her greeting, but with no enthusiasm. The smell of beer and smoke, and the heat of the fire was the same as it had always been, and as good as it had always been.

She slid on to a high stool resting her carrier bag on the bar. Joe had resumed his television watch as though she was invisible. But she wasn't. Not any more. She knocked on the bar. 'Shop!'

He flicked a look. She said, 'I come in peace.'

For a moment he faltered, then smiled, but it didn't altogether reach his eyes. 'That's not what I heard this afternoon. I suppose you need some polythene?' He was wiping ashtrays as though his life depended on it.

She nodded, 'And scampi and chips for two, to take away, and a nice cold Chardonnay. That's one of Isaac's favourites, isn't it?'

Joe shook his head. 'He won't do it, and why should he?

259

Besides, he's busy, he's brought his voyage forward. He's anxious to be off. He understands the sea, finds its dangers comforting, especially after . . .'

'He doesn't need to do it, I can handle tape and polythene quite well, thank you. And a glazier will sort it out properly.' There was pain, a twisting hurt. He was leaving. 'Please, Joe, I need to see him.' Her voice was no longer calm. 'Please.'

Joe was staring at the screen. 'It'll take twenty minutes to cook the scampi and cool the wine,' he murmured at last, not looking at her but flicking his tea towel to the other shoulder which was a sure warning of imminent action. Still with his eyes on the screen, he picked up a glass and poured a double measure of gin, topping it up with tonic and sliding it along the counter. 'Get that inside you while you wait, but if you want lemon, you can whistle for it.'

With that, he was gone, heading through into the kitchens. She called after him, jubilant, and her voice miraculously strong, 'Don't forget the polythene.'

His departing gesture left something to be desired.

At the boatyard Molly was illuminated by two electric lanterns. Beside her a small generator was humming. There was no sign of life other than that, not on Molly, or anywhere else in the yard. Kate stood at the open gates. Joe had packed the polystyrene boxes containing the scampi in newspaper before putting them into an insulated cool box, grumbling all the while that though it might stay hot any crispness would be a long-forgotten dream. In her other hand the carrier bag was cutting into her fingers.

Joe had also told her that one of the three stooges would post the polythene through her letter box when he left in about an hour, and some tape that he had just happened to find.

Kate had kissed him and hurried out of the pub, almost running down the road to the boatyard until the banging of the box against her leg forced her to slow down, regain control of herself and her breathing, but now she was here, and all seemed deserted, and so dark and quiet, except for the generator. She took a step forward, then stopped again.

She looked around, checking for movement, for ghosts and ghouls, wanting to break and run, but needing to see him. She approached Molly, who was bigger than she'd thought, and beautiful even in the eerie light, like a graceful greyhound. Behind the generator there was a tarpaulin tied down over a mound of objects. Were those Isaac's?

Should she call? Should she just go home? What the hell was she doing here?

She waited a moment longer then heard a scratching sound from Molly. Rats? She stayed quite still, then heard Isaac's voice. 'Bloody hell, come on, you asinine, idiotic piece of garbage.' She started forward, coughing instead of calling, but would he hear that over the generator? He must have done because he was on deck when she reached the foot of the ladder, wiping his hands on an oily rag, his navy jumper snagged just above the elbow. He said nothing, just stared.

She lifted the carrier bag. 'I bring bribery and corruption to the boatyard. Chardonnay, pâté, crispbread and black olives.' She lifted the cool box. 'And Joe's scampi and chips, sodden, but warm.'

He still looked down at her, his face hidden in shadow, whilst she was caught in the flickering lights like some scared rabbit. Well, that was a pretty accurate description. She set the cool box on the ground, more uncertain than ever, knowing she must say why she was here, but not finding the words in spite of having rehearsed. In the end she said, 'A peace offering. I'm so . . .' She snapped her lips shut, knowing that her control was fading, wanting him to reach out to her, wanting him to . . . She didn't know what.

He came to the top of the ladder, gesturing to the cool box. 'Welcome aboard.'

She handed it up. Their hands met. His were warm, hers were cold. For a moment they stayed like that, then he took the box, and still she couldn't see his face. She started up the ladder as he swung the cool box on to the deck, but then he reached down again, and she held up the carrier bag and this he also took. He reached down again and his grasp was firm and warm as he guided her on to the deck, and now she saw he was smiling, and it reached those wonderful eyes, and still he held her hand, and was too close, but only for a moment, for then he scooped the provisions off the deck.

It was not a varnished deck, but one painted green. She

261

stooped and ran her fingers along it. He said, 'The owl and the pussy-cat went to sea in a beautiful pea-green boat, and very wise they were too. Saves an awful lot of puking – nothing worse than glare. Saves an awful lot of slipping, too – nothing worse than a broken ankle.' He was leading the way down into the cabin and once there she saw why Molly had seemed deserted. The windows were boarded up on the inside with plywood, so the light from the large kerosene pressure lamp hanging near the bunk was not visible from outside. 'It saves loss of heat,' he said.

'What heat?' she shivered.

'Sit,' he commanded. 'Just shove them along.' She slid on to the bunk which was piled high with a sleeping bag and all sorts of clothes, and boots. He wasn't looking at her, but unpacking the provisions at the small flap table hinged to the foreward end of the bunk. He clucked appreciatively over the bottle of wine and lost no time in removing the cork. Behind him was the galley and there was an electric light over this, and another over the navigation table, but neither was on.

In the galley cups hung clear of one another on hooks screwed into the deckhead. These cups were pint-sized, broader at the base than the rim. The walls were a soft green. The galley stove must be kerosene burning because she remembered him telling her it was the best; obtainable almost anywhere ashore, and bringing little risk of fire. The heating stove, placed between the mast and the table, was unlit but somehow she was no longer cold.

Two small watercolours hung above the bunk behind her, depicting a tractor and two skipping children in one, Fowey in another. There were books on an enclosed shelf. It was like a home. It was, of course. It was his home.

He was pouring wine into the two glasses, but as always they were only half full. 'Why?' she asked, pointing, knowing he would know what she meant, just as he always did.

He handed one to her. 'Who wants to scald themselves out on the ocean deep? If I lose a hand, I lose half my crew.' He clinked her glass. 'Cheers.'

He was smiling, but wary, and who could blame him? She sipped. The Chardonnay was certainly cold enough. She said, 'There are plates in the carrier, and cutlery.' She had meant to say she was sorry, she had been wrong, but so had he, a little. He found the plates, sorted out pâté and crispbread, and used the ring-pull to remove the lid of the olive tin, draining the brine into a bucket, smiling up at her. 'All mod cons will materialise by the time I set off. What you see here is organised chaos.'

When he set off. She said, 'It looks fine.' What she meant to say was – come back and help me. I can do it alone, but I miss you.

He tipped too many olives on to the plate which rested on her lap. He came to sit beside her, shoving the clothes into an even higher pile, and throwing the boots into the galley. 'I always say I should get a proper table, but when there's just one of you, that seems fine.' He nodded towards the flap table. She could feel his thigh alongside hers.

Beside her he munched his way through the pâté, the crispbread, the olives, and went back for more, before taking her plate, looking from it to her. 'Aren't you hungry?'

She shook her head. He tipped the food into a brown paper bag, and then into a black bin bag, saying gently, 'You look tired.'

She said, 'That's the way to a girl's heart.'

He brushed the words aside, looking at her intently. 'Did he hurt you?'

'No, not in any way at all, inside or out.' It no longer surprised her how news got about.

He said, 'I wanted to come down and check.'

She said, 'It's all right, I borrowed polythene from Joe.'

He turned away, opening the cool box. He tipped the soggy scampi on to their plates. The chips looked worse than the scampi. He returned to his seat, but now he too seemed unable to eat, and finally put his plate on the flap table, taking hers too. He sat back, resting against the boarded window, staring ahead as he took her hand and put his arm around her shoulders, pulling her back with him, kissing her hair.

'I'm so sorry,' he said. 'So sorry for fouling up. I've missed you and . . .' He stopped.

She shook her head, loving the feel of his arm, the feel of his hand. 'You didn't foul up, or if you did, I let you. I should have made it clear what I wanted, and from now on, I will, to everyone.'

His arm tightened. 'The dark night of the soul, eh?'

'Something like that.' It seemed so strange to be sitting against the body of a man other than Peter. So strange, and so wonderful, and she fitted, absolutely fitted, and she could smell sawdust, and his hand was rough as he held hers, and it was warm, and gentle, and it tightened as she told him of Peter.

She told him of Jude.

He explained that he hadn't thought he was trying to turn her house into his, but perhaps he had been subconsciously. All he really wanted was to make everything good for her, safe for her. 'Paint it over, as I tried to say.'

'I have, but I know it's there, taking care.'

She shifted slightly, just so that she could feel the movement of her body against his. 'But I can decide what help I need, from now on.'

It sounded bald, even though her voice was soft. His arm tightened. 'I know.'

They just sat, and everything seemed right, and enough, and they talked of the unfinished sail repair that he would continue with tomorrow, after three o'clock. And of the voyage he would still make, but no longer bring forward, of the flying fish that he would trap on board in the tropics by hanging out a white night light and the bony breakfast they would make, of the dolphins and porpoises which were too oily for him to eat.

It was only when she beat at him that he confessed that actually it was because he couldn't bear to hurt them, and she was mollified.

It was then that he took her up on deck where the moon and the stars were out and still with his arm around her he talked her through the mechanics of planet sights, and then the moon sight, and she didn't understand a word, but she wanted to be able to imagine him navigating while she was here, or somewhere.

Slowly she became aware of the cold which even his arm couldn't keep at bay. Here, or somewhere?

His grip tightened as he turned her to him, holding her close, pressing his body against hers, kissing her forehead, her cheeks. 'I'm here for you,' he said.

She knew that, but not yet. He kissed her again and his lips were such tempting lips. The music ran through her mind. She had thought she wouldn't know how to kiss after so long, because she and Peter didn't. It was only their bodies that had bumped into one another from time to time.

But she did, and the moment her mouth opened beneath his she knew that he was someone she had been waiting for all her life.

They stayed together for what seemed like hours, with the Fowey sky above, and the Fowey trees all around, and the sound of the river. Just standing together, arms around one another, lips touching now and again. And it was enough.

Isaac walked her back through Fowey, stopping at her door, taking her key from her, opening the door, accepting that she wouldn't be asking him in, touching her face, as she touched his, taking her hand, kissing the palm. 'You're not Barbs, you don't need the cloak.'

This time she knew just what he meant. 'I know, but I've decided I want to practise.'

'Then that's good enough.' His eyes were serious as he held her hand to his cheek.

For a moment she weakened, but there was tomorrow, and the next day, and she wasn't ready. This was what she told him, and again the truth sounded bald, though her voice was soft.

'I know. Sleep well,' he said, kissing each finger. 'I know.' He smiled and stepped back. 'Eight thirty or nine thirty?'

'Eight thirty, and may I borrow your hammer?'

She heard his laughter in her dreams that night, and Barbs's rollicking guffaw, and her own.

He arrived at eight thirty prompt, and the glazier at ten. After measuring and pursing his lips and generally making a mountain out of a molehill, Mr Fraser said he would be back the next morning at midday to replace the glass. She saw him to the door, stepping over Isaac's lengths of two by two and four by four bunk bed pieces, then made coffee, calling to him to join her on the bottom step.

He did, and again his thigh was next to hers, and his arm around her shoulder, and she wondered how it had ever been otherwise.

At lunch they walked as they had done so often, but nothing was as it had been before. Now they were hand in hand, and in step, and as one they stopped by the boulder, sat and ate sandwiches and talked of the bunks that would be finished by the end of the day, and the ships she must paint tomorrow, and Molly's refitting. But not her marriage. Not her family.

They returned via the pub, and she drank Dry Blackthorn cider, whilst he stuck with lager, and though it was crowded with walkers, and some Emmets, and more than a few locals, they managed to find two high stools together and watch the flickering television with Joe. Her mind, however, was on the hand he placed on her thigh, and on her fingers which interlaced with his, and she wondered if there was a similar yearning in him.

Their drinks finished they smiled at Joe. 'Work to do,' Isaac said, pulling her from the stool, walking behind her, his hands on her shoulders. Joe's laugh followed them to the door.

One of the three stooges called, 'All work and no play makes . . .'

'Yeah, yeah,' Isaac called back, reaching past her for the door, his body brushing her arm. She stepped into the light and the fresh air, but he was with her, his arm about her. Together they walked to Journey's End, and up the stairs and across to the window, discarding their waterproofs. The polythene was billowing, but the tape was standing firm.

He stood behind her, pulling her back against him. She felt the warmth of his breath in her hair as they watched the craft which pottered beneath them, and the cows in the meadow, and cars which roared off the Bodinnack ferry and geared up the hill, and all the while the yearning intensified, growing keener as he kissed her neck, his hand stroking her throat. She kissed his palm, tracing the calluses, the weathered lines, kissing it again, then stepped out of his reach. 'Work,' she reminded them both.

He groaned, checked his watch, then shook his head. 'Molly,' he reminded her.

'Is it that time already?'

He nodded, snatching up her hand, gripping it hard. 'I have to go.' She knew.

★

266

That afternoon she traced pictures of ships from the book she had borrowed from Joe, then enlarged them, using graph paper, then cut templates out of cardboard. By the evening the ships were outlined on the sea, and, free-hand, she attempted a gull. It was successful. Then a lighthouse. That also worked.

In the morning she left Isaac to tackle the hall and admit the glazier whilst she found appropriate paint at the DIY store, where the manager greeted her like a long-lost friend, as well he might considering the money she was putting into his coffers.

At lunchtime, the glazier and Isaac were still struggling with the window, so she distributed coffee and returned to her ships, but the sun was out, the air was fresh. She called up the stairs. 'I'm taking a breath of air. Is that OK?'

Isaac called, 'Have one for me. Of course it is.'

She walked their usual route, and though she missed him, she still found beauty in the gorse, in the wake of the fishing boat returning home. She watched the gulls, and there was no sense of haste, no gut-wrenching panic that he might be bored, that he might be annoyed, that she would return to tension. That would be *his* problem, not hers, if it happened. But it would not, with Isaac.

She walked further still, finally making her way down to the bay, standing at the shoreline, watching the gulls. Was Barbs up there, watching her? She wouldn't put it past her. Was she cheering her on? She knew she was. Dearest Barbs. They'd come a long way, the pair of them, and for Kate there was further to go, and the thought was exciting.

She picked up a pebble and prepared to skim it across the gentle sea, but instead dropped it in her pocket, finding another, and another, until she had enough to bring the sea into every room of her home, enough so that one could be spared to accompany her wherever she went.

She found one more, and it was this she skimmed. 'For you, Barbs.'

On Tuesday she and Isaac viewed the sale, because soon the house would be complete, soon it could be furnished, soon she could leave.

On Wednesday they bid, he for his, she for hers, and took their booty home in Joe's van, piling hers into the hall, and his into his room at Joe's. Kate had not been admitted behind the green baize door before, or been allowed entry into Isaac's inner sanctum. But it wasn't Isaac's room, it was Joe's. It didn't have watercolours, a soft green decor, functional mugs, a navigation table, but it did have the trolley, half restored, the Feng Shui colours in situ. She smiled as she touched it. Smiled as he touched her. She came into his arms, feeling that she knew his every contour though she did not, yet.

On Thursday Penny phoned. 'Just touching base,' she explained.

Kate laughed. 'I'm fine, Journey's End is on course.'

'And you?'

'I'm on course too.'

On Friday morning flowers were delivered, from Peter. 'Come home, let's start again.'

She eased them out of the Cellophane and placed them in a bucket, for she had no vases yet, but they were on the list. Isaac watched, standing in the kitchen doorway. 'They're beautiful,' he said.

The fragrance of the white lilies filled the kitchen and seeped into the rafter-dome. How amazing that he'd remembered lilies were her favourite. Did he have it in his Filofax, under W for wife? 'Yes, exquisite.'

By lunchtime the hall was almost finished. It was bright and cheerful, a mixture of mild yellows and daring red. 'Auspicious,' Isaac said, shrugging into his waterproof.

'Welcoming,' Kate suggested, reaching for the door.

'Same thing,' Isaac insisted as the phone rang.

'Maybe you're right,' she said, answering the phone. 'Yes?'

'It's me.' She stepped into the street as Isaac shut the door behind them.

'Hello me, thanks so much for the flowers.' She walked along with Isaac's arm around her. The Glovers approached. Kate waved, Isaac too.

'Oh, I knew you liked lilies. Kate, come home, let's sort this out. You're mistaken, there's never been anyone but you. Please, let's just talk it through.'

They had reached the post office. Isaac mouthed, 'Shall I make myself scarce?' She grabbed his jacket, keeping him with her. He took her hand, kissed it, and they walked on.

She said into the phone, 'Peter, there really is nothing more to say. You're still lying, there *has* been someone else for you.'

'It's over.'

'Then there will be a replacement found fairly shortly.' They were passing the church. It was a terrible line.

'Come on, you can't mean that. We had something good together, you can't chuck it away like this, just when life could be getting so much easier. Hey, the kids are almost off our hands, we could sell Journey's End as a going concern at the end of the season, you could take a cruise, something like that. It could be good again, Kate. Come on.'

Kate was striding up the hill and now the esplanade was in sight. She said, 'It was never good, it still isn't. It was hardly bearable, in fact, and is now quite unbearable. I don't love you any more than you love me. Neither do I like you. I was going to come back tonight to sort out some stuff, but I've things to do, so it'll be next Friday evening instead. I have a key, of course, so you might prefer to be absent. I'll bring Jude and Simon completely up to speed, of course.'

'There's someone else, isn't there? You wouldn't do this without a hole to crawl into.'

'Of course there is someone in my life, but that isn't the reason. You are the reason, and I am the reason. Goodbye, Peter.' But he'd already gone.

She slipped the phone into her pocket, unmoved. Totally unmoved, but hoping he wouldn't phone again because he had no place here. As they reached the path round the headland the wind snatched at their clothes and hair, buffeting them into one another. Isaac laughed and kissed her, full on the mouth. Out to sea, a boat was beating towards the horizon. Soon that would be Isaac, and this was where she would stand until he was out of sight.

The waves were white crested; the gulls stalled in the air then swooped away. Isaac's strong arm was around her, the smell of sawdust was on his clothes, his blue, blue eyes were searching the sea and the sky, his mind reading it like a book. Soon he would be gone.

'Come back with me,' she said, grabbing at her hood.

For a moment Isaac stood quite still, and then pulled back, examining her face, his eyes serious. 'Are you sure?'

She didn't answer, just set off along the path for Fowey. He caught up with her within three paces, and now there was an urgency to their movements, and by the time they reached the post office they were running, hand in hand, laughing but not really.

They scrambled for the key at Journey's End, managing to open the door on the third attempt, falling in, panting, clinging to one another and the yearning had become a roar and she kissed him as he stripped her of her weather gear, and his own, and they kissed as they climbed the stairs, and as they reached the landing, and then the rafter-dome, and then the platform bed.

They made love and for Kate it was something quite new, something quite free and wonderful, and she couldn't get over his slim, taut body, and he couldn't get over hers, and soon she forgot that she had hidden herself, liking the light off, dreading that look in Peter's eye. They made love all afternoon, and talked, and made love, and then it was the evening, and they pulled the duvet over themselves and lay together, and it was as though they'd been born for one another, as though there had never been another past, and could only be one future. 'At last,' they both said, as they lay in one another's arms. 'At last.'

They woke at dawn to the river, the sky, and one another, and knew they would never be lonely again.

From his office Peter phoned all the glaziers he could find in the Fowey area. At last he reached Mr Fraser. Then he rang DS Meadowes, explaining that his wife would not be returning this Friday, but next. Reaffirming his complaint, he asked DS Meadowes to make a note that his wife's violence had culminated in an attempted assault with a hammer. A Mr Fraser could verify a glazing job he had just done at Journey's End. He gave the details.

He replaced the phone with a shaking hand. Bloody police. They sounded so bored, so damned uninterested, but at least they were coming, and a damn good thing too. He'd regretted phoning them the first time, bloody well regretted it, could you believe that? He flung himself back in his chair, refusing to look at his in-tray. How could he be expected to cope with all of that, while this shit was going on? He stared at his Filofax.

270

Lilies, he'd sent her lilies, and all the time there was someone else. He felt too hot, and loosened his tie, then undid his button. At her age, and a mother, and she dared to give him stick, and walk off with his property. Well, she had another think coming. And *she'd* tell the kids, would she?

He reached for the phone, stabbed out Jude's number. She was in. 'Why aren't you at lectures?'

'I've a free.' She sounded angry.

He said, 'I've bad news. Your mother's gone off her head, some sort of mid-life crisis. She's got another man, and she's leaving.'

There was a pause. 'Jude?'

Jude said, 'She's been keeping me in the picture, and now I've got to go.'

'But you said you had no lectures, and what bloody picture?'

'Everything, Dad. I've got to go.' The phone went dead.

He didn't phone Simon. Instead he called in Miss Simmons. She was only a temp, and a silly little thing, but quite pretty. She held her notebook at the ready but he waved her to a chair. 'Take a seat.'

She did so, her legs together. Her ankles were a bit thick, but who looked at those when . . .

'Mr Maxwell?' Miss Simmons was shifting uncomfortably, staring all the while at his collar.

He remembered and did up his button, and adjusted his tie. 'The heating's on too high.'

She nodded. He smiled, sitting back. 'I was wondering if you were free this evening? There's a nice little French restaurant just outside Yeovil and I think you said you went to France last year? You could advise me on something for a cold February evening.'

Miss Simmons shifted even more, a blush rising. 'I'm going to *Les Miserables* with my boyfriend, but it's kind of you and Mrs Maxwell to think of me. Now, if there is anything else?' She wasn't looking at him, but at the picture behind him. Well, her loss. He sent her away, had a look through his in-tray, worked for half an hour, kneaded his neck, sighed, and then rang Jan. With a bit of luck it would give her time to sort out something good for dinner.

CHAPTER TWENTY-SEVEN

It seemed so long ago that she had driven down this road and into the drive. So long since the harsh security light had blasted her, and she longed for the soft lantern that welcomed her to Journey's End, the breeze, the gulls. She stopped thinking and switched off the engine, hating the familiarity of her knotting stomach, hating the fact that she had allowed it to be part of her life for so long, hating the fact that it could seep back so quickly.

She opened the car door, not wanting to be here, just wanting to be gone without having to do the going. She checked her watch. She had made good time, but deliberately so. This way she could pack before Peter returned from work. This way she could pass him on the stairs, as it were, and leave him to it.

She reached for her handbag, gathered up the roll of black bin bags and clambered out. Opening the boot, she collected up the cardboard boxes and balanced one on top of the other.

'*Déjà vu?*' called Penny from behind the *leylandii*. 'It's not so long ago that we did this for Barbs, and now we're doing it for you.' Inside the New Vicarage Bertie busied himself barking. Penny hushed him. 'It's only the scarlet woman.'

Kate, her chin wedging the boxes, smiled slightly. 'Don't just stand there, put your money where your mouth is.'

Penny was already on her way round. She took the top two boxes from Kate. 'Just tell me you've already got your keys out or we'll be doing a juggling act for the next five minutes.'

Kate hadn't, of course, and while Penny muttered unseemly things about the mental powers of menopausal women they started again from scratch, and by the time Kate stepped over the threshold the knotting had stopped, pushed aside by her friend's chattering, and by the comfort of her supportive presence.

The house seemed so quiet, and smelt of dust, not of Jude, or Simon, or the Maxwell marriage, or their lives as they had lived them. Had Mrs Anderson been given her cards? Well, that was his business. She flicked on the hall light. It looked the same, just not hers any more. 'So many years,' she murmured.

Penny was opening the sitting room door. 'Boxes in here?' It was her chin wedged on the boxes now; Kate had got off lightly as keeper of the key.

It was photographs that Kate wanted, though she was scrupulously fair, and only took half of those in frames, but gathered up all the negatives from the photograph box under the stairs. These were her history and she would make copies for him.

'What about the kids?' Penny queried as they moved upstairs to the wardrobes.

Kate started to divide the clothes into two piles. 'Simon's got all that he wants, and Jude is happy to leave her stuff here until the next vacation, then she'll move what she wants down to Fowey. She volunteered to be here tonight, but the front line is no place for innocents.'

Penny nodded, folding the ball dress Kate handed her, putting it on the charity shop pile. 'Are you sure? You could still cut a dash . . .'

'Hardly, in Yellowstone Park, and my backpack is only so big.'

'You're going for three months?'

The wardrobe was empty; the charity pile was twice the size of Kate's, and beginning to topple. 'Probably. Journey's End is only let for that long, so that it can be available for Jude, whether I'm there or not. She's happy with that.'

Penny touched her arm. 'I know. And I know all this is for the best, under the circumstances.'

Kate held the first bin bag whilst Penny stashed the clothes and muttered, 'Action Research will think their Christmases have all come in one.' Kate knew that inside Penny the knowledge of the life she and Peter had lived and the impossibility of it continuing vied with her faith. A faith which though lightly handled was nonetheless fundamental to all that Penny lived and breathed.

Finally they tied up Kate's solitary bag then checked the

273

time again. 'You'd better scoot with your booty, Pen.'

'You're sure?' Penny was panting a little, and her hair was awry.

'Quite sure.' Kate's voice was strong, as strong as she felt as she loaded Penny up, slapping her bottom lightly, and pointing to the door.

'You'll still let me take you to the airport?' Penny looked like a demented Father Christmas as she tried to ease her way through the door, whilst the swollen bin bags did everything to thwart her.

'I'd love you to take me, and wave me off, and shed a few tears, and rend your clothes, and issue instructions . . .'

'Shut up.'

Kate followed her downstairs, guiding Penny's bags past the pictures on the walls, dragging her one bag behind her. 'Jude will collect the car from you at her convenience after I've flown. Is that still OK?'

Now Penny was struggling out of the front door, and whispered, though who she thought would hear Kate didn't know, 'Of course, and you're sure you'll be all right at Yellowstone?'

'I'll be fine.' And she would, because she and Isaac would be under the same sky, and Barbs would be up there cheering, and she would have the purple dress.

She checked her watch, then carried her clothes to the car, opening the boot. 'You're sure?' her friend repeated, pausing beside her.

'Never been more so, now scoot. Peter will be home soon.'

'Oh, Kate, what a mess.' The security light was far too harsh for two ageing has-beens; it etched their lines too deeply and bled them of colour.

Kate shook her head. 'It was. It isn't any more.'

She leaned forward and kissed Penny. 'Now go, there really are some things you can't help me with, and saying goodbye to Casanova is one of them.'

'Do not feed the bears, d'you hear me?'

Peter still hadn't arrived by seven thirty, and Kate paced the hall, tapping her fingers on the top of the two cardboard boxes which she had filled with odd bits and pieces to fill in the time.

She could always put them in the car, but she wanted him to see how little she had taken.

As well as the photographs there was the cockerel that sat on the kitchen shelf and had been given to her by her mother. There were the candlesticks, a few crystal tumblers given to her by an old school friend, a couple of tapestry cushions she had worked on during the long, lonely evenings, a rather strange pottery ashtray made by Jude at primary school and Simon's football.

The knock on the door startled her. She tried to see who it was through the window, but there was only a looming shape, or was it two? It was like receiving a letter in a strange hand, one that you turned this way and that to assess its contents before finally opening it, almost as a last resort. She looked again. Perhaps they were Mormons? Well, she could tell them to call back when Peter was here. Now that would be sweet revenge.

She opened the door and almost laughed, because they were Mormons, surely, with that short hair, those suits. One held out a plastic wallet. 'Mrs Maxwell? I'm sorry to disturb you, but I'm Detective Sergeant Meadowes, and this is my colleague, Detective Constable Torrence.'

She stared at the identification card, a great shuddering coldness developing. 'One of the children?' Her hand was at her throat. Jude? Had she been driving someone's car? Simon?

DS Meadowes's hand was up. 'No, no, nothing like that.' He looked horrified. She relaxed, shaking her head, rubbing her brow. DS Meadowes looked young at first but actually his temples were grey, and he was probably in his late thirties.

Kate said, 'Oh, I'm sorry. When your kids are away . . .' She petered out.

DS Meadowes said, 'We just wanted to clear up a few things, if you have a moment to spare.'

'Just a couple of minutes.' DC Torrence was a younger man, probably early thirties, but he too gave the impression of being younger still, almost a boy. Was it the short hair? He was shifting from foot to foot, until a glance from Meadowes stilled him.

Penny hadn't mentioned burglaries, but maybe she'd overlooked it, under the circumstances. But it was Peter who

275

was on the Neighbourhood Watch committee, so it was him they should see. She said, 'Clear up?'

DC Torrence looked behind him, then back at her. 'May we come in for a few moments, Mrs Maxwell?'

Mrs Maxwell? Yes, the other one had called her by name, so it must be Neighbourhood Watch business.

She stepped back, gesturing them in. 'Please come in.' She nodded towards the open sitting room door. DS Meadowes paused by the boxes, and looked at her. 'Bit of a clear out?'

Kate shut the front door. 'Yes.'

She followed them into the sitting room. 'Please, sit down. May I get you some tea?'

DC Torrence looked to DS Meadowes for the answer. 'No, that's quite all right, Mrs Maxwell.'

DS Meadowes took the settee, whilst DC Torrence remained standing, his back to the television, his hands clasped behind him. Kate sat in the armchair opposite DS Meadowes. 'Is it Neighbourhood Watch? You see, my husband is the . . .'

DS Meadowes interrupted. 'So, you're having a clear out?'

Kate nodded, wanting to turn to see what DC Torrence was doing, because he had moved to stand behind her. 'Yes, I've a place in Fowey.'

'That's nice.' DS Meadowes seemed very relaxed, and he had a nice smile, and eyes that crinkled at the corners. They were light blue.

Kate turned to DC Torrence. He wasn't moving, but was busy nonetheless, looking around the room. His gaze settled on the mantelpiece. She said to DS Meadows, 'I've just packed up some photographs.' She pointed to the mantelpiece, then stopped. She didn't have to explain. She said, 'Please, what's this all about? How can *I* possibly help you?'

DS Meadowes stared at her for what seemed like a long while, and then up at DC Torrence before examining the palm of his hand closely. 'We have a few queries regarding the death of Mrs Barbara Maxwell.'

DC Torrence had moved quietly, and now he was standing by the door, his hands still clasped behind him, his eyes locked on her face. Had she paled? Had he noticed that she was no longer breathing? She didn't move, though she wanted to grip both hands together until her knuckles showed white.

DS Meadowes waited. She had to say something, anything. But no, not anything. 'Barbs?' Her voice shook. She pressed her lips together and swallowed.

DS Meadowes never took his eyes from her face as she felt the weight of Barbs in her arms, felt the touch of her lips as she placed one capsule on her tongue, and then the cool of the glass, and Barbs's slow sip. Another, and then more water.

'Barbs died in the autumn.' Her voice was little more than a whisper. Now she let her hands grip tight.

DS Meadowes nodded. 'I gather you nursed your mother-in-law until her death. It must have been a very trying time.'

Queries? They had a few queries? Where had these come from? She made herself take deeper breaths. 'No, it wasn't trying, not with Barbs. Barbs was . . .' She paused.

DS Meadowes was looking at her closely. DC Torrence prompted, 'Was?'

'Special.'

DS Meadowes was still looking at her closely. 'Have you had the Fowey house long?'

'The house?' For a moment Kate was confused. She'd been back with Barbs in the garden, watching the tennis. 'No, not long.'

DC Torrence asked, 'Have you always had the Fowey house?'

She turned to him. 'No, not always. It was bought with Barbs's legacy.'

DS Meadowes said, as though mildly interested, 'Nice little surprise?'

She turned back to him. 'Well, yes.'

DC Torrence spoke and his voice was harder, though not unpleasant. 'You didn't know about the legacy, didn't know that the will was to be changed just before her death?'

Kate shook her head, looking at neither of them, just at her hands. 'No.'

DS Meadowes leaned forward, his elbows on his knees, his fingers lightly clasped. 'So, you didn't expect the house?'

Kate rubbed her forehead, feeling very tired, very cold though the heating was on. 'No, I hadn't thought about what would come afterwards. You never really think someone you love is really going to die, even when you know it. You just

277

can't get past the "now". You don't want to, you see.' Again it was a whisper. Did they see?

Her mind was numb, slow, painfully slow. 'But you are a nurse, Mrs Maxwell?' DS Meadowes's voice was almost gentle.

'I'm still a human being, Detective Sergeant, and I loved her very much, but she had so little time. Keith Maxwell was a difficult man, and she always said her life began when he popped his clogs. She had this way with words, you see.' Her mouth wasn't working properly. It was stiff and awkward and her throat was full, and she didn't know if it was fear, or grief, or utter confusion, because where had these men come from? How did they know? *Did* they know? How could they?

DS Meadowes still sat forward, his fingers still clasped. 'Why did you nurse your mother-in-law? It was quite a task.'

'I've already told you, I loved her, and what's more she wanted to stay at home. It was important to her.'

'You nursed her alone?'

'We had cover when necessary.' Her voice was clear now, her throat less thick, her mind less numb because she needed to be sharp.

Again his tone was almost gentle. 'Were there any of Mr Maxwell's morphine capsules left, and were they in the bedside cabinet drawer?'

Kate let the words play inside her head, then settle. The drawer had opened easily, it was the top of the bottle that had been the problem. Poor Barbs. For all those weeks she had hidden the fact that her hands hurt so much, that her strength had ebbed, so much. Poor Barbs, having to beg for release when her independence had been all important. Poor little Barbs. Her throat was thickening again.

DS Meadowes's voice was almost regretful. 'Mrs Maxwell, were you aware that there was morphine in the cabinet drawer?'

She nodded, swallowing. 'Yes, I was aware. Barbs kept it, just in case. It was important to her to be independent, to have the final say, to choose her moment of death.'

It wasn't lies. None of it was lies.

'Where are those pills now?'

There had been twenty or so. More than enough to depress

278

the respiratory centres in the brain, more than enough to do as Barbs wanted. She could still feel the capsules she had shaken out into the palm of her hand, still see the two that had spilled on to the coverlet. It was all Barbs could do to swallow them. 'Bless you, Kate. Dearest Kate,' she had said.

'Thrown out, I expect,' she said, clearing her throat.

DC Torrence's voice was harsh. 'Don't you know?'

DS Meadowes raised one eyebrow at the younger man. 'Do you know?' he asked.

'I cleared the house with Penny, the vicar. I remember tipping the drawer out, seeing the bottle.'

'Was the top on or off?'

On or off? Which would be better? On or off? The truth. 'On,' she said. 'On, I think. I wasn't looking really.' She had made it her business not to look.

DS Meadowes sat upright, his fingers no longer clasped. 'You left your job at the surgery. Why was that?'

'Hard to go back after her death, was it?' DC Torrence had moved behind Meadowes.

She stared at him. He was hard, his eyes didn't crinkle. He knew. An awful fear gripped her. He knew and soon Jude would, and Simon, and Penny. He knew, and her life was going to be taken away from her. He knew and she hadn't wanted to do it, shouldn't have had to do it. She felt her breath squeeze in and out, felt her heart almost die, but then she made herself think of Fowey, Isaac, of the cool wind, the water, the cows grazing, made herself hold on. Made herself remember that Barbs had said she was to lie.

'Barbs had left me her house. I thought I'd just take time off to get the house in Fowey ready to let.'

'Thought?' DC Torrence snapped.

DS Meadowes didn't move, but his eyes still crinkled as he nodded slightly and repeated gently, 'Thought?'

'Barbs was big on thinking. She wanted everyone to be able to stand back, and assess.'

'And you've assessed?' DS Meadowes looked interested.

'Yes.'

'You'll be returning to nursing?' DC Torrence sounded impatient.

'No.'

DC Torrence had walked round behind her again. DS Meadowes looked weary and he almost exchanged a 'Some people are very trying' look with Kate. DC Torrence barked, 'Mrs Maxwell, do you think it is ever permissible to take a person's life?'

She directed her answer at DS Meadowes, who seemed to be somewhere else for a moment, just a moment, and then he was back with her, waiting. She said, 'We nurse people, DC Torrence, day in and day out, and they have to trust us to do our best for them, and we do.'

'But do you think it is ever permissible to take a person's life?' DC Torrence was insistent.

Again she directed her reply at DS Meadowes. 'I've just done my best, that's all.'

There was a silence.

DS Meadowes stood. 'Thank you for your time, Mrs Maxwell. By the way, the name of Mrs Maxwell's doctor is Stuart Duncan?'

She felt cold again. 'That's right. Look, my husband should be home shortly, if you need to ask him a few questions too.'

Too quickly they said, 'No, that won't be necessary.'

DC Torrence led the way to the front door, followed by DS Meadowes, who thanked her for her time before stepping gingerly out into the drizzle. Their car was parked outside the house. It too was plain-clothed, which was a blessing, or Penny would have been round, and what could she say to her?

Just before they walked away DS Meadowes said, 'If you're thinking of leaving the area you will keep us informed of your movements, won't you, Mrs Maxwell.'

It wasn't a question.

'So it's not over?' she asked.

He shook his head. 'Not really.' His voice was regretful.

Whilst she waited for Peter to come in she phoned Joe, hoping that Isaac was there. He was. She told him about DS Meadowes and DC Torrence, and she told him the truth. 'Then you have as much courage as I thought you had, and as much compassion,' he said.

'I can't come home until this is over.'

'I know. Shall I come to you?'

She shook her head, looking at the cardboard boxes. 'Three would be a crowd.'

'Did Peter lodge the complaint?' Isaac asked, his voice carefully controlled.

'Oh, yes, I'm sure of that. They knew her doctor, where the capsules were, everything.'

There was silence. He said finally, 'I can raise enough from the sale of Molly to fund any lawyers you might need, and I can be with you any time, day or night. I really, honestly, love the ground you walk on.'

CHAPTER TWENTY-EIGHT

It was Saturday morning, and Kate rolled over, her hand reaching for the clock, her back aching from a sleep so heavy that she had barely moved. It was eight. High on the opposite wall Keanu Reeves's lids were as heavy as her own, but he was no doubt more sexy. Did Jude still fancy him?

Kate sat up, laying her head on her knees. How uncomfortable were prison beds? Had this been her last night in something sprung? But Isaac loved her enough to sell his boat and that was why she had slept. He loved her. She was not alone. She would never be alone again.

On the landing she could hear Peter tippy-toeing downstairs, just as he had tippy-toed up last night at one in the morning. She shook her head. He'd gone into their bedroom, then into Simon's old room, into the spare room where the beds were not made up, and then finally into here, Jude's room. She'd played at being fast asleep and he'd closed the door quietly. Let him wonder all night, she'd decided. Let him try and decide if the police had been, and if they had, what had been decided. Or did the police inform the complainant?

She bathed and dressed and was downstairs by eight thirty. Through the open door she could see Peter in the dining room, eating his toast and marmalade. He only liked Old English and cut his toast into diagonal halves, putting on a blob of butter, then a larger blob of marmalade, eating a mouthful, then loading on another blob and so on. Once she had worried about his health. She sipped her coffee standing against the sink.

She arched her back but the ache persisted. She should call Jude and Simon and confess. She should talk to Penny, but poor Penny, what would she say? In the garden the night frost had turned the perennial beds into stark sculptures. Would Fowey be frosted? Would Isaac be leaning back against Joe's Aga clutching his huge tea mug?

Peter had done it to reclaim Journey's End, of course. All this to regain his property. All this to . . . She let the mug drop into the sink. It didn't break, it just splashed the remains of the coffee up and over her beige polo neck. Damn, damn.

She grabbed her jacket from the kitchen chair, unlocked the back door and stood in the shelter at the rear of the garage where on summer days they had barbecued hamburgers. She could smell them now. She leaned back against the wall, giving panic its day, but not for long, because Peter must not know he had touched her, he must not know that she cared that he had diminished what good memories there were, and jeopardised her future. He must not know. She buried her head in her hands. He must not know.

Peter finished off the last slice of toast, though it tasted like ashes. He had heard her leave the kitchen for the garden. Phoning that sailor, no doubt, weeping it out? He had phoned DS Meadowes from his own mobile at Jan's. 'We're pursuing the matter, Mr Maxwell,' DS Meadowes had said. When Peter persisted he replied, 'Yes, we have spoken to your wife, and, as I said, we are pursuing the matter.'

He had broken the news to Jan that the police were not happy with Barbs's death and Kate had been interviewed. She had been taken aback, amazed. He'd prompted her, affecting distress, reminding her of the capsules, of poor Barbs's hands.

Now he shoved his plate aside. He was playing golf at nine thirty with Alan but his limbs felt leaden. What had he done? What the hell had he done? He left the plate and mug where they were, and slammed from the house.

At the golf club he drew alongside Alan who was taking his clubs from the boot of his Peugeot. He joined him, turning up the collar of his jacket. Alan said wearily, 'I hope you've come prepared to talk.' His face was thinner than last week, his eyes more sunken. 'I hope you've bloody come prepared to talk because the shit is rising, my friend. Something's got to be done, or you are in deep trouble and will lose the Old Vicarage.'

By the time they'd taken their first step Peter knew why he'd done it, and none of it was his fault. It was his bloody mother, and bloody Kate, and they had no right to cock up his life like this.

DS Meadowes was in the driving seat. He preferred to drive as Torrence was the sort of bloke who felt that his manhood was in doubt unless he took every bend just that bit too fast. He was probably quite safe, but it made life bloody uncomfortable. Ben Meadowes estimated that they were about five minutes from Miss Janette Seymour's flat. The frost had cleared and the sun was too bright. He reached for his dark glasses, finding them in his breast pocket, but without the case.

His mother had hated it when he did that. 'The lens will scratch,' she'd say. Even as late as last September she'd said it, but then she'd worried about them all until she couldn't concentrate because of the pain. But he didn't want to think about that.

DC Torrence issued instructions to turn right. Ben already had his indicator flicking. Tom was a bit keen, a bit too hard. Would he settle? Who knew? He shook his head. Bloody thinker today, are we, my son?

'She did it, you know.'

Ben knew. He always knew, or usually anyway. There was a sort of gut feeling, a sense of questions being ignored, or answered on a slant. Yes, he knew.

He said, 'Maybe, but that husband's malicious. OK, let's think about it. He makes the complaint. There are packed boxes in the hall. She's definitely leaving him, and having met the shit, who can blame her? She's leaving and she's taking a house bought with *his* mother's money, when we know he's overstretched.'

They parked outside the flats, and as he switched off the engine Tom Torrence asked, 'How *did* you find that out?'

Ben tapped his nose. 'Ways and means.'

Tom sighed and stepped out into the cold. 'So we're back to the recovery of property bit you were going on about last night.'

Ben locked the car. 'Going on? Suggesting is a better turn of phrase.' But Tom was walking towards the entrance. Yes, keen, very keen. Ben followed, wondering just how well Mr Maxwell knew Miss Seymour.

The flat was furnished with a strange mix of furniture. Some

284

of it was new, some old. There was a nice Capo di Monte piece on the mantelpiece. His mother had . . .

He turned to Miss Seymour, his voice mellow and kind. He didn't like her – too much lipstick at this hour of the morning, and a tan that was obscene. Mr Maxwell had a tan, he'd positively glowed when he came to the station to reinforce the complaint.

He let Tom run the questions, not caring this time that the tone was too abrupt, because this woman reminded him of the Sister in charge of his mother's ward. Oh yes, undoubtedly efficient, but without compassion, whereas Mrs Maxwell had compassion. She cared. He knew that, because she still did.

Jan crossed her legs. Nice pins. Ben could see why someone like Mr Maxwell might like to get his leg over. Bloody fool, though, when he'd got a wife like that. Good-looking, warm, sexy. He took out his notebook and scrawled, *Check ownership of flat*. There was no reason to, of course, but some man visited, that was clear from the books, the coat on the back of the door, a million things.

Mr Maxwell had said they could find Jan Seymour at the surgery. He had been too insistent, and anyway, Ben liked to speak to people in their own surroundings, if possible.

Tom had an eye for the girls, and now he was becoming less hard, and settling back into the chair as though for the duration. Ben moved to the bookcase. Books on golf, on computers, interior design, romantic novels. At the end was a photograph album. Slid in on top was a packet of photographs. He turned and listened to Jan as she said, 'Well, yes. Poor Barbara Maxwell, she was arthritic. She could barely move her hands at the end.'

Ben interrupted gently. 'How did you know that her hands had deteriorated so badly?'

Jan Seymour hesitated, looking at her own for a moment, then replying to Tom, not to him. 'I visited just before she died. It was all very sad.'

Tom's voice was encouraging. 'And there definitely was a bottle of capsules in the cabinet drawer?'

'I've already told you. Yes.'

Ben cleared his throat. 'Miss Seymour, I know this is a pain but any chance of a glass of water, or even a coffee?'

He was aware of Tom flashing him a look, but good as gold he came in on cue. 'That would be great. It's been a bit of a rush this morning. Perhaps I can help?'

Tom began to stand, but she waved him back. 'Fine, that's fine. Is instant all right?'

Ben smiled. 'Perfect, just what the doctor ordered.' She sort of laughed, but only sort of, and it was with a degree of reluctance that she left the room, the same degree of reluctance with which she had dealt with the whole proceedings. Could just be, of course, that it was the professional not wanting to discuss a case, but who knew? The interesting thing would be to see if Tom had noticed, or if he'd been too busy prostrating himself before the tanned legs.

Tom obviously had noticed, because he raised his eyebrows at Ben and took up position at the kitchen door as Ben pulled out the photos and flicked through them. There were scenes of a pool, a bar, a hotel, all in blazing sun. There were photographs of her, but no one else. He counted them. Thirty-four. He snatched a look at Tom, who listened at the door, then mouthed, 'OK.'

Ben took out the negatives now, holding them up to the window. Thirty-four from thirty-six left two. He found the missing two. A man by the pool. Difficult to say who, but not impossible. Over by the door Tom clicked his fingers, jerking his head towards the kitchen. Ben whispered, 'Maxwell, I'd lay my bottom dollar on it.' He replaced the negatives and prints and was standing by the window when Jan returned.

There was too much milk in the coffee, cooling it quickly, which was all to the good as they were anxious to be off, anxious to talk. Tom concluded the interview, then chatted about a holiday he was taking in a month's time, wondering whether she had any suggestions where he could collect a tan like hers.

'Try the local health club,' she laughed. 'They've a good sun bed there, as you can see.'

She'd answered at a slant – and now she's wondering why she didn't just tell the truth, Ben thought.

He let Tom drive to the Medical Centre where they had arranged to meet Stuart Duncan to discuss Barbara Maxwell's medical record. They'd said midday, and twelve thirty was pretty close. By now Tom had flashed a gamut of conspiracy theories past Ben, eager to think they'd stumbled on a murder conducted by a son and his lover, with the fall guy being the wife.

Dr Duncan met them at the glass doors. He wore moccasins and cords. Ben didn't like moccasins himself – they always became too floppy, sending him arse over tit at inappropriate moments. He wouldn't hold that against the guy, though, especially as he was built like a tank and had a face that had clearly seen its fair share of scrum bums.

They followed the Doc through to his room, and Ben took the only patient's chair while Tom had to stand. Well, rank had its advantages.

Dr Stuart Duncan's chair had arms, and a cushion. Ben's was hard, but then patients weren't supposed to linger, were they, or their relatives? They weren't supposed to question, to say, 'Do something to help her, anything. I wouldn't let my dog suffer like this.'

Stuart Duncan read Mrs Barbara Maxwell's notes, belligerently and defensively as though he guessed at the line they were taking. Ben liked him for that and listened carefully to the progress of the disease, to the adequate pain control, and death as anticipated, the constant compassionate attendance by Kate, the visits by the community nurses, the visits by the Macmillan representatives. Stuart signalled his closure of the matter by sitting back and throwing the notes on the table. Ben asked, 'What about her arthritis?'

Stuart was startled. 'Arthritis?'

Tom chipped in. 'Yes, in her hands.'

Stuart shook his head, reaching for the notes again, saying as he did so, 'Arthritis? She had it, but her hands were pretty formidable, right up to the end, or at least they were when she gave me a good slap for being cheeky the morning before she died.'

'And you're sure there was no sign of an overdose?'

Stuart Duncan was rereading the notes, but now he stopped, and looked up, his face wary. Then he resumed his reading, 'Just a moment.'

Good for you, cock, Ben thought. You keep these whipper-snappers in their place.

Stuart spoke to Ben, not Tom, when he put down the notes with an air of finality. 'No marked deterioration in her arthritis. No sign of overdose. Why would there be? The pain was under control, incontinence had not yet occurred, so dignity was intact, and what's more I don't take kindly to a matter like this being dragged up. Kate Maxwell was devoted to Barbs and worked her butt off for that lady, and never resented it.' He was jabbing the table. 'Moreover, I arrived soon after the death. I would have noticed something, believe you me. There was no need for an autopsy because everything was expected, and a professional was in attendance. Or are you about to question my judgement of that professional?'

Ben Meadowes gestured to the notes. He knew what he believed but nonetheless he wasn't about to query Duncan's competence, especially in view of the relief he was beginning to feel. 'It's this arthritis I'm interested in. You are quite sure that Mrs Barbara Maxwell had sufficient strength to give you a slap? You did say a slap?'

Stuart laughed. 'Yes, and a bit of a shake. Grabbed my wrist and called me a naughty boy, all because I said that if I was twenty years younger I'd have wrapped my legs around her, and tandem skydived her myself.'

'Skydived?'

Stuart told them of Barbs's list, of Kate's support for that list. But he fell quiet when asked of Peter Maxwell's attitude. 'He's different from Kate,' he said finally.

They were out of the Medical Centre by one and it was Ben who suggested they visit the local pub. They shouldn't drink on duty, but hell, they had to get rid of the sour taste somehow. They decided to eat as well. Tom had a baked potato with prawns and Ben had one with tuna – but then I'm not a high flyer, he told his DC.

Neither laughed, because they were too busy thinking. 'She killed herself,' Ben said finally. 'The Doc won't admit it, but that's what happened.'

Tom agreed. 'You just had to look at Mrs Maxwell to know there was something odd. But suicide?'

'Suicide,' Ben said firmly. Something else had happened, but he didn't quite know what. Whatever it was it involved Kate, and there was no way that good woman was going to be dragged into that shit's mire.

The baked spud was good, the low-alcohol lager not bad.

As Tom wiped his mouth on his napkin he asked Ben if he was still going to check out the ownership of the flat. Ben shook his head, staring into the lager glass. 'No need, no point. If we go after him for wasting police time we'll drag Mrs Maxwell into it, and why hold her up any more? She's leaving, isn't she, so let her get on her way. But I might just let her know the name of the opposition, if she doesn't know already.'

'But I still don't understand why the old girl killed herself, if her pain was controlled, if there was no lack of dignity.'

Ben said quietly, 'But there was. This was someone who lived life to the full and was tied to a drip. Think about it.'

Back in the flat Jan was packing. Her hands were shaking as she folded the clothes. Her hands were strong and tanned, and capable. Barbs's hands had been capable, right up to the end they had been capable. She knew that, deep down. Suddenly she sat, exhausted. Stuart had just rung to warn her that the police might be calling. He had read out the notes just so that everyone was clear about the facts.

The facts. Those that Peter had told her were not. God, oh God. She pushed the case on to the floor, and the clothes spilled out. Where else could she go? Who else could she love? The cream satin coverlet was cool as she lay on it. She was thirty-five and what else was there for her? She loved him, and he had meant no harm. Surely he had meant no harm. He had merely been suspicious of Kate, that was all.

She lay for hours, until the darkness began to fall, and it was only then that she took the clothes and replaced them, knowing that she must never allow him to stop loving her, or he would destroy her too.

Peter drove past DS Meadowes's car, and roared too fast into the drive of the Old Vicarage. In his mirror he watched the Detective Sergeant get out and walk up the drive, and take hold of the handle of Peter's door, opening it, bending to speak to him. 'We've investigated your complaint, Mr Maxwell.' His side-kick was there too, now.

Peter fingered his seat belt. They were too close. He released his belt. DS Meadowes did not step back, just leaned closer. Peter pressed into the seat. 'We've investigated your complaint, Mr Maxwell, and have decided not to charge you for wasting police time on this occasion. If this matter should be raised again, however, I doubt that we'll be so lenient. Incidentally, the photographs were nice, though I feel your wife was not quite as enchanted as Miss Janette Seymour.' He straightened, then bent again. 'One further point, on the matter of the hammer. I consider it a case of justifiable violence and nothing more, not that justifiable violence exists in the rule book, of course. But let it drop, Mr Maxwell, there's a good boy.'

Only now did DS Meadowes and DC Torrence step back and allow him to leave the car, turning their back on his bluster, and walking briskly down the drive. He watched, aware now that Kate's car had gone, and hearing that bloody Bertie barking under the *leylandii*. He tried to walk to the front door but staggered, his legs weak, his mouth dry, his heart pounding. He leaned against the car. He was cold, so very, very cold.

He stared around him as though he had never seen his home before. The beds were only just under control, the *leylandii* cast a great shadow. He took great gulping breaths, his head pounding, beating his fists again and again on the car roof. It'd have to go, the whole bloody house would have to go and he'd be stuck in that flat, with that stupid bloody bitch, and God . . . He turned and buried his face in his arm, and that horrible noise was him, sobbing, and he couldn't stop, and he wanted his mum and dad, he wanted Kate, and his kids. He wanted to feel safe.

Kate stood on the deck with Isaac. It was March, Journey's End was let, her backpack was in the car, near the Bodinnack ferry, and Isaac's arms were around her. His grip tightened. The wind was fair for him, she knew that. It was fair for them both. Over his shoulder she could see the cows grazing, above the gulls were calling. She would miss them, and him, miss the weight of him on her, his love; the muscle below his collarbone, the curve of his neck. She would miss waking up to find his arm around her, miss looking out across their beloved river.

'You'll be all right, Kate.' It wasn't a question.

'You'll be all right,' she replied. Neither was that.

'I'll see you in San Diego.' He was speaking into her hair.

'I'll give your love to the bears.'

'You'll bring me a sticker. Yellowstone Park.' He was kissing her cheek and her eyes.

'I'll insist it's stuck to the mast.'

'Over my dead body.'

'So be it.' They laughed.

'I must go,' he said, against her mouth.

'I know.' It was what he did, and she might sail with him after San Diego, complete with acupressure bracelets. She hadn't decided yet.

'Jude's coming to San Diego?' he murmured, reluctant to let her go.

She clung to him, the boat wallowing beneath them. 'Yes, for a while.'

'That'll be good. And Simon?'

She nodded. 'We'll come down together from Yellowstone.'

'Peter's instigated the divorce?'

The gulls were insistent above them. The ferry was trawling across. 'Oh yes, Jan's seen to that.'

They kissed again gently. He released her. She stepped on to shore. 'Be careful.'

'I will.'

She didn't wait for him to cast off. Joe would see to that. Joe who was waiting patiently to one side. Joe whose arm she touched as she walked away, not turning, not looking back, just hurrying through Fowey, heading towards the coast path from where she would bid him Godspeed.

She rounded the headland and the wind dragged at her purple dress. For a moment she watched a gull soaring higher and higher. 'Watch me now, Barbs,' she whispered. 'Just watch me now.'

She turned, dragging her hair back from her face, waiting for his yacht. She watched as he made his way out into the seas, watched until she could see Molly no more. Watched until his wake had dissipated. Only then did she leave.